Ghost

THE HALLOWEEN BOYS

KAT BLACKTHORNE

Author's Note

Dear Halloween Lover,

If this book is in your paws then you likely have some idea what you're getting into. You read the blurbs, saw the cover, and thought *yeah, I'm into that*. It's my every hope that you find this tale to be cozy and comforting in all its darkness. It's not gore. There is violence, villains, red-substance play, graphic love scenes with non/dubious consent and more.

This is a cozy-spooky-spicy halloween why-choose monster romance with lots of fun creatures, occult and satanism themes.

This book is intended for mature readers 18+. *Please check the content information on katblackthorne.com for an extensive content warning list.*

Each immortal character, being, and creature in this book was written under the careful advisement of an esoteric and occult master. The depictions, likenesses, and proclivities, among other things… are real.

Enjoy every spooky bite.

xoxo,

Kat

To the demons throwing birds at my window while I wrote this. You can stop. I think I made you proud with this one.

&

To the girls like me who wear black, sleep with stuffed animals, and don't quite fit in.

I wrote this for you.

Choose your monster.

And I really hope you pick the one inside yourself.

Vibes

Ghost Spotify Playlist

Halloween Boys Mood Board

Story Keeper

Citrus singed in blue unholy flame.
No one knows who ,where, or why they came.
And when the darkness took notice
Of the Death that was there
Generations would hear stories
Of new evils to fear.
The slaughter was grace
Compared to the survivors fate.
Return to the burning grove
All you wicked
Pray, pray.
damned and depraved
gods pity the soul
that finds its way . . .
Amidst the monsters of hell
They cannot be saved.

The above verses were traded to a pirate from an Original Witch. The first known recorded story of Ash Grove and The Halloween Boys. *Year unknown.* Captain Vex Beard III *Story Keeper of The Pirates of Ashes*

CHAPTER 1

Blythe

SLEEPY HALLOWS

> I am pretty fearless, and you know why? Because I don't
> handle fear very well; I'm not a good terrified person.
> *Stevie Nicks*

That day, it was a cell phone ringing that made me want to die. Two weeks ago, it was a laugh. A distinct, grumble of a chuckle that sent my pulse through the roof. A month ago, it was a rusty red pickup truck.

But that day, it was a cellphone I had to contend with. My mouth went dry as panic flooded my system. I searched the diner, scanning every patron before landing on a petite old lady. The breath that left my lips was shaky, uneven, as I tossed a crumpled twenty on the greasy table and grabbed my purse. I sucked in a breath of September air while I scurried to my car, checking under it before I got in. As always, I surveyed the back seat before I even touched the leather interior. Clicking the locks three times, just to make sure, I fished my phone out of my bag and called. I doubled clicked the only number in my contact list. The only number in my recent calls log. Once, twice, just a voicemail.

I drove to the blandly-colored office building in the middle of town, parked, and power walked inside. If I kept moving, I wouldn't break. If I kept moving, I wouldn't cry.

If I kept moving, he wouldn't find me.

The elevator beeped and I stepped in front of the receptionist. I tapped my fingers anxiously along her desk while she finished a call. Finally, she faced me with a wary smile. "Miss Pearl," she coaxed as if I were a child. "We don't have you down for an appointment until next week."

I could feel my breaths coming in shorter bursts. My hand jittered against the desk of its own accord now. "It's an emergency. Please, if Dr. Omar could just squeeze me in—"

"She's not in today. All our doctors are booked."

I ran a sweaty palm through my hair, feeling strands loop free from my claw clip, messing it up thoroughly. "I'm begging you. I have to talk to somebody, any—"

"I can see you," a deep male voice boomed from behind me. "My one o'clock is a no-show."

"Thank you," I responded, turning on my heel. I usually preferred female therapists but I'd take what I could get right now. I halted in my tracks, staring up at him. Thick-rimmed glasses were perched on his stoic face as he crossed his arms and assessed me. Something fluttered deep inside my belly despite the rising panic in my chest. Suddenly, I became aware of my appearance. My face was blotchy, my hair askew, my white T-shirt stained with my morning coffee.

"Dr. Cove, that's very generous of you, but I haven't pulled Miss Pearl's clinical notes. I'm afraid nothing is ready."

"That's alright, Shannon, I'm happy to take this one on the fly. Please, step into my office." He gestured with a wide, strong hand. Why did I have an unnatural fetish for man hands? His were perfectly huge and worn. I gulped before nodding and scurrying past him. "Have a seat. Can I get you some water?"

He was pouring a glass of ice water and sitting it in front of me before I could respond. I perched on the loveseat adjacent to his leather armchair and took a small sip, letting the cold cup alleviate some of my rising heat. "Thank you," I breathed, staring at the ice.

Dr. Cove's chair squeaked, and I caught his black loafers in my periphery. Maybe this was worse than enduring the panic attack. How could I possibly talk about this with such an attractive man? I considered faking an excuse to leave when he broke the silence. Dr. Omar never broke the silence first.

"Overrated band," he remarked.

I glanced up and arched an eyebrow, unsure what he was referring to. He flicked a lazy finger toward my breasts. Thank God my face was already flushed or I would have been as red as a beet in that moment. Then I realized he meant my T-shirt. "Fleetwood Mac? Are you kidding me? Stevie Nicks is one of the greatest lyricists of all time. Why don't you like them?"

He shrugged, offering only the hint of a half smile. "I'll educate you on how you're wrong if you tell me why you were so desperate to get in here today."

With a sigh, I clutched a pillow and slumped back into the loveseat. Somehow my anxiety was lessening since I'd first walked in. Maybe just being around mental health professionals calmed me. Maybe it was because Dr. Melissa Omar had been my only friend since I moved here. Well, not really a friend, but the closest thing I had to one. "I guess I'm only seeing you for today, so I'll give you the nutshell version." I fidgeted nervously with the tassel of the pillow. "My childhood wasn't great. My mom had a bunch of guys in and out. She finally settled on this one real winner of a human, who beat her, and sometimes me. I spent most of my teenage years being afraid to close the refrigerator door too loud or look at him wrong . . . ," I trailed off, feeling my chest tighten again. "My mom's death was ruled a suicide but I blamed him. He either did it and covered it up or he drove her to it. Either way, it's his fault. So when I was nineteen, I packed a small duffle of everything I owned and took off."

His dark gaze held mine with intensity as I glanced up at him. His black button-up shirt and tie did nothing to conceal the evident strength beneath formal attire. But his stare . . . I had to look away. "On my way out of town I made a call to the police with an anonymous tip revealing his cocaine and narcotic stash. They busted him that night."

"That's a lot to live through, Miss Pearl." Dr. Cove's tone was soft and sincere, making me want to cry and hug him and run away all at the same time.

"It's not the worst part though, if you can believe it. I made it as far as Tennessee and settled in for a few months. I got part time job and was even starting to make friends when the letters started . . ."

"What kind of letters?" he asked deeply, his voice like molasses and silk.

I took a deep breath. I'd only ever told Dr. Omar, but this felt easier than telling her for some reason. Maybe practice helped. "First, they came from Alabama State Prison. An envelope was addressed to me with a blank page inside." I bit my lip, remembering that first jolt of terror. "He'd found me. I have no idea how, but it was his handwriting. So I left that night. Eventually the same thing happened in Pennsylvania. And New York. Wherever I go, he finds me."

The room was silent. When I looked up from the threading and lint I was hyper focused on, Dr. Cove was gripping the sides of his armchair. "Did you come here because you felt unsafe?"

"I never feel safe, doctor. But that's not why I came. I was sitting in a diner and heard the same ringer his phone used to have and I lost it. It's stupid, I know."

"Not stupid. Normal, natural. Your brain is evolved to keep you safe. Anxiety and trauma are all mechanisms meant to keep you alive. But sometimes they go haywire; sometimes they interfere with our lives in ways that we can't control. I'm glad you're talking to someone about this and seeking therapy, Miss Pearl, but have you informed the police?"

I huffed a sarcastic laugh. "Yeah, I tried that three states ago. There's nothing they can do."

His jaw tensed into a hard line and I could feel his tension radiating toward me. Dr. Omar never showed emotion. I'd never felt anything from her other than maybe sympathy. "What do you do for fun?"

His question caught me off guard. "Go to bed before eight?"

He raised that sexy eyebrow again. All of a sudden, all I could imagine was him occupying my bed. I'd never been with anyone in a bed. *What a stupid realization.* I'd never even had proper sex, only making out and above clothing touching in the backs of cars or under school bleachers. Now I was in front of a professional psychologist who was only talking to me because it was his job and I was going feral. I needed to get laid. If only I ever felt safe enough to seek such a thing out.

"Panic and anxiety can be helped when you have an anchor tied to better feelings. Some sort of moment or activity that grounds you. Have you heard of Hallows Fest?"

What he was saying made sense. I'd been running and afraid for so long, I'd never considered that my brain needed something nice to hold on to. "What's that? I've only been here for a few months."

"It's Ash Grove's month-long dance party. They meet at The Brew Pump every night in October. Then on Halloween . . . Well, you'll just have to go and find out."

"Aren't you supposed to recommended meditation or some shit? A rave doesn't seem very therapeutic, doctor." I grinned. I liked him.

He made a sound of amusement. "You'd be surprised how therapeutic some people find wearing a mask and dancing their asses off for a month. You'll find this town takes Halloween very seriously."

I nodded. "Maybe I'll check it out. I work most nights at Garden of India, but maybe." I glanced at the clock on the wall. "It looks like I've wasted your time long enough." I stood, clutching my purse. "You may have no musical taste but at least you seem okay at being a psychologist."

He stood, towering over me, looking like he wanted to say something else but chose against it. "I hope today was helpful, Miss Pearl. I'll leave a note for Dr. Omar about our visit."

"Thanks." I hesitated by the door. I'd only known him for an hour and I wanted to wrap myself in his arms. I wondered what he looked like without his thick glasses. "And um . . . Blythe. You can call me Blythe, even though I won't be here long. You know, I'm kind of a ghost." I shrugged. "See ya."

I left Dr. Cove with a pensive expression across his stubbled face. The moment the door clicked, I felt both relief and sadness. What would have happened if this weren't my life. If I'd just met Dr. Cove in a bar, or in college. I'd considered studying social work before I had to run. Maybe he and I could have been friends. Or maybe more . . . I silenced that small, insignificant piece of my heart.

If I kept moving it wouldn't hurt so bad.

And maybe dancing was the sort of movement I needed right now.

CHAPTER 2

Ames

JACK THE STALKER

People think that I must be a very strange person. This is not correct. I have the heart of a small boy. It is in a glass jar on my desk.
Steven King

It had been eighteen months since my last kill. Nothing excited me anymore. It was getting harder to get my blood pumping. To satiate the gnawing fucking beast in my ribs. Onyx had been throwing me scraps and they weren't enough, but now . . . Now something may have stumbled right into my office. Something about five foot three inches, as curvaceous as Aphrodite, and with the ripe smell of fear on her breath. It shouldn't have made my cock twitch. The tremble in her little voice. Her dainty red fingernails pulling at the strings of the cushion. I wondered how they'd look wrapped around my dick. We had an instant chemistry. She felt it. I felt it. I hadn't met a new woman in . . . a long time. How'd she fly under my radar for months?

The moment the sound of the elevator doors closing reached my ears, I grabbed my jacket and whirled out of the room. "Email me Blythe Pearl's file and cancel my day," I ordered at a wide-eyed Shannon. I didn't care that I had another client in thirty minutes. They didn't make me feel alive. It was Brandon Peters and all he did was drone on and on about his hedge fund and hookers and why he couldn't settle down. Pathetic. The current batch of newly lured in townies had so much money they bought themselves problems to solve so they'd have something to fill their brainless days. Those clients didn't have any real problems. Except, you know, being trapped here. My other clients . . . Well, their problems were my fault anyway. The least I could do was talk to them. There were no skeletons in their closets. Predictable, boring, tragic. But Blythe . . . She spun in like a desperate tornado on the verge of destruction. I knew that look; I tasted and recognized the fear. It was all I could do to remain somewhat professional. To walk her down casually, so casually, from her panic attack. As if I were just another nerdy, gentle giant of a therapist. My mask.

Blythe Pearl knew what true horror felt like. And I was all sorts of fucked up for finding that sexy as hell. Her ass helped too.

I took the stairs, walking out the moment her long golden-brown hair floated behind her through the revolving doors. Reaching into my briefcase, I pulled out my black beanie and tugged it on, sure to keep my gaze downward—though it was an effort not to watch her walk. I should be reining myself in, therapizing myself into better behavior, but I wasn't kidding myself. I was long past that. The guys and I were too far gone. I'd accepted my reality, my need to feed.

I almost stumbled as she stopped and turned to the side. Recovering, I quickly pushed up next to a brick building, partially ducking behind a garbage bin. She was looking in a shop window, considering for a moment, like she may have wanted to go in. She turned and kept walking to her car. Slinking out of my spot, I eyed her getting into her Honda. My car was parked right outside the shop she was looking in. I paused a beat to see what caught her eye. A costume. Perhaps she would take my advice and go to Hallows Fest. I was counting on it.

Her forest-green beater rolled past as she looked forward. Oblivious. A sitting duck. An easy target. No family, no friends, no roots. No one to miss her if she vanished.

Blythe was perfect.

Following a good two car lengths behind, we took off toward the south side of town. I dialed with my thumb and jerked my phone to my ear.

"The fuck do you want? I'm in court."

I smirked at the mirth in Onyx's voice. "I got one, brother. I got a really fucking good one."

"Really?" His tone was hushed now.

"Meet at the underground later. Call the guys."

"Well goddamn, it's been months since The Halloween Boys found a victim. I'm salivating."

With a huff of laughter, I ended the call. Finally. Fucking finally.

My sweet, innocent, rosy-cheeked target crawled to a stop in a residential driveway. A small, seventies townhome. I sat with my foot on the brake across the street and leaned my seat back, watching. She grabbed her bag and stopped to pet an orange cat before walking down the gravel and to the side entrance. Not the front door, huh? I pulled out my phone and did an internet search on the address. Like I suspected, a basement apartment. Could be a smart move for a girl like her. Old Man Moore and his wife resided upstairs, and by the looks of the advertisements, something possessed him to rent out his tiny studio basement for extra cash. She'd never be alone with him right above her. Plus, she was in the suburbs, which posed another obstacle. Neighborhood watch and busybody joggers and soccer moms were better security than most law enforcement. It was pretty good; I'd give her that. She'd mastered her routine.

But it wasn't good enough. Not nearly enough. An illusion of safety was all it was when monsters lurked everywhere. And one had followed her home.

She called herself a ghost. But I was the one that was going to haunt her.

CHAPTER 3

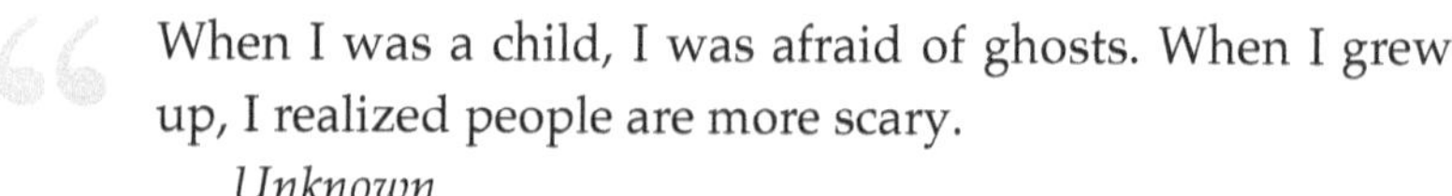

DON'T SCREAM

When I was a child, I was afraid of ghosts. When I grew up, I realized people are more scary.
Unknown

The purple tint of my lava lamp greeted me as I collapsed onto my bed. Well, it wasn't my lava lamp, it was the Moore's, and it probably really was from the seventies. My entire basement apartment was covered in shag carpet and daisy wallpaper. The only window was the one above the squeaky door, and my only furniture was a rickety white metal daybed. It was a nice neighborhood, though, and knowing Mr. and Mrs. Moore were upstairs, hearing their slow and steady footsteps and the vacuum roar to life promptly at eight every morning, had offered me some level of strange comfort. My panic had waned and left me exhausted. Anxiety was like being on a treadmill while being chased by a lion. I was constantly spinning my wheels but getting nowhere but closer to the carnivore's maw. Dr. Cove had helped though. My heart fluttered while rolling his piercing stare around in my mind. The way his knuckles went white and the muscles in his hands flexed. He pulled me from my dark place with a snide comment over my favorite band. I wondered if that was a therapist trick or if he was flirting. Likely the former. It had been so long since I'd had any sort of meaningful interaction with a man, my body was short-circuiting. Embarrassment flooded me at how frazzled and weak I probably looked to him. He took me in out of pity and had likely forgotten all about me by now. But he was all I could think of. I closed my eyes to imagine I had the nerve to actually hug him goodbye and thank him. And maybe I'd pull back and look up and gently brush his shaggy black hair out of his eyes, off his glasses. My thumb would graze his prickly five o'clock shadow eliciting that damn smirk . . . My core warmed at the fantasy.

I vowed to wear something cuter to my next appointment with Dr. Omar, hoping I'd run into Dr. Cove again. Here I was, in an old couple's basement, fantasizing about the first man to acknowledge me in years, and I didn't even know his first name. I groaned. Dr. Cove. Blythe Cove. Blythe Pearl Cove. Sitting up, I puffed an annoyed sigh and pulled a bag of tortilla chips out from under my bed along with my phone from the pocket of my jeans. I searched *Ash Grove Hallows Fest* and waited for the page to load. The Moores didn't have wifi so my little track phone struggled like an old dial-up computer to access any sort of data. The tenth salty triangle crunched between my lips when pages of results displayed on the screen. Articles and headlines galore. "Why Hallows Fest Should Be Banned," titled one local article. "Man Responsible For Several Murders Found Dead Outside Hallows Fest," "Hallows Fest: The Month-Long Halloween Dance Party. Do You Dare?" Skipping the less savory and more scary sounding links, I clicked the latter and snacked more while waiting for it to load. Why would Dr. Cove suggest I go to something so . . . controversial? He was a bit odd for a mental health professional. Maybe his casual style of practice was some sort of genius tactic. Maybe the flirtatious attitude was a part of it too. I'd probably fallen right into his trap. Repositioning to a cross-legged stance on the bed, I stretched, removing my hair clip, and laughed at myself. I was most definitely overthinking the entire interaction. That was how socially awkward I'd become. I'd started making theories on how every person who spoke to me was either some mastermind working for my stepfather or was in love with me. Truly, I probably should have taken a break from talking about my childhood with Dr. Omar and mentioned these delusions instead. I should have told her about the way growing up isolated in an abusive household and thrown into an adulthood on the run had left me inept at human interaction. My brain was dysfunctional. For some reason, the reality of that felt more shameful than spilling about my abuse and fears. Like not being able to carry a real conversation was somehow more taboo than being hunted across the country by your criminal ex-family member. Or maybe that was just in my head too. And, obviously, my head wasn't a very reliable place to spend time in. Even Dr. Dreamy Cove had mentioned my mind had evolved to keep me safe and was misfiring. Making me jump at every noise and question every stranger's glance.

The prospect of putting on a mask and dancing my ass off for a month was sounding better and better. I considered the costume I'd peered at in the window of the spooky local shop. It was late September, yet the whole town was transforming into some sort of Halloween village. Every shop window was adorned with bats and cobwebs. Bright orange pumpkins lined the sidewalks flanked by hay bales and skeletons. I'd never seen a town so serious about their Halloween decorations. It was eerie but homey in a way too. And the costume I saw in the window . . . It was as hard to get out of my mind as Dr. Cove's Adam's apple was . . . .

The article loaded and I scrolled greedily, already sold on the idea without the journalist's opinion. This article was recent, written only two days ago.

"Hallows Fest: Ash Grove's Trick and Treat Dance Party for Adults."

By Wolfgang Jack

Something wicked this way comes . . . To the delight of masked ravers and to the horror of local killjoys, the fiftieth annual Hallows Fest is underway. If you're new here, Hallows Fest is a month-long, Halloween-themed masquerade dance party. The bands are always a secret, and only the costumed-beyond-recognition are allowed entry. Insiders claim it's harmless fun, while some local Ash Grove residents have expressed concerns for, well, fifty years that the event is a stain on our picturesque mountain town. But the festival isn't just a grown-up trick-or-treat or excuse to party. Its roots go beyond that to our town's unique and some would say haunted history.

The Brew Pump, where the event is held, is claimed to be the most haunted and spiritually charged spot in Ash Grove. I mean, I thought it was just an old ass gas station, like the other dozen in this town, but who knows? The stories vary and each festival goer will give you a different account of its significance. All this lowly journalist could find was old newspaper clippings from the first event where it's noted as an event to honor the town's ghostly ancestors by confusing October's evil spirits. Some say the monsters come out to dance and play, too, at Hallows Fest. Others say the event is just an excuse to dance and get wasted. To each their own, yeah?

I wouldn't know, because my job here at the Ash Grove Gazette forbids my attendance. I am to represent our great city and its newspaper at all times and would never do anything to jeopardize my career. I'd never, say, sneak in abiding by Hallows Fest rules and conditions in a mask and costume. That's not something I would ever consider doing, folks, sorry. Anyway, if you go, be sure to shoot me an email and let me know how it went.

Article details:

Ash Grove's Hallows Fest is an eighteen and up masquerade dance festival spanning the whole of October. Begins when the sun goes down and ends when it ends. Come hidden, come spooky, come ready for tricks and treats. If you see a ghost, don't scream. Or do. No one will care.

Wolfgang Jack is a lifelong Ash Grove resident, chief journalist at Ash Grove Gazette, and law-abiding citizen

A snicker escaped my throat and I dusted off my hands on my jeans. I was sold. I'd be hidden and masked, no one would know me, and even if I were followed by "he who should not be named," he'd have a hard time finding me amongst a horde of fully costumed adults. In fact, it was sounding more and more like this may be the safest place I'd been in a long time. How odd that a controversial and, frankly, sort of creepy-sounding event could be the first place I'd found refuge in years. I was willing to give it a try. My adrenaline pumped at the thought of seeing what it was all about. Dancing, being free, maybe even talking to people. Maybe I'd meet someone handsome. My mind was falling into immature fantasies again, but this time, I allowed it without chastising myself. Why not? Why not allow myself to dream just a little. Fun. The prospect of fun was so overwhelming it made me jittery. Searching under my pillow, I tugged out my stuffed bat, the only tangible remnant from my childhood. My mother bought me the stuffed animal after I begged and begged in a grocery store line at five years old. I'd slept with him every night since. Benny the bat. My only family.

With a sigh, my mind drifted to Hallows Fest.

A costume. I needed something epic to wear.

Maybe being a ghost for a night would actually benefit me for once. Besides, who would notice me anyway?

CHAPTER 4

Ames

WAH HA HA

> I put a spell on you now you're mine
> *Hocus Pocus*

I didn't want to leave her there all alone. Everything in me screamed like a banshee, telling me to kick down her door and be done with the song and dance. But the song and dance was my favorite part. The anticipation. The hunt. I hadn't gotten to hunt in so long. I wanted, no, needed, to drag this out. Make it last. That meant a trip to the tech store. Reluctantly, I shifted my '69 Mustang into drive and made another call. The static on the other end was the only greeting I received. My only indicator that someone was listening was the call dial ticking forward, second by second. Judas was a scary motherfucker.

"Hi, sweetie, so nice to hear your voice," I drawled into the silence. "We got a gig. The boys are meeting tonight. The usual spot. You in town?"

A moment passed and I checked the phone to make sure the call was still connected. The seconds droned on. "It's a fun one, Judas. A scared, lonely, girl on the run . . . ," I said as if I were taunting a dog with a bone.

He bit.

A low, graveled voice growled. "Fine."

The line went dead.

With a chuckle, I turned up the music. This was so much better than listening to whiney ass Brandon Peters for an hour. I added *psychologist* to my collection of careers to help . . . myself and my boys. It began as an intel gathering mission on newcomers. Though, there hadn't been a new batch in a very long time. The older residents, if they ever stumbled into my office, the haze would make them forget who I was. I spoke with them to attempt to assuage some lost part of myself that needed help a long time ago. I thought I could deny who I was. What I did. What we did to this place, these people. I thought maybe I could guide the new and old with words, through unravelling their damage, walking them through the darkness.

What a load of shit.

I was the darkness. I was worse than any of their problems. Scarier than any of their mundane fears. My past was always worse than theirs. My mistakes . . . jewels in my crown. Where people like Brandon would shrivel up and die under the weight of the char on my soul and blood on my hands . . . I thrived on it. I got off on it.

Unfortunately, the light filtered in after a while. Eighteen months ago, I was laughing my ass off, dirt on my knees and under my finger-nails, drunk off the beers the boys and I drank. We shoveled as slowly as possible, relishing feel of metal stabbing into earth, the scattered rain-drop sound of dirt hitting the firm and filled garbage bag below.

The morning after I murdered Spencer Warbler, I ordered a bear claw and doppio espresso. With a spring in my step, I walked to work instead of drove. The air smelled cleaner, my body felt as if I'd just fucked the hottest woman alive, and my mind was clear. In the weeks that followed, I almost hoped for a missing person's report. A news story. Maybe a stray dog would dig something up or a hiker would stumble upon the makeshift grave. I checked the local media outlets every day, but of course, nothing. We were too good. Our skill sets were molded by the god of death herself. The chase was over. There were no follow-up endorphins to be had. Goddamn, there was nothing like that post-homicide feeling. The high was like none other.

And I was about to get that feeling back.

But first, I had errands to run.

———

THE TEENAGE BOYS WORKING the tech store didn't bat an eye when they scanned my items. The devices I purchased should have been illegal. I was lucky they weren't, but still. Bad guys could buy them. A bad guy *was* buying them. I looked the part of the hometown geek. I looked like someone who built computers from scratch and lived in his mother's basement. My oversized clunky glasses and shaggy black hair were more of a mask than the one I wore to Hallows. That one at least mirrored what I really looked like. I didn't grow up academic and professional. I'd lived long enough to see the world change, speech adapt, ideas shift. Being smart wasn't the byproduct of books. It was more a self-taught survival skill. When I went to college, I wasn't only studying the courses. My attention often fixated on my professors and how they carried themselves. Brainy yet . . . doofuses. No one ever questioned them if they ran late or changed clothes between classes. No one batted an eye at their short responses or eccentric interests. Smart, dopey, harmless. I could wear that skin. That wouldn't frighten the locals. The ones who didn't already know. My height could even be concealed by slouching in the right way. My muscles hidden behind pink polos and khakis. *Gag me.*

But it was a worthy disguise. No one suspected good ole Doctor Cove. The guy who brought doughnuts to the office every Monday and never wore jeans on casual Friday because *it just wouldn't feel right.* I loathed every moment of it, instead daydreaming in crimson, in screams and the smell of burnt and poisoned skin. Ash Grove was a pendulum town swinging between Mayberry and Gotham. But I loved that. I'd lived here my whole life, as did my father and my grandfather. I wouldn't abandon it even if I could.

My next errand was unconventional, but I was hoping it would pay off. Hopefully I didn't turn into a slug when I stepped through the threshold. Like Marcelene would even try me. Bells jingled upon my entry and a skeleton holding a plastic scythe on the cobwebbed wall laughed a buzzy, *wah ha ha*. "Hi! One moment, sir," Yesenia chimed.

I pretended to browse. Every shop in town was itching to transform by August, as if Ash Grove didn't already look creepy as fuck on a hot July day. October first brought a special pinch of spooky. It highlighted the gothic architecture and narrow little alleys and roads. Orange and black swathed every store front. Our old cobblestone walkways added to the eerie aesthetic, and hundreds of weeping willows blew and snaked their tendrils as if to snatch you from your stroll. The old pointy stone church with its ominous gravestones behind wrought iron covered their front and back with pumpkins. From their blood red door to the fencing and gravestones, every patch of grass held an orange orb, free for any child to pluck and carve and call their own. It was a charming, if not quirky, town when it came to Halloween. Hallows Fest was only the start of it. October thirty-first, on actual Halloween, shit got even weirder. It was sadistic, really. No one was aware of what they were actually celebrating. What really happened. I was feigning a perusal of a knight's costume when I was blessedly interrupted. "Oh, Dr. Cove, I didn't recognize you when you walked in. Sorry about that. Can I help you find anything?"

I nudged up my glasses and bounced on the balls of my feet. *Aw, aren't I cute?* "Ames, please. Yeah, I have a kind of strange request."

"I love strange." She smiled. "Do you remember me? You came to my high school to counsel the new kids."

I chuckled, already tired of the interaction. "Of course I remember you, Yesenia. How's Javier and the kids?" She was older now. A good five years past high school. And I still looked exactly the same . . . Luckily she didn't notice. She wasn't an original, an old Ash Grover. But Marcelene was.

She giggled. "As crazy as ever. I swear to God, I'm going to kill him in his sleep if he doesn't get the front decorated soon. We'll be the only house on the block without as much as a jack-o'-lantern if he doesn't pull himself away from soccer one Saturday and actually get it done. Oh, and the kids. They're very excited for the festivities, like every year.

But enough about me. Is there . . . anyone special in your life these days?"

Ha. Fuck no. Never. Not in a million years. "Ah, I wish. Hearing about you guys and the kids . . ." I sighed. " . . . makes me wish I'd found that same love too."

Yesenia took me off guard and gripped my hands. "You'll find your person, Dr. Cove. I know you will. In fact . . ." She flipped my hand over and pulled it closer to her dark-brown eyes.

I laughed nervously. "My hands dirty or . . .?"

She traced a line down my palm, clicking her tongue. "Not what I was expecting . . . You've got some secrets, don't you, Ames Cove?"

My jaw tensed on instinct, but my mask remained intact. "Caught me, I have a major sweet tooth. Don't tell my trainer."

Her brow furrowed, ignoring my rehearsed dwebery. "I definitely see a woman coming into your life. You've already met her. You both fall hard and fast in love . . . but this line next to it is very strange to me."

"What's it say?" I ask, a little curious what meaning someone with her distinct bloodline could pull from the ridges in my skin, even if she were tragically and laughably wrong. Love wasn't in the cards, or palms, for a thing like me.

She hummed and shook her head. "I must be reading it wrong. Most people's love lines cross off or end, you know, with dying. Normal, let's grow old together stuff. But your love and life partner line runs *parallel* with death. Like, side by side as if...," she trailed off until finally pulling her gaze away and dropping my hand. "Like I said, I probably am reading it wrong. My abuela would know more than me. She taught me to read palms and fortunes."

"Neat party trick." I chuckled nervously. "So, um, onto my unorthodox request?"

"Yes! Sorry, just knock me out next time I start talking too much."

Don't tempt me.

"So there's this woman . . . She's new in town—"

Yesenia jumped up and down, clapping. "I knew it! See? I told you.

And you're only, what, thirty-something? Plenty of time to get married and settle down. Now tell me about the lucky lady."

Thirty-something. Lucky lady. If she only knew.

"I'm going to need this to be a secret. Can you do that for me?"

After thirty more minutes of agonizing, chatterbox, over-fucking-excited discourse, Yesenia was on board. On my way out the door, she called my name. I turned and a tiny, bright-orange package flew to my chest. I caught it with one hand. "Candy?"

"Sweet tooth." She gave a small smile.

With a wave, I nodded. "Oh, yeah. Bye."

Sugar. A normal vice. If only. No, my addiction went deeper. Was it our affliction or the years that made us strange? I opened the pack and shot back the candy corn, the waxy, chemical residue sticking to my teeth. *Fuck, how do kids like this?* My treat was coming soon. And it wasn't fucking candy.

CHAPTER 5

Blythe

THE SWEEPING

> A person should always choose a costume which is in direct contrast to her own personality.
> *The Great Pumpkin*
> *Charlie Brown*

The week passed in a blur of sameness. I passed by Mr. Moore on my way up the driveway to my car. Standing on the sidewalk with his broom, like he did every day, he swept . . . the road. Smiling, I gave a polite wave. I hadn't spoken to the elderly man who lived upstairs very often since moving in three weeks ago. Mr. Moore gave me the tour of the tiny basement and gave me free rein to the washer and dryer. He only asked that I not play loud music or have friends over late at night. Neither would be a problem, of course. I never listened to anything loud, preferring subtitles even on the Tim Burton movies I streamed on my phone. A part of me knew I needed to be alert at all times. That was probably where my dark circles came from and why they were permanently imprinted under my eyes. I rarely slept. Instead, I was a night owl, rationalizing that if I stayed up late, there were fewer hours of night. It made sense in my head. Fewer minutes of vulnerability where he could find me. He was going to find me. And the sick thing about that was . . . I deserved it. I deserved what he was about to dole out. It was why he was chasing me: punishment.

Sometimes I'd jolt if something banged upstairs, Mr. or Mrs. Moore dropping a pot or something. It may as well have been an intruder. To my body and mind, every bump in the night was him. While most girls my age were excited to have turned twenty-one and were planning their careers while bar hopping and looking cute, I rolled my inevitable murder around my thoughts. Over and over, I envisioned it. Would Mr. Moore find me at the beginning of the month when he came to collect rent? Depending on what time of the month I died, the smell may alert them sooner. Would my stepfather come in through the upstairs? Would he harm my landlords too? That reality scared me most. The awareness that I was putting a sweet old couple in danger just to claw at some level of peace I would never be afforded. It was selfish and cruel of me to endanger people like that. I was truly a monster. If I had any nerve at all, I'd stop running. I'd let him find me, preferably somewhere secluded, and let him end me. Or maybe I should just end my life myself and let him show up disappointed.

My option, either way, was only death. The only question was, how much longer would I be a runaway coward recklessly putting innocent people at risk because of the demons that haunted my every move?

But for now, for this brief moment, I had October. I had this new thing . . . This strange Halloween-crazed town with its peculiar residents and unnerving vibe. Hallows Fest. Where I could wear a mask and show myself for the first time from the comforts of obscurity. If this were the last month of my life, this was where I wanted to spend it, dancing with the ghouls to my early grave.

A small part of me, a girlish, desperate, stupid, naive piece of me, hoped that maybe I'd find someone to dance with. Maybe even a kiss too? Man or woman, it didn't matter to me. If only for a night. For one night, I could pretend to be a normal twenty-one-year old. I guessed that was what you'd call a dying wish. It was probably a lame wish. Climbing Everest or soaring above the world in a hot air balloon were better goals. But I'd always been subpar. Muted. And out of all the better things one could hope for before their last breath, dancing with a stranger was mine. And maybe finding a decent slice of pizza.

As I pulled out of the driveway, Mr. Moore raised a withered hand and I stopped, rolling down my window. "Young lady, how are ya getting settled in down there?"

"Oh, um," I stammered, gripping the steering wheel. "Just fine, sir, thank you."

"Well, you're quiet as mouse down there, just checking on you. My wife Betsy and I wanted to invite you for dinner. How's that sound?"

Dinner with my landlord . . . and his wife. Questions about my life, about me, conversing with adults . . . sounded horrible. But I couldn't exactly say no. They knew where I lived and all. "Sure, that sounds great. I work every weekend, but maybe a week night?"

"We'll plan a nice supper. You drive safe and try not to blow any leaves onto the road I just swept." He smiled a toothy grin and backed away, clutching his straw broomstick he may as well have stolen from a witch with how ancient it looked.

I gave an anxious laugh. "Yes, sir."

Don't blow leaves onto the road? This town was nuts. Nuts, but gorgeous in an odd sort of way. The drive into downtown was crisp and fragrant with the aroma of earth and warm spice. The brick and cobblestone walkways rumbled in every direction, propping up jagged buildings. Actual fire lanterns lined the streets, held by black iron lamps. I wondered if someone came to snuff them out each morning. This place somehow seemed frozen in time. Almost like a horse and buggy appearing wouldn't feel out of place in the slightest. Now that October was coming tomorrow, even more pumpkins, hay bales, and plastic crows had appeared even since I was in town last week—like the town even needed a stitch of decor to look holiday ready. Ash Grove looked straight out of a horror film on any ordinary day. But somehow, I liked it. Somehow, I felt safer here than I had in more traditional towns.

I thought I may have liked to stay here, if I could settle somewhere and stop running, or if I would live long enough.

Clicking my car lock five times, I arrived outside the shop that caught my eye earlier. I'd gotten my first paycheck last week. It was meager but enough to pay my low rent and stock the plastic bin under my bed with non-perishable foods and snacks. Things I could grab and throw in my car in a hurry if needed. With what cash was leftover, I could splurge, just this once, on a costume.

The moment the door swung open, I startled at the mechanical laughter that greeted me. My heart sped up but waned as I realized it was a stupid hooded-skeleton prop. "Hi there! Sorry about that. I hate that stupid thing but my abuela owns the shop and insists he stays there. He's supposed to scare away the evil spirits." A beautiful woman with long, thick brown hair giggled. "Can I help you find anything?"

I fidgeted nervously with the braid over my shoulder. "I'm new in town so I'm not totally sure what exactly I need . . . but I was hoping to find an affordable costume for—"

"Hallows Fest virgin!?" She squealed and I jolted. "So exciting. We never get fest virgins anymore. Not after . . . well," she trailed off. "Anyway, I'm Yesenia and I'm the girl to help pop your Hallows cherry."

Wow, she had a lot of energy. But she radiated kindness and warmth, things I wasn't accustomed to anymore.

"Thank you. I'm Blythe. So, I read you have to be unrecognizable to enter?"

The friendly store clerk gently took my wrist and guided me farther into the store. I ducked under dark-purple fabric draped from the ceiling and rubber bats bouncing and swaying from all heights. The shop smelled like herbs and cinnamon. "There's a lot of rules, some more enforced than others. You know, what's unrecognizable for me might be different from you, ya know?"

It sounded like a riddle. "I don't think I'm following. I'm sorry," I admitted.

Yesenia smiled a dazzling white smile. "Don't worry, I got you. Here, I'm going to pull a bunch of outfits and put them in the changing room for you." She looked me up and down, clicking her tongue. "You look about my size . . . twenty? Twenty-two?"

Surprise curved my lips slightly. If she could make me look as good as she did, I'd be doing okay. Yesenia was gorgeous. Her eggplant-purple, form-fitting, long-sleeved dress hugged tight to her curves and brought out the bright golden hue of her brown skin. "You have a good eye. Yes, I'm a size twenty, sometimes up to a twenty-four. It just depends."

"I got you, and of course since I do the ordering, most of the best clothes are in my size. You know, just in case I want to borrow something." She winked. "And all the skinny bitches have plenty of options. We need witchy cute shit too, ya know?"

I couldn't help but smile. "I really appreciate your help. I'm totally lost and don't want to look like an idiot."

"Honey, with your ass? You couldn't look like an idiot if you tried. You look a little . . . alternative. Is goth your vibe?"

A chuckle escaped my throat at her directness. Despite being on the run and having a yearly shower pass at truck stops, I did make an attempt at personal style. I'd always leaned toward blacks and fishnets and anything a little rock and roll. Black and red chipped polish adorned my chewed nails, and before I'd left this morning, I'd done a pretty good cat eye with charcoal liner.

"You guessed right again." I grinned. "I love anything weird. I guess it's why I like it here."

She clapped her hands together like a delighted child. "I knew it. You're going to be perfect for A—" she cut off, her eyes widening. "I mean, you're going to love Hallows Fest," she amended before scurrying away.

Feeling lighter, I ran a finger over the shelf lined with glittering crystal balls and onto the boxes of holographic tarot cards. Yesenia buzzed around me, grabbing garment after garment. "Oh," I realized, embarrassed. "I don't have a lot of money so if you have any clearance items maybe—"

"No worries, it's all taken care of. You're going home with a lot of shit today."

My brows furrowed in confusion. "What? You really don't need to do that."

"I didn't. It's been paid for. The town's tourism board gives us a set amount every year we give away for free, you know, to encourage tourists to come and stay and spend money everywhere in October. I haven't gotten a newbie in years. So it's your lucky day, Blythe."

"Oh," I mumbled, registering the information. It made sense, I guessed, for such a weird place, at least. "That's amazing. Thank you."

Immediately I was shoved into a fitting room and ordered to show her each thing I tried on. Yesenia may have been the scariest thing I'd encountered in this town. I smiled to myself, and I peeled off my shirt. Full length mirrors were scarce in my day-to-day life. A wince scrunched my face as I caught sight of myself in the mirror. The bruises along the soft flesh of my ribs were transforming into a muddy green color. With how fair skinned I was I'd stay marked forever. Lovely. But at least I was alive. For now. Live each day like it's your last took on a whole new meaning when someone was literally trying to kill you. Unfortunately, what they didn't tell you about those last days was they were either incredibly tense or incredibly boring. Except today. Today had been special. And it was all thanks to Dr. Cove. My heart fluttered at the thought. I imagined him sipping tea at that moment, smiling and nodding with his next patient. I imagined he got off work and did all of the sexy ordinary things a grown man would do. I bet he went to the grocery store and bought organic vegetables to cook in his three-story home. My heart dropped at the thought of him opening the door to a wife and dog. He seemed like a dog guy. Instead of dwelling on the jealousy I felt for this hypothetical lucky bitch who nabbed him, I fantasized that instead it was me who opened the front door. *Wearing a black, frilly apron, I clutch a cherry pie. Dr. Cove wraps his arms around my waist with that smirk of his. He then sticks his finger right into the pie. I hit him playfully, laughing as he brings the sticky red filling to his lips and sucks.* My pussy clenched at the image. *Then his lips lower to mine as his hands softly untie the strings of my apron . . .*

"Blythe! I'm dying out here. Show me something, woman!" a voice demanded from outside the curtain, jolting me from my daydream. Swallowing, I ignored my arousal and vowed to store that fantasy away for later that night.

Quickly yanking an orange leotard off its hanger, I shimmied it over my hips, stuffing my boobs into the fitted corset top. Something fluffy fell between the back of my thighs. "Yesenia, you've got to be kidding me with this one." I groaned.

"Show me, show me!"

Sighing, I stepped out, feeling naked and exposed. She squealed. A good squeal, I thought? "You're the sexiest fox I've ever seen. If I weren't married with like, a horde of kids, I'd do you. Now spin," she ordered, walking up to inspect me. "You're getting this one for sure."

"I don't know . . ." I hesitated, afraid to look at myself too long in the mirror.

Just then, something dropped over my vision and positioned over my cheeks. "Here, try it with the mask. Now, see the vision?"

To my surprise, she was right. The mask did change the whole look. Instead of looking like a go-go dancer, suddenly I looked mysterious and dark, even in an orange and black corset with a ridiculous fox tail dangling over my ass. "I guess this with some black stockings and boots would look pretty cute," I admitted.

"Exactly, you're getting it now, girl. A lot of people will wear the same costume each night, or some variation of it. You can sort of . . . take on your own persona at Hallows. You may meet people by their masquerade alone. I'm hoping to run into the zombies I met last year. They're a fun crew. Oh, and the vampires are a trip, just don't drink anything they give you. They can make it weird."

My heart pattered in anticipation. "I think being a fox is growing on me." The costume was supposed to be the opposite of me. I couldn't think of anything more different from me than a fox. Foxes were clever, swift, and cunning. Foxes were vicious. In this costume, I looked sexy and confident. My breasts were overflowing, and my ample hips and ass were sticking out just right. Each curve was on full display. My face was completely hidden. I didn't even recognize myself. Good. I didn't want to. I wanted to be anyone else.

"I think it's perfect. But just for fun, I threw some other costumes in there. A black cat, a witch, and some fancier stuff. Oh, that reminds me, on the last night, on actual Halloween, everyone dresses in traditional eighteen-hundreds garb. Wear the masks still, but the clothing is a traditional gown for people who identify as women and trousers and top hats for those who identify as men. Of course, if you're nonbinary, you get to do whatever you want." Yesenia rambled on as I smiled and nodded, eventually excusing myself into the dressing room. I tried on a slinky cat-like costume, eyed a long purple dress much like the one she was wearing, but I didn't see the old-timey gown. "This is all so generous. Thank you so much for your help. I don't see the traditional gown back here though?"

"I keep all those safe at my abuela's." She winked. "But come back here the morning of Halloween and we'll get you all sorted. I would love to play with your hair if you let me. You know, curl it and pin it up."

Something close to happiness beat its creaky wings in my ribs. "Will I see you? At Hallows?"

"I don't know, will you?" With another coy wink, she spun on her heels, pausing by a crystal ball and glancing inside, as if seeing something I couldn't.

Curiosity got the better of me as I gazed over at it too. "Hey, was that one cloudy like that earlier? Is it motion activated like the skeleton guy over there?" I quipped, my awkward attempt at long forgotten humor.

But Yesenia didn't return my mirth right away. Instead, she stared at the smoke-filled lavender orb for a moment before paling slightly. Something cold washed over me and pricked the back of my neck. Her earlier bubbly light shadowed for the briefest moment . . . until she pulled her gaze away. "What was that, dear? Oh, here, take some candy with you. The local kids are always afraid to come in here. We hardly get trick-or-treaters inside the shop anymore. They say it's too scary." She chuckled and shoved a handful of tiny packets into one of the bags I was gripping. "Which is funny because I swear to god, Old Man Pine's haunted house is much scarier than my abuela's tacky, old decor. But kids, ya know, they're weird. They have all month to trick-or-treat anyway."

"The kids here trick-or-treat all month?" I asked, still a little unnerved by the sudden change of atmosphere. The smell of cinnamon had even disappeared somehow.

Yesenia smiled softly. "You've got a lot to learn about Ash Grove,

Blythe. You're about to discover all of our secrets," she purred before holding open the door. I scooted out, thanking her and promising to come back in to say hi.

A chorus of maniacal laughter and bells jingling faded behind me as I hopped in my car. I checked the back seat and rearview, like I always did. And despite a rather pleasant interaction, and my passenger seat filled to the brim with new clothes, an uneasiness settled in my shoulders as I clicked my seat belt and cranked the engine. I hadn't received a letter yet. Not here. I wouldn't dare let myself hope that maybe, maybe just this once, I'd outrun him. That maybe the monster wouldn't find me here. Pausing, I checked the rearview again. Townspeople milled about, placing pumpkins and buckets of candy outside their storefronts. Women fluffed hay bales and men stood on ladders securing lights and maple leaf garlands to buildings and door frames. It all looked like a Halloween wonderland. Innocent enough.

So why did I have the heavy, distinct feeling that someone was watching me?

GARDEN OF INDIA was only a short drive, a mile or two from the shop. I wished I felt safe enough to walk, but that was too risky. By the time I arrived and clocked in, my uneasiness had waned in a cloud of vindaloo and rice. At least Raja let me eat on the job. He was actually the nicest boss I'd had in a very long time. He didn't hover; most of the time he just sat in the back doing the restaurant's bookkeeping while the chefs watched sports on the kitchen's television between orders. Being to-go only had its perks. No one lingered. No one talked to me, really. The cooks and Raja all spoke to each other and left me out completely, but I didn't mind. I liked it, actually. It was nice being near conversation but not weighed down by having to think about it. I changed out of my black shirt and slipped on my India Garden T-shirt, tying it at the small of my back so it wasn't so baggy. The only shirts that fit me were men's sizes. I kept meaning to distress it and cut it up a bit to make it more me, but I always forgot by the time I got back to my basement dwelling at the end of a shift. After the dinner rush, a calm blanketed the space, and I leaned on the counter. Suddenly, a plate of samosas slid over, tapping my elbow. I looked over at one of the chefs, Dhruv, and smiled. "Thank you, Dhruv. My favorite." I took a big crunchy bite of the crispy triangle and suppressed a moan. Shit, the food here was good. He gave me a grin and disappeared into the kitchen. I wondered if he was single. He was definitely handsome. Would Dhruv be at Hallows Fest? I thought about asking him, but even if he answered, he'd probably give me the same coy riddle of a response that Yesenia did. This town was bonkers. But I wouldn't lie, I was excited and eager to see what this party was all about. As I was dusting samosa crumbs off my fingers, my gaze caught on something in the parking lot. The flickering streetlight revealed what looked like a man bending over the side of my car. My heart jumped into my throat. What if it was my stepfather? Here? All my illusions of being somewhat safe while on the job dissipated. Would he hurt the guys here too? I could run out the back door like the coward I was, but where would I go without a car? Panic threatened to paralyze me when the stranger began walking toward me. A black beanie concealed his features. I couldn't be sure, but he didn't have the same heavy gait as my stepfather. My pulse thrummed up to my throat . . . and then dropped to my core at the sight of who walked in. He pulled off his beanie, letting his black hair fall across his forehead and dangle over his glasses. Dr. Cove offered a lopsided smirk that made me clench my knees together in ache.

"Why hello, Blythe."

I rushed a napkin to my face, hoping my lipstick was still intact. *Why hadn't I made this stupid work shirt look cute already?* "Hi, Dr. Cove. In the mood for Indian?"

He chuckled, walking over to my counter in that slow, sexy way. He leaned forward and rested on his elbows. "The vegetable korma here can't be beat. I'll take one of those and a chai to go, please."

Vegetables. See? I knew it. Straight-laced, uncomplicated, normal, professional Dr. Cove.

"Oh, and please, call me Ames. You make me feel like I'm one hundred years old when you call me that."

I felt my cheeks heat, though I wasn't sure why. The comfortability we seemed to share so soon, so instantly, wasn't something I was familiar with coming across. I rang up his order, fighting past my jittery fingers, and Raja appeared with a bright smile. "It's on the house for Ames Cove, always," he chimed, handing him his bag and a paper cup of tea.

"You know I just pay double each time you do this, Raj," Ames goaded, tossing a large bill on the counter.

"Anyone who offers service workers and people in need free sessions gets free food from me forever, my friend. Blythe, why don't you take off early. I've got it here."

My shift was over in fifteen minutes anyway, so I thanked him and grabbed my purse. "Free therapy, huh?" Though it wasn't a complete shocker. Dr. Omar had been seeing me on a sliding scale. Such a steep sliding scale that I hadn't even paid yet. I probably wouldn't even get around to paying before I took off again. Add thief to my list of sins, right under coward.

"I'd do anything for a free meal," he said lowly, taking a sip from his cup. "Is this your car?"

I nodded. "Yeah, I think I saw you looking at it?"

"Your rear tires are low on air. When was the last time you filled them?"

"Oh, uh . . . I don't know. Five states ago?"

He rolled his eyes. "Come on, there's a gas station two miles south. I'll fill them up for you."

Somehow, instead of panic I felt . . . butterflies. He wanted to help with my car? Why?

"No, seriously, it's okay. I can do it."

He put his food in the back of his car before holding out his palm expectantly. "Come on, it'll give me a chance to talk to you more anyway. You ran out today before I could offer you more resources."

Well, resources didn't sound so bad. It didn't sound so *sexy* either, but whatever.

I dropped my keys in his large hand. "You're not a serial killer, are you, Dr. Cove?"

He huffed a laugh. "Only sometimes."

When we were situated and pulled out of the parking lot, I broke the nervous tension that I was sure was all in my head. He was just being nice. He probably came by just because he felt sorry for me. He'd said as much already. Resources. I was a charity case. "Is this against some doctor and client code or something?"

He raised a dark eyebrow from the driver's side. "Putting gas and air in the car of someone who's not my patient? No, not an ethics violation."

We stopped outside the ancient-looking gas station with one rickety pump and busted overhead lights. "Wow, fun gas station. Is this where you kill me?"

He gripped the wheel for a moment, staring out into nothingness, before turning to me with a grin. "No."

With that very reassuring reply, he exited. The hiss of air soon emitted outside before he filled my tank with gas. I got out then and leaned against the car. "Hey, I didn't agree to you getting me gasoline."

"I can't use their free air and not buy fuel."

"Oh, right."

After he went inside to pay, he returned with a toolbox and plastic container. He popped my hood and began tinkering. "Are you a mechanic now, too? What are you doing?"

"Fixing your headlight, one's out," he responded. I tried not to stare at his hands. I failed. His big, strong hands were smeared with inky residue. He noticed me staring and shot me a dark look I didn't quite understand.

"Your food's getting cold," I scolded, knowing there was no point in objecting to this headstrong man's goodwill. I knew my car needed it just as well as he did.

He said a beat later, "I have a microwave."

In the silence that followed, I surveyed the empty lot. Across the way was a cornfield. Its stalks were high and swaying in the light of the moon. Cornfields always freaked me out. There was no way to see more than one stalk in front of you. Imagine the things you could bump into . . .

"So, you going to the rave of lunatics tomorrow?"

I pulled my gaze from his rolled-up sleeves and muscular forearms, storing *that* image in my private brain file for later. "Maybe. Are you?"

"Overrated rave."

"You seem to think a lot of things are overrated. Why'd you suggest it then?"

He tightened something with a wrench, entirely focused on his work while he spoke. "A lot of things *are* overrated, and I thought it might be fun for you because it's what kids your age do around here. And well, every other nutcase in Ash Grove. Which is everybody."

"So are you going? And you can't be that much older than me, Dr. Cove. You're what, thirty?"

"Ouch, thanks for that. I'm twenty-eight, and to answer your question about Hallows, I'm not allowed to go. Most prestigious businesses here forbid their employees from attending. Especially prominent folks like myself."

"Yeah, you didn't answer the question. Are you going?"

"Like I said, overrated. But even if it weren't, I'm afraid not. I'm not into all that Halloween stuff."

I laughed. "You moved to the wrong town then, didn't you?"

He shut the hood with a slap that made me jump. "Didn't move here. Born and raised. First generation, actually."

I watched him wipe his oily hands with an old rag. "No shit? So you can trace your family all the way back to the first people?"

"Sure can. My grandfather had a big family tree mapped out that went all the way back to the beginning. The beginning where all the ghost stories began."

"What ghost stories?"

He smirked that infuriatingly handsome smile. "Oh, you'll hear about them. Anyway, that brings me to what I wanted to tell you about. I host a free therapy group every Saturday at Lamb's Blood Church downtown. It's open to anyone needing support." He shrugged. "There's stale pastries and really shitty coffee."

I chuckled softly. "Yeah, maybe. I don't know how long I'll be in town for."

His lips narrowed into a hard line. That angry sense from earlier overwhelmed me. "Did I say something that upset you?" I dared to ask.

He shook his head and rubbed the back of his neck. "I met my best friends at a church. I was in a really low place. They're like brothers to me. Just give it chance. Perhaps give Ash Grove a chance while you're at it." He finished, sliding back into the car after returning the tools. I couldn't even see anyone inside the dim gas station. Was it empty?

"Ash Grove isn't the problem, Dr. Cove. I am."

His grip tightened on the wheel. "From what you told me earlier, it sounds like your stepfather is the problem, not you."

I shrugged. "If I stay, people could get hurt. Whether the hurting comes from me or from him, it's still my fault."

"What if he doesn't find you this time? Have you thought of that?"

I looked out the dark window as we stopped next to his car. "I can't allow myself to dream like that. Not anymore."

He didn't immediately get out like I thought he would. Maybe him being a therapist felt like a free pass to share openly with him. More openly than I would anyone else. It felt . . . different, though, than it did with Dr. Omar. He was so close I could feel his warmth. I could smell his pine cologne and see the stubble on his cheek. I wanted to rub my fingers against it. I wanted to rub *other* things against it too.

"Listen, Blythe, I know you hardly know me. But I also know that a girl as young as you shouldn't be living like this. It doesn't take a psychologist to see that you have PTSD, and for good fucking reason. You need support. You need a community. If you get a letter here, if you see or hear anything from your stepdad, tell me."

Tears pricked the corners of my eyes and I hoped the darkness concealed them. No one had ever asked me to stay. No one had ever offered to help. I'd only just met Ames Cove and already he was kinder than anyone in fifteen states combined. If he knew the truth, he wouldn't be offering his help. The truth I tried not to think about. The truth that made this entire situation even more terrifying than it already was. I nodded. "Okay. But I don't want to put you in danger."

He chuckled darkly and looked away. "I mean, I'm useless in a fight.

I was the punching bag in school. But I have buddies in law enforcement. Let's just try, alright?"

"Thank you . . . Ames."

He smiled and I swore it glowed with moonlight. "See you tomorrow, Blythe."

CHAPTER 6

Ames

THE FIRST RULE OF MONSTER CLUB

 Monsters are real, and ghosts are real too. They live inside us, and sometimes, they win.
Steven King

I waved my Little Ghost off with a dopey smile as I hunched into my Mustang. My Mustang that smelt like a delicious coriander explosion. Worth it. She drove off in a functional vehicle, not the death trap she rode in on, and I scrolled my phone, satisfied. I watched as the little blue dot turned onto Crescent Drive and blinked in the direction of her apartment. My gaze didn't falter until the blue dot stopped right outside 154 Locust Road. Home safe . . . for now.

She was smarter than I thought, catching me fucking with her car in the lot. I didn't think she'd see me in the dark. But I guessed a life on the run had sharpened her senses somewhat. That was valuable information for me to have. I stuck one tracker near the back of her tire. The other I put deep under her hood when I was changing the dangerously broken headlight. Seriously, the girl was going to get herself killed. Good thing I came along. I shouldn't have to do this. My skills alone should have been enough to track her. But I didn't feel her at all. Why?

I watched the blue dot for a moment longer before reversing and speeding down the highway. It didn't matter. Tonight was boys' night. *Finally*.

An hour and several rural back roads later, I spun into the lot of withering grass. From there it was a short hike through the pines before reaching the old, dilapidated structure. The moon was my only source of light. Creatures of all sorts murmured in the forest. I wondered if there was anything out here more dangerous than me. Unlikely. My cell lost signal, but it didn't matter. I'd already emailed the file out and the guys undoubtedly read it. They combed through every detail the same as I did. I never cared that there was no signal out here. It had always been a positive, especially for the bodies we put in the ground throughout these acres. The bodies that didn't make it to my graveyard. But tonight, unease pressed against my spine. I futilely pulled up my phone but couldn't access the blue dot. It felt . . . wrong.

I wanted to watch her. Needed to watch her. I'd stalked people before and enjoyed the thrill. This was different, though, somehow. I couldn't put my finger on it, and it was pissing me off.

The therapist in me said in a calm and cooing voice in my ear to sit with that sensation and quietly get curious about its origin. But I wasn't the therapist tonight. Tonight, the mask was off. Under the moon on a vacant piece of dead land, the monster prowled beneath my skin, itching to be set free, let off its leash, thirsty for blood. The monster wouldn't be stretching its claws in its psychologist's chair tonight. No, these feelings would be set free by one thing and one thing alone: pain.

Glorious, mind-numbing pain. A blood sacrifice to the monster in the woods, offered in front of the bonfire burning outside the damned barn I stalked toward. My little piece of Hell, right here and now . . . It was beautiful.

Even the chilled breeze stilled upon my approach. The crickets' chirps were long gone now, even the fireflies hiding with their lights off, while the cockiest crow and most judgmental owl kept silent, watching the predators descend.

Stopping by the raging fire, I unbuttoned my shirt, letting it fall to the grass. I stretched my triceps and popped my neck and knuckles. I knew what awaited me inside the barn and I was eager, wanting, needing. The moment my first step touched the rotted wood plank . . . it attacked.

They attacked, rather.

My jaw ached from the surprise slam to my jaw. The tangy taste of blood invaded my mouth. I took a moment to spit before sensing the follow-up blow. This one I dodged. Tonight, I'd be battling a dragon, a wolf, and the Devil. If I could defeat them, they'd hear me out. If I could defeat them, they'd join my cause. Dragon stumbled, not expecting to hit air instead of flesh. It was the opportunity I needed. With a jolt of energy, my fist made contact with his face before my other fist hooked him in the abdomen. He lurched forward with a grunt.

And then a thick arm wrapped around my throat. Wolf didn't go easy. He never did. He was a beast who never showed mercy, and I fucking loved him for that. "Kill me if you can, motherfucker. I *want* you to," I gritted out through the lack of air. Instead of pulling against his grip, I pushed in it, feeling the tight flurry of lightheadedness. The treat of blessed darkness.

"You're a deranged bastard," he growled in my ear. The Beast.

I couldn't stop the quirk of my lips as I said goodbye to the temptation of unconsciousness. With a balance of my stance and turn of my broad shoulders, I hauled Wolfgang over my body. He dropped with a thud and I gave him a sharp kick for good measure. But I knew I couldn't linger and beat the piss out of him like I wanted. The scariest of them all waited. He wouldn't lunge. He wouldn't bother trying to surprise me or take me off guard. No, The Devil wanted me to know he was there. He wanted me to see him coming. The Devil didn't need the element of surprise. He didn't want it. That evil fucking being got off on terror. I guessed I could relate.

Awareness pricked the hairs on the back of my neck and I turned. His shadow encompassed the musty space as he leaned casually against the splintered frame. The jagged crescent moon hung in the corner above him like horns. "Come on, fucker, give me all you've fucking got." I growled, steadying my breath. The smallest hesitation flashed through me as he took one slow step forward. We were all big, but he was bigger.

He was bigger but I was more ruthless.

Not willing to play into his cat and mouse that night, I charged with a rebel yell. He didn't bother to step aside, instead letting me ram into his solid front. Any other man or monster would have fallen back with such force, but not this immortal son of a bitch. One step back caused me to grin as if I'd just defeated a giant. *He didn't step back last time.* He noticed, too, and it made him angry. A rough hand curled around my neck and gripped hard, lifting me off my feet like I didn't weight over two-hundred-and-thirty-some pounds. "Fuck," I gargled out. Instinctually when air supply is threatened, when a monster is holding you by the neck like a living gallows rope, you want to kick and claw and scream. The animal inside of us says get air, panic, flail. But part of my training, part of what happened here, was a relearning. A slap in the face to the basic human body and a call to something greater. My weapons of weight and gravity were useless on such an opponent. I'd have to resort to, well, cheating. I shot the hard part of my palm forward, feeling the sting when bone hit me hard. An ounce more of force and I could have broken his nose; if he were anyone else, I would have. The Devil tossed me forward. My back screamed against the wooden beam of the barn. The entire dilapidated structure moaned at the impact. Likewise, I assessed that an ounce more force from him would have broken my spine. If I were anyone else, he would have.

The man's looming presence stood over me looking murderous. I wondered if this was how my victims felt when I towered over them before the kill: helpless, tired, defeated. He reached out a hand. I stood with a grunt, feeling the trickles of blood beading down my back. I slapped him on the arm. "Good to see you too, old friend."

He didn't respond. He rarely did.

"You promised something good," Wolf stated, crossing his arms.

Onyx, or Dragon as he was called here, tossed me a glass bottle. "Let the man have a beer first, for fuck's sake."

I chuckled, popping the cap and taking a swig. "It's been a while. I know you're all as bloodthirsty as I am right now."

"Our welcoming ritual helps," Wolf said, grabbing two beers from the cooler in the corner and passing one to Devil, or Judas as he was known in the mortal world.

"Speak for yourself. How am I supposed to explain a shiner when I show up to court tomorrow morning? I can heal it myself, I guess. But next time paws off the face." Onyx grumbled, sitting on a log. He ran a hand through his messy black hair. We could have been brothers we looked so similar, though he had a more pretty-boy facade where I'd adopted nerd-core as my persona. We sat in companionable silence around the fire, Onyx stoking it every few moments. Judas stood at the corner, still in shadow, listening, watching. He was six feet six inches, easy, and massive. His dark skin only just revealed the whites of his eyes in the fire's flickering flame. I was glad he was on our side. Or at least I hoped he was. Sometimes it was hard to tell as he rarely spoke. But he knew who and what I was. And he was his own form of dark, too. Around this fire with my chosen brothers, I was me. Collectively, we breathed in the freedom of that awareness. All of us were shirtless, beaten, bloodied, and probably the happiest we'd be outside of slitting throats or whatever each of our own preferred brands of bloodlust were. Our monster names were our true titles, revealing more about us than the letters stamped across our counterfeit birth certificates. On our third beers, I spoke. "What'd you all think of her file?"

Wolf tossed his bottle into the bonfire with a shatter. "I was skeptical but you're right. She seems perfect. Alone, fearful, utterly fucked in the head according to the therapist notes." His long hair was tied at the nape of his neck. He looked animalistic in the raw orange firelight. Maybe his parents were giving us all a clue when they named him Wolfgang Jack.

"This killing is going to be fun. And right around Halloween, how cute." Onyx grinned. "I did some research on this guy, her stepfather. She wasn't exaggerating to Dr. Omar. He's a right nasty motherfucker. Maybe more so than she even knows."

"What'd you find?" Wolf asked, zeroing in. I could see his excitement building. He loved the chase as much as I did. It was why he spent his days as an investigative journalist. It was basically legal stalking and prying into lives, but he had the charm to pull it off.

Dragon stoked the fire, eliciting a peppering of flame and ash into the night sky. "Mr. Simon Seth Glen had a fuckton of court filings. The dude's got everything from assault and battery to stalking and harassment. He was sued for the involuntary manslaughter of Judy Pearl, this chick's mother, but wasn't charged due to a fucking technicality. I dug through the filing and he actually got away with making it look like a suicide. He's been in and out of Alabama State Prison, but he's currently out on parole. Which makes me wonder how he's chasing this Blythe girl across state lines and getting away with it. I don't get the impression he's a mastermind. He seems like your common wife beating piece of shit. But, you never know."

We pondered in quiet for a moment before I dared ask. "Any thoughts, Devil?"

Each of us waited patiently, knowing by now that when you speak to the Devil, you sure as hell wait for his answer. Or dismissal.

The ground crunched beneath his boots as he stepped forward. "Looks can be deceiving," his deep timbre rumbled. "Don't underestimate, men. A checkered past that halted its paper trail after the death of his wife . . . It's as if he disappeared, which is uncommon for someone so patterned. Something's changed in Simon Glen. He's not just looking for her. He's scaring her, hunting her. He's in this for the chase just as much as we are."

"You think we're dealing with a fellow killer?" Wolf asked in surprise.

Judas didn't answer.

"Ames, you wild motherfucker. You really did bring us a treat this Halloween, didn't you?" Onyx purred with glee. "Not like it matters. We can all sense anyone with bad intentions the moment they cross town lines. We'll all feel it. However, the chase is still the best part of the killing."

"Do you think the town will let him in?" I asked, stilling, mulling over Devil's guidance.

Wolf cracked open another beer, peering into the misty tree line. He sniffed once, assessing something or other with his keen beastly senses. "It let her in. It'll let in whatever's following her."

Onyx snorted. "Fucker picked the wrong town, didn't he? We might not be able to leave, but pretty soon, neither will he."

The fire cracked and hissed like the Gates of Hell were rattling at our discovery. Maybe they were. Simon Glen would be joining us in Hell, that was for certain. But more than that, he'd never see me coming. I'd be the chill in his spine. My tactics would make him feel the same fear he inflicted on his victims. Blythe's stepfather would see me out of the corner of his eye and turn to see no one and nothing. I drove my targets mad with terror before I ended them. I salivated at the thought of that taste of horror . . . There was nothing like it. I wanted him to be afraid not because of some sense of justice, but purely because I got off on it. The fear made my dick harder than any woman or man ever had.

Dragon, Wolf, and Devil were who I called my found family. My chosen brothers.

And me?

I was Ghost.

———

We talked strategy for a while before departing, each of us itching to exercise our skillsets. Things got boring for creatures like us. We were lions in a cage. We'd see each other again soon. Though Devil was absent the most, never staying in one spot long, traversing the coastline in search of . . . well, none of us knew for sure. He wasn't trapped here like the rest of us. *Must be nice.* Regardless, I was looking forward to donning my war paint again. Hallows Fest breathed life into the year. In the dead of night, I crept toward my blue dot, parking down the road but in view of her house. From my vantage point, I could see a purple glow emitting from her tiny window in the basement. I wondered if she'd show at support group the following day. Not like it mattered, I'd see her that night. All of us would.

I should have gone home. My knuckles were chapped, my back scabbing over, and I was in desperate need of a shower. My shirt was dirty and unbuttoned, revealing reddened abs. But fuck did I feel alive. The beatings were part training and part self-harm. We liked it: the pain,

the struggle, the promise of death by the hands of a friend. It was a difficult need to explain to a non-psychopath. Our human bodies needed the
beatings. The lashings were like cool breezes on our true forms. But
where was the fun in that? We understood each other. We'd all killed
hundreds of times and we'd kill hundreds more. I imagined we'd still
be doing our monster shit well into the end of the world. When we
didn't have the luxury of roaming the earth like Judas, The Devil, kills
were harder to come by. But I found this one, this target that fluttered
straight into my web, so it was my time to take the lead. Whoever
brought in our prey got the killing blow; the others played assist. They
typically got their blood lusts fulfilled as well, but the operation was in
my charge this time. I was already mulling over how and where. There
were unknown variables to consider with this mark. The Devil's
warning over Simon Glen's underestimated skill level didn't concern
me. He wasn't better than me. A mortal was too easy as it was. That was
why we dragged it out. It was why I usually killed them as a man and
not a monster, unless I felt like shifting at the very end just to scare the
fuckers. This deadbeat sure as fuck wasn't better than the four of us. But
I didn't have a current location on him, and neither did the boys. That
was unusual but not unheard of. We'd handled targets like him before.
The letters intrigued me. It was poetic, cryptic, artistic, even, to send a
blank letter to every address she landed. It seemed too creative for him.
But Devil was right, this man liked the chase. Just like I did. I got off on
the kill. That darling girl's fear had my cock straining against my pants
the day she stumbled into my office. It danced and tingled on my forked
tongue. I imagined the taste of her fear if she knew what I was. What if I
showed her a glimpse, forced her to look . . .

But I didn't hurt women. The thought was unfathomable and sent
pulses of rage through my blood. My mortal prey were capable, overgrown bullies, abusers, fellow psychopaths. They deserved to be
haunted by me. My paranormal opponents were a different story, and I
supposed I'd be seeing a few of them at Hallows Fest soon.

What interested me personally, what dragged me into fixation right
now, however, was her. That wasn't supposed to be. She's wasn't a part
of the plan, not really. I didn't change the oil for Florence Jenkins before

I slaughtered her old teacher who molested her. I didn't invite Jordan Kerr to a support group before I buried his ex-boyfriend for beating him. When the security footage plastered across every news station showed a man in a hat abducting a teenager from outside a car wash four towns over, I didn't check in on the parents after I let Onyx feast on his blood while I cut the sicko to pieces and dumped several bags of his worthless body into Lake Ash. That asshole fled right into Ash Grove; we didn't even get to hunt him.

So why was I talking to Blythe?

Why couldn't I leave her street and go home? I told myself I'd track her because following her meant finding her stepfather. If he were watching her, I'd be fucking watching him. But hell if I could drive away. She was just a mark. A means to an end to get my need to kill fulfilled. I was bored, restless. My abilities were waning from dormancy so badly I couldn't even sense her without the help of technology. This was my pathway to offering the monster inside me his blood sacrifice so he didn't strangle me in my sleep. This was purely selfish. A desire born of blood and violence and chaos. I cared for nothing and no one, least of all some human woman I'd just met.

But the thoughts shook their chains and rattled in my mind.

Why'd I stay up all night staring at the purple glow?

CHAPTER 7

Blythe

HORROR MOVIE WALK OF SHAME

I enjoy tremendously every single moment of my life because death, all the time, is very close watching me and death might catch me. And every five minutes death don't catch me, I enjoy tremendously.

Salvador Dali

I dreamt of Ames all night. The way he wiped the engine grease from his thick fingers . . . That stupid tuft of hair I wanted to push back to see his face. I wondered how I'd fit in his lap, straddling him in his office chair . . . I awoke wet.

Literally.

Sitting up, I rubbed my eyes and pawed at my drenched comforter. I wondered if I'd slept with my water bottle open, as half of my queen-sized bed were soda cans and makeup. I peeled off my blanket, my bare feet hitting the ground with a squish. Murky cold water puddled around my toes. I swore, dropping to my knees and pulling my box out from under the bed. Water had crept through the holes in my container. Any opened foods were ruined: a lidless, half-eaten jar of peanut butter, a loaf of bread, a bag of chips. I pulled out a dripping envelope stack: the letters. I'd saved each blank letter I'd received from my abuser. There was no reason to save them, but I did, if only to remind myself it was all real should I get too complacent and forget. *I can't settle down. I can't stop hiding.* Ames made me promise to tell him if I got another letter here. He said he knew people who could help. No offense to him, but I didn't think Old Man Winston down of Ash Grove's Sheriff's Department would be able to do anything about my rageful and vindictive stalker. Sheriff Winston picked up takeout last week atop his lawnmower because the police cruiser's battery died. Was he going to mow my stepdad to death?

I was on my own, alone, as always. Though I appreciated the semblance of someone caring about me, even if it was a stranger and it was his job. The small bit of interaction I'd had with Ames Cove left me feeling like a lovestruck middle-schooler. Apparently, all it took for me to hopelessly fantasize about someone was the smallest amount of human decency. Embarrassment washed over me with the mucky basement water. He probably had a girlfriend or boyfriend already. He certainly wasn't going to give the likes of me a second look even if he were single.

And it didn't matter. I'd either be running away or dead in a few weeks. The truth of that fact hit me like a cold wave of dread.

I hoisted my wet box of everything onto my soggy bed with a thud. "Dammit," I breathed, turning around to find my clothes I'd left strewn along the floor all soaked with filth. Slipping on my boots and shrugging on my gray robe, the only thing I had hanging, I grabbed my bag and keys. Stumbling out the creaky door, I marched up the gravel lot, the crisp first morning of October eyeing me like the crows that sat in a line on the oak branch above my car. My legs were chilled, exposed in black and white striped sleep shorts. My Radiohead T-shirt was peppered with holes, my pale skin shining through. I was about two seconds from ducking into my Honda and screaming when my eye caught on the front yard. Early morning fog blanketed the withered grass, stretching out across the neighborhood. Locust Road was like any other quaint, small-town street. I'd seen only elderly folks and a couple of young families with kids. Across the way, past the aging homes already sprinkled with jack-'o-lanterns in various sizes, stretched a tree line to a dense forest. A raven cawed above me, startling me as I blinked to make out the shape. The distinct outline of a man stood at the edge of the forest. *It's a neighbor; it's just a neighbor.* Whoever it was, he was staring right at me. I couldn't make out any features from such a distance, except he was large and seemingly unmoving . . . like a statue. Nervously, I lifted a hand and waved. Not even a sway greeted me. Whoever it was just stood preternaturally still and staring. I swallowed. *It's not him. It's not him. What if it's him?*

Suddenly, a hand clamped down on my shoulder.

I screamed.

Mr. Moore stumbled back a step. "Sorry, darlin', I didn't mean to frighten you. I'm not used to seeing folks out this early. Honey, I'm afraid we've had a leak downstairs. I hope it didn't ruin too many of your things. We'll get that cleaned up today. I'm sorry for the trouble."

My pulse beat in my throat as I took in Mr. Moore's red plaid shirt and wrinkled eyes. "I was just wondering who that was over there." I swallowed, turning back to point at the tree line. The gravel crunched as Mr. Moore stepped next to me and put a hand over his forehead, squinting. But whoever it was, they were gone.

"Your mind must be playing tricks on you. I get up at five every morning and I've never seen anyone else around. Especially not near the trees. Did nobody ever tell you not to look into the trees, girl? The woods here are ugly even on a good day. Don't go out exploring in these woods, alright? Easy to . . . lose your way."

An eeriness settled in my bones. It was so quiet I heard the ruffling of the bird's wings above us as it watched with more interest than any bird should have.

"I'll keep that in mind," I replied, my breath like smoke between us. "And don't worry about the leak. I don't have much stuff anyway."

Mr. Moore clutched his broom and nodded. "Well, we'll wave this month's rent all the same. You have a nice day, young lady. Keep your wits about you. It's October in Ash Grove." He chuckled before rasping a cough. "Get ready for the ghosts."

"Yes, sir." I wrapped my robe tighter around my waist and slid into my frosty car. My gaze hesitantly went to the tree line again, despite his warning not to look. Empty. I cranked my engine and turned up the heat when a knock on my window pulled my attention. Rolling it down, I smiled. "Hi again, Mr. Moore."

"I forgot to tell ya, this came in the mail for you yesterday."

My heart sank into my soggy boots and a cold fear paralyzed me as I reluctantly took the letter from Mr. Moore's veiny hand. He gave the hood of my car a friendly tap as he slowly walked to the street and began sweeping. I held the letter with a tremble. I didn't need to open it. It would be blank. And it was from him. He knew I was here. I knew it was coming. It always did.

Shoving the envelope into my purse, I rolled out onto the street, giving my landlord a polite wave. Every moment I trailed through the fog, I felt eyes on me. It seemed that this town itself had eyes. It watched me through the crows, the shop windows, and rustle of the wind in the trees.

What would I do this time? Run again? Hide in place? I had to decide quick. Because someone was watching. Something was always watching.

PEOPLE SAID cockroaches would survive the apocalypse. That was probably true. But I'd say diners would too. There was something about old diners that stayed the same in every small town I traversed. They were always hardy yet looked like they could collapse at any moment. Grimy even through the disinfectant shine. I slumped into a booth, clutching my second refill of coffee. My mind was blank, lost in the steam and idle chatter of the restaurant. I wasn't safe here. I wasn't safe anywhere. But I didn't want to leave. For the first time, I'd landed in a place I didn't want to flee. Something about this weird-ass town fit. Maybe its odd matched my own.

But right now, all I had was a blank letter from a psychopath and a soggy basement. I had no escape plan, no way to defend myself, and no one was coming to save me.

"Excuse me." Knuckles vibrated lightly against my table. I glanced up to see a tall, good-looking man in a suit. His hair was black and slicked back. He reminded me of a more self-assured Dr. Cove. "You look like a person who knows about letters."

My breath caught. "Excuse me?"

"May I sit?"

I swallowed down the fear threatening to overtake me and nodded, frozen in place. "What do you mean letters?"

The man gave a lopsided smile and slid into the adjacent booth. "Letters of the alphabet, what else would I mean?"

My cheeks heated. "Great, another stranger to toy with me."

He chuckled darkly. "You mean I'm not the first local weirdo to bother you this morning?" He looked at his watch. "It's seven-thirty. I guess I need to be quicker next time. I need a six-letter word for how the victim in a horror movie walks so their predator doesn't hear them."

He *was* toying with me. "Who are you?" I asked, my fear easing into curiosity. Something about him felt familiar but wild, unpredictable. He smiled a smile that told me he knew more than he'd ever say.

"I'm a friend." Silence hung between us for a moment.

He scribbled on his crossword for a moment, obviously comfortable sitting across from a woman he didn't know. He reminded me of the football players in high school who just assumed that every female wanted them around. The fact should have annoyed me, I should have moved, but I was too tired, too stunned, and maybe a small part of me liked that I wasn't sitting alone for once. "So you're a local? Can you tell me what the hell is up with this place?"

He snickered, not looking up from his page. "Well, Tim's Diner has the best burgers in Ash Grove if you get here on Wednesday mornings at eleven right after the meat shipment drops—"

"Funny. You know that's not what I mean," I interrupted. He was irritating, but in that way a guy who's been your friend for a long time was. I couldn't help the grin that pulled at the corner of my mouth. "The obsession with October, this Hallows Fest, the ghost stories everyone alludes to but won't tell me about . . . the lack of tourists. What's the deal?"

"Good questions, you'd make a fine attorney. I'm hiring a paralegal if you're interested."

I crossed my arms and sighed. It was hopeless. "It doesn't matter. I'm not going to be here very long anyway." The words chilled me because in that moment, I truly didn't know if I meant I'd leave or I'd die soon. Either or both were inevitable.

The man's stare caught mine, his green eyes gleaming the most vibrant shade of emerald I'd ever seen. "A lot of what stories say are monsters are really just people. Like the story of this town. Ash Grove, the tiny little gothic town that was slaughtered on Halloween in eighteen twenty-three." Chills nicked my arms as he continued, "Some say it was beasts from the forest, some say it was an army attack, the others . . . think maybe it was the Devil himself. But does the answer matter? I think people would prefer a human variety of bad guy. Something they can explain. But regardless, there are scary stories of people . . . that are really monsters. Something else, something unholy, something unexplainable. Those are scarier than anything in our woods or campfire tales."

My breath caught in my chest. "Just spooky old ghost stories, I guess."

The man rolled up his paper and stood. "Court awaits."

I replied, staring at my lukewarm coffee. "Tiptoe."

"Pardon?"

"The answer to your crossword. To get away from a predator in a horror film, you tiptoe."

With a grin, he unrolled his paper and filled in the squares in accomplishment. "See? I knew you'd know." The man turned and took a carafe from the bar counter and refilled my cup. "You're not alone, Blythe."

I opened my mouth in surprise, but before I could say a word, he'd walked out. In his wake, the old waitress toddled over and sat a heaping plate of pancakes, eggs, and bacon in front of me. "Oh, I didn't order this—"

"Courtesy of Onyx Hart, dear."

Tears swelled in my eyes as I inhaled the salty sweet aroma of a freshly cooked breakfast. Something terrible, awful, and ghastly was happening now.

I was beginning to love it here.

RAJA ALWAYS PAID me in cash after each shift. Without having to pay for rent or breakfast, I had enough to buy some new clothes. Ironically, my backseat was filled with bags, but they were costumes for Hallows Fest. Yesenia fully stocked me with sexy outfits for Hallows so I wouldn't have to repeat too often. The festival was kicking off that night. The anticipation tempered my anxiety over being found. I knew my stepfather would make a move eventually, but I was hoping to maybe get another month in first. Regardless, I needed something to wear other than my sleep clothes and robe. I stumbled into Yesenia's shop, embarrassed over my attire. I remembered seeing some casual smocked dresses and knit cardigans on my last visit. This time I was prepared for the dangling skeleton that greeted me. More decorations had popped up since last time, though the shop didn't need it. The entire ceiling housed hanging dried herbs and flowers. Crystals, bones, and runes lined the shelves between garments. And I was pretty sure the bones weren't Halloween props. Maybe it all wasn't so entirely strange. Many towns I'd travelled through put huge emphasis on Christmas, and decorations and festivities would stretch throughout November and December. Ash Grove's focus was on being a Halloween town, which even made sense with its old architecture and bright red, orange, and yellow trees. The townspeople were a bit kooky, but they seemed to mean well. I really hadn't met an unkind person since my arrival. But the man this morning's, Onyx's, words played in my head. The history of Ash Grove sounded brutal and mysterious. An entire town slaughtered on Halloween and hundreds of years later there's no consensus on how it happened?

If those stories were true, why would the town celebrate Halloween so heavily? It seemed more natural it would be a day of mourning, not a month of celebrating. Then again, it was probably all just a scary story meant to frighten children. Made and told to keep children out of the woods at night.

Some say it was the beasts of the woods.

That was . . . an oddly specific statement. And eerie after what I saw this morning standing at the tree line. It was probably my mind playing tricks on me and I was reading too much into it. Onyx was an attorney, I presumed, so he thrived off fucking with peoples' heads. But then, how'd he know my name if I were just some random to mess with?

I wondered if I could ask Mr. and Mrs. Moore at dinner the following week. Would they think I was crazy for asking about old stories? Something didn't quite add up, and not in that usual way that legends were a bit outlandish. But something was off that felt specific. It felt as if everyone knew but no one wanted to say. I hoped dancing that Hallows Fest could shed some light on the mysteries that were surrounding me.

The oddest thing about this entire situation was probably the fact I was thinking about stupid ghost stories instead of things like, oh, escaping a violent death by the hands of my criminal stepfather.

But also, I was considering stopping by the support group Dr. Cove told me about. It was only a short walk through the town from Yesenia's shop, but I couldn't show up in my pjs. I already looked like enough of an invalid as it was. "Hello, dear," an older woman's voice croaked as I thumbed at a blue dress. "I'm Marcelene. Please let me know if I can help you find anything."

The older woman was short with long and wild gray hair. Her rosy cheeks glowed as she smiled warmly. She only looked to be in her forties, and not like a grandma in the slightest.

"Hi, I'm Blythe. I'm new in town. You must be Yesenia's abuela?"

She cackled softly. "Yes, child, I am. And everyone here knows who you are." She looked me up and down. "Your legs must be freezing. I hope you're here for a pair of our wool-lined leggings."

"Oh, those sound perfect, thank you. I'm renting a basement apartment that flooded overnight. All of mine are ruined, unfortunately. Is Yesenia around?"

Marcelene pulled four pairs of thick leggings out of a chest in the corner. "No, not today, but I'm sure you'll see her soon." She winked. "I hear you're our new fox. Don't worry, I'm sworn to secrecy. I would never reveal someone's identity at Hallows."

I clutched the leggings to my chest, already absorbing their cozy warmth. "Is that another festival rule? You can't share someone's identity if you know?"

Marcelene plucked a long-sleeved maxi dress off its hanger and passed it to me. "Yes and no. Who we are changes at Hallows. Even if you knew who someone was, they may not respond to their regular name within the celebration. They may not even remember it. Some would say the grounds of Hallows are bewitched."

That was . . . interesting. "Wow, this town takes its cosplay very seriously, huh?"

She cackled again. "You're about to find out just how seriously, dear."

"Should I bring anything other than my costume?"

"Just your wits," she said coyly, and I could see the resemblance between her and her granddaughter. They had that same feisty charm.

I grabbed a pair of wool socks to add to my stack of clothing. "So do you believe it was serial killers, an army, or monsters that took out the town in the legends?"

Marcelene's smile faltered as she tucked a strand of hair behind her ear. I got the impression I'd said something wrong. "I'm sorry. I didn't mean to offend . . ."

"Who told you that?" she asked, tone somber as she straightened the row of crystal balls.

"Someone I met this morning at the diner. His name was Onyx Hart."

She snorted. "He would know."

Ames had mentioned that everyone here had their own version of events, their own ghost story they believed about the town. What I didn't realize was how seriously some seemed to take it. It was just an old spooky story, right? A silly tradition.

I paid for my items with what I suspected was a steep discount. Marcelene was kind enough to let me change in their dressing room before leaving. My ugly bruises still on full display, I pulled on a long-sleeved navy dress that hooked around the thumbs and a thick beige cardigan. The luxurious fabric fit my curves perfectly, making me look more adult than my usual band T-shirt and ripped jeans combo. Dodging the white envelope of doom, I pulled my eye makeup from my purse and did a smokey eye complete with burgundy lipstick. My long, wavy brown hair fell nicely over my shoulders. I thought I looked like someone who lived here. Like if you were passing through, you might stop and ask me for directions. I'd be holding Dr. Cove's hand as we took our morning walk with our dog, and I'd tell you exactly how to get to India Garden. The tourists would drive off and Ames and I would chuckle about how I used to work there. He'd say he stopped by just to see me that night so long ago when he worked on my car. Then he'd sweep me into his arms and swoop down for a movie starlet kiss . . . *And I was daydreaming again.*

Gathering the rest of my things, I thanked Yesenia's abuela and headed out, but then something strange happened.

As I turned the knob and pushed out, the door wouldn't budge. Thinking it must be jammed, I pushed harder. I may as well have been shoving against a brick wall.

"I think the door must be jammed—"

Marcelene walked slowly toward me. Her gaze was set on mine, not paying attention to the door. "It seems you have more ghosts chasing you then we have stories."

"What do you mean by that?" I didn't know why, but I tried the door again. It wouldn't move. It wasn't locked, but it was immovable. *I came in just fine . . .*

"I love my granddaughter and don't want to see her or her family in danger. We don't get many newcomers, and I know a girl as young as you is either running from something or someone."

I swallowed, nervous now. "You're not totally wrong about that. But I promise you, the last thing I want is for anyone to get caught up in my shit."

She hummed as she stopped a foot away and leaned against a table of tarot decks. "We're wary of outsiders here in Ash Grove. Always have been."

My chest tightened. I wasn't in danger, I didn't think, but this conversation while I wiggled the door handle was unnerving to say the least. "I understand, ma'am—"

"But . . . ," she interrupted, walking over and reaching towards my neck. I froze. "If you choose to stay and your intentions are pure . . . you'll find that the town protects its own. It's possible to find some level of peace. But no harm should befall my Yesenia, understood? Not from you or . . . *him*." She spat the last word like a curse at the same moment she tore a sales tag from my collar with a pop. I jumped and decided not to ask questions.

"Um . . . thank you," I squeaked as her gray-violet eyes surveyed me. As if she'd decided something in her mind, she jerked a short nod.

"October in Ash Grove is like none other." She smiled. "Enjoy."

I thanked her again, and this time when I turned the knob, the door swayed open with ease.

THE WALK across town was decidedly less tense than my conversation with Yesenia's abuela. Her words rattled in my mind like bolts in a tin can, each word bringing on only another set of questions. Her wanting to protect her family was understandable, and I did look like a shady character. She was spot on about me running from something. But I guessed that wasn't too difficult to decipher. The town would protect me? That choice of words unnerved me for some reason I couldn't quite describe. And then finally, the way she spat *him*. *Him* who? My stepfather, maybe? How would she know? Or maybe she assumed a man was chasing me. But something about the way she said it . . . made me believe she knew him. Whoever he was, she must have been mistaken. I hadn't gotten very close to anyone here, especially no man. Not that I wouldn't like too, however . . .

I stopped outside the jagged and looming stone church in the center of town. Ames's old vintage Mustang sat parked off the street, the sharp wrought iron fencing behind it creating a giant cage of orange and black amongst the . . . gravestones. *Jesus, this town was creepy.* Two additional vintage model cars were parked alongside the Mustang, and I wondered if they were support group attendees too. I was about to find out. I opened the gate with a squeak and a raven cawed. My gaze locked eyes with the bird sitting on a low branch in the middle of the church's courtyard. "Are you the same crow from earlier?" I asked, stepping over a pumpkin. "Are you following me?" I almost tripped over another pumpkin. "Join the club, bird," I scoffed, stomping up the narrow stone steps. With a glance over my shoulder, I saw the crow remained fixated on me. Shaking off the eerie cloud that had seemed to form over my head since this morning, I clicked open the huge, blood-red door. The murmur of voices inside laid my path before me. I wove through a broad corridor, past crimson crucifixes and paintings of blood-stained lambs. Lamb's Blood Church. The name was almost as off-putting as the vibe. Churches had always freaked me out, though. My mother dragged me to Catholic mass every Christmas Eve and Easter. Most kids fell asleep in the pews. I sat fidgeting with my fingernails, counting down the prayers until time to leave. Thirty-five prayers on Christmas Eve, forty-one prayers on Easter, if you were wondering.

The male voices grew louder, though their tone was hushed. "It shouldn't have been so easy to get in," a low voice, I think it was Dr. Cove, said. "We know one can be followed in, but until now only by those with good intentions."

"Unless someone, or something, brought him in. That's a loophole, too," a raspier man responded.

Ames huffed with the sound of a chair scuffing the floor. "Impossible. They're all accounted for, plus Cat is always on watch."

Cat? Was that his girlfriend? My heart dropped. Yes, the conversation itself should have concerned me more than the mention of another woman, but the thought of my fantasy-world being destroyed so quickly was painful.

"But you're sure he's here?" a familiar voice asked, but I wasn't sure how I knew it. "I haven't picked up anything."

"He's under the radar somehow, and fuck if that isn't pissing me off." Ames cursed before the chair scuffed again. I crept closer to the room's entrance . . .

Suddenly, the ancient creaky door swung open. I startled, putting a hand to my chest. Ames cocked his head to the side for a moment, his blue eyes catching the dusty streams of light. For a moment, he looked like he could be an image etched along the beautiful stained glass of the sanctuary. A dark angel. Lucifer in a black beanie and glasses. "You came." He smiled, gesturing me inside. "Welcome."

"Hey, Blue dot," a tall, muscular man with long brown hair pulled into a low ponytail jeered. He poured two paper cups of coffee and walked toward me.

Ames shot him a death glare and the guy chuckled. I looked to Dr. Cove. "Blue dot?"

"Inside joke," he replied through gritted teeth.

I accepted the coffee from the smirking guy, noticing the golden wisps throughout his gorgeous wavy hair. He was beefy, with sun-kissed bronze skin. Black tribal tattoos curled around his thick biceps. It was an effort not to gawk. He was gorgeous. Ames cleared his throat, sounding annoyed for some reason. "This is my buddy who apparently really wants his ass kicked."

The muscled gorgeous guy scoffed, "That didn't work so well for you last time, did it?" He directed his attention to me. "Since my friend here has apparently forgotten how to act around a lady, I'll introduce myself. Hello, I'm Wolfgang Jack, but everyone calls me Wolf."

Wolf felt like an intuitive and appropriate name for him.

"Nice to meet you. I'm Blythe Pearl," I replied softly, letting his massive hand swallow mine in a shake. Then it occurred to me. "Hey, you're the journalist. I read your article on Hallows Fest the other day."

"Wow, look at that, Wolf. One person reads your ramblings," the familiar voice sounded as he made his way nearer.

Then I pieced it together. "Onyx? From this morning?"

"Yes, ma'am. Great job *tiptoeing* down the hallway like we couldn't sense you the moment you stood outside." He winked a dark-green eye and grabbed a danish. He'd unbuttoned his collared shirt, giving him a sexy, ruffled look.

A rush of heat invaded my cheeks.

Wolf elbowed him in the ribs. "Dude, stop being weird to the one person who reads my shit."

"Technically, I only read one article, and to be honest, I skimmed it," I replied, staring down into my bitter coffee.

Silence spanned a beat before laughter erupted. It shook the dust from the rafters it was so loud. When was the last time I made a joke? It felt nice. And their reaction was like a warm blanket on my heart. I couldn't help but smile and let out a giggle myself at their collective merriment. Ames put a hand on my shoulder. "You're going to fit in just fine, kid."

Kid. There was that word again. That was all he saw me as. A child.

We all took our seats in cold metal folding chairs arranged in a circle. It just occurred to me that I didn't know what to even say here. But I felt comfortable with them. Even though we'd just met, it felt like we'd all known each other forever, as cheesy as that sounds. Or maybe my lack of real human connection from years of running was finally catching up with me. My daydreams were getting harder to control and definitely getting worse. I almost forgot where I was for a moment while changing clothes earlier.

"Welcome to support group," Ames began, crossing an ankle over his knee. "This is an open forum. We chat about whatever. But whatever we say stays within this group." He was wearing black jeans and a V-neck black T-shirt. I couldn't help but notice his sculpted arm as he raised his mug to those perfect lips. *God, I needed to get laid before I died.* These men were sending me into a frenzy. I pushed out the fantasy that was trying to shove its way into my mind. *Later,* I told myself. "I thought we could talk about self-care today. Things that can be done to help ease the stress and tension that post-traumatic stress can bring on."

Onyx made a noise and Wolf gave him a rough shove, causing the chair to shriek at the movement. Ames stared daggers at his friends while I suppressed my grin with a sip of dark roast. *I knew how I'd like to relieve some tension . . . .*I forced another daydream out.

Onyx spoke up. "Like what, Ames, things like *following* your passions? *Pursuing* your dreams—"

Wolf kicked his shin, eliciting a groan and a laugh from the green-eyed trickster. Onyx removed his jacket and rolled up his sleeves, revealing a scaly tattoo wrapping around his arm and disappearing up his sleeve. When I glanced up, he was looking straight at me, suddenly serious. I quickly flicked my glance away and back to Ames.

"If you assholes don't take this seriously, I'm kicking you out," he said with a quirk of his lip. Honestly, I would have been fine with just sitting and watching them all goof off. There was something comforting in their brotherly banter. Ames reached over, putting a hand on my knee, and my heart stopped. "Sorry, I told them to behave."

Tearing my gaze away from his blue stare back to my coffee, I swallowed. "No, it's okay. I like it." I could feel the warmth spreading across my cheeks and hoped my meager makeup was enough to at least make it a little unnoticeable. His hand retracted and I wanted to whine for it back. My knee pulsated, my inner thigh cold and screaming for more. One more touch like that, please.

Wolf spoke, taking a bite of pastry. "What do you do for fun, Blythe? Tell us about yourself."

"She's damn good at crosswords, I know that." Onyx grinned, shooting me another wink. My heart fluttered. *God damn.*

Fiddling with my thumbs, I felt their attention fixate onto me. I hoped my dress looked okay. "I'm not sure I've ever done anything for fun, if I'm honest. I wanted to be a therapist or a social worker, but college wasn't in the cards for me. I don't stay in once spot long enough." I shrugged. "I like music, even if Dr. Cove seriously doubts my musical tastes." I dared to shoot him a playful glance. The corner of his lip quirked in the sexiest way. I could tell he wanted to say something back but instead stayed quiet, still giving me the floor, letting me speak at my own pace. It was probably just a therapy trick, but it made the butterflies in my belly flutter all the same. In my experience, most people spoke over the quiet girls. "Running from state to state doesn't leave room for many friends or hobbies." When I worked the nerve to look up, I expected to see smirks or eye rolls. *Oh, poor little Blythe.* Or maybe they'd poke fun at my lack of social skills and friends. I couldn't maintain eye contact for anything. But what I saw etched on each of their expressions took my breath away. Onyx's and Wolf's expressions were steely, jaws tense as they listened. Wolf straightened with a loud exhale and ran a hand through his hair, as if he'd just had a tense internal conversation with himself and came out angry. Onyx's deep emerald gaze looked to be plotting, sorting through the Rubik's Cube of my predicament.

And Ames . . . The look on his face was pure fury. Like the day we met when I told him about the cause of my panic attack. It chilled my blood, and for a brief moment, I wondered what lay under the thick-rimmed glasses and shaggy black hair that masked his strong features. Was there more than the mild-mannered doctor lurking beneath his skin?

"Have you received any communications?" Ames growled. "I hope you don't mind, but I did share your story with Onyx and Wolf, hoping they could maybe provide some insights into resources for you. They're both very well connected." Maybe I should have been annoyed that he shared my biggest secret with them, but I wasn't. My heart took comfort in my fear being revealed. It made me feel like perhaps my shame wasn't too much for people. At least, it didn't seem to be too much for these guys.

My previously heated heart iced over as I pulled the envelope from my purse. I passed it to Dr. Cove. "My landlord gave it to me this morning. See for yourself," I breathed, trying to calm my shaking voice.

I wasn't just telling someone now; I was showing them. I'd never shown anyone the letters. No one had ever asked to see. No therapist or cop. And what did it matter? They couldn't do anything. Even now, what could a shrink, an attorney, and a writer do to scare off my attacker? I was screwed no matter what.

Ames tore the envelope open with malice, quickly surveying the folded paper inside. It was always the same. Blank.

When I glanced up, he was still holding it, staring at the white sheet. His face paled slightly before his jaw tensed. Something dark flashed across his gaze as he looked to his friends. Something unspoken passed between them as the tone of the room grew heavy.

"Blythe," Onyx began, softer than I'd ever heard him speak. "You're sure the person pursuing you is your stepfather?"

My brow furrowed in confusion. "Yes, I um . . . We had a run-in before I came here. He didn't hurt me, at least not in any big way. But it's what drove me to take a million weird turns and end up here in Ash Grove. My phone's navigation still says this place doesn't exist." I gave a weak laugh, but no one smiled. They were figuring it out. *Shit. No.* They couldn't find out what I did. If they knew what was happening, they either wouldn't believe me or they'd be horrified. Probably both.

"Did he hurt you?" Ames said with lethal calm.

My heart fluttered at the tone of his voice, like he . . . cared. It was likely me confusing therapist with more, again. "No, not really. I tripped while running. But he's here now, so." I shook my head.

Wolf spoke. "Are you certain he's acting alone?"

"Wolfgang," Ames chastised, as if to keep him from saying more . . . but what?

I looked, confused, between the two of them. "Yeah, I mean, I've never seen anyone else. I've never really thought about it. You don't think he has a friend helping, do you? Oh shit, new anxiety unlocked." My heart pounded in my chest as my breath quickened. I couldn't be sure what happened, but before I could see anyone move, all three men surrounded me. "I can't breathe," I rasped. "I hate it when this happens," I whined, suddenly embarrassed to be having an episode in front of them.

"Panic attacks are normal, Blythe. You have complex post-traumatic stress disorder. There's nothing wrong with you. We're not judging you. We want to help. Deep breaths in." Ames took a deep breath as if to show me how to inhale. It helped as I imitated him and sucked in a breath.

My hands shook as if they were freezing. Onyx enclosed both of my hands in his palms, giving Ames a look. With a short nod, Onyx got whatever answer he was seeking and suddenly warmth flooded my body, as if I'd just drunk hot chocolate and been wrapped in a blanket by a fire. My eyes drifted closed and my daydream sucked me into its grip. *I'm cuddled by a fireplace, clutching a mug of cocoa. I take a sip and nibble at the marshmallow foam. Voices carry in from the kitchen. Men joke with each other while soft, fluffy snow floats out the window. It smells like roast beef and potatoes, and my mouth waters. "Where's my Little Ghost?" a deep voices coos.*

When I turn around, smiling, hoping to see them—everything goes black.

CHAPTER 8

Ames

CAT BLACK SCORNE

> Tis the night—the night of the grave's delight, and the warlocks are at their play; Ye think that without the wild winds shout, but no, it is they—it is they.
> *Cleveland Coxe*

It was risky, but I was desperate. Even without the blue dot, I could taste her fear roaming through town. All day, it imprinted on my tongue. Her fear tasted like pomegranate and black tea. Sweet, strong as hell, and intoxicating as fuck. It was all I could do to let her into that shop while Marcelene stood post. The old bat. When the door locked, I was about two seconds from kicking it in when she stumbled outside. I ducked behind a scarecrow and watched for a moment before booking it over to the church. I took the side entrance and joined the boys in the sanctuary. This was one of the only places we could talk, really talk, without the threat of someone hearing. Onyx's serpentine eyes met mine the instant I knew she was near. He raised his eyebrows. "You weren't kidding. This bitch is always terrified."

Yeah, no shit.

I didn't like using him to sedate her. But she was safe with me, with us, even if she didn't know it yet. Wolf scooped her sleeping body into his arms and shouldered her purse. "Looks good on you," Onyx jeered, crossing his arms and cocking his head at me. "Well? What now, boss?"

With Judas absent, I was the boss, and Judas was rarely here. If something involved talking, you could count him out. As much as I wanted to take her to the attic, it wasn't the wisest choice since I'd be leaving her alone. If she woke up in a strange place all alone, it could bring on another panic attack. I also didn't trust myself around her. She was hard enough to resist with the boys within arm's reach. If she were in my bed . . . I may chain her there and never let her leave. The thought sent a lightning bolt to my dick and I hardened instantly. Onyx's property was in the middle of nowhere and took forever to drive to. She'd wake up in the car and think she'd been abducted. She *was* being abducted, but she didn't need to be afraid. "Wolf?" I questioned.

His eyes roamed her slowly, his grip tightening ever so slightly. Not sure how I felt about that. Or the sudden interest Onyx seemed to take in her, either. But those were thoughts to sort through at another time. "I'll take her. She'll be safe with the pack."

I had no doubt that she would be. Looking to Onyx, I could hardly contain my rage. "Let's go kill a motherfucker."

His answering smile was pure evil, revealing a glint of those legendary fangs. "You know I'm dying to get my hands on this prick. But damn, humans die so quickly, and then you're the only one who gets to have fun."

He wasn't wrong.

"Speaking of human . . ." I jerked out the letter. ". . . look at this." Wolf raised an eyebrow and pressed in next to Onyx. They recoiled at the same moment, as if slapped. "My reaction exactly."

"What the actual fuck?" Wolf rumbled, his voice turning straight carnivore. "How is this possible?"

"Devil was right, apparently. He's either like us or he has help from someone like us. No one else could read this shit. No one else could see it."

Onyx crumpled the paper and shoved it in his pocket. "She gets a letter everywhere she goes? Where are the others?"

"Her apartment is a shoebox. Shouldn't be hard to find if she's kept them. But I don't care about that now. We can read them as we toss them atop his burning corpse."

Onyx hummed. "Damn, now you're speaking my language."

Fucking pyro.

I HELPED LAY Blythe gently in the back of Wolf's Corvette, her hair soft as velvet, her dark-painted lips like a blackberry in a jar of milk. I wanted to bite them, and then I wanted to fuck her, hard. I wanted to fuck every ounce of fear out of her. I wanted to fuck her brave. Because she could be brave now because she had me, and I'd kill anyone trying to hurt her. She'd been through enough, she'd run long enough, and it was time to stay. But also? What in the ever-loving fuck was I thinking? I couldn't get involved with her. I couldn't live a normal life. What would she think if she knew the truth? She'd be more afraid than ever. I wouldn't blame her. But as much as I loved the taste of her fresh fear on my tongue, to think of the source of that fear being me . . . It wasn't something I thought I could put her through. To open someone's eyes to the terror of our existence . . .

Blythe was running from a criminal, and possibly more. I couldn't allow her to fall into the arms of something worse than either of them. She was a little white mouse hiding from an owl in a snake hole. And I was a whole pit of vipers. No, for once in my cursed life, I was going to do the virtuous thing and not touch her. I'd kill the asshole and send her on her way to wherever she pleased. To meet a nice guy who could give her the white picket fence life. Not the graveyard and haunted house I had to offer. This was just another obsession. I was prone to fixation which was where my proclivity for stalking originated. Blythe was prey. It was natural to want to chase prey. But I wouldn't let myself destroy her life further. She needed freedom, a white knight, not me. Not Hell's reject.

"Where to?" Onyx asked, cracking his knuckles once Wolf peeled out in the direction of his community. "This town's so fucking nosy, surely someone's seen the bastard."

"Something tells me he's thought of that. We need to think one step ahead and not fuck around." I kicked at the tire of my Mustang in annoyance. I really needed to kill someone. And fuck someone. In whichever order. "You know what really pisses me off?" I shook my head. "I slept in my car outside her place last night. I was there, all night, and I didn't sense the motherfucker. I can't sense her. This letter didn't come by post. It was hand-delivered. He was right outside and he's just fucking with her. If I had been thinking with something other than my cock, I could have ended him then and there."

Onyx's brows rose. "Interesting. Now I want to go feel around her place, see if I pick up on any imprints left behind." He paused, shoving his hands in his pockets and looking in the direction of Wolf's place. "So . . . you're into her, then?"

Anger rose in my chest at the question. The last thing I needed was the boys sniffing around her like she was a piece of meat. I shot him a warning glare. "It doesn't matter. Stay away from her."

He raised an eyebrow, about to object, when I slid into my car. "I'll catch up with you later."

"Where are you going?"

I gripped the steering wheel, feeling the magnetic pull before I even uttered the words.

"Cat."

CHAPTER 9

Blythe

RUNNING WITH THE WOLVES

> There are nights when the wolves are silent and only the moon howls.
> *George Carlin*

Crickets chirping and children laughing drew me from my deep slumber. When was the last time I slept so soundly? I sat up with a stretch and my fingers brushed the wooden ceiling. Confusion rattled through me as I took in my surroundings. This wasn't my bed. The dark gray sheets weren't mine and . . . Was I elevated? I looked over the edge of the small banister to a wooden ladder. I could see the entire space from up here. It was small, maybe even smaller than my basement living situation, but cozy and warm. A small kitchenette sat on the farthest wall, and a petite loveseat was in the middle of the room. The ceiling of the main area was just two giant skylights, letting in the purple tinted hue of . . . What time was it? Where the hell was I? The last thing I remembered was support group. My panic attack . . . Oh my god. A knock on the door made me jolt, and I quickly climbed down the ladder, fruitlessly trying to fix my hair on my descent. Why, I don't know. Wolf walked in with a warm smile. "Morning, sunshine."

"Where—"

He must have sensed my rising panic because his amusement faded quickly into something much more tender. He rested two heavy palms on my shoulders. I didn't flinch from the contact. "Everything's alright. You passed out back at the church. We weren't sure where you lived so we brought you here. It's about seven-thirty."

"At night?" I screeched? "Jeez, I slept a long time. I'm sorry—"

"Hey, nothing to apologize for. My home is your home."

"You live here?" I looked around at the miniature dwelling. Wolf encompassed the space with his massive form. It made sense why the ceilings needed to be so high.

He smiled, and it was dazzling white. I noticed his canines were prominently pronounced. "Not here, in this house specifically, but in the commune, yes."

"Commune?"

He gently took my elbow. "Come see." Wolf was a very touch-feely guy from what I could see. But I didn't mind it. It was comforting, actually. In fact, everything about Wolf seemed comforting, warm, and safe. He helped me down the steep, two cinderblock steps into the grass and gestured in a wide circle. "Welcome to Fenrir Point." He beamed. It took me a moment to make sense of what I was seeing. There were dozens of tiny houses scattered throughout a large, wooded plot of land, though it didn't look like any trees had been cleared. All the homes were simply positioned between and next to mighty oaks and bright-red maples. Orange and yellow leaves coated much of the ground. In the center blazed a giant fire, where women sat chatting and bouncing babies on their knees. Several men were knocking away with hammers, building decks and nailing in shutters on various homes. The smokey aroma of wood and coal tickled my nose and reminded me I was starving.

"This is amazing," I breathed, already feeling the love pulsating from this little community. "Are these all family or friends?"

"Can't they be both?" He winked. Just then, two children burst forward, screaming. I jumped back as a little red-haired boy launched himself at Wolf. Wolf fell over with a flourish. "Whoa, sneak attack!" he announced before grabbing at the boys' ribs. The child giggled and fought back.

Then a little girl with bejeweled braids jumped onto his back, hanging on by his thick neck. "I got you this time!" She cackled.

Wolf flipped her upside down and stood, somehow holding each child by their ankles. The kids laughed and wiggled. I couldn't resist my own giggle that erupted at the sight of it all. "You little wildlings need to mind your manners. We have a guest. This is Blythe." He grinned, sitting them down softly. They straightened, still echoing with residual hilarity.

"Hi, Blythe. I'm Lem, and this is my brother Leif. We like attacking Wolf." The little girl grinned a toothy smile.

I laughed. "I can see that. I'm sure he deserves it." Wolf gave me a mock shocked expression before I continued. "Are you two excited for Halloween?"

"Oh yeah, we are! Gonna get all the candy in all the land!" Leif announced. "Nice to meet you, Blythe," he yelled, already chasing his sister across the field.

Wolf put a friendly arm around my shoulder. "Come on, B, let's feed you. We got campfire specials tonight. Hotdogs, burgers, steaks, chicken . . . pretty much any meat you can think of, to be honest."

My stomach rumbled in gratitude, but I didn't want to impose. "Oh, I shouldn't stay. I've already taken up enough of your time—"

"Nonsense, any friend of mine or Ames is family here at Fenrir. I'm gonna make you a huge plate, so I hope you're hungry." He paused a moment as we walked toward the fire. I actually kind of liked the feeling of his arm wrapped around my shoulder, though I knew it was a brotherly sort of touch. It was nice all the same. "You're not . . . ," he whispered, "vegetarian, are you?"

We stopped outside the fire, catching the attention of several couples and a few ladies who eyed me with curiosity. I replied, "Oh, um . . . I'm vegan, actually."

I swore even the fire stopped crackling and the crickets stopped chirping. Everyone's eyes were wide. I could see Wolf's panic as he tried to sort through what to feed me. It was then I laughed. "I'm kidding. I love meat, and food, any food."

The crowd around us roared to life as women covered their mouths in laughter and a few men clapped. "You got yourself a good one there, son," an older man said, walking past and hitting Wolf on the arm.

Wolf tousled my hair a bit before letting go. "I'm going to have to watch out for you, Blythe. You're trouble, I can feel it," he said before retreating in the direction of the men at the barbecues. He returned, passing me both a kabob of steak and chicken and a long stick with two hotdogs speared at the end. We stepped closer to the fire, and I nibbled my chicken while roasting my hotdogs. The community joked and laughed as if they'd all been friends, or I guess family, forever. The men served the women their food, chased children, and cleared plates as the women talked around the flames. Wolf looked right at home in the blaze of the inferno's heat. I kept catching his glance when he didn't think I was looking. I wondered what he was thinking. I wondered what his long hair felt like between my fingers . . .

I thought he was wrong about something, however.

I wasn't trouble.

But he most certainly was.

***

THE BLAZE from the bonfire wasn't the only thing keeping me warm in Fenrir Point. I listened as a young woman shared funny anecdotes about tiny-house and communal living. I heard as the men set about their weekend chore schedules. Each person looked different, from skin colors, to hair, to a spectrum of gender identities, yet everyone here worked and lived in loving harmony. I'd never seen anything quite like it. It was if they were from a different world. A better world. After my second mouthwatering kabob, Wolf nudged me with his thick, tattooed elbow. "Whatcha thinking about?"

My lip quirked in a grin. "I'm thinking you have a very special home. I'm thinking I'm a little jealous." I sighed.

"What was your home like?" he asked gently. I watched idly as a little girl ran across the tree line, trailing a long pink ribbon behind her.

"Tumultuous. It was that even before my mother met . . . him. And just got worse after. She died, and I couldn't get away from him fast enough. If only I hadn't done what I did—"

"What did you do?"

Bad things . . . but let's stick with— "Got him sent to prison."

Wolf leaned back on the log, eyebrows raised. "No shit? That's badass. Don't regret that for a fucking second." He reached up a palm and I giggled, tapping him with a weak high five.

"Yeah, well, a lot of good it did me. Now I'm running from a psychopath, no family, no friends, no roots."

He leaned on his knees. "I wouldn't say that. I know we've only just met, but I think we're friends. Or we could be, if you want?"

His simple sincerity was like a glass of sweet tea on a summer's day. I nodded genuinely. "I'd like that very much."

Swatting me lightly on the shoulder, he beamed. "Then it's settled, bestie. Fenrir accepts all peoples. You'll notice the men do the cooking, cleaning, and kid chasing. The women here are our alph—" He cleared his throat. "Leaders."

My eyebrows rose in surprise. I scanned the property again, seeing clearly what he was saying. The women were calm, strong, happy. They were dispersed within the groups, but what Wolfgang was saying was evident. The men were scrubbing the grills clean, braiding little girls' hair, and otherwise working within the community. I liked the idea of a woman-run space. No wonder it felt so safe and peaceful here.

With that, he stood, gesturing for me to follow. I tossed my stick into the fire and stepped clumsily over the log that looked like a twig beneath Wolf. We stopped outside the tiny house I'd napped in, and I looked up at him, puzzled. "Here, your new home."

It took me a moment to register what he was saying. "Wolfgang, no, I can't live here."

"Why not? I've already talked it over with the Fenrir Elders. Everyone's cool with it. We've got snacks, laughs, everything here is free, and everyone is kind. We all help each other—"

I put a hand on his bicep, surprised at the jolt I felt from the contact. He seemed to notice too, his gray eyes swirling with some emotion I couldn't place. I quickly retracted my palm. "That's very generous, and everyone here seems wonderful. But I couldn't risk putting anyone else in danger. There are so many of you . . . At least in my basement apartment, there's only the Moores upstairs, and even that I feel guilty about. There are children here. What if he came . . . ?"

"If your stepfather tried to come here, he'd be dead before his feet crossed the threshold. There is no safer place for you, Blythe."

I swayed, taken aback at his tone. "You all look after each other, I know, but even if you have some sort of security set-up, my stepfather is . . . crafty. He'll find a way to get to me. He always does."

Wolf snorted, crossing his thick, bronze arms. "I'll give you some time to think about it. But trust me when I say, we've got *security* down to a science here."

After offering him a weak smile, I just wanted the conversation to be over. The sun was slowly sinking past the flaming red treetops. "I should go," I whispered.

He stood for a long moment, arms still crossed, staring me down. It was as if he wanted to argue, like he didn't want to listen to me. But after a breath, he inclined his head. "Alright, I'll take you back to your car. But you know about October, here, yeah? The town goes a little kooky."

I giggled, sliding into his white car with chipped paint. "You don't say? No, I haven't noticed anything at all."

With a playful roll of his eyes, he made the engine roar to life, and we took off down the mountain. "As a someone who's lived here forever, and a journalist, I bet you know a lot about this town's history, huh?" I asked as we rounded a steep curve.

"Sure, yeah."

"Do you want to tell me your version of Ash Grove's ghost story?"

His masculine face remained impassive as he stared ahead. "Didn't you get a good enough history lesson from Old Lady Marcelene?"

"How did you—"

His lazy smile caused me to shake my head. "Nosy townspeople," I scolded jokingly. Was *everyone* here talking behind my back?

The rumble of his chuckle vibrated through the car. "You're only getting a small taste of it now. Just wait."

We pulled to a stop outside the church, which as expected, was even more unsettling at night as it was during the day. "Well, thanks for looking after me today. Are you going to Hallows, too?"

Wolf put a hand to his chest. "Me? I'm not allowed to go."

It was my turn to roll my eyes. "Uh huh."

I clicked open the door when his hand shot across the console. "Hey, think about what I said? I got three hundred and fifty square feet of happiness with your name on it at Fenrir."

He was so sweet it was almost unbearable. I'd never met a man so kind. Very large and very kind. "I'll think about it," I said, stepping out. "Thanks again."

He kept his car in park next to mine as I climbed in. I was going to have to change in the backseat if I was going to go straight to the festival. My pulse quickened in anticipation as I rifled through my choices. I landed on the fox corset and mask I'd tried on the other day. When I looked up, Wolf was still parked next to me, the blue light of his phone the only light inside. Clutching my costume, I knocked on the window. "I'm good. You can go. I, um . . . have to get changed."

The window rolled down. "Go ahead. I'm not leaving until you're rolling."

"That's not necessary," I argued, not particularly wanting to change clothes in front of him.

He grinned. "Those are my orders. So change or don't, but I'm not leaving until you do."

"Orders? Who gave you orders?" I put my hands on my hips indignantly.

He pointed to his watch. "Tick tock, you're wasting time, my dear. Hallows awaits." He made a spooky *ooooo* and I tried to hide my grin.

"Fine, but don't look at me."

Retreating to the other side of my car, I opted to dress between the church and my trunk. I shimmied my corset up under my dress and buttoned the clasp at my pelvic bone. That was the hardest part. The stockings and everything else I could do in my seat. Finally, I revved the engine, giving Wolf a big wave in send off. He smiled a wolfish grin before finishing on his phone and shoving it aside.

As I drove away, I realized I hadn't felt lonely with him. Not once.

Though I was wondering what Ames was doing. Why hadn't he been the one to take me home with him?

CHAPTER 10

Ames

HELL AND HER THREE

The well-worn path snaked through the indigo tinged forest. The trees near this cursed place had already lost their leaves. Or perhaps even the foliage knew that any display of beauty was wasted here. Closer and closer I crept toward the cold, fog-soaked plot of despair. I arrived at the towering spikes of wrought iron. No rust or decay showed on the sharp enclosure, unlike what writhed within. When they didn't immediately part, I growled. "Open."

"For whom?" a female voice, too feminine and delicate for this place, asked.

"You know for fucking who." I'd run out of patience. This was supposed to be an easy kill. A fun kill. A murder to blow off steam. The boys and I should have known the second that sack of shit crossed our borders. But the motherfucker probably slithered right by me and put a letter in Blythe's mailbox. Now I was racking my brain, wondering who he may be, what he may be. The gates swung open with a high-pitched scream and I walked through. "Dramatic much?"

The gates slammed closed. No one in the stories include the part about Hell's Gate being into melodrama. Once fully inside, I felt it, tasted it. I took a deep inhale of my favorite scent, especially here. *Terror.*

"Cat," I called, leaning against a tomb. "I know you're watching me from a tree or some shit. I'm not in the mood for games."

Leaves rustled as Cat stepped out from behind a barren plot. Her black fur gleamed blue in the light of the rising moon as she jumped onto a gravestone. "How nice of you to stop by." She licked a paw. "Come to make a deposit or withdrawal?"

"Neither tonight, unfortunately. I'm having an . . . issue."

"I'm sure there are doctors who can help." She swished her long feline tail over the stone.

I cut the animal a sharp look. "It seems you haven't been doing your job very well. Perhaps I should be looking for your replacement."

She stopped licking a paw. "What? I'm impeccable at my job. These bastards are burning, tortured day and night. And the ones in the cemetery are comfortable. I'm cat-ing both forts while you leisurely walk in whenever you please."

Annoyance burned my throat. "I did not hike all the way out here to argue with a house pet."

Cat hissed, baring her gleaming white teeth. "And I didn't plan on playing assistant to a pathetic haunted skeleton for all of eternity, yet here we are."

I rubbed my temples, feeling the headache build behind my eyes. "You've let someone out, haven't you?"

The black cat straightened. "Of course not. Why would I do that?"

"You tell me."

She paced up and down the narrow stone. "That doesn't make sense. Why would you say that? Is this some sort of test to see if I've slipped up? I've been here or there every single wretched night—"

"Calm down, you're not in trouble. Unless you're lying."

Cat hissed.

"Perhaps you can answer this riddle for me then. Ash Grove sucks in a girl running from her abusive stepfather. He finds her. I plan to kill him."

Cat narrowed her yellow eyes into slits, listening instead of talking for once. "If you planned to kill him then where is he? I've gotten no one new in months."

"Exactly the riddle. Where is he? Because—" I pulled the letter out of my back pocket and held it up to her whiskers. "—she got this in the mail with me right outside her door."

"That's impossible."

"None of us can feel, see, or scent him. Either he's something like us or he has help."

She perched into a little black loaf, tucking her paws in. "Then let him have the girl. It's not worth the trouble. What does it matter if one human dies?"

I gritted my teeth. I wanted nothing more in that moment then to toss that stupid cat into the well. She noticed my anger and cocked her head. "You like a girl?"

I crossed my arms, remaining silent. Cat tossed her furry head back, baring her fangs in a cackle. "Well, I'll be damned."

"You *are* damned." I sighed. "Just give me a hint. I know you know something. You always do, you little fucking creep."

Her sandpaper tongue licked her paw as she straightened and preened her whiskers. Vain little creature *loved* that I was asking her for help. "I'll keep an ear out and see what I hear. But word of advice? You might want to reconsider trusting this human at their word. Because anything that's caught the attention of something like that, the thing that wrote that?" She shuddered. "That's not some normal girl."

"Thanks, you're ever so helpful, as always. I'll let you get back to chasing mice and coughing up hairballs."

She jumped down gracefully, hissing. The hollow ground beneath us rumbled. Suddenly the top layer of earth pushed up like it was mere carpet and not hundreds of pounds of dirt. We jostled and I kept my balance on my favorite tomb. Cat paused a moment, one paw frozen mid-step, considering. "It's happening more and more. If you could only shift, perhaps you could make them behave."

"Thanks for the advice but I've got it under control. Go catch a rodent or chase your tail."

A meow screeched before she cursed, "Prick," upon her sashay away.

I, at least, got one answer. Whoever, whatever he was, it didn't come from here. All my souls were accounted for and screaming gloriously for their release. It eased my headache immediately, the melody of all of them together. Sure, things beyond Hell's Gate were becoming more and more . . . disgruntled, and my inability to fully access my true form was unfortunate, but what could happen? I'd figure that out later. For now, there was a greater threat than meddling dead psychopaths. There was a real live psychopath chasing an innocent girl. I'd tear the town apart stone by stone tomorrow and find this motherfucker. In the meantime, the guys and I could easily keep Blythe safe. Shoving aside the top of the tomb, I pulled out my change of clothes along with white and black paint. But tonight was October first. The beginning of Hallows, the one time of year I could be free—we all could. I'd don the skeleton paint and creep through, though few knew how much worse my true form even was.

After combing back my hair and shrugging on a black leather jacket, I painted my knuckles and checked myself in the hand mirror I kept in the tomb of Joseph Watts: The Dismemberer. One of my longest sufferers in this graveyard. It made me nostalgic.

I checked my phone, and as expected, my blue dot was parked in the lot of the field far below. I'd see her soon. I'd see her every night for as long as she stayed here and perhaps beyond. My fascination with Blythe Pearl was only growing. Her fear called to me like a siren. Devils, it tasted so sweet. I wondered if the taste of her pussy matched that of her delicious terror. I could never find out . . . but the thought alone had me feeling feral.

And tonight, I was on the loose in these woods.

And I knew exactly who I wanted to hunt.

CHAPTER 11

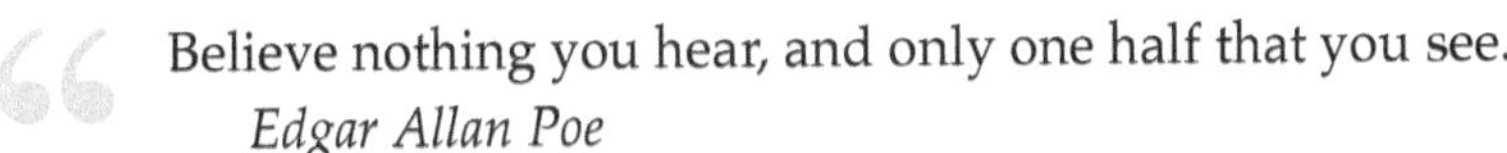

THE NIGHT SHE MET MURDER

> Believe nothing you hear, and only one half that you see.
> *Edgar Allan Poe*

The lot was suspiciously empty, and I wondered if I was in the right place. Did a lot of people carpool? Maybe Hallows Fest wasn't as populated of a festival as I'd imagined. I guessed that would make sense, being its elusive, mysterious reputation. Nevertheless, I hoped there would be enough people there that I wouldn't feel awkward and even more alone than I already did. I kicked my car door open and struggled into my pull-up fishnet stockings, securing my pointed fox mask tightly with its black ribbon. Standing and surveying myself in the reflection of the windows, a grin tugged at the corner of my eggplant-colored lips. I looked like a fox. I felt like a fox. Sultry, cunning, and crafty. Odd how a simple, albeit slutty in all the best ways, costume could elevate my confidence. I hadn't had a reason to get dressed up since prom, and to be adorned in October, at a Halloween festival . . . Well, this was as good enough as my dying wish fulfilled. A sigh escaped my lungs. I'd try for tonight, and however many nights in October I was afforded, to enjoy this. My last hoorah. If I were to quit running and stay in Ash Grove, I would surely be murdered here. I wondered if he'd take me here, to the woods. Or maybe he'd do it on the side of the road. I half hoped it would be nearby in the forest. It was creepy as fuck here, but comforting too. For some strange reason, the odd, the strange, the dark and gloomy had always comforted me. Like an inky blanket of night, it soothed me more than any warm summer's day.

I turned to check the back of my corset, trying to reach around to my shoulder blades and failing. I looked great, but my ample breasts pushed the strings loose and they needed a good tug and tie. However, that was nearly impossible to do alone. That didn't stop me from awkwardly trying to defy my anatomy and do it, though.

A cute ripple of laughter pinged my ear. "Need some help?"

Startled, I glanced around thinking I'd missed a car pulling in. It was only me and two other vacant vehicles. "Um, sure, thanks." We were standing in a patch of gravel, yet I didn't hear her approach.

"Closing a corset on your own is a bitch, I know." The woman with long red hair floated over. Her skin was so white it glowed in the moonlight, and her eyes glinted deep crimson. When I met her gaze, she smiled a sharp smile, her incisors defined and long. "You make a sexy fox," she purred, giving the strings a firm pull, and my cheeks flushed.

"I appreciate that. You're beautiful . . . .Vampire?"

Her touch skimmed my shoulders like ice as she turned me around and assessed my fit. "That's right." She lightly bit her bottom, candy-apple-red lip. "Want to head in together?"

My gaze flitted over the lot again. *Where did she come from?*

I nodded. "Sure, I don't really know where I'm going. It's my first time."

"You don't say?" She giggled, looping her elbow in mine. "You're lucky I'm the one who found you and not some other monster. We've got lots at Hallows."

I swallowed, not sure if she was being facetious or not. Even still, I was desperately curious. "Oh, really? Who should I stay away from?"

The vampire woman huffed as my heels moved from gravel to grass. "You'll learn quick enough. We each have our . . . vices. But I'd say the worst of us? That would be The Halloween Boys. They're nasty mother-fuckers in sunshine and moonlight. There's no break for them. They'll chew you up and spit you out and then do it again for sport. Us vampires at least retreat to our coffins occasionally." She smirked.

"How do I know who they are? Wh-what are their costumes?" The last thing I needed was to unintentionally anger a *Halloween Boy* and be on yet another angry dude's shit list.

The vampire hummed thoughtfully. "That's one of the things about them that makes them so unpredictable. They don't stay with their own like many of us do. We all chat and hang out, don't get me wrong. The pirates, for example, are a fucking blast. But at the end of the day, we all have our own little—" She gave me an assessing look before continuing. "—families. But The Halloween Boys . . . They're just a mix of the worst of us. One of each. Though we can never really be sure how many of them there are."

A chill slithered down my spine. This all sounded way more serious than just a dance festival. I shook my head and huffed a small laugh. "It's almost like this is all real."

Her returning smile was pure feline. "Yes, almost."

I noted how incredibly realistic her pointed teeth were and was thankful monsters, vampires, didn't really exist. We trudged through a dark and winding path in the forest that seemed to go nowhere. The way was dotted with only a carved pumpkin every several feet, the only indication we were walking into anything more than a haunted wood.

Only the sound of crunching leaves and twigs peppered our walk when I spoke up. "How many years have you been coming here?"

My red companion laughed fully this time. It seemed everything I said was part of a joke I wasn't in on yet. "Many years, dear." The trees began to clear as we passed the last flickering orange pumpkin. "Welcome to Hallows Fest," she purred sweetly, looking from the scene to me. My eyes grew wide as I inhaled sharply. I was expecting a small-town carnival, a little party, or at best something like a concert. This was . . . It was its own city. A living breathing thing. Hundreds of masked people milled by in the most realistic suits and getups I'd ever seen. A man on stilts in a jester costume juggled past as my vampire friend twirled away with another laugh, her deep-red hair fanning around her like a cape. Beyond them, it was hard to know where to land my focus.

Tents and lanterns jutted between mossy trees where people ate and drank and mingled. People wasn't the right word. Werewolves, vampires, witches, ghosts, pirates, zombies, ghouls, and animals of all sorts went about their activities. There were so many of them.

"In the center is The Brew Pump. My band plays all week at ten. Say you'll watch me play?"

After picking my jaw up off the ground, I nodded, wide-eyed. "What's your name?"

"You can call me Ezmerelda." She stepped closer and tugged at my wrists. My pulse quickened and she flicked a quick glance from my chest to my gaze and grinned, the moonlight sparkling on her vampire teeth. She'd perfected her bit as a blood-hungry being. If I didn't know it was all a performance, I'd have wondered if she'd *sensed* my heart speed up. Before I knew what was happening, she planted a kiss on my cheek. "Come find me if you want to have some fun, Fox."

Another twirl and she disappeared into the crowd, leaving me blushing like a fool. Maybe she would be the one to dance with me at some point tonight . . .

From what Ezmerelda said, The Brew Pump sounded like where the bands performed. At least my worry about no one being here was unfounded. There were so many people, all fully in character. It was like stepping into a different world. The tents were draped, and old fabric hung between the trees. Lanterns and torches blazed along the dirt maze of pathways while pumpkins took up the remaining vacant patches of grass. It was a Halloween lover's dream. My mask and smoky makeup shielding my eyes was a blessing, hiding me from my obvious gawking. Everyone looked *so good*. The costumes were like something from a movie set. The fur of a wolf man brushed my arm as he stomped past with a grunt. The feel of it was soft and gritty in that way a wild animal feels against the skin. I wondered if it was a real pelt repurposed. A man with crimson eyes exactly like Ezmerelda's caught my gaze. His white hair shimmered in the torchlight, and he lifted a goblet of dark liquid in cheers when we met looks. I swallowed, and he grinned, taking a step forward. Something in me told me to run. Some sort of second sense, like when you see a bear in the woods. But that was crazy, wasn't it? He was just a man in stage makeup. And I did want someone to dance with . . . and maybe more . . . tonight. "Beautiful fox, why are you all alone, darling?"

His voice was as smooth as snakeskin and soft as his long white hair looked, though his face was young and strong, with a classic handsome edge. The red of his eyes against the pale was . . . mesmerizing. "I'm new to Hallows," I replied.

Another smile exposing fangs. They must all shop at the same store. He extended his long arm and gently swirled a lock of my hair around his leather-gloved fingers. The movement froze my breath in my chest and an unwelcomed warmth burned into my shoulders. He didn't attempt to conceal his long glance down and back up my body. I felt naked and exposed under his heavy stare. "Come have a drink with me and my brothers and sisters—" Suddenly, the vampire swiftly dropped his grasp on my hair. He straightened, looking over my shoulder. "I did not know," he remarked, tilting his head to the side.

"What?" I glanced behind me, following his gaze. My heart jumped into my chest. Something . . . No, that wasn't possible. *Someone* stood a few yards away. Tall, muscular yet lean, he was painted in the blackest paint, wearing a leather jacket and a . . . skull face. His blue eyes shone with a lethal glare within the black around his eyes. My breath caught in my chest, and all of a sudden, I felt I'd be safer with the white vampire than with whoever this was behind me. But the vampire seemed just as alarmed as I was. And judging by the small, lithe steps he was taking backwards, he was unwilling to assist me. Because the skeleton man's attention was fixed on me. And that seemed to convey something that I didn't understand because the vampire gave a short bow and stepped back. "Have a nice evening, Fox." He turned in the same sort of flourish as Ezmerelda had, his dark cape revealing a deep ruby underside as he glided back to his group. I was nervous to turn around, to see whoever this was again . . . but when I did, he was gone.

I felt I could explore for hours, days, maybe even years and never grow tired of what I saw. The smell of clove and earth and sugary rum. The sound of laughter and fires crackling. The feel of soft fabrics and furs brushing past me. Some glanced my way; others didn't notice me at all. Yellow slitted eyes and crimson glares black as night assessed me as I wove through the pockets of festivalgoers. In the distance, I spied what looked to be an abandoned gas station—the roof of one, at least. Below was old gasoline pumps. Squinting, I made out forms walking across the top of the roof. "Check, check, check," resounded through booming speakers.

"Hi, Fox!" someone said cheerily from behind a beaked mask. They flapped their long ebony feathers and I grinned. "Hello . . . ... Raven?" I smiled at the dark-beaked person. "So, is that the stage?"

"Oh, yes. That's The Brew Pump. It's a haunted gas station. We have a few of those in Ash Grove."

I chuckled. "Is there any place in Ash Grove *without* a ghost story?"

They cocked their head thoughtfully. "The old lady who's house I live above, maybe, though her washing machine does start on its own sometimes."

I laughed for the first time in what felt like forever. "I want to tell you my name and ask for yours, but I know that's not allowed," I lamented, gazing at the long beak and intricate feathers. Eyes large and soulful looked back at me.

"Well, I can tell you I'm a he/him or they/them, and I'm called Raven or Crow here. The Murder all go by the same names. I'll call you Fox if you'd like, but I already know your name."

I opened my mouth to respond when the trill of an electric guitar radiated outward. A mass of characters had gathered around and under the abandoned station. They cheered adamantly as the band greeted them and played a hard rock melody. "Do you want to go down or watch from above?" Raven asked.

The bravery to join the bustling mosh pit wasn't immediately appealing, and I liked my new friend, so I opted for the latter. "Where to?"

I couldn't make out any facial expressions from behind his large, pointed mask. Standing just over my height, their face was completely covered, and long onyx feathers shown purple in the mix of moon and firelight. He took my hand. "I'll show you."

We broke off from the main area and trudged up a grassy knoll. "So I take it you're a Hallows Fest regular?" I asked.

"You could say that. I mainly enjoy watching, though."

I grinned. His voice sounded exactly what I'd imagine a raven to sound like. If, you know, ravens could speak human. Raspy but with an airy kindness about it. "People watching sounds nice for my first night. I feel like I don't know enough to get too involved right now. It seems I've already wandered into places I shouldn't."

A beak turned, interested, in my direction. "Oh? Who'd you piss off so soon, Fox?"

"Some guy in a vampire costume with long white hair. One hell of a wig, if you ask me. And those red contact lenses."

Raven halted our walk, cocking his head to the side again and ruffling his shoulders. "You didn't go with him anywhere, or let him touch your skin, right?"

"No, no. I mean, I might have, but then this other guy showed up and scared him away."

"Who?"

"I'm not sure. Someone with a skeleton face."

Raven coughed a squawk of a laugh. These people always remained in character, I was learning. "I'll be damned. Just don't tell him what we do up here, got it?" We had reached the top. The feathered-person tugged at a rope ladder attached to a thick maple. He climbed a few rungs and looked down at me.

"Don't tell who?" I asked, confusion furrowing my brow.

He only motioned for me to follow. "Alright, I'm following a bird costumed guy into a tree. This is fine," I mumbled to myself, impressed with my hilarity. We made our way up through vibrant orange branches, finally setting foot on a platform. "Wow," I breathed. "It's all connected?"

"That's right, Fox. Come on, we've got snacks."

I followed him across a bridge connecting trees to several larger platforms until finally we ended at the farthest space. "This is like one giant tree house," I said in admiration. "It's remarkable. How did you build it?"

"Magic," he answered plainly. The sound of music was louder here, and I noticed four others in the treehouse with us.

Raven gestured around the room. "Fox, meet The Murder."

Four beaks, just like his, turned toward me. I wished I could see their eyes, or mouths, or some sort of expression. But their true faces remained concealed. I could only see the outlines of their forms, which were almost identical to Raven's.

"You're all called . . . Crow or Raven?"

They nodded.

"I'm going to have a hard time telling you all apart, but it's nice to meet you all. Thanks for sharing your treehouse with me tonight." I walked over to the ledge. It was a close and perfect view of the band but completely hidden from sight. No one even looked our way as we sat elevated above them all. Just another shadow in the trees. "This is amazing."

The bird-people looked between each other and nodded. "Glad you like it. Help yourself to food and stay as long as you like," Raven said with a smile in his voice. "Though . . . don't stay too out of sight. We don't want any trouble from you know who."

"Are you going to tell me who you keep referring to?"

"Shh," a crow interrupted. "I love this song," a meek feminine voice squeaked.

My gaze drifted back to the stage, and I spotted Ezmerelda playing bass. Her red hair glowed in the bright strobe lights and she looked even more beautiful in clearer light. At that same moment, her gaze found mine, even at such a great distance. Or maybe she was only looking in my direction. It would have been impossible for her to see me from so far and in my dark hiding place. But she smiled that radiant pointed smile all the same as she played. The Crows passed me a plate of food and I nestled into bean bag chairs with them as we watched the show. I let the music thump through me along with the band's hypnotizing melodies. After my second helping of nut and berry loaf and a wooden cup of mead, Raven said to me from where he perched near the ledge, "That's who I mean, Fox."

The others peered over. "It was only a matter of time," the soft-spoken one crooned.

"Who—" I looked over to see him leaning against a boulder: the skeleton man. He surveyed the concert before flicking his gaze up to us in our elaborate treehouse. "How did he find me? He's the guy I told you about that scared the vampire guy—"

Raven let out a high-pitched laugh again, flapping his long feathers. "I wish I could have been there to see Vincent's face when he realized who you were." The treehouse erupted in similar cackles all while the man below glared up at me.

Pulling my attention away, I said, "Thank you for everything. I hope I see you later." I waved goodbye to their flapping wings and made my way down the rope ladder. Something stirred in my chest. But for once, it wasn't fear. It should have been fear, but it was something else. Something I couldn't name. I'd come to Ash Grove running from something, someone. From my past, from my mistakes, from my stepfather. My death awaited me. It was inevitable. I'd been to countless cities with various levels of hope each time I started again. And then a letter found me, followed by a rusty pickup truck. He kept finding me. He kept following. And I kept running. Now, I'd decided to stay and dance until I died. I'd go every night to this damn, weird festival until he caught me and killed me. Until I couldn't come the next night. And god damn, if I weren't being followed in here too. This was supposed to be my safe space. Where I could wear a mask and blend in. A space I could celebrate my favorite holiday one last time. And this asshole was trying to scare me. I resolved to confront him and tell him to fuck off, but when my heels tapped the ground . . . he'd vanished again. Annoyance roiled through me as I stomped and slid ungracefully down the hill and made my way into the crowd of concert goers. An energetic song played, and people danced. And I joined them. I danced, head buzzing from the tangy mead. I lifted my hands to the sky, shook my ass, and dipped low and popped up. I danced until my neck was slick and soaked with sweat. I danced until my corset and fishnets felt wet with perspiration. No one cared. No one looked at me like I was anything but one of them. This wasn't like prom or any function I'd ever been to. This was something entirely new. The music had a life of its own. This place, Hallows, Ash Grove, had a life of its own. And I existed inside of it like a soul or racing blood. I became a part of it all that night, if even for the briefest moment. The fast set slowed, and the crowd roared with applause. I rested my hands on my knees, panting and laughing. A wolf man lifted his palm and smiled with fangs. I high-fived his leathery paw, catching my breath. The band announced they were sending us off with a slow song. Something romantic, the lead vampire man proclaimed. Everyone around me coupled up, and then it did feel like prom. It didn't matter. I'd gotten so much more than I'd come for. And I wanted to do it again the next night, and the next, for as long as I was . . . here.

I turned on my heel to weave through the dancing couples. The hint of piano wafted through the crowd. It was gorgeous. All of a sudden, the crowd parted like a wave, making way before me. I looked around in confusion, and then I saw him.

He straightened the collar on his leather jacket and strode forward with all the confidence of any predator. I stood my ground and crossed my arms. My ghostly stalker. "What the hell do you want?"

He stopped a foot in front of me, silent, and even the music paused. Everyone's gaze unabashedly fixed to us. I could have sworn the side of his mouth curved slightly. It was hard to tell under the heavy white and black detailed paint of his skeleton mask. Without a word, he extended a palm. When I raised a brow in confusion, he bowed slightly, putting his other arm behind his back. "You're . . . asking me to dance?"

The soft piano melody began again as all sorts of creatures around me smiled or giggled. *What the hell, I'm going to die anyway.* I placed my hand in his and he straightened. Gripping my palm, he pulled me with force into his hard chest. Air escaped my lungs upon warm impact, and we began to move with the music. The couples around us went back to their dances as the enchanting tune played. He was hard, and warm, and silent. When I finally got the nerve to look up, his deep blue gaze fixed to mine immediately. I gasped. He was beautiful, even hidden by paint. His black hair was brushed black and shone blue under the moon's glow. Something in his stare softened and my heart quickened. Losing my step, I tripped over his foot, but he held me up firm, as if I weighed nothing. "Joke's on you. I can't dance," I whispered. He was so close and towering over me. I should have been telling him to fuck off, to get away from me, but I couldn't. I didn't want to. His aroma touched each breath I took: bergamot, lavender, and oakmoss. It was a heady, addicting scent. The desire to bury in my face in his chest and kiss his jaw was so strong it overwhelmed and disturbed me.

His mouth quirked again as he crisscrossed my wrists and pulled my back to his chest. My core heated at feeling his hot breath on my ear. He then pushed his nose into my hair and sucked in. *Was he smelling me?* Before I could say anything, his rough, white and black painted finger softly trailed down the curve of my neck. Goosebumps pricked my skin as warmth found the space between my thighs. I was panting again, and this time from a completely different kind of dancing. One that heated me from the inside. I leaned my head back onto his chest and sighed. "That feels nice."

Abruptly, he spun me around and out, letting go of one hand. When I spun back, expecting to crash into him, only air met my back. I turned around, searching, but he was nowhere to be found. Only the shimmer of a fine blue fog was left.

After winding my way through the masses, I walked down the main path. Pockets of folks chatted and laughed, some glancing my way, others oblivious. I hugged my arms to my ribs to beat the oncoming, late night October chill hitting my damp skin. My dance partner's smell still lingered in my hair. Unashamed of looking like a fool, I brought a lock of golden brown to my nose and inhaled deeply, savoring the lavender and woodsy and leather. Whoever he was, following me was annoying, and I planned to confront him if he continued to do so. But a small longing inside me hoped he would. Maybe he was watching me weave my way back to my car. The skin on the back of my neck prickled in awareness of danger, or hope, or maybe both. That dance . . . He was likely just toying with me. It meant nothing to him. Not even a fraction of what it meant to me. To have my dying wish fulfilled . . . to be taken in by the land of misfits and to dance, and laugh, and explore was everything. Ending the night with my body pressed to a mysterious and intoxicating masked man . . . It was more than I ever could have dreamed of. Death was always on my mind. Death was always nearby.

But if only for tonight, I didn't mind so much.

CHAPTER 12

Ames

WHY IS THE FOOTAGE ALWAYS BLURRY?

> This is my costume. I'm a homicidal maniac. They look just like everyone else.
> *Wednesday Addams,*
> *The Addams Family*

Change was its own form of amnesia. It crept in like a stealthy killer and crowned its victims with false security. For better or worse, things evolved, and we all accepted it for the most part. I'd borne witness to a lot of change over my years. I'd evolved too. I'd become a different thing than I was back then. But sometimes a touch or sound could release an arrow of remembrance. Something my brain long forgot but my psyche recalled. There was a time when I believed sex should be reserved for marriage, but I'd long abandoned that belief. Both the notion of waiting and the idea of marriage wasn't possible for someone like me. So I'd fuck around here and there. Why not?

But tonight, when Blythe took my hand . . . when her soft body molded inside mine and we moved together . . .

Something inside me remembered.

A long time ago, dancing was the most intimacy we were allowed outside of the threat of marital vows. Dancing was passion in plain sight. A dress rehearsal for what we hoped would transpire between cotton sheets. And Blythe, my Little Ghost, tasted like fear, and sadness, and hopelessness. As I pulled her to my arms, it burned my throat and made my mouth water. I wondered if her cunt tasted like fear, too. I wanted to find out. To rip that too fucking sexy corset from her perfect body. I wanted to run my true tongue along every curve, divet, and dimple. Perhaps I'd search for another taste besides terror hiding somewhere between her folds. Maybe what dripped from her when she wanted me would taste like something else entirely. What would she taste like if she didn't want me?

I could have stayed with her there all night. Having her in my arms sure beat watching her from afar, watching that loathsome Vincent blood-drunk bastard zero in on her. If The Ravens hadn't stepped in, I would have sent them. Thankfully they were smarter than anyone gave them credit for and they sought her out. I made a mental note to reward them later.

Maybe I'd feed them Cat.

An amused breath escaped me as I leaned against her car, waiting.

If I hadn't left her when I did, I wouldn't have had time to wash up and change. And I needed to see her home. I should have been there when she arrived—but of course, Ez took the opportunity. The vampires could smell someone needing to get laid a mile away. They fucking loved their partners wanton and needy. Anger swirled in my chest at the thought. Ez could back the fuck off, along with all these other assholes. *Mine.*

My mind startled at the realization that I'd just referred to her as such. Was I claiming her? No, I couldn't. It wasn't possible. Blythe was a target, a game, a means to an end. Nothing more. And no one could fuck with her except for me. Not until I was done with her, at least.

The aroma of fear and darkness drifted through the rustling autumn leaves. Orange and yellow maples floated around me like confetti as she stepped out of the shadows. A fox in the night. A fucking vision of a woman. I quickly readjusted my cock for the twentieth time that evening. She held her elbows and looked down, a dreamy sort of grin hinting at her dark lips. I wondered if it was there because of me. Or *him*, rather.

Her footsteps paused when she finally glanced up, and her shoulders jumped back a fraction. *So jumpy, Little Ghost.* But the blood returned to her cheeks once she realized who I was. Who she thought I was.

"Ames? What are you doing here?" She stopped just an inch too close before taking a small step back. *Interesting.*

"Making sure you get home safe," I replied, straightening the collar on my dorky blue button-up.

Her brown eyes narrowed beneath her fox mask. "How'd you know I'd be here?"

I shrugged off my old varsity jacket and wrapped it around her shoulders, noticing the lovely rose blush that illuminated her cheeks at the soft brush of my fingers. "Wasn't too hard to guess. Plus, I saw your car. How'd you like it? You seem to still be in one piece. That's better than most first-timers."

"Thanks, I guess I know to bring a jacket next time. It was . . . bizarre. In the best sort of way." She giggled. *Wow, what a lovely sound.*

I couldn't help my grin. "Glad you had fun. I'm here to see you home." I held out my palm in silent command for her keys. She really shouldn't give them to me. She shouldn't have trusted me at all.

"Why are you really here? You came all this way at this hour just to make sure I get home safe?"

I shrugged. "I'm the town nice guy. Wolfgang dropped me off a minute ago, so technically you're my ride, too."

She shook her head and looked at her feet before fishing a key out of her cleavage. *Her cleavage. Fuck me.*

"He's a funny guy, but I don't think I'm going to live with him."

Red flashed across my vision. "Excuse me? Live with him?"

"Yeah, he didn't tell you when he brought you over? He asked me to stay in his community with him. There's a tiny house he says I can use and everything. But, I don't know. I don't want to impose, and with everything going on in my life right now—"

"The elders wouldn't approve of that anyway," I cut her off, trying to mask my irritation with my friend. We never discussed her staying with him. Fucking animal just wanted to mount her.

Blythe made her way to the passenger side and, before ducking into the car, responded, "They did though, apparently. But it doesn't matter."

What the fuck? Fenrir was run by their females, the collective alphas. Though every so often they'd choose an exceptional male to be an alpha alongside them. They'd had their sights set on Wolfgang for years and probably would agree to anything he wanted at this point to stay on his good side.

Once I was inside the old Honda, I clutched the steering wheel, thankful the darkness concealed my emotions. Onyx and Wolf needed a swift kick to the balls for each trying to fool around with her. She may have been gorgeous, and I may not have been the guy for her, but they sure as hell weren't either. And I wouldn't let them hurt her.

I turned up the heat for her and she exhaled. "By the way, I'm sorry for passing out at your therapy group. I'm pretty embarrassed."

Shooting her a sidelong glance, I replied, "You have nothing to be embarrassed about, Blythe. It's that psycho stalking you that should be embarrassed. And punished."

Did I say that last bit out loud?

"Punished? I'm afraid the good state of Alabama has already tried and failed to punish my stepfather. At this point . . . it's just inevitable."

"What's just inevitable?"

"He's going to find me, Ames. You saw the blank letter. He's here. Or he will be soon. It's only a matter of time before he catches me and it's all over."

Without thinking, I veered off the highway. Blythe shrieked, bracing herself on the dash. "What the hell?"

The car came to a screeching, dusty halt on the side of the road. Unable to hide in that moment—maybe it was the moon, and her, and Hallows, and that goddamn dance— I couldn't fucking bear sitting here and listening to her talk about being murdered. I took her chin and tilted it toward me. Her brown eyes went wide, but she was still wearing that stupid mask. I loved her dark makeup, but I hated the fox in that moment. She wasn't a fox. I wanted to paint her in my skull mask so everyone knew she was mine. Take her out of orange and put her back in black. She wore a lot of black and I fucking loved it. "That is *not* what's going to happen, Blythe. I can fucking swear that to you. This fucker isn't touching you, finding you, speaking to you, fucking nothing."

"How can you promise that?" she whispered, her voice a small tremble between hope and fear. I'd never wanted to reveal myself before. The urge to share my story and true self had never emerged. Until now. In that moment, all I wanted to do was offer her every one of my secrets slaughtered on a silver platter. For her to consume, or wear as jewelry, or discard entirely, if it was her doing it, I'd be okay with that. The thought tightened my throat and screamed at me that I was losing control. My resolve around her was already hanging by a thread, and those puppy dog eyes didn't help. Perhaps I should have told her then. Perhaps it would make things easier if she ran away in terror, seeing me for the monster I truly was. But I wanted to hang onto the fantasy a little longer. For now, I could be her gentle therapist. Her awkward acquaintance. A part of me wished I could really be him. That one day I'd wake up and the darkness would be gone and this skin I'd shrugged on could be mine permanently. Those were the rare days I allowed myself to pretend that was what I wanted. When in truth, I wanted my monster. I was the monster.

The truth wouldn't set me free. The truth would damn me. The air between us grew heavy as my glance dropped to her mouth. *Oh, to feel her sweet tongue* . . . Her lips parted as she sucked in a breath. Did she feel it too?

Against every instinct, I dropped my grip. "You'd be surprised at the things I can promise, Blythe."

The sound of her puff of breath as she repositioned in her seat and pulled my jacket around her were the only sounds in the car as I pulled back onto the main road. "Nineteen forty-one," she mumbled, tracing a finger over the faded navy embroidery. "This is a vintage jacket?"

"It is," I replied, trying to shake off my gnawing emotions. What was she doing to me?

"I like it."

"Keep it."

"That's okay—"

I interrupted. "Would you like to stay with me tonight? If you're worried or afraid, I'd rather you be somewhere you feel safe." I ran a hand through my hair. "If you feel safe with me, that is."

Her eyes narrowed slightly, assessing me. For a moment, worry panged me. Did she think I was a creep? I was, but still. She didn't seem to notice that I was the masked asshole dancing with her, so that was a point in Ames's favor.

"I do feel safe with you," she answered after a moment, and my shoulders relaxed. "But I need to do this on my own. I appreciate your kindness, but I can't drag you into this."

I scoffed. "I'm already in it. I'm invested."

"Because you care about me as some client, or charity case, or whatever you see me as," she murmured, though her voice sounded stronger than I'd heard her speak before. Even if I didn't like the words, I liked the small flicker of fight I sensed behind them. Like when I asked her to dance and she looked like she wanted to kick me in the balls. There was still some fight left in Blythe Pearl, and the least I was doing was assisting in coaxing it out. If even out of sheer annoyance.

We stopped in her driveway, but she didn't get out immediately. "You're wrong about all of those things. And you might not want my help, or my idiot friends' help, but you've got it. We aren't about to let someone bully one of our own."

"I've only been in Ash Grove for a few weeks."

"I don't care." I watched an orange cat trot across the lawn.

She huffed suddenly and crossed her arms. "You called me a kid."

I grinned, glancing over at her. I didn't even remember calling her that, but clearly, she did. She remembered things I said. "Everyone's a kid to me. I'm ancient."

Shaking her head, those beautiful brown eyes glittered. "You're only seven years older than me. You're hardly Mr. Moore. He sweeps the street, Ames. Everyday, he sweeps it."

I chuckled. "How do you know I don't do the same?"

The grin etched across her face made me wish I could remove her mask and see her without all of her coverings. "Give me your phone number. I'll text you so you have mine. If you change your mind about a place to stay, text me. I've got a spare bed. It's not a problem."

She took my phone and typed before handing it back. "Do you want to take my car home?" was all she asked. *No, I want to take you home.*

"I already called a ride and they're waiting down the street." I got out and made my way around to open her door. She took my palm as I helped her out, and her gaze shot to mine for a moment. Dropping her hand, I readjusted my thick glasses, letting my hair fall over the frames. Straightening my *other* mask. The good guy masquerade. She didn't recognize me from earlier, did she?

If she did, she didn't say, and I had a feeling she was the kind of person who would call my deceitful ass out immediately. "Hey, how'd you know where I live?"

Shit, in my fit of rage, I forgot to pretend to be normal and not a fucking stalker. "I'm an old friend of the Moores. He told me you were staying here a few weeks back."

She nodded.

We walked silently around to the side entrance, a faint purple glow emanating from the sheer curtain on the door.

"Lava lamp," she said, fidgeting with the lace on the end of her corset. "It came with the room. It's like a seventies time capsule in there. Do you . . . want to come in?"

Yes. No. I want to take you back to my place and fuck you, not in a basement. But I couldn't do that. This couldn't happen. She wasn't just a girl to fuck. I wasn't capable of love. Not after all I'd done. I didn't deserve it. I sure as hell didn't deserve her.

I gave her a dopey smile and shoved my hands into the pockets of my jeans. "Thanks, but my ride's waiting. I should get going. See you around . . . *kid.*"

She huffed a small laugh as she opened her door. "Goodnight, Ames."

The door closed and I let out an exhale. Breathing out who I really was. *The Ghost.* "Goodnight, Blythe," I whispered to myself. Of course there was no ride waiting. I wasn't going home. As I turned to leave, motion in the trees behind the house caught my attention. I stopped and peered into the darkness.

There was no monster in there scarier than me. The fact that I couldn't sense this criminal, deadbeat motherfucker was what was pissing me off. I couldn't wait to get him under my blade and venom and make him squeal like a pig. He may be invisible to me, but the fucker would still bleed all the same. I looked forward to ensuring that happened. *Slowly. Painfully.*

If he were hiding in the woods right now, watching me, all the better. A rat wandering into the viper's pit. Glancing over my shoulder, I checked to make sure Blythe wasn't within sight. My Little Ghost had disappeared into her purple glow. I strode into the darkness. All forests grew dark, but Ash Grove's woods . . . the darkness here . . . was different. Deeper, heavier, with a fullness that could cause even the bravest of men to quicken their steps. *I fucking loved it.*

Ten yards into the forest and anger gripped my chest. *Motherfuck—*

A slash of wide paws and dripping fangs tackled me to the ground. I grabbed the beast's snout, having to use two hands and more force than I was proud to admit to close his snarling maw. "Get the fuck off of me, Wolf," I hissed.

When I stood and picked up my glasses, he was only a dark mass. A black shadowy outline of a monstrous wolf. And then the shadow took the form of a man, and the black faded into my bone-headed friend. "Someone's got their undies in a twist tonight. I wonder why?" he said, tone dripping with sarcasm. "Sounds like jealousy to me. When was the last time you shifted?"

"What are you doing out here?" Onyx's voice drifted near, and I spotted him carrying an armful of firewood.

"What am I doing here? What the fuck are you two doing outside

Blythe's . . . ," I trailed off. "No, absolutely not. You can both go fuck right off. I'm watching her tonight. And I don't need to shift. I'm not some carnivore with zero control of my urges."

Wolfgang huffed and took a seat on a mossy stone. "Sure, whatever you say. And like hell am I leaving that girl all night."

"Just some girl, huh? Some girl you invited into your goddamn pack after knowing her all of a couple hours. Typical, overeager canine—"

His answering snarl threatened me with another shift. And as much as I liked kicking his ass, I wasn't in the mood to wrestle a beast tonight.

Onyx arranged the logs in a triangle. "How about you both quit bickering like an old married couple and we actually settle on a game plan for how we're going keep Blythe safe when we can't find this asshole. Oh, yeah, that's what Wolf and I were doing while you were off playing dress-up and having a dance party all evening." Onyx's typical joking was edged with a sharpness he didn't display often. The reason why he was so sharp, I didn't even want to think about.

I picked up a stone and threw it into the dark woods, wishing I could punch something instead. "I don't have time to argue with you clowns. Blythe is mine. End of story, so paws and claws off. Both of you."

Wolfgang crossed his burly, tattooed arms and stared me down like he was dying to challenge me but resisting. Onyx simply looked up at me as he leaned over the fire and blew a breath. Green fire erupted, dancing on the logs and simmering into a blazing orange inferno. "So you've claimed her then?" he asked carefully. Ever the attorney.

"No, I haven't claimed her. I'd never do that. It wouldn't be fair to anyone, least of all her, and she's been through enough."

Wolf huffed. "If you haven't claimed her then she's fair game."

I stalked over to him, popping my knuckles on the way. "No, she's fucking not," I spat. He stood, puffing out his chest. Onyx jumped between us, placing a flaming hot hand on each of our chests. Suddenly peace and clarity washed over my senses. I was seventeen and back on the farm, skipping rocks in the creek. My heart rate slowed, and I watched as Wolf's shoulders relaxed. "Both of you calm down, shit."

Onyx dropped his hands and went back to his fire tending. "We have bigger things to talk about other than dick measuring tonight . . . and how I'm going to be the one to fuck her and not either of you."

Wolfgang and I both shot to respond, but he only waved us off with a hand. "You two are calm as sleepy kittens right now. Don't try to pretend otherwise."

"We've talked about you using your abilities on us," I said softer than I meant. I wanted to kill them both. I wanted to *want* to kill them both. But his stupid emotional manipulation would last for at least twenty minutes. On a human, much longer.

He huffed in amusement, poking a stick at the flame. His eyes glowed green in the orange light, and my thoughts briefly drifted in his direction. We might have made some sort of sense together, Onyx and me. We'd explored it for a few nights here and there over the years. But we always landed somewhere between friends and more. We were both comfortable there and I wasn't looking to change it anytime soon. Plus, all my cock could think about at the moment was Blythe. That seemed to be my friends' affliction at the moment as well. Something about this girl had a chokehold on us all. It'd be best if we killed this guy and sent her on her way so life could go back to normal. We could all go back to punching the shit out of each other and being your average serial killers by day and . . . whatever by night.

"You found something," I stated, knowing the tension around Onyx's jaw only appeared when he was pissed off or worried.

"I pulled every security camera from surrounding towns and ours. Though as you know, our technology in Ash Grove is . . . temperamental. A truck registered to Simon Seth Glen stopped outside Candor about a month ago. Footage at a truck stop shows . . . Well, just fucking watch it." Onyx passed me his phone, and I held it up so Wolf could see over my shoulder. I wasn't about to go sit next to that asshole right then, calming, peaceful emotion energy or not. Tapping the screen, the black and white security camera footage rolled. A truck pulled up next to her car. The door opened. Wolf's presence loomed behind me as he rose from his brooding rock and walked closer, leaning in over my shoulder. "You need a shower," I muttered.

"You need to get laid," he growled.

He wasn't wrong.

A boot appeared outside the truck and then—

The footage blipped forward, the truck door closed now. "What just happened?" I asked, looking to Onyx for an explanation. His stare remained fixed on his beloved flames. "Keep watching."

A girl walked out, clutching a duffle bag. Blythe. Something moved behind her. I squinted to look harder.

Wolf grumbled low. "What the fuck?"

We could only make out the faintest imprint of a gray shadow. She fell and heat rose in my ribs, and I gritted my teeth. She scrambled up, clutching her side, running to her car. She sped off moments later. Wolf snarled behind my ear, a deep, feral and terrifying rumble. I clutched the phone until my knuckles were white. The shadow stood unmoving in her wake. As fixed as a carved statue. Then suddenly, it spun, shooting toward the camera with lightning speed. The camera jostled and then went blank.

Onyx's peaceful demeanor concealed his rage. His anger tasted like a shot of scotch. It was all I could do not to slam my friend's phone into a nearby oak. "How?" I demanded.

Onyx simply nudged a crackling log with his fireproof hand. "I don't know. But it looks like Judas was right all along."

I glanced back to get Wolfgang's reaction. Only, the massive silhouette of a wolf greeted me, pacing along the tree line. His desire to kill was so strong right now it threatened to inebriate me. God, the taste of murder was rich and lush. Like a perfectly cooked filet mignon. "It's not possible. He can't be. Blythe's stepfather is mortal. You saw his criminal record."

"That I did." Onyx shrugged a shoulder. "It's either tampered with or he . . . became what he is later on. But I-I haven't heard of that happening in a very long time."

"Not since us," I breathed.

Replaying the footage in my mind over and over, it only pointed to one thing. And if that was the case, we were all in for more of a fight than we anticipated. And Blythe was in more danger than she realized.

A green flame snaked into the sky, the only show of emotion from Onyx so far. "He's like you, Ghost. One of yours." I met his stare as the green light flickered around him and Wolf paced, circling us like a shark. Then Onyx spoke the unthinkable. "Blythe's stepfather is a goddamn demon."

CHAPTER 13
Blythe

SPOOKY GIRLS LOVE LIBRARIES

> Walls have ears.
> Doors have eyes.
> Trees have voices.
> Beasts tell lies.
> Beware the rain.
> Beware the snow.
> Beware the man
> You think you know.
> *Catherine Fisher*

My heels sloshed into the still sopping, green shag carpet. Pumps were not my smartest idea. First the climbing and walking and now this. I didn't care if it clashed, the rest of Hallows I'd be in sneakers. I splashed over to my bed where a pink post-it note was stuck to Benny. Snatching up my beloved stuffed bat, I read the cursive scrawl.

People coming to clean the basement tomorrow. Please feel free to stay in our spare room. First door to the right at the top of the stairs. - The Moores

I let out a sigh. What other choice did I have? After digging a discarded, roomy T-shirt from the dry portion of my sheets, and fishing out some clean underwear, I trodded up the stairs. *What choice do I have?*

Oh, two other big, sexy choices. One with my therapist crush and the other on an idyllic compound with Mr. Beef Cake. Why hadn't I just gone home with Ames? Or I could have agreed to stay in my own little house near Wolf. I'd been running so long that any sort of kindness or show of friendship unnerved me. Why would they care? I knew I looked pitiful and hopeless, but that didn't mean I wanted pity. Especially not from Ames Cove. I wanted him to look at me and see a sexy, sure, strong woman. Not some pathetic wanderer. If he had invited me home because he wanted me . . . I knew I would have said yes in a heartbeat. But the moment I stepped through the pitch black doorway and into the shockingly pink and frilly spare room, I started to doubt my decisions. Maybe beggars shouldn't be choosers. And maybe accepting a bit of charity would be better than this pink pom-pom and lace twin bed. The sickeningly pink wallpaper didn't help matters, but what was more disconcerting were the old, vintage photographs splattered across the wall in dusty white frames. Struggling to unhook my corset, I inspected them and kicked off my pumps. The same little girl stared back blankly. Blonde pigtails in ribbons and poofy, lacy gown in each photo. A man, woman, and cat sat posed next to her behind one frame. I half wondered if they were the Moores and maybe she was their daughter. Then I noticed a horse and buggy in one scene behind them and decided these must be old relatives of theirs. Heirloom pictures. An intricate vanity sat next to the bed, complete with carvings of cherubs in the wood and a mirror blackened with spots to where it looked like old silverware. A blonde doll with pigtails tied in blue ribbon sat in the center, her head cocked to the side. Add that to the list of things that creeped me out, right under churches and cornfields. I shook off my eerie feeling and tore off my tight clothing. Thankfully, there was a tiny en-suite bathroom and a little pink-tiled shower. I washed off with a bubblegum scented bar of soap and tried not to think about how old it was . . . or who had possibly used it before me. After pulling on my Danzig band T-shirt that skimmed the thickest part of my upper thighs, I shut off the lights and tucked myself into bed. In the dark and with the moon shining through the sheer curtains, it wasn't so bad in there. And I supposed I should be grateful that the Moores offered the room to me.

But I couldn't think of my wet heels or the sugary scent of my skin. I snuggled my plush bat close to my chest and inhaled, pulling out my favorite memories of the night like silk from a drawer. The friendly vampire that walked me in and her flaming red hair. The Ravens brought a sleepy grin to my face. A grin that faded when I remembered the white-haired vampire and his less-than-friendly crimson eyes. And then, I slid out my favorite memory . . . and my palm slid down my stomach. When I turned and saw the skeleton man, his leather jacket and that malicious look in his blue eyes. I slipped my hand under my panties. I thought of Ames and his sideways grin when he rubbed his hand through his black hair. I could marry them both together for this fantasy. My fingers found their mark. My mind drifted to the butterflies that erupted when the crowd parted and I saw him again. The way he extended his hand and pulled me close. Our dance that took my breath away. I slipped a finger inside and pumped slowly in and out, stealing a gasp, and I tilted my head back. And then in my mind, Dr. Cove opened my car door and didn't step back when I stood up. He was so close I wanted to wrap myself around him. His hair moved off his thick glasses just long enough I half wondered . . . God, wouldn't that be something? If Ames Cove were my mystery skeleton man? It was absurd, and impossible, because he was standing next to my car right after. No man was that fast, not with how far away were were from my car at The Brew Pump. But in my fantasy, Ames donned the skeleton man's face and wrapped an arm around the small of my back, tugging me flush to him. It was his hand, not mine, that snaked between my thighs and found me wet and wanting. A small orgasm built, and then in my fantasy, he pressed his lips to mine. *God, I wonder what his kiss tastes like .*

. . My climax rippled through me like a pebble tossed in a pond. With a soft sigh, I pulled my hand out of the fabric's hold. How I wished for something thunderous and loud and not small and timid. But that would have to be enough.

Sleep took me as I hoped my monster would find me in my dreams for another dance.

THE NEXT DAY began with an alarm clock of the vacuum cleaner roaring and buzzing across, what I assumed was, more shag carpet. It was rude of me, but I waited for the sound to grow faint before sneaking out of my room and back downstairs into the swamp. I pulled on a pair of ripped jeans and enclosed myself in Ames's varsity jacket. Even in a hurry to escape my surroundings, I took a moment to indulge in a breathful of his aroma. Oaky and slightly floral like . . . lavender. Awareness pricked at my senses as the smell brought back the memory of my dance with the skeleton man. No, that wasn't possible. Clearly, my daydreams and night fantasies were merging in a fantastical and unhealthy way. The man I danced with was probably some town bad boy and I'd never know his true identity. I guessed he'd probably forgotten all about me.

My stomach grumbled and all but shoved me out the door in search of something other than the crumbly granola bars stashed in my bag. Droplets of chilled rain speckled my cheeks as I trudged up the gravel to my car. Mr. Moore, on queue, was sweeping the road, even in the rain. I hoped to avoid getting stuck in an awkward conversation with him, so I quietly clicked my door closed. Just as I thought I'd made it past the point of contact, their orange tabby cat jumped onto the hood. I rolled down my window and shooed him. "Hey, you're going to get wet, go on," I hissed.

The commotion was enough that after a few moments, Mr. Moore appeared with his broom tucked under his arm. He scooped the feline off my car and gave a small nod. "Good morning, Blythe. We hope you slept well in Ellie's room last night. We should get an estimate on how long it'll take to fix the basement later today."

"Thank you, sir. I appreciate you letting me stay upstairs last night." I hesitated a moment before asking, "Is Ellie your daughter?"

My landlord scratched under the cat's chin, seemingly unaware of the rain that was picking up speed around us. "Yes, Ellie May is our daughter."

Something about his forlorn tone made me not want to ask any more questions. "Well, tell her thanks for letting me use her room last night."

"I'll tell her." He smiled faintly. "You still planning to join us for dinner on Monday?"

"Yes, sir," I replied, turning the crank on my manual window and rolling it up slightly as rain poured down now.

Mr. Moore sat the cat down, who walked off, very un-cat-like, through a puddle. We wished each other a good day and I rolled slowly out the drive, my windshield wipers flapping like crazy in the sudden storm. I checked my rearview to see Mr. Moore standing where I left him, broom still lodged under his arm. He could get sick standing around in the rain. I considered turning around and urging him to go inside but decided against it. The man was old but seemed of sound mind. Maybe he liked the rain.

My landlord was eccentric, no doubt, like the whole of Ash Grove. But the look on his face when he mentioned his daughter Ellie . . . was what made the hair on my arms stand up. She couldn't have been the girl in the photos; that would be absurd. Maybe she collected vintage family heirlooms. For some reason, I found that hard to believe but a good enough excuse to stop thinking about it for a while.

"Gold Dust Woman" by Fleetwood Mac crooned on the oldies radio station, and I cranked up the volume as I drove to the diner. I had five dollars and some change after filling up my Honda's gas tank. That was enough for coffee with free refills and some buttered toast. I'd take it.

I claimed my usual cracked leather booth, and my favorite waitress, Doris, greeted me with a fresh mug of coffee. "'Morning, dear. What can I get you today?"

"Hi, Miss Doris. Can I get some butter toast, please?" I asked, thumbing at the dollars and change in my purse, making sure my math was right.

Doris's wise and wrinkled eyes followed the movement before putting a hand on her hip. "He told me not to tell you, but I don't take orders from that boy. Your tab is paid off indefinitely. Order whatever you want, sugar."

I furrowed my brow in confusion. "What do you mean? Someone paid for me to eat here?"

"That's right, honey. We've got his card on file."

"Who?"

Just then a man's voice interrupted as he wrapped a gentle arm around the old waitress and tugged her close for a kiss on the cheek. "Doris O'Malley, you are looking particularly radiant today. Did you get a fresh perm?"

My waitress blushed and swatted Onyx's arm as he slid into the seat across from me. She shook her head and gave me a pointed look. "Who do you think? And a word of advice? Order the most expensive things every day and make this troublemaker pay big."

Onyx chuckled and I grinned, feeling a rise of embarrassment warm my face. "I don't need you to pay for my food," I mumbled to Onyx, who had casually draped his arm over the back of the seat, his dress shirt peppered with dots of rain. Little glimpses of the muscles were hiding under his formal attire. "I've got more money than I know what to do with. Let me buy you unlimited waffles and coffee, will ya?"

Doris snorted. "You've got more money than sense is more like it."

"That too." Onyx smirked.

Rolling my eyes, I gave up the fight. I was starving, and this was the nicest offer I'd probably ever gotten. And someone picking up my breakfast tab was innocent enough, even though I hated being a charity case to these boys who'd decided to interject into my life in the smallest ways. "I'd love a Belgian waffle, please. Thank you, Miss Doris."

"Add bacon, eggs, and a fruit bowl onto her order. I'll have the same. Thanks, cutie." Onyx batted his long dark lashes. Doris snapped his ribs with a rag before she smiled and walked off. He chuckled before pulling out his newspaper and pencil. "She likes me. I know it."

I couldn't help the smile that tugged at my lips. He may have been cocky, but he was good breakfast company. "Thank you for picking up breakfast. You really don't have to. I don't need you or your friends' pity."

A green gaze met mine in seriousness as he paused his crossword. "We don't pity you, Blythe, not for a second, okay? We want to do it. We like helping. It . . . helps us to help you. Trust me on that."

I huffed a laugh. "So you're all selfishly buying my food and offering me places to stay. Sure, I believe you."

He shrugged, "Can't we all go a little crazy trying to impress the town's prettiest girl?"

Heat flooded my face and I looked down, tugging my jacket closer. I didn't know what to say. But Onyx seemed like a shameless flirt, so I was sure compliments like that rolled off his smooth tongue regularly. "I've got a jacket like that, too."

My interest was piqued. "Your grandpa went to school with Ames's?"

He gave a half smile, revealing the slightest hint of a dimple as he filled in a word on his puzzle. "Sure, if that's what he told you."

"What's that supposed to mean?"

His piercing emerald stare leveled me again, like he was debating on what to say next. "Have you been to our library?"

Random.

"Um, no. I didn't know Ash Grove had a library."

"I'll take you after breakfast. You should check it out—"

Another gruffer male voice interrupted, "Where are we going after breakfast?"

In a wet, dirty T-shirt and dirt covered jeans, a bulky Wolf pushed into space next to me in my booth. His thick arms brushed up next to mine. I swallowed back the butterflies in my throat. Onyx shot him an annoyed look. "Blythe and I are going to the library after what *was* a lovely and quiet breakfast."

"I haven't agreed to going anywhere," I protested weakly, but I could feel the giggle on my lips. I felt like the new toy between dogs. The feminist in me should have hated it, but I didn't. I liked the attention these impossibly attractive men were giving me.

Another man's voice interjected while the table was filled with plates of sweet and salty smelling food. "Blythe didn't agree to hanging out with either of you idiots because she's coming with me back to my place today." The butterflies in my stomach shifted into pterodactyls at the sight of Ames. He looked freshly showered with wet shaggy hair and a tight black T-shirt and dark washed jeans. He gestured a thumb over his shoulder at Wolf, who let out an exasperated sigh as he stood. Ames took over his very large friend's seat as Wolf shoved in beside Onyx. I struggled to run a few fingers through my braid, hoping I didn't look too disheveled. "Good morning, beautiful." He smiled a megawatt smile behind his thick-rimmed glasses, and I could have fainted. *Did he just call me beautiful and say he wanted to take me back to his place?*

"Let the woman eat, Jesus Christ," Onyx complained, positioning my waffles, eggs, and meat in front of me. My mouth watered as I unwrapped my silverware. Before I could ask if they were going to order, several more plates of food arrived before them. Doris swatted at them as they fussed over her. *Her perm, her new apron, her pretty smile.* I giggled at their playful banter in between bites of strawberry waffles.

Onyx and Wolf ate their eggs and sausage while casting irritated glances at Ames, which I didn't quite understand. Ames rested an arm on the seat behind me and leaned toward my ear. "I didn't mean to presume, but I'd like to show you my place today. Like I said, I have plenty of room if you ever want to stay."

Taking a sip of coffee, it was an effort not to tremble being so close to him. Our knees softly touched under the table, and my mind drifted to my naughty fantasy from the night before. Wolf asked while my face turned red, "So how'd you like Hallows last night? You don't seem to be missing mass amounts of blood."

I giggled, wiping my face with a paper napkin. "I loved it. But yeah, I did get cornered by a couple of vampires," I said jokingly, though the boys' faces only looked serious at me.

"Did any of them touch you?" Onyx asked, his jaw tensing.

I furrowed my brow and shook my head. "No, not really. Well, I met one named Ezmerelda and she was flirty but nice—"

Wolf scoffed and crossed his arms. I wondered if he knew her. The thought of her being flirty toward him made something in my chest boil with jealousy. The feeling made me uneasy. I had no business worrying about these guys' conquests. I continued, "And then I ran into one with long white hair. I think someone said his name was Vincent. He was a little more insistent."

Onyx's mouth dropped and he gave Ames a pointed look. Ames only leaned back, arm still positioned protectively over my seat, looking as impassive as ever.

"Don't worry. I have a guy dressed like a skeleton stalking me. He seemed to scare the vampire guy away. And then I just hung out with the Ravens," I said, taking a bite of crispy bacon. I chuckled softly. "That may have been the weirdest thing I've ever said."

"Interesting," Wolf grumbled, his thick arms crossed over his wide chest. "What are your plans tonight?"

I looked between them, each so focused on me it was both flattering and unnerving. "Well, I need to check in with Raja about my work schedule. Apparently, they close early all of October. And they don't serve breakfast. So I don't know if that job is going to pan out. But I'm never in one place long anyway, especially now . . ."

Ames spoke. "You're not running this time, Blythe. You're going to let us help."

"You guys are really generous and sweet, but I don't see how you could help me in this situation. I've dealt with being followed for so long."

"Do you want to leave?" Onyx asked. "Do you want to run again?"

I swallowed down the emotion in my chest. I knew the answer. I'd known the answer the moment my bald tires hit the pavement in Ash Grove. "No, I don't want to leave. For the first time in my life, I want to stay. Ash Grove feels like home, somehow," I said sadly. If I didn't run, I'd die here. And maybe I was ready for that, now. After Hallows, after meeting these guys, maybe I could die somewhat happy.

"We have a plan," Ames said decidedly. "You're staying here and you're going to be okay."

Wolf's gaze eyed me pointedly. "No one is going to hurt you."

Onyx rolled up his newspaper and put his pen behind his ear. "We're going to protect you."

My heart warmed as emotion swelled behind my eyes. "I can't—"

Ames put his rough palm over the top of my hand and squeezed. "You can and you will. We've decided, and there's no arguing with us when we make up our minds. You're ours now."

The heat from my cheeks dropped like a weight between my thighs. Onyx smirked. "Don't bother arguing. Stick with us and see what we can do."

God. Damn.

"How can I say no?" I gave a breathless laugh. "At least if I die it's around a place . . . and people . . . that I like."

Wolf leaned forward, making strong eye contact. So strong I felt his fervor in my bones as a chill of intensity traveled down my spine. "You are not going to die, Blythe. You can be sure of that."

A breath lodged in my throat and I realized Ames was still holding my hand. "Okay," I agreed meekly. We finished our meals and the guys cleared our plates, marching them to the back as if the diner were their home kitchen. Judging by the smell of soap on Wolf when he returned, I gathered they actually washed the dishes too. Admiration pooled in my heart. These boys were dangerous with their easy smiles, charm, and kindness. I realized then that I was at great risk of falling for each of them. Something deep inside me whispered that not only did I want to stay in Ash Grove for Hallows, but for them. And I wanted to stay alive for them, too. It was a feeling I hadn't experienced in all my travels. But then again, I'd never met anyone like them before.

Something about these boys made me want to live.

CHAPTER 14

HELL RIDER

> The real world is where the monsters are.
> *Rick Riordan*

My possessiveness was growing. Blythe was afflicting me like slow and steady frostbite. The mask I'd crafted to hide my true form from the world was cracking. Piece by piece, it fell at her feet like a bloody offering. Did she notice? Could she see the way I couldn't pull my eyes from the crook of her neck? Did any part of her sense that I didn't close my eyes once last night in fear of missing her assailant again? The way her lips wrapped around the grape on the end of her fork . . . How she sucked the juice before taking it in her mouth . . . I was hard in the booth next to her. Her golden-brown hair was tied in that sexy, tousled braid and her ripped jeans hugged her ass just right.

I called her beautiful, I held her hand, and none of it came even close to being enough. Even our dance paled in comparison to what I wanted. To the growing ache in my core for her. I'd fought it the entire time she'd been in town, and I should have kept fighting it. If I held out a little longer, her stepfather would be dead, and she'd change her mind and want to leave. With safety and possibilities ahead of her, why would she stay? I needed my mind clear. The Halloween Boys and I had already proven ourselves to be sloppy and out of shape with age. Perhaps our supernatural abilities had made us slow and overconfident. Because this had been a challenge from the start. An annoying challenge. And we still had no real leads. If I lost sight of this fucker, if somehow he slipped past us again, if he touched her . . . Losing this target meant losing her. And that wouldn't, couldn't, fucking happen.

I may have been slipping, and falling for her, but I had to keep it together. I had to maintain some level of distance so I could see straight. Otherwise, I was afraid of getting far too deep. And where could we even go? I wouldn't drag Blythe to hell with me. She couldn't haunt graveyards and thirst for dirty blood like the evil inside me did. Being with me would mar her. She was dirtier just by association. Everyone at Hallows knew. They all feared us, as they fucking should, but they also knew we were the most wretched of them all. The reason the town was what it was. The source of the suffering.

They were right.

I knew Blythe's stepdad deserved every ounce of punishment I was about to rain down upon him. I knew because I deserved it too. If we were marking our sins like tallies on a wall, mine would outweigh his by miles. But that didn't change the fact that the moment I found him, he would die slowly, painfully.

My Little Ghost walked outside, her eyes wide as I extended the helmet and revved my engine. I wasn't a total idiot. I knew girls liked the bike. My ride was a black on black Ducati Multistrada V4. Sharp, powerful, and fast as hell. "Those assholes can drive your car behind us. You and I are taking the scenic route to the library."

"Playing dirty, dude," Onyx complained as Blythe fished out her keys and handed them to him.

Wolf shook his head. "Should have known you'd bring her out soon. Man, I haven't seen you ride in a good many years."

"Why is that?" Blythe asked, gripping my waist and hitching her leg over the back of the bike. Her perfect, soft thighs pressed around me, and her breasts grazed my back. *Fuck me. What was her question again?*

"Haven't felt like riding until today." I shrugged, though Wolf and I knew better. We both knew it was her. She made me want to ride. Even on that cloudy-ass day where a downpour could have caught us at any moment. It didn't matter. It was still somehow a beautiful October day. The oranges and reds shone deeper in hue after the morning storm.

She tugged on her helmet, and leaning forward, she whispered in my ear, sending tingles electrocuting straight to my already hard cock. "Go fast, please. I can take it."

I was about to go fast alright, ditching the boys and taking her home to my bed. But Onyx was right in the plan we hatched last night. I had to trust that if anything, the guy was smart.

She needed to know about us. And the gentlest way to do that would be to lead her to finding the truth by herself. She needed to discover it and piece it all together. If she had all the cards in her hand, maybe she wouldn't run away screaming. She sure as hell would if we sat her down and just told her—which was what Onyx advocated we do. Wolf thought we'd be keeping her safer by keeping her ignorant.

If Blythe's stepfather was just your average criminal, I'd agree with Wolf. In that instance, she wouldn't need to know about us. He'd die, and she'd move on with her life. But being that we highly suspected now that her pursuer was an actual demon . . . Demon hunting required more . . . everything. More tact, more energy, more eyes, and she had to be told what was truly after her. And it also seemed she needed to be told that so we might compel her to accept our help. If she knew what she was up against and what we were . . . If she wasn't completely horrified and disgusted by the truth about us, then we stood a chance of catching this bastard. But if we somehow failed . . . The consequences of a demon catching Blythe were too ghastly to even think about. And that was coming from me, a demon myself. I knew how dark and depraved my kind were. It certainly explained him enjoying the hunt. The sicko was probably drinking up her fear. So was I, but, you know, I wasn't trying to actively kill her.

There also seemed to be pieces missing. Like how'd she get mixed up with a demon stepfather? She recognized him on the surveillance and ran, so she knew him, yet he was displaying demonic qualities. Something didn't add up. We couldn't keep hiding much longer, and we needed more answers from her. Perhaps a perusal through the archives at the old library would be enough to softly introduce her to our past. As my motorcycle screamed to life, I jutted us onto the road, grinning at her squeal of excitement. Little Ghost wasn't kidding; she wanted to go fast. I was happy to oblige. Not happy she'd ask someone she assumed was a mortal guy to drive fast. These things were not safe for humans. But me? I'd keep her safe. I could fly us into the night with my eyes closed and she wouldn't be harmed. To any onlooker, we'd be a phantom wind. A puff of smoke impervious to harm. We could ride through trees or buildings if I wanted us to. That was part of my talents, though. Onyx called them gifts, Judas called them curses, and I landed somewhere in the middle with my assessment of our unique abilities, even if my own capabilities were waning for some reason. Perhaps I truly was reaching ancient status, like I told Blythe. Even the elderly in this town looked like kids to me. I didn't tell her that, though.

There was a lot she didn't know and that she'd probably be better off not knowing. I would have been content to leave her in the dark. I'd sure as fuck never disclosed anything about my true nature to any woman I'd been with over the years. Though those encounters began and ended in bed. But Blythe was different in so many ways. Not only did she call to me like a siren and I felt a deep and unending desire to protect her, but she had another demon on her tail. *Another* demon. Did she call to another like she did me? The question had me digging my nails into my handlebars as we leaned into a curve on the highway. Why was he after her? Out of all the humans in the world, why her? Maybe she held the clue and she didn't even know it.

I wanted her to know. A part of me was thrilled at the idea. Another part of me wanted to keep her in the dark. I could live in this world where I was her friend who changed the oil in her car from a haunted gasoline station and who she unknowingly danced with later as her ghost. Couldn't we stay in this purgatory a while longer?

"Is this fast enough for you?" I shouted over the wind. The sound of her giggling as her legs pressed firm around me sent a jolt down my front.

"You could go harder," she replied.

Thank the Devil I wasn't a regular man because I would have lost control of my bike at that point. We would have been goners. Who could stay upright at a response like that?

With a raspy laugh, I instructed her, "Loop your fingers together around me and lean in to the curves, not away, got it?" *I'd like to lean into her curves.*

"Got it," she said with excitement

I pushed past a moment of doubt and let the speedometer crank forward until it disappeared. My bike was made for this, and it purred in appreciation. But even more so, I was made for speed. She had no idea how fast we were truly going, but we were torpedoing between worlds. Blythe laughed behind me, thoroughly enjoying herself as we raced down the winding roads of backwoods Ash Grove. When we arrived at the old library attached to the abandoned high school, I jumped off and offered her my hand. "Looks like we beat the guys here," I remarked, pleased with that fact.

Her hand trembled slightly as she took mine and got off. I helped her unclip and remove the matte black helmet, and when I did, alarm washed over me. "You're crying. It was too fast. Blythe, I'm so sorry—"

She sniffled and shook her head. "No, it wasn't too fast. It was perfect. I loved every second." And then her arms wrapped around my waist and she buried her head in my chest. If I had a heart, it would have stopped. This was . . . *a hug?* I wasn't sure I'd ever gotten one from a woman before. "Thank you, Ames," she whispered.

I wrapped my arms around her in return and gently stroked her hair. "It was my pleasure, Little Ghost." The words left my mouth before I could stop myself. A hint. A plea.

She looked up, still holding onto me, her brown eyes speckled with . . . black. They were like marbles. Remarkable. "Little Ghost?"

"You called yourself a ghost the first day we met in my office."

A small sad smile swooped over her pink lips. "I guess I'm haunting you, then."

"I'd love to be haunted by you," I replied, surprised by the breathlessness that had overcome me, and it wasn't from the ride.

Her eyes sparkled, the black streaks dancing. Before she could reply, the sound of two dumbasses interrupted. "Way too fucking fast, Ames," Wolf chastised.

"What were you thinking? Shit, are you okay, Blythe?" Onyx asked, wholly annoyed. But I couldn't even be mad, and I couldn't let her out of my arms, even when she tugged back slightly. *Mine.*

"I'm fine. It was my idea to go fast," she admitted.

Wolf grinned his positively canine smile. Once you knew what he was, you saw it in every part of him. How he walked, interacted, and spoke. He was the living embodiment of a mythical shadow beast. "Our girl's got a need for speed, huh? You're fitting in just fine, baby."

"Yeah, yeah, let's get inside. It looks like it's going to rain again soon," Onyx muttered, walking past us. I would have apologized for stealing Blythe away from his breakfast and library date, but I wasn't sorry. And they weren't listening to my warning to not get overly emotionally involved with her. Onyx needed a reality check.

"My jacket looks nice on you," I commented as we made our way inside.

She blushed. "Thank you. It's comfortable. Was it from your grandpa?"

"No," I replied absently as the cold, stale air of books and memories smacked me in the face.

Blythe broke away from our group, exploring, running a delicate finger over musty leather spines. "This place looks like it's frozen in time," she said, picking up a book. "This can't be a first edition from eighteen-twenty, right?"

She and Onyx exchanged a gentle look before he answered, "What you see is what you get in here. No tricks."

"This place is all new to me too," Wolf joked. "I sure as shit didn't spend any time doing homework in here."

"You went to school here? Wait, all three of you went here together?"

Wolf nodded. "Yep, a long time ago."

"Couldn't have been that long ago," she replied, distracted by a wall of browning newspapers. "Are these real?" she asked.

The boys and I paused, looking to each other. "They are," Onyx replied carefully.

She immediately reached for the paper we were all hoping she'd get to last. She read the headline out loud. "The Massacre. A Town in Mourning . . . Holy shit . . ."

I shifted anxiously on my feet, waiting for her reaction when she pieced it together.

"The date on this is November eighteen twenty-three. Is that even possible? Were there printing presses back then?"

Wolf answered, taking a small step closer. "Ash Grove was one of only about two hundred newspapers in America at that time. So yes, it's real."

"Wow, I feel like I shouldn't be touching this, like it should be in a museum or something." She squinted her eyes as she carefully unfolded the paper, revealing the photo on the front. We all cringed. I was sure the guys were cringing from our wardrobe; the caps and suspenders weren't our best looks. I was cringing for my crime. Our crime. "It says the town blamed . . . . . . The Halloween Boys for the massacre on Halloween . . . almost the entire town slaughtered in cold blood at the hands of the three men." She brought the paper closer to her face. "The names are so small I can barely read them . . . and this photo—" She stopped, and I could see the way her throat tightened. I felt the budding blossom of her tangy fear. "They look exactly like you guys—"

And then Onyx cut in.

With a panicked voice, he put an arm around Blythe's shoulder. "I think all this dust is giving me a headache, how about you?"

The taste of her fear evaporated as Wolf and I stared at our friend in alarm. Blythe giggled. She *giggled*. "Yeah, the allergens are pretty bad in here. Maybe we should get going. Wow, I'm really craving sugar right now. And I'm suddenly super tired . . . ."

Onyx continued, "Wolfgang, buddy, why don't you take Blythe back to her car. Ames and I will catch up."

She giggled again and batted her eyelashes at the dark-haired dragon hybrid. I was going to kill him. "Sure thing," Wolf growled, hardly concealing his rage. I was right there with him, shooting him a stern look that said I'd handle it from here. He escorted Blythe out, who kept casting little glances back. Onyx smiled like the Devil and gave a short wave as they disappeared behind the swaying door.

In an instant, I had him by the collar. I lifted him off his feet, slamming him into the newspaper wall and holding him steady. Periodicals and dirt fluttered down around us as Onyx's green eyes stared at me head on. He didn't attempt to manipulate my emotions; he knew better than to try that right now.

"What the actual fuck, Dragon? Her finding out this way was your idea."

"I know."

"So you blow it at the last possible second? Explain before I ram my fist through your face."

He sucked in a breath, "I don't want her to know yet. I know I said I did, but being with her . . . Can you blame me if I want to keep . . . this . . . going a little longer? She likes us and I haven't seen you or Wolf like this in a long time."

I held his neck tighter, my rage not subsiding. "This isn't about us. You know that. What about her? Have you forgotten there's a fucking demon on her scent right now?"

Onyx shoved out of my grip and I let him, taking a frustrated step back and running a hand through my hair.

"I think we're jumping the gun out of fear. This is one demon and there's three of us, four if Devil shows up. We haven't battled a paranormal in a while, granted, but we aren't weak. Even if your powers are lagging, you're still the strongest fucking demon I've ever seen. You used your disappearing speed shit on your bike with a mortal on the back and she didn't even notice."

"You saw that?"

"Yeah, of course I did. Using your demon prowess to impress a girl is a new low, even for you."

I scoffed, "Oh, and using your vampire touch to make a girl into you for the day wasn't the scummiest thing you've ever done?"

He shrugged. "I won't lie about liking her. I'm pretty sure Wolf does too. But that isn't the whole reason I want to keep a lid on us for now. Just for now, Ghost. We've barely put in any effort to hunt this fucker. We're just scared because we actually like his mark. But think about it, he's been tailing her through several states. He's finding her address and stalking her with those demon letters of fucking nonsense. I snuck into her place and found the others. Badly water damaged but from what I could make out, they're all the same. The legible ones all say, *"I'm not going to let you. I'm not going to let you."* Over and over again. The demon's fucking lost it. Why put in that effort? Why not just kill her, or possess her, or whatever the fuck your kind like doing."

"So you think he's crazy?"

"All signs point to yes. Maybe he's just into the hunt, like you are."

I sighed, exasperated. "I'm into the kill more."

"Precisely. And he hasn't killed her. Why? I think we stand a better chance of catching him then you think. Let's not blow our cover just yet. Maybe we can eradicate him and save the day."

I leaned on an old table and crossed my arms. "You think you stand a better chance with her by pretending to be a mortal, huh?"

He shrugged. "Don't tell me you don't think the same goddamn thing."

"I told you to leave her alone. Both of you."

Onyx's green eyes glowed in the dim light of the library. "And you told us you haven't claimed her. Is that still true?"

Fuck. He knew I couldn't claim her. I wouldn't do that to her. "How could I damn her like that? Tie her to a demon. You know what that would mean."

"Yeah, I get it. But if you haven't claimed her, it's not fair to tell us to stay away for no other reason than you have a crush the same as we do. Grow up."

"I'm almost two hundred years old, dickhead."

He scoffed, reaching under the cabinet of the newspapers and pulling out a bottle of amber liquid. "A hundred and seventy some-thing, give or take a few years. I, however, am over two hundred."

I rolled my eyes, taking the bottle when he offered it and downing a hefty gulp of whisky. "Fuck, how long have you had this in here? Since high school?"

He chuckled, inspecting the bottle. "Which year? The first time we graduated or the fiftieth?"

"I'm glad we quit the high school scene. Geometry got old after the first thirty years."

Onyx took another gulp before hiding the bottle back in its spot. "Practicing law is more engaging than taking sex education for decades, that's for sure. Luckily humans moved on and accepted our charade of, ironically, being older than our bodies look. Though, the new towns-people do look at us odd when they met us when they were thirty, and they die at ninety while we look the same."

I shrugged. "It's not like they can leave and tell anyone. And we haven't had a new batch of townspeople in a long time. Blythe is the first who's passed through in, what, seven years? It's been us and the originals for what feels like eons."

Onyx snorted. "Right, so you can see why it's not fair that you call dibs without claiming her."

"Since when do you think I give a shit about fair?"

Onyx considered me for a moment. "You seem to be concerned about what's fair for Blythe. I've never seen you care about a girl so much."

"Don't read into it," I warned. Though I could see it in his eyes as well as he could mine. My resolve was slipping in regard to the town newcomer.

We walked out slowly, seeing Wolf leaning on Blythe's car, scrolling his phone as gray rain sprinkled around us. "You've found loopholes. Ash Grove lets you leave for court in neighboring towns. You could find willing partners," I said eventually.

"I can get laid, sure, but you know as well as I it gets old. Sex and no relationship, never bringing them home, never being honest about what we are. Knowing that if we ever risked claiming them they'd be fucking doomed? I wish I could get in contact with my parents, find them some-how. If Judas could find a way to break this wretched curse . . ."

He was right, and I couldn't argue. Onyx had more reason to want to leave than Wolfgang and I: his family he'd worked so hard to regain memory of. But here we were. Stuck.

We stopped in front of a pissed off Wolf. "Well?" he asked impatiently. I envisioned a large ball of shadow fur and suppressed the smirk that threatened to cause him to shift right there on Rose Street.

"Dragon and I agree we can give it a little more time. There's no need to scare her right now when we can catch this guy if we pull our heads out of our asses long enough."

Wolf huffed and began pacing. "Starting with you," he growled, pointing at me. "And you." He pointed at Onyx. "What the fuck did you do with your sex hands?"

Onyx put a hand to his chest in mock offense. "My *sex hands*? You mean my half vampire gifts?"

I put a palm over my mouth and pretended to scratch my jaw as Wolf walked over, towering and brooding over Onyx, who didn't as much as flinch. I'd pay good money to see them battle it out both in full shifted form. Somehow, though, that had never happened. "You know as well as I do," Wolf said lowly, "vampires are the most deviant, sex-obsessed maniacs on this planet. That's why you all have the touch: to seduce your lovers into bed."

Onyx tsked. "I'm only half vampire, and that half is very offended you think me some sort of nymphomaniac. I am a consent king. Many vampires are. Our touch is to enhance sex with willing partners, not to coerce people into things they don't want to do. That's no fun. Besides, who wouldn't want me?"

Wolf waved a hand to the backseat of Blythe's car. "She just talked my ear off asking if you had a girlfriend or boyfriend, how old you were, your interests, and other things I was too mad to answer. Now she's sleeping off the effects of your *sex touch*. Sounds real consensual to me. And her finding out was the plan. You don't take it upon yourself to break the fucking plan without telling the pack."

I raised a skeptical eyebrow at Onyx who only gave a lazy shrug. "I made her happy and calm . . . and maybe believe I was as attractive as her first crush, whoever that may have been. Harmless, it'll wear off, so wipe those murderous looks off your faces. You'll continue to be on a level playing field to throw yourselves at her. She was getting scared, and I freaked and made her happy."

"Will she remember the newspaper?" I asked.

"No, any human would forget. She'll only remember coming here, browsing, and waking up from a nap in her car."

Wolf huffed and stomped around the vehicle, slamming the car door as he took over the driver's seat.

Onyx looked at me, emerald eyes glowing slightly again. "I'm going to find this fucker. I'm done with this shit. We kill him and we move on."

"Agreed. We'll split up. One of us stays with Blythe, the others comb the town. Demons can be creative in where they lurk but they're messy. He'll fuck up and leave clues."

I glanced into the backseat at my Little Ghost sleeping peacefully. I couldn't even be mad at Onyx because he made her happy for a moment. Even if it was artificial. The look on her face . . . She deserved happiness. And I may have been a rotten, evil, damned soul . . . but I could save her. Today may not have been the day she discovered us. Perhaps she never needed to. Could it be that for once in our existences, we could make a friend who didn't have to be mortified by learning about who we were? About what we did to this town?

I may have been a demon, but I was her demon now. And I wouldn't rest until my graveyard echoed with the sounds of her stepfather's wails of pain and terror. The thought lit a flicker of joy in my murky consciousness. Wherever this fucker was, he had the three deadliest beings in the world on his ass. And we never missed . . . demon or not.

CHAPTER 15

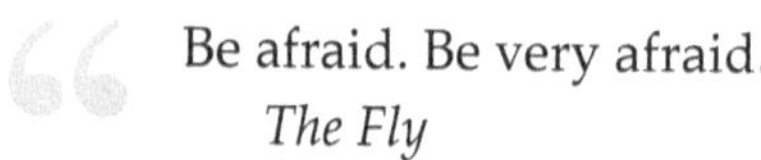

CHAINS IN THE CHURCH ATTIC

Hushed voices pulled me from sleep, but somehow, I had the good sense to keep my eyes closed. I knew I was in the back-seat of my car because I was lying on top of piles of my hoodies, costumes, and jeans. "I don't get why you're being so pissy about this. You didn't want to tell her anyway. You got your wish."

A low guttural sound vibrated. "Making an agreement and going against it isn't something a pack does, Dragon."

Dragon?

Memories were like misshapen splotches in my mind. I remembered my waffle breakfast with the guys, and then the sexy as hell ride with Ames, browsing the old library . . . and then I got so tired . . .

"You're right. I'm sorry. I just panicked. I'm not a were—"

Onyx grunted like something whacked him. Silence followed us to our destination and my car slowed. I assumed we were outside my apartment. Pretending to only then wake up, I yawned and stretched. "Wow, I didn't mean to fall asleep like that," I said, trying to not show how unnerved I felt. This was the second time I'd blacked out around these guys and it was starting to feel . . . odd.

"Ah, no worries. Onyx and his books are pretty damn boring. I could use a nap myself." Wolf grinned, opening my door and helping me out.

"Oh," I said in surprise. "We're going to . . . church?"

Onyx chuckled. "Ready to confess your sins, Blythe?"

My chest tightened. No, I was very much not ready to confess the sin that followed me everywhere I went. He must have noticed my anxiety because he put a gentle palm between my shoulder blades. "I'm only teasing." Calm trickled down my awareness like water on a window-pane as I looked into his deep green eyes. Onyx was tall, dark, and handsome in a debonair and stylish way. The way he spoke always left me wondering if he was being truthful or only charming. He smirked, as if reading my thoughts, and I blushed. Just then, the rumble of a motorcycle engine pulled up behind us. Ames strode over, adjusting his glasses. "I hope you had a nice rest. Sorry Onyx bored you to tears. He tends to do that."

"You guys should take this comedy show on the road, really," Onyx replied, stepping over dewy pumpkins.

Ames gestured toward the ruby-red door of Lamb's Blood Church.

"Support group?" I asked, swerving around a pumpkin. They still littered every inch of the lawn and trailed up the narrow stone steps.

"Not exactly," he replied. "Come on, I'll show you."

I followed them up the stairs and down a corridor. Goose pimples dotted my arms. "All these crucifixes and bleeding lamb paintings are creeping me out," I whispered to Ames, who'd lagged behind with me.

"Really? I love them. I considered becoming a priest a very long time ago."

"You're kidding. I didn't know you were religious. Why didn't you?"

He only looked ahead, the darkness of the dusty shadows revealing nothing of his expression. "Sometimes God's not the one who comes knocking."

We finally reached a tiny wooden stairwell leading up. After scaling what felt like several floors, we reached the top. A splintered door opened to reveal an attic. Red light illuminated every surface, filtering in from stained-glass windows. "Welcome to my humble home," Ames said with an easy bow. "Please make yourself comfortable."

It took me a moment to take in my surroundings. A small kitchenette and a boxy Dolmeire refrigerator sat in the corner nearest the entrance, while the rest of the room sprawled out like a studio apartment. A worn leather sofa on a red Persian rug was positioned under the stained glass and across from a clunky, old television. Only a single lightbulb dangled from the middle of the room with a tiny, beaded chain attached. A queen-sized bed with black silk sheets sat in the farthest corner, and another twin-sized bed was against the wall across the way. I was suddenly glad I didn't agree to staying with Ames a few nights ago. Not that I judged him for his older furnishings and living in the attic of a weird church, but there were no walls for privacy. There would be no way I could sleep knowing his bed was right across from mine. "It's not fancy," he said, and I realized he was watching me. Suddenly I felt like the rudest person in the world.

"It's lovely, really. I just wasn't expecting, you know—"

Wolf interrupted from the sofa. "You weren't expecting to be hanging out with the ghost that rattles chains in the church attic, huh?"

Ames shot his friend a glare and I choked on a laugh. "Something like that."

Onyx replied, pulling a beer from the fridge. "You're all heathen sinners. I quite like being in the Lord's house."

Ames and Wolf chuckled. I joined them in the living area as Onyx passed me a bottle of stout ale. "How long have you lived here?" I asked, taking a sip. I strolled over to the stained glass. From a tiny crack in the red, I could see to the pumpkin-cluttered ground far below.

"Several years. Father Joseph and I have an . . . agreement."

"A mutually beneficial understanding, I'd say," Onyx added.

Wolf switched on the black and white TV and it buzzed to life. A controller nudged my elbow, and I turned to see him cross-legged on the ground like a little kid. Well, a not so little kid. A very large man who even sitting came up to my waist. I took the rectangle from his hand before a laugh emerged from my throat. "You have an old school Nintendo? I haven't played one of these since I was a little kid."

Ames rubbed the back of his neck. "I know there are newer game systems out there but—"

"No, I love it." I smiled. Was he . . . insecure bringing me here? Something warmed in my chest at the thought that he might be hoping to impress me. No hope necessary, I was continually impressed by and attracted to Ames. The ride he gave me earlier made me want to ride him in return. It wasn't only sexual attraction, though. There was a tenderness behind his blue eyes I'd never experienced before. It was as if Ames had seen and lived a thousand lifetimes yet still looked at me as if I were the only person in the world. It felt easy with him. I felt like I could trust him. Trust that he wouldn't lie to me or screw me over. Ames Cove seemed like the most perfect angel of a man. Maybe that was why, unlike me, he felt at ease in holy places. He was an angel; I was a demon. My sins burned at me with the alcohol on my throat. Someone like Ames deserved better than me. For the sake of my newfound friends, I pasted on a smile and bounced on mushrooms in *Super Mario Brothers*. Being around them was a warm blanket of comfort I'd never experienced before. I found myself loving their banter and loving it even more when they included me in their teasing and jokes. These strange boys somehow felt more like home than the one I'd fled in Alabama. They felt so right that fear sprang up like a weed in my thoughts.

What would they think of me if they knew what I did?

CHAPTER 16

Ames

IF YOU THINK YOU SEE ONE . . . NO, YOU DIDN'T

> Terror made me cruel . . .
> *Emily Bronte, Wuthering Heights*

She looked good in my place with my friends. I liked having Blythe in my space, watching her smile and laugh. She deserved happiness. She deserved a life. That was the one thing I couldn't give her. All I could offer Blythe was death. And I was a bastard for considering it. Just as I clicked on the dangling lightbulb, Wolf jerked his head up in alarm. Onyx and I noticed immediately. The Wolf stare. He smelled something. I shot Onyx a pointed glare toward Blythe, who was sticking out her tongue in concentration as she played. He understood, moving to sit beside her on the couch as Wolf stalked toward me, the floors creaking under his weight. "Animal, demon, death," he said.

"Where?"

"Everywhere."

"What do you mean everywhere?" I glanced over his shoulder at Blythe, who was already nodding off from the touch of Onyx's palm.

"Let's go find out. Onyx, you got her?" Wolf ordered, but I was already halfway out the door.

"She's having tranquil dreams. Go."

I stopped on the church steps. Claws pricked my palms, and my knuckles shook. *My demon awakened. Angry.*

"Motherfucker," Wolf hissed. "How many?"

"A dozen." Blue smoke settled around me. My blue smoke. Finally. But the satisfaction I felt at my abilities finally waking the fuck up was short-lived—stabbed to death by the scene before me. Interspersed amongst the orange pumpkins was bright orange, white, and black fur. Their lifeless bodies lay perfectly around the courtyard.

Foxes.

Wolfgang rumbled forward, kneeling by one of the slain. He touched it softly before inhaling. "It suffered in death . . . .They all did." He swallowed, surveying the dead foxes. "The one who did this will suffer more." I wasn't certain if he was speaking to me or the fallen animals. I didn't really care.

"He knows we're here in the church. He knows Blythe is dressed as a fox at Hallows. The fucker's been watching her . . . right under our nose." Blue mist permeated the ground now, rising, slithering, sensing. I closed my eyes and breathed in every ounce of my power's intel. Something demonic but somehow smells of human too—a ghoul."

"I got a scent. The ghoul went east," Wolf barked, his form already rippling.

"The alphas would have scented a ghoul. How could we miss this?"

When my smoke faded, the carcasses were gone, pressed back into the earth. The threat of death to Blythe in such a poetic way . . . seemed unlike a ghoul. But maybe this was an outlier. They had the ability to take on their kill's skin and walk in it, though it was strange that one would do it for as long as this one. They typically used their bodies as bait to lure more humans, latching onto, and repeating, the victim's last words. *Help. Save me. Somebody.*

I'd catch this one and question its fixation for Blythe as I tortured it slowly.

WOLF WAS a big guy in his human form. As a werewolf, he was massive. We always laughed at the films the mortals made about his kind. They envisioned overgrown rabid dogs, which couldn't have been further from reality. Though Wolf and his community could shift into wolves at will, their true forms were closer to what a human would call a four-legged demon. Like a monster made of black smoke with thrown back pointed horns, he'd stalk through the forest, bigger and more sinister than any imagination could muster. Following behind him on my motorcycle, I could make out his black, hunched back and claws as they propelled him forward. As much as we teased the guy, I was glad he was on our side. I'd hate to go up against him in a battle. I'd win, of course, being what I am, but it would be painful.

We trailed the highway deeper toward the coast, which was several hours from Ash Grove. Though with our abilities it only took half an hour. Thankfully my hell-rider powers were back, thanks somehow to Blythe. On the outskirts of a dirt path, Wolf's shadowy form halted. His snout turned toward me and then the woods, signaling that I follow on foot. The moment I stepped into the woods, I felt it. The birds had gone silent. Even the yellow leaves on the maples didn't dare to flicker in the wind. It was the way the woods acted when one of them was around. Wolf led the way with the stealth of a seasoned predator, while I was content to stroll. I wasn't anticipating that this being would put up much of a fight when it saw us. If anything, Wolf would get all the fun of chasing it and shredding it to pieces. I was just here because I couldn't stay in Ash Grove after what it pulled. The way she was just upstairs as the innocent animals were slain and arranged around us, the threat on her life, the way it was toying with her right under our noses . . . It pissed me off. If I could get even a single blow in the creature would be ended. Wolf stopped abruptly, and I slammed into his smoky backside. "Of course." I rolled my eyes. The putrid aroma burned my nose. "These things love swamps. Like I told Onyx, these fuckers aren't creative. However, we should have checked here earlier."

Wolf growled, sniffing around the perimeter of the marsh, but the smell of rotting eggs invaded my senses. "I wouldn't have thought it would come so far east just to hide from us. Pathetic." I kicked a stone into the murky water. "It's not here. I may not be able to track this one, but I'd feel it if it were out here."

Wolf snorted and brushed past me, back the way we came. When we made the loser-walk-of-shame back to the side of the road, I put a palm on the top of my friend's shadowy, monstrous shoulder. "Go on ahead. I'm going to ride mortal on the way back. My abilities are still . . . lagging." I hated admitting it out loud, but they knew. Though none of us knew why. I could still access my gifts, but I'd become drained over time, whereas I previously was a wealth of never-ending power. Using them in the churchyard and on the way here had them stunted for longer than I would have liked. Wolf cut a nod, his snout the size of my ribcage, and bolted off like a mist of black. We couldn't communicate if I was in my human form. Sighing, I grabbed my handlebars.

And then I felt it.

Anger roiled beneath my chest and a brief hint of the milky bones along the black of my demon form became visible on my hands. I turned slowly and leaned against my bike, crossing my arms. "Ah, there you are, you little coward," I taunted.

Only twenty yards away, it stood as fixed as a statue. Its gray skin and hollow eyes were both dull and reflective in the sunlight. The thing hunched forward on long, lean limbs, bracing itself on its bony knuckles. It was the size of a horse on all fours. Not as big as Wolf, but he wasn't here. A few possibilities played in my mind as it assessed me. I could kill it outright and be done with the thing. That was what the rage inside me was begging for. But this wasn't an average kill. This thing knew something. It had a motive and I wanted to find out what that was. In that case . . . immobilizing it would be harder than killing it. And I was weakened from the ghost ride over. I'd have to egg it on. Get it to act recklessly. "I know what you are," I said thoughtfully, rubbing my jaw. "You're a fucking ghoul." I pushed out a raspy laugh. "I thought you weaker demons died out eons ago. But no, you're busy chasing little girls and joining the filth in swaps, aren't you? What, stealing farmers' chickens get too tedious?"

That got its attention.

The ghoul rose on its haunches, its long but muscular frame

stretching out to that of a juvenile tree. "Ghost." Its whisper echoed in my ears. "Ghost," its hiss of a whisper repeated. This is where humans would scream and run, activating its prey instinct as it drank their terror as if wine before its meal. It would get neither flee nor fear from me. Though it had been a while since I'd seen one of its kind and I had to admit . . . it was a ghastly creature.

Finally, I felt the shift take hold in my hands, traveling slowly, too fucking slowly up my forearms. "Yeah, that whispering someone's name in the forest shit only works on mortals. You don't fucking scare me and you fucking know it."

Then it did something awful. It's wrinkled, hideous face curved into something resembling a smile. "I was not sent to scare you," it whispered. "I was sent for her."

"Sent? Who sent you, ghoul? I have hierarchy over you, you pathetic scumbag."

It took a step forward, yet somehow its body remained stoic. As if the statue had just rolled forward a yard. Ghouls were eerie as fuck, I'd give them that. "It will have gotten closer to her by now," it whispered.

Fury panged in my consciousness, and it was the push I needed to change. This thing wouldn't hurt her. If something had indeed sent this ghoul, I'd hunt and kill it too. Even still, worry crept into my thoughts. *Onyx is with her. Nothing can get to her.*

"I can taste your fear," it hissed, moving another yard closer. "You taste human now, Ghost."

Suddenly, I felt the weight of my mortal form lift. My muscles and body expanded and elongated. In an eclipse of darkness, my power coursed through me as I watched the creature's dead eyes follow me up, up. I wasn't as tall as him at seven feet tall, but I didn't need to be. "I'm going to enjoy making you squeal like a gutted pig." The words were pushed from my throat but not in Ames Cove's voice. This voice, my real voice, was ancient and otherworldly. It held power in itself.

The ghoul was stupid enough to charge first, which I dodged with ease. "Is this the best the surviving lesser demons can do?" I chuckled in a deep rasp.

"You haven't been able to find me. Or it." The creature sneered, turning on its pointy heel. "Because of her." It wrenched a smile again. "And you don't even see because she makes you blind."

Before I could speak, it disappeared. Two seconds later, I felt its cold presence behind me. Its razor-sharp, scissored hands swiped at my back. Pain radiated as the distinct feel of their poison trying to make its way in stung at my demonic tendons. The poison would paralyze a mortal, who would be frozen, but conscious, as the ghoul dragged them deep into the forest to feast on their bodies and souls. I spun on my heel. "Now you've pissed me off," I gritted out. The poison in such a low dose wouldn't affect me other than with sheer annoyance. To me, or any of my kind, it was merely a bee sting. The thing reached its arm back, baring its jagged brown teeth. Before it could come close to landing another blow, I shot up into the air in a curtain of night. Black befell every surface from the pavement to the treetops, and a thick fog snaked along the ground. Hovering over it, I tasted it then. *Fear.* Demon fear pricked like acid on my tongue, bitter and tasteless. It looked up at me, and I smirked just as the coils of smoke attached to its arms. It shrieked, a high-pitched, odious sound. "Oh, shut the fuck up," I snapped as the ropes of smoke slithered up its body, searing its gray flesh. It bellowed again, and I sent a snake of blue to cover its mouth. A mass of darkness enveloped the space under me as it ground to a heavy stop. A black snout turned upwards, and I floated down to greet him, landing beside Wolf, as he had returned. "Where the fuck did it come from?"

We could communicate now too, which was also a benefit of me shifting into my demon form. "Coward was waiting for you to leave, I suppose. I guess he didn't want to play with the big bad wolf today."

The creature's lifeless eyes grew wide as they assessed the beast next to me. It struggled and the taste of its fear grew more potent. Ghouls were terrified of werewolves, and for good reason. Where I'd have my fun and kill the thing, to the wolves, killing ghouls was a mercy they didn't deserve after plaguing their forests, stealing away everything from their young to their livestock. Wolves had a bone to pick with ghouls. They didn't send them back to the fire with death. They punished them. Some legends said for eternities. I wasn't sure how that was feasible, but I was a young demon still and had a lot to learn. I didn't believe everything I heard, but I did when it came to the wolves. If anything, the stories were underplaying their power. And that was how they preferred it. But the ghouls knew firsthand the skill and prowess my friend and his kind possessed. That was why the creature was now fighting, attempting to bring his razored fingers forward to impale himself. I tightened the fog and his muffled shriek made me chuckle.

Wolf, however, stared the creature down with vengeance. "Did it say anything?"

"It claims it was sent by someone. I haven't yet gotten to the part of extracting who or if it was a lie to save its wretched skin."

Wolf looked to the ghoul. "Are you the one who's been terrorizing the girl? Wearing her stepfather's skin?"

The ghoul didn't answer. I tightened the fog around its neck, pulling it backwards and contorting its long form into an abnormal and painful shape. The sounds of its shrieks made me smile. I'd missed killing.

Wolf circled, zeroing in on its head. "Ah, good idea, friend. Chew on its skull a while, then it'll sing like a canary."

The ghoul flailed fruitlessly, shaking its head and poking its forked tongue, pushing against the fog wrapped around its mouth. "It was me, yes," it whispered. "I followed her from Alabama and took the form of her stepfather because that was the human I found in her nightmares. He was following her but I took him."

My jaw tensed and I shot a barb of smoke and inky darkness into the bottom of its spine. It gargled a screech as my power twisted, hooking onto its decaying flesh.

Wolf snarled and shot me a look. "It's not dead. You can have it when I'm done."

"Kill me, please, Ghost," it begged.

I rolled my eyes. "Now you really are pathetic. And you will suffer for what you've done to her."

Wolf straightened and howled, low and long. I smirked. "How fun, now you get to meet the whole pack."

It writhed as if it were being electrocuted. "Please, it talks about you. I heard it. I know the way to break the curse on your home," it strained in a whisper. "You can free the souls and complete your contract. Just set me free—"

Just then, another shadowed beast pounced from behind the tree line. The creature screamed as the werewolf took it by the throat, yanking against my chains. "Wait," I told the wolf. "Tell me," I demanded, loosening my power's hold.

"It's right in front of you—" The ghoul screeched as the werewolf clamped its maw harder around its neck, spilling black, oily blood onto the pavement. Wolf looked to me. "It's saying whatever it has to and trying to manipulate you, Ghost. You know that. Let my people take it. It belongs to us."

I stared at the ghoul's vacant eyes as it tried to shake its head in disagreement. I dropped my ties, and the smaller werewolf gave me a small nod before it pulled the creature by its neck into the forest. A chorus of howls echoed through the twilight, and the sounds of nature answered. The rustling of leaves and scurrying of animals reemerged. The forest was safe again.

Wolf looked at me assessingly. "You shifted."

I held out my long black veiny hands marked white with bone. "Is that what this is? I thought my Venom cosplay just got really good."

He snorted. "Glad to have you back. Thanks for . . . saving the ghoul for us."

"As much as I considered killing it, I know it belongs to you."

"We won't forget that consideration, Ghost."

When Wolf spoke like this, his destiny was clear. He was an alpha, whether he wanted to claim his title or not. The first male alpha in generations. He was worthy of it too. I let out an exhale. "Do you believe that was it? Is it all over now? The surveillance footage was hazy, but this looked like it could have been the same foul creature."

"We got his scent on the foxes. It confirming it knew Blythe and where she came from seals it for me. Don't you think so?"

My violet-blue fog crept along the forest floor, coating the dead grass and then the pavement. I closed my eyes and felt every branch, squirrel, insect, and stone. My fog and darkness rippled around the pack, each sinking their fangs into a different limb of the ghoul as they roughly carried it away as it screamed. "I don't feel anything else here," I said when I opened my eyes. "But I want to check farther into town, too."

"If you insist. But I think we can rest easy and Blythe can be free. And hey, we didn't have to reveal our monsters to her. I think we fucking owned it. Now, let's head home and grab a beer and a burger. I'm starving."

"I need to get back to Blythe before she snaps out of Onyx's mood-touch."

I'd shot a text checking in after the ghoul's erratic threats. Dragon assured me nothing demonic was in their sphere. He didn't seem worried. And now that my powers were in a more stable place, I could get home quicker. My abilities had come back, and they had reappeared stronger… for her.

I should have felt more peace. The ghoul was caught and currently experiencing a fate worse than death. I'd protected my little ghost, like I promised I would. My powers had returned, even if momentarily. They'd returned out of a need to protect her, which was . . . different. I should have been ready to celebrate and breathe a sigh of relief. Maybe my distrust of demons was getting to me, and the adrenaline of the fight and the poison my body was fighting was throwing me off. I shook off my hesitations. Wolf was right. We did it.

We could set Blythe free now.

It was what was best for her. What I'd been fighting for and working toward.

So why did something in me shatter at the fact it was now all over?

CHAPTER 17

I WANT YOU

Is evil something you are? Or is it something you do?
American Psycho

After several beers and rounds of vintage Nintendo games, the low flicker of candlelight lured me into a nap on Ames's worn sofa. I was still feeling the effects of our library trip. Wolf said I may have breathed in asbestos, a toxic chemical used in older buildings. I guessed that made some amount of sense, but something was still nagging at me. I couldn't quite place it. Maybe it was their conversation I overheard in the car, or maybe it was the number of times I'd blacked out while being around them. It didn't seem plausible it was all an accident. Then again, I'd been on the run and skeptical of everyone from the truck next to me at a stoplight to the barista at the coffee shop. My trust instinct was broken and looking for any reason to not believe these guys were sincere. Was it so crazy to believe that I felt so safe around them that I got sleepy? I'd been alone and in fight-or-flight for so long that finally having human interaction in the form of beefy men put my mind at ease, at least for the time we were together. Their jeering lulled me into a fitful sleep.

. . .

His boots crunch through dried leaves as he kicks a jack-o'-lantern off a winding path into the dark forest. A path I recognize from the night prior. He's whistling the same tune he did when I was a teenager. The sound of it is so real, I want to run. I want to hide. The crunching stops in the middle of the path and he looks up, his face more worn and grayer than when I saw him last. He still has huge swatch of dried blood on his ragged flannel shirt. It's still soaked on the spot below his left shoulder, right where I left it. Wearing it reminds me of what I did. It reminds me of how I failed . . . somehow. Even though I was sure he went cold and stopped breathing . . . he survived, and he wouldn't stop until he returned the favor. Fear gripped my throat and squeezed. No, it was him. It was his freezing cold hand. How could I feel it in a dream? "Caught you, just like I said I would," he whispered.

SOMETHING GRABBED my shoulder and I startled, opening my eyes. I expected to see the woods, the crushed pumpkin. I'd expected the smell of his rancid breath in my face. But instead, a crocheted blanket covered my legs and dripping taper candles illuminated the church attic. Next to the stained glass was a beautiful scene that looked like it belonged in a different time, like I had stepped into an era long past. It was oddly comforting feeling like I'd escaped my time period for the briefest moment. I wondered if Halloween here felt the same, with everyone dressing in eighteen-hundreds attire. I'd find out in a couple weeks. The sight slowed my breathing, and the man that was still touching my shoulder . . . only sped my pulse back up again. His jaw tensed and his blue eyes shone with concern beneath dark brows. "You were having a nightmare. You've been asleep a few hours."

Sitting up, I weaved my fingers between the holes in the blanket. "I was talking in my sleep? I'm sorry I passed out. It seems to happen a lot around you guys."

"Trauma can make a person weary. Please don't apologize for that. I consider it an honor you feel secure enough to rest around me." He slowly moved his touch down my arm to my hand. "You were so . . . frightened just now."

I must have been thrashing or talking in my sleep. I'd never done that before. However, I hadn't been asleep around anyone long enough for them to ever tell me. So, I guessed that was a new trauma development. "Sometimes the dreams are so real that I can't breathe."

"Flashbacks can be difficult for any survivor—"

I stopped his therapist speak. "They aren't flashbacks. I know you're going to think I'm crazy. I'm sure Dr. Omar does when I tell her during my sessions, but the dreams, they're . . . happening now. In real time, it seems. Sometimes in places I recognize, sometimes I don't. Sometimes he sees me and interacts briefly. But he's different than he used to be. It's hard to explain." I searched his eyes for judgment and found nothing but attention and sincerity. My chest warmed and I continued. "He's freezing cold, and wearing the same clothes, and . . . "

"And?" Ames's jaw ticked and I wished I could look into his mind and know what he was thinking. *Probably poor pitiful girl with her self-inflicted drama . . .* I took a deep breath. "It's nothing. It's stupid."

"You can tell me," he urged. Maybe it was the doctor in him, but he seemed insistent to know all the things I could never share with him. He'd hate me and never speak to me again if he knew what I'd done. So instead of telling him, I elaborated on my stupid nightmare. "When he talks to me, he's always whispering. That's it. I know it doesn't sound scary, but it is."

Ames turned his face away and tapped his foot against the creaky hardwood floor. I'd made him angry. "I'm sorry. I'm not trying to—"

It happened so fast. His hand cupped my jaw in an instant, rushing the breath from my lungs as I gasped in surprise. He was so close I could smell the exhaust from his bike that lingered on his black T-shirt. "Stop. *Apologizing,*" he bit out. His breath was ragged as his lips parted. "I want you," he rasped. It sounded more like a threat than a kind request, and my chest quenched. Shoving the blanket off, I pushed his hand away and stood. Pulling myself from his touch, from his angry demand and declaration was difficult, but I knew it hurt something inside me, hearing him like that. "Am I getting on your nerves sharing my past with you? You want me to stop apologizing, and what, suck your dick because you want me? Is that it?"

I could feel the anger radiating from him as he stood. Had he always been this freaking tall? "Is that all you think I'm after? You think we're doing all this so I can fuck you? As if I couldn't have already if I'd wanted to."

Ouch.

Stomping across the room, the floorboard protested as I snatched my keys off his tiny butcher block countertop. "You only want me because you want to save me. I don't need saving. And you can go fuck yourself, *Dr. Cove.*"

A guttural sound flew from his throat as he strode after me. My heart rate quickened, but I wasn't afraid of him. My body, my idiotic body, wanted him. I wanted him to slam me against the wall and fuck me hard. I wanted to feel his rough hands between my thighs and slipping inside the wetness pooling there. I backed against the very door I wanted him to take me against when he stopped inches in front of me.

"You don't want saving because you're resigned to die. I'm not letting that happen." I jumped as he slammed his fist on the doorframe. His other hand propped up next to me, caging me in. All I wanted was to slap his smug face . . . and wrap my legs around him and suck his bottom lip until it bled.

On a shaky inhale, I forced my gaze to my shoes as I replied, "That's right. I'm okay with death more than the average person. Go ahead and psychoanalyze me all you want. I haven't been running because I'm afraid of dying. I've been running because I'm afraid of not living. But I'm ready to stay. And either die, yes, or have a shot at living some sort of life. Have I fantasized about a hero? Sure. But I don't need you."

"That's where you're wrong. So fucking wrong about everything, Blythe." His mouth was open as he breathed heavily, and a small sigh escaped me at the feel of his breath on my neck as he leaned in, brushing his lips against my ear. His voice didn't even sound like his as he growled. "I'm not the hero. I'm the villain. I'm so evil I make the gates of Hell shudder. And you do need me. You need me more than you know."

An infuriating and heady mixture of anger and desire surged through me. I'd never felt so mad and turned on at the same time. Who did Ames think he was? "The villain?" I choked a laugh as my gaze faltered on his broad shoulders caging me in. "Mr. Town Nice Guy? The therapist who works for free? You're perfect, Ames, too perfect. I'm not. I'm fucking damaged."

A raspy chuckled emerged from his throat—not what I was expecting. He looked at me over his glasses, his blue eyes glimmering through dark lashes. My breath hitched as he flicked his tongue over his full lips, the darkness and amber flicker of the room making him look like someone . . . something else entirely. The possessive tilt of his head as he surveyed me sent a jolt to my core and made me question my assertion. Was Ames Cove truly as good as he portrayed himself?

"That's what you think of me?" His whisper was rough and velvety.

I swallowed down my conflicting emotions, the urge to hit him, to drop to my knees and explore his cock. My mind went dizzy with the heat of confusion. "Let me go."

His hands balled into fists next to me, and his shoulders tensed. "I'd rather watch over you here, tonight," he whispered after a moment.

What?

"I said, let me go," I repeated, willing my voice to sound stronger than I felt. For the briefest moment, I thought he'd say no. He could easily overpower me, force me to stay, take my keys and lock me up here like some counterfeit princess in a tower.

With a long and frustrated exhale, he pulled back swiftly. He ran a hand through his hair and shook his head. I turned on my heel, my hand on the knob, when he said softly, "The door to the church and my room is always unlocked. You can come here whenever you need to, no questions asked. This church is . . . a protected space."

To add to my inner chaos, tears welled in my eyes. I slammed the door without saying goodbye.

I choked on a sob as I walked to my car in the pale glow of stars and fire lanterns. A crow sat perched on a branch above my old beater of a Honda. The bird angled its head and cooed softly. I sniffled, looking at the creature and remembering seeing it before. "You are following me." I sniffled. "That reminds me. I brought you something." I fisted a hand into my jeans pocket and pulled out a handful of shelled peanuts. The crow eyed me curiously as I placed them on the roof of my car. "I heard crows like gifts." I shrugged, feeling like an idiot for talking to a bird. I'd found a bag of bird and squirrel food in the Moores' backyard. I refilled their feeders and kept a handful in case I came across the inky feathered creature again. I startled as the bird hopped from its branch onto the roof next to the nuts. It tilted its head, and I realized it was much larger than it appeared in the trees. My mind flicked back to remembering the Ravens and their treehouse at Hallows Fest. I grinned in remembrance, and it was then I was sure of what I wanted to do that night. My plans to continue attending Hallows Fest weren't going to be deterred because of a maddening interaction with Ames. A pang of sadness held my heart as I morbidly wondered if that was the last time I'd see him. Why would he bother after that fight?

I carefully opened the backdoor of my car as the bird pecked at my offering. "Please don't bite me," I said nervously. I swore the creature laughed in bird, it's caw almost bringing a smile to my puffy face. I dug through my costumes and decided on something warmer and easier to walk in, but still festive and fox-like. I plucked out a lacy black crop top with a matching mini skirt. I paired it with black stockings, boots, and a long, black trench coat. I clutched the items and my makeup bag and fox mask and shot the crow an exasperated look. "Any ideas where I can change that's not here or in my car?"

The bird ruffled its feathers and shot forward. I screamed and ducked as the wind from its wings blew over the top of my head. My mask and makeup clattered to the pavement. I groaned as I knelt to gather it altogether. As I strained to reach the mascara that had rolled under my back tire, I paused. The sound of footsteps echoed through the abnormally empty street and my breathing stilled. My heart froze in my chest as I recognized the sound of boots in the darkness. My hand trembled as I clutched my things. I should have dropped them and gotten into my car. But in the pile, I'd lost my keys. *Shit, shit, shit.* I scrambled through my costume, frantic to find the keys when the foot-steps stopped. Crouched, I peered under my car at the black leather boots that appeared there. One foot tapped and my mouth went dry. *This is it. This is where I die. By my car, clutching my favorite tube of mascara.*

The footsteps resumed but I couldn't make out where they were going.

Something touched my back and I shrieked, whipping around.

She jumped back, putting a hand to her chest. "Oh my god, Blythe. I didn't mean to scare you," Yesenia said, kneeling next to me and helping gather my things. "I thought I saw your car over here and I thought to myself, that girl is not changing in her car, is she? No way, come on over to the shop. You can get ready with me."

I put a trembling hand to my forehead and exhaled a shaky blow of air. "I'm a little on edge, sorry." I forced a laugh. "I'd love to get dressed at Magia, if it's not too much trouble."

Yesenia took my makeup bag from my hand and the tube I was gripping so hard it had grown slick with sweat. "This is the best black mascara ever. I might have to raid your beauty kit." She smiled warmly and placed a tender hand on my back. "Let's go, girl. I've been meaning to catch up with you anyway."

We walked in the lantern light of Ash Grove as the friendly shop owner chatted my ear off about everything from that week's sales, local divorce gossip, and the mood-color-changing lipsticks she'd ordered for the store. I only smiled and nodded, my body relaxing at the sound of her cheerful, lithe voice. I loved girls that talked a lot. I loved women with lots of opinions and so many thoughts their words flew faster than their minds could keep up with. For someone quiet, like myself, it was the perfect escape from my inner world of turmoil. The cool October chill danced with the smell of fallen leaves and apple cider. "Anyway," she said, opening the shop door with a jingle and *wah ha ha* of a skeleton. "My abuela says no one will buy the lipstick, but now I know you will, right?"

"Oh, absolutely."

The shop was different at night than during the day. Violet candles swayed their flames, casting little orange orbs onto the dozens of crystal balls along shelves of tarot cards, bones, and colorful glass vials. The dried herbs dangling from the ceiling mixed a floral, herbal scent along with that of cinnamon and clove. Magia Eclectics was sultry Halloween in physical form. "I love it here," I murmured, following her toward the back. "I certainly feel more at ease here than I did in that godforsaken church."

She looked over her shoulder at me. "Ah, hangin out with Ames Cove and his boys, I take it?"

I sighed, "I was, but probably not anymore. Ames and I got into a fight tonight. It's one of the reasons I'm so scattered right now. He said the church is always open, though, and safe, so maybe I'll need to go back at some point . . . I don't know."

She snorted. "That dead old building isn't nearly as safe as Magia." She led me up the stairs to a sprawling apartment and office area. "Hey, what are you doing for October since Garden of India closes for Hallows?"

I shrugged, perching on the arm of a gold and pink lounge. "Eating ramen in the Moores very pink guest room, I guess. My basement apartment flooded so they waived rent this month, but I'm not sure how I'll cover next month being out of work." Not that it mattered because my stepdad was near, probably just buying time until he caught up with me.

"Well," Yesenia began, motioning for me to follow. We stopped in a small but cozy room with a white metal bed frame, chest of drawers, and dark purple rug. "My abuela and I were talking, and since I'm not able to man the shop as much while my boys are in school, we thought we'd make you a deal."

I raised my eyebrows and she dropped my things on the lavender comforter. "What kind of deal?"

"You work here and watch the shop during the day. We can't pay you a lot, but we can give you a decent-sized check, along with free rent here." She nodded toward the sitting area. "There's no stove but there's a microwave, computer, and bathroom with a shower. I know it's not much, but it has to be better than staying in a soggy basement out in the suburbs."

My jaw dropped in surprise. Without thinking, I wrapped her in a hug. She laughed immediately and squeezed me tight. "I take that as a yes?"

The hug reminded me of when I'd launched myself into Ames's

arms after our motorcycle ride. I'd felt so alive and real that I'd cried. This feeling, this offer, was comparable to that experience.

"Are you sure it's not too much?" I asked, skeptical that Yesenia's abuela would be okay with this arrangement after her stern words during our first meeting.

Yesenia smoothed my outfit out on the bed and then placed my makeup on the dresser, unzipping the bag and helping herself to a perusal of my eyeshadow palettes. "Girl, you're doing us a favor. We need someone downstairs, and we never use this office anyway."

"Wow," I breathed, slumping onto the bed. "Thank you so much, Yesenia. Please tell Marcelene thank you from me too."

"I will." She smiled. "I like your sexy black fox look for tonight. I have a lacy black fox mask downstairs that would go perfect with it. I'll go grab it. And then I want you to do my eyes all smoky like yours were the other day. I'm going for sexy, spooky ho tonight. Which isn't too different than my everyday look but, you know."

I laughed, feeling the unfamiliar but welcomed warmth of female friendship. A new, free, and gorgeous apartment and a new job had found me in one night.

It almost sated the pain I felt from potentially losing Ames and the guys.

Almost.

CHAPTER 18

Blythe

IF GHOST HASN'T KILLED YOU, YOU'RE HIS FRIEND.

> A world in which there are monsters, and ghosts, and things that want to steal your heart is a world in which there are angels, and dreams and a world in which there is hope.
>
> *Neil Gaiman*

As promised, I gave Yesenia the smoky eye look of her dreams. Her golden-brown skin glowed magnificently under bronzer, and the deep purple lip I'd added made her sensuous features come to life. My outfit was sexy and comfortable, though the skirt was a little too short. The trench coat would protect me from my ass falling out, at least. After taking it upon herself to haul in my clothes from the back of my car and hanging them in the room's white vanity, Yesenia put her hands on her hips in appreciation. "Well, I'm hot and you're hot. My work here is done. I'm going to scoot home and get changed."

I laughed. "Thanks again, this helps me more than you know."

My new friend scanned me with a compassionate and considering gaze. "I don't know if you've figured this out about me yet, but I'm a nosey bitch. You want to tell me about what happened with Ames Cove before I leave?"

I buzzed my lips on an exasperated exhale. "He's been so nice and sweet since the moment I got to town. He's handsome and just perfect."

"Wow, sounds like a real problem," she said playfully. Rummaging through the tiny office closet, she pulled out a bag of tortilla chips and an unopened jar of salsa that she brought over to the coffee table in the center of the room. We'd already devoured a pizza we'd ordered while doing makeup, but I was still starving. "These are my favorite, thanks." I appreciatively scooped a mouthful of salsa, careful not to spill on my delicate crop top. It would be like me to be in a sexy get-up with food stains "It is a problem, because I'm very *not* perfect, and I feel like he's only interested because he wants to save me and score more good boy points or something."

The confession rolled off my tongue so much easier than the stuttering first conversation I'd had downstairs with Yesenia. This town and its people had grown on me and helped me in such a short period of time. "I get what you're saying. Sometimes good guys are too good to be attractive." She eyed a chip as she broke it in half. "But Ames isn't *such* a good guy."

I raised an eyebrow. "How so?"

"I don't know, really. But I do know my abuela and the older w—" She stopped herself. "Women," she stated carefully, "don't like him, or his friends, but especially him. None of them will tell me why except to warn us all to stay away from him."

"Huh," I pondered. "That's strange. And you have no clue why? Haven't you known him for a long time?"

"I've known of him since high school. He'd come by to counsel whatever new kids arrived in town. But I have no memory of him or Onyx or Wolf before high school." She shrugged. "Dr. Cove was just kind of a quiet nerdy guy. Not much to tell. But the reaction from my abuela and her . . . friends . . . makes me wonder what I don't know."

Bewilderment but also a strange sort of confirmation unraveled at her words. I'd known there was something about Ames and his friends. Even if I were no closer to figuring out what that something was, it was validating to have it confirmed by someone else.

I shook the salt off my hands. "Well, when he was angry at me this evening, he did say he was the villain. Something like he makes the gates of Hell quake." I chuckled. "So he's a little melodramatic, if anything."

But Yesenia didn't join my laughter, or even smile, as she tucked a brown wave of hair behind her bejeweled, multi-pierced ear. "He said those words? The gates of Hell?"

"Yeah, along those lines. Why?"

She shook her head softly, lost in thought.

"Oh, I overheard him talking about a woman once. Someone named Cat. Do you know anyone by that name?"

Yesenia straightened, the usual mirth vacant from her gorgeous features. She sucked in a breath before standing. "No, sorry. And I have to get going, but um . . . stop by the willow tree later for a drink."

"Is that a bar?" I asked, but Yesenia was already halfway to the door. "Well, thanks for everything—"

"Fresh linens are in the office closet. You'll find anything you need in there if you just ask for it—I mean, whatever you want should be in there," she fumbled her words. Why was she all of a sudden acting so unlike herself? Before I could respond, the door clicked closed, followed by the mechanical laughter and the jingle of bells. I walked to the window overlooking the decked-out Halloween town, but I didn't see which way she went. It was as if she'd evaporated. I leaned against the cool windowpane for a moment and watched children with sheets over their heads clutching orange pumpkin buckets. They giggled and weaved through the streets as shop owners came out to toss handfuls of candy into their loot piles. A soft smile played at my lips. I loved that they trick-or-treated all month here. I loved Halloween. The crisp air, the bright foliage, everything changing and growing a shade darker . . . I wondered like a child as I inspected my costume what Hallows had in store for me tonight. Would it be tricks or treats?

My mind spun into a vivid daydream.

I'm kicking piles of leaves in a forest I don't recognize. Green fire burns in the distance as the shadow of a humungous wolf blurs past me. I reach out and touch coarse fur as it crosses my path. I pick up into a jog, chasing after it, when blue fogs laps at my knees. It's odd and eerie, but I'm not afraid. I stop and reach down, swirling the now purple fog into my palm where it wraps and spins softly around my wrist. Eventually it clears and leaves behind a circle of shimmering periwinkle smoke dancing around my ring finger. Sighing, I thumb at it softly. "I love you too," I whisper.

DR. OMAR CALLED my daydreams a form of dissociative disorder. She said they elicit a disconnect between thought patterns and even identity. My dissociative disorder was beginning to interfere with my functioning as the flashes became more and more intense and real feeling. I wasn't even sure how I arrived at Hallows Fest after the jarring and uncontrollable daydream of the strange forest and blue fog. It was an effort to shake free of the heaviness that pressed in on my shoulders as I walked through the trees to the Halloween festival. The caw of a bird yanked my attention upwards, and as I suspected, bouncing on branches above me sat my raven friend. Knowing he, or she, was with me brought about a strange measure of comfort. When I looked down to continue my walk, I startled at the slash of red only two feet in front of me. "I think you've made a familiar," she said, grinning that pointed smile.

I placed a hand over my heart. "Ezmerelda, hi. I didn't even hear you walk up." I glanced around at the dry leaves that blanketed the ground and found it strange that once again, I didn't hear her. I heard even the soft patter of new leaves floating down to join the ground. Maybe it was because I was so distracted. That was what I told myself, lied to myself. I was doing that a lot lately . . . "What's a familiar?"

She looped her arm in mine like she did the first night we met, and my body instantly calmed. My fear and nerves settled into excitement, curiosity, and a rosy sort of bliss. Strange how she had that effect on me each time we walked together. "A familiar is a tiny, cute little demon who assumes the form of an animal. They show up around beings who are just coming into their powers. Usually they prefer witches, but anyone powerful will do. They're very protective of the being they choose . . . or are gifted to."

"You know a lot about this stuff. Where'd you learn all this?"

Ezmerelda kicked a stone with her pointed red boot. "Old stories from my family . . . By the way, I heard you ran into Vincent. He wanted me to tell you he's sorry if he frightened you or . . . angered your friend."

"Oh, you mean the skeleton guy? I wouldn't say he's my friend, more like he stalked me for an evening."

She giggled and twirled, fanning out her long crimson hair. "If Ghost hasn't killed you, you're his friend."

I rolled my eyes as I followed her. "That's comforting."

As we reached the clearing and the festival sounds and energy blazed to life before us, Ezmerelda winked. "Vincent says you're welcome to come find us anytime. We don't bite unless you beg us to." As she smoothed out her long, flowy red dress, she added, "Oh, and your familiar isn't the only one following you tonight, it seems." With her fangs on full display, Ezmerelda blew me a kiss. "See you soon. Killer outfit, by the way. Your tits look yummy."

Blush rushed to my cheeks as bright as her hair as she skipped away through the crowd. I turned to look around, expecting the skeleton man, Ghost, he was called. But I saw no one. Maybe she was just messing with me. *She's just playing a game. This isn't real.*

The heaviness returned as I slowly meandered through the crowd. I came for a distraction from earlier, only to find my mind wanted to burrow into the fight I'd had with Ames and replay it over and over again. What did he mean he was the villain? How could someone as good as he was think such a thing? Yesenia's reaction to something I'd said regarding Ames was just as jarring. Or maybe my lack of social skills had me reading wrong into everything others said or did. It was very possible I was the weird one in each of these encounters.

Someone dressed as a furry sheep-like creature with twisted horns walked by on stilts. I jumped out of the way and looked up, marveling at its height and the dedication it took to craft such a realistic and long costume. The goat-like-snout looked down at me and winked it's rectangular yellow and black pupil at me as it continued its long strides. It brought a grin to my lips as I continued along the path. A group of white, red, and black jesters danced and bounced flamboyantly over a game of cards as a few folks in wolf costumes watched, taking bets.

Twenty pale-skinned and tall vampires strode past in a single file line, seemingly in a somber hurry. I didn't see Vincent among them. Despite myself, I kept glancing over my shoulder for the skeleton man, whom I hadn't spotted yet. Maybe he was sitting tonight out. Maybe I'd never see him again. For some reason, the loss of Ames and the potential loss of my skeletal stalker made my heart drop into my boots. I was truly good at pushing people away. The few people that ever dared try to get close to me . . . I'd shoved so far away so they wouldn't get caught up in my shit. So that they wouldn't get hurt. But Ames, and even Onyx and Wolf, had disregarded those walls with reckless abandon. They didn't seem to care at all that associating with me could put a target on their backs. What if my stepfather decided to go after them first? The thought made me shudder with worry. A flash of blood-stained carpet invaded my vision. I imagined the waitresses he slaughtered at the diner I worked at in Tennessee . . . and then the old couple from the flower shop I worked at in Philadelphia. I'd pushed those horrors so far from my mind because if I dwelled too long, I couldn't keep moving. Couldn't breath from the weight of shame and terror. But there was a road of blood behind me, following me in his wake. His next target very well could be my new friends. I shuddered at the thought, feeling guilt burn my throat. The pattern was the same. A letter, killings, and then I'd see him somewhere following me. But so far there had been no killings, so maybe . . . just maybe he'd been thrown off my trail.

The distinct and spicy aroma of clove grazed my senses as I weaved between tree roots, tents, and booths. A giant willow tree swayed in the distance, the source of the lovely smell.

A large, purple open-air tent stood erect under its lanky ropes. I inched closer to find what looked like a circle of intricately masked witches. Some were in long flowy garb and pointy hats. Two were topless, wearing only long sheer skirts that billowed with their every movement. Their skin and breasts glowing in the moonlight. No one gawked as one of the topless women stood to stir the caldron in the middle of their circle. One of them waved me over. I looked over my shoulder and saw no one. Pointing to my chest, I mouthed, *Me?*

She giggled. "Yes you, clever Fox. Come here."

I tentatively made my way over and stopped outside the circle, unsure if it would be impolite to cross their sacred threshold. The topless woman wore a huge peacock feather mask and smiled at me warmly. "Brother, sister, or sibling?" she asked, taking me off guard.

"Um . . . ," I stammered, glancing nervously at the swaying willow vines. Was this some sort of test? A riddle I didn't know about?

The witch that called me over whispered, "They're just asking your pronouns, sweetie."

"Oh!" I replied, relief relaxing my shoulders. "Sister, please. And yours?"

"Sister too," she remarked, delicately stirring a thick stone cauldron over their fire and picking up a coffee mug. "Or sibling. Both or either. Welcome to Hallows Fest, newbie." She handed me a steaming mug.

"Is this a magical potion?" I asked, glancing around at the others. The scent of nutmeg and spice warmed my nose along with my chilly palms.

A melody of soft giggles surrounded me as the dark-purple-robed witch next to me put a reassuring hand between my shoulder blades. "You could call it that, or you could call it a pumpkin spice latte." She winked.

I laughed along with the others and took a sip. "Thank you, this is delicious." The brew expanded in my chest and warmed my soul.

"Feel free to find us and sit with us whenever you'd like, sister," an older witch with a black pointy hat and a glittering silver mask crooned. "We haven't had a new visitor in a very long time."

"We know lots of tricks too," another softer-voiced witch said. She lightly shuffled what looked like a deck of tarot cards. It was then I noticed all the iron lanterns surrounding them. They flickered amongst the grass while several hung from the trees. Their setup was lovely, and spooky, and homey all at once. Just like Magia Eclectics.

A beautiful witch approached as I sipped my drink. Her long beaded braids cascaded down her back. The golden hues of her black skin sparkled in the firelight.

"It must be fun being a witch," I said.

She giggled. "It definitely is. Though, anyone who identifies as a witch is one in some way. You just have to find your thing. Maybe you always find the best deals thrifting, or the weather is always nice when you make plans. Magic is everywhere. Us witches just notice it more. We harness it."

I smiled over at her, enjoying the breeze and the break from the chaos and bustle of the Hallows crowd.

Her curious voice broke the silence. "Step into the firelight for me? Something about you is bugging the shit out of me."

"Sure."

Squinting and looking me up and down, she took a step back. "I've never seen this before. I thought it was just the dark night. Can anyone else see?" she asked the circle. Everyone only stared with the same furrowed brows and silence.

"What is it?" I asked, unsure if I wanted to know the answer.

"Y-you don't have an aura."

I cleared my throat, the cinnamon lingering on my tongue. "Is that bad?"

I had so many questions, but then the quiet witch interjected. "We are not alone here. I think someone else has laid claim to you for this night."

Confusion furrowed my brow until I noted everyone in the circle looking over my shoulder. Air lodged itself in my throat as something beat heavily in my chest. When I turned, a white face and black painted eyes stared back at me. The skeleton masked man leaned casually against an adjacent tree. He was cleaning his nails with a knife in between intense glances at me. *A knife. Lovely.*

"He's following me," I whispered breathless. "Maybe I should stay here?" Though I couldn't deny the cocktail of relief and excitement that washed over me knowing he'd found me. He was here.

The witch next to me giggled, meeting my eyes and taking my hand in hers. Recognition flashed through me. Yesenia? I couldn't be totally sure, and I wouldn't say her name and out her even if I were certain. I thought I noticed the glitter from the smoky eye I'd done for her earlier. Why was it so difficult to decipher just about anything at Hallows Fest? It was like moving under water or being on heavy narcotics.

"I promise you're safe with Ghost, clever Fox." She grinned and flipped my hand over, trailing a gentle finger down the center. Her smile faltered as she studied my clammy palm. Her gaze shot to mine and then immediately to the skeleton, or Ghost, as I guessed he was called here. No words were spoken, yet it seemed as if something were said between the two of them. The atmosphere of the circle grew quiet, eerie. She looked to the older witch who simply stared at me. *Okay, this is getting a little weird.* I gently tugged my hand away. "Your palm, it's . . . ," she trailed off, as if losing her breath, before sitting down on a log.

"Are you okay?" I asked with concern.

The older witch answered, "She will be fine. Run along, Fox."

Too many feathered masks peered at me, seemingly knowing something I didn't. I nodded and took a step back, tenderly setting my mug on a patch of brown grass next to a lantern. "Thank you for the drink. I'll find you guys again another night."

No one spoke a word as I turned to walk away, but I could feel their stares boring into my back. What just happened? But the sight before me was as unnerving as the one I was leaving. The tree was empty.

The skeleton man was gone.

Like a ghost.

<hr>

After meandering around pockets of partygoers and accepting a meat kabob from a tent of people dressed as werewolves, a whistle pricked my ear. I ignored it, thinking it wasn't my business, but when I heard it again, I turned to find a rough-looking man with an eye patch staring me down. He held a finger to his lips and waved for me to follow. After shooting a glance over each shoulder, looking for what, I wasn't sure, I inched forward to follow him. I'd already met so many people, and they'd all been friendly, so I had no reason not to trust this stranger.

What a strange feeling to be surrounded by folks cloaked as monsters and feel safer than I did on normal, day to day, human life. If only I could pitch a tent in October and live in this month forever.

My curiosity was piqued at realizing I hadn't seen anyone dressed like him before, and I worked to piece together his costume in my mind as I followed him through a curve in the woods, away from the bustle of the crowd. The man walked with a wobble, and it wasn't until we arrived at our destination that it clicked for me who they were.

A group of men and women and folks sat around a fire near a sprawling pond, or maybe it was a lake; it was too dark to tell. I didn't know there was a lake in Ash Grove. Various jewels of emerald and rubies glinted from their knuckles and necks as dangly gold earrings jingled from their lobes. Another rugged, bearded man with beads and flowers weaved through his long beard strummed a guitar, and when I stepped closer, I noticed the parrot perched atop his shoulder. "Pirates?" I asked as the man with the wooden peg-leg motioned toward the fire. He didn't speak, just smiled broadly and nodded. "Sit? Are you sure?" I asked.

"Get over here, new girl, let us have a look at you," the bearded man demanded, his voice thick with mischief. "This is the newcomer that this godforsaken town is abuzz about, eh?"

"Hi, I'm Blythe," I replied weakly, meeting the gaze of a dozen pairs of eyes, well, some patched, so maybe that was an uneven number in reality. "I was led here by . . . ," I trailed off, looking for the man who brought me.

The bearded man spoke up gruffly. "That would be Scully. He had his tongue cut out by a rival ship. The bastards." The others around the fire grumbled and grunted curses. "We showed 'em what happens when they mess with The Pirates of Ashes, though, didn't we?"

"Here, here!" someone yelled as flasks and goblets clanked.

Scully took his seat next to me and nudged a glass under my nose. "Oh, for me?"

He nodded enthusiastically, his one, unpatched eye twinkling amidst his fuzzy white hair and short beard. I gave the amber liquid a sniff. Whatever it was, it smelled like gasoline. "To hell with it, sure," I replied, bringing the drink to my lips. Knocking my head back, I chugged the alcohol in six big gulps. When I finished, I wiped my mouth with the back of my sleeve and noticed the quiet that befell me. The circle had gone silent, all watching me. "What," I whispered to Scully. "Did I do something wrong?"

The bearded man's parrot squawked as he marched over in his heavy boots. "Devil himself, that rum didn't burn your face off, girl?"

I shrugged. "Clearly it doesn't do that to yours either." I gestured to his beard, which hung well past his ribs. I noticed several keys hidden amongst tiny beads, daisies, and charms as they dangled around the brown coils. First a woman chuckled, and then the man beside her. Suddenly, the bearded man began howling in laughter, even his parrot joining him.

"You might be dressed like a . . . Well, it doesn't matter." He beamed. "You're a pirate if I ever saw one. Blythe, my girl, you're welcomed on my ship anytime." He gestured at one of his men who promptly refilled my glass with more. "Come and listen to our stories and poems. We're a hell of a lot better company than the band of critters and dick bags out there."

More grunts and clanks of agreement.

"Stories and poems," I repeated. "That sounds really good, actually. It's hard to get anyone in this town, or Hallows, to give me a straight answer on anything. Maybe you guys can answer some of my questions?"

"That we likely can, for a price, that is." The bearded man reached out a handkerchief-wrapped hand. "I'm Captain Vex Beard III. I'm the Story Keeper of The Pirates of Ashes with the most tales of anyone these cursed seas ever saw." He gestured around the fire. "And this here's me crew of merry assholes."

I smiled as he held his hat to his chest and bowed. "It's nice to meet you all. I didn't know there were pirate cosplayers here. Your outfits are so authentic . . . ," I trailed off as the noise level died down again. A few whispers fluttered between crackles of the blaze, and I realized my misstep. "Sorry." I swallowed. "I know I'm not supposed to . . . "

The captain looked at me consideringly. His parrot cocked his head as if he, too, were sizing me up. Their costumes truly were, like everyone's at Hallows, immaculately crafted. These pirates weren't in your typical polyester and plastic. The swords and daggers at their sides glinted and seemed scuffled with not only weight but age and use. Their clothes were missing threads and covered in stains. Many of them donned hats of sun-stained and worn leather to go with their eye patches and various wooden prosthetics that, by my casual observance, weren't hiding or attached to actual limbs. Many of them were truly missing a hand or foot. And when Scully knocked back his own drink, I noted that he indeed seemed to be missing a tongue. The truth to what I was seeing with the pirates was bizarre and unnerving, even more so than the animalistic costumes. Though I couldn't find anything beneath the fur on those either, no zipper tracks or tags peeking through. I couldn't find any holes or slip ups in these guys' getups either. It was almost as if it were all real. Which was preposterous, but how could it be that each and every person at Hallows had such exquisitely detailed finery?

"Ask your question, girl. I know Seaman McGee over here is eager to share his poem of the evening." He flipped a gold coin in the air, idly catching it and repeating the process.

I took a long sip of my rum to settle my nerves. It tasted like sweet, gritty razors in my throat, but it helped steel my resolve. If I could ask only one question and hope for one straight answer, this one stood out in my mind the most. This question shouted the loudest in my psyche.

"Who is Ghost?"

CHAPTER 19

Ames

CLAWS

Emily Dickinson

My demon was so close to the surface, skimming his claws along my consciousness until it was an effort not to shift. A woman had never made me want to turn before. I'd never met anyone who could coax out the Devil in me. And I wasn't sure that was a good thing. It was at the very least a dangerous thing, especially for Blythe.

I told myself I'd been so close to turning because I'd turned and killed only an hour prior before returning home to a pensive Onyx who'd kept Blythe in a serene slumber while Wolf and I caught the wretched ghoul. My power thrummed through my tendons, aching to be set free again, pulsating, wanting to show her. Saying over and over in my mind, *let us out, let us out, let's play with her.*

I'd seen and done some disturbing shit in my years as a damned soul, but tasting Blythe's anger, the warm spice of it, like mulled wine, sent a jolt of desire straight to my cock, and this time, my demon wanted to play too. We were the same, him and I. If anything, I was more Ghost than Ames. I'd just suppressed that side of me for so long, only coming out to kill when the ideal target presented itself. When Onyx lost a case against a rapist or a pedophile, we'd assemble like bloodthirsty gargoyles and torture and maim in whatever way assuaged the evil within us all. That's when my demon came out. But tonight, he wanted to fuck her . . . and that was . . . new.

An angry woman should not have my demon dick throbbing.

But Blythe was angry. *Finally.* Finally, I tasted something other than sadness, and fear, and loneliness, and resignation. I wanted to shake her and scream, *you don't have to be afraid anymore. You have me.*

And then chain her to my bed and yell, *you should be very afraid now that you do.*

Both were true. And I didn't have a goddamn clue what any of it meant.

The moment she slammed my door, I called Judas, who sent me straight to voicemail. The ever-absent fucker. Some leader. Some Devil.

Clearly, I'd pasted on too thick of a Clark Kent facade if Blythe thought me pure and innocent. No, worse than pure and innocent, average. An average, self-serving, horn dog frat boy who just wanted in her pants. That was what she thought of me. And that fucking hurt. It hurt. Nothing fucking hurt me. Not the cries of the bastard dredges of this Earth as their blood spilled onto my hands. I didn't hurt for the howls of torment I heard the moment I walked into Hell's Gates. I liked it. I loved it, even.

And what did I feel for Blythe? Hurt, and need, and . . .

Devil damn me.

I was disgusted at the part of myself that pinned her against the doorframe. All I wanted in that moment was to let my beast free. I wanted to stand at seven feet tall, skin like the night, glowing bones of the horrifying skeleton, only tendon and terror. The desire to push her down onto her knees and see how much of my monster cock she could fit in her mouth rode me hard. I wanted to make her gag, make her jaw hurt for days after. I wanted to flood her mouth with my seed and put a hand over her lips until she swallowed it all.

I was no better than the cowards I murdered.

And I couldn't stay away from her.

Not when she stormed off, not when she spent several hours with Yesenia, and I sure as hell wouldn't let my eyes off her as she walked with Ezmerelda or accepted a protection drink from the witches or was whisked away by the pirates. *Mine.*

But my Little Ghost was angry with me. My Little Ghost had me all wrong. My Little Ghost in that goddamn *motherfucking* mini skirt and fishnets . . .

I knew my demon was bloodthirsty. I didn't know he was now a sex-craving lunatic. I might as well have been a vampire with how badly I wanted it, how badly I wanted her.

But who did Blythe the fox want to play with tonight? She was mad at Ames, but what about Ghost? Was he too fucking pure for her? Yeah, I guessed not. If she wanted bad, I could give her bad. It would be up to her just how much she could take.

With the ghoul chasing her gone, I could relax. Her earlier night-mares could only be from trauma. There was no other explanation. Ghouls could look into nightmares but they couldn't create them. They couldn't interact or move within them. Only powerful demons could manage that, and even then, they rarely bothered. None of us gave a shit about mortal consciousness, awake or asleep. Blythe was wounded and psychologically unwell, but she would recover, especially now that the threat was gone. Once she discovered that . . . I didn't want to think that maybe she'd leave. She had to stay. Ames had to make her. Or perhaps . . . Ames and Ghost could work together to convince her to stay. Together they were me. The blessed and the damned.

I caught the gaze of the captain and jerked my chin at Blythe, shaking my head slightly. He stilled for a moment, not betraying a single emotion, though I tasted the faintest hint of fear—like sugar cane and salt water. Far less fear than anyone else at Hallows had for me. Except maybe the crones. The elder witches hated me. And I wasn't too fond of them and their pious, judgmental attitudes either.

Getting the message, he tipped his hat in my direction and plucked Blythe's half-full second drink from her hands. "That'll be enough of that," he said smoothly. "Can't have ye drinkin' and sailin'."

The pirate folks laughed and guffawed. I rolled my eyes and blended back into the shadows. Being tipsy was fine, being drunk wasn't. There were demons, some I knew personally, who hung out at bars just to prey on drunk mortals. Drinking lowered humans' poor mental barriers to non-existent. It was like a bleeding seal in a sea of sharks. Certain demons and entities went into a frenzy over it; sometimes just to fuck with them, and sometimes to inhabit them. To wear human skin for the evening or, you know, forever. Messy business.

I never got the point, really. Taking on human form was easy enough. I did it, and I'd done it for hundreds of years. But we all had our particular kinks, I guessed. But hell if I were going to allow Blythe to become inebriated and vulnerable. Not tonight.

She seemed to enjoy our dance. Perhaps I'd cut in again and afterwards we could—

My thoughts were interrupted by the meow of a stupidly intrepid feline. "What are you doing all the way out here? I've been looking for you everywhere," Cat hissed. "We have a problem. I need you now."

I glanced at Blythe. She was laughing, laughing. Devil, she was beautiful when she smiled. The taste of her amusement on my tongue was like the juice of fresh peaches. "Hello? Daydream much?" Cat insisted.

"What is it now, Furball? A dog's off its leash in the graveyard—"

"A damned has escaped," Cat said, low and serious. "I don't know how it happened. I did my checks as always and came up short somehow."

"That's impossible. No one can escape Hell's Gate. You counted wrong."

"You thought it possible last we spoke. And I didn't miscount. If you don't pull your head out of your girlfriend's ass, he's going to wreak havoc on your precious little town."

Motherfucker. I ran a hand through my hair. "There's no one here to watch her but me."

"I'll look after her," a soft, uneven voice wavered from the darkness of a high branch. By time I looked up, a thud sounded and he walked forward. "She is safe with me, Ghost." Raven bowed. "We're friends," they added.

I'd always liked the Crows. They were weird as fuck but smarter than they let on. The crows were the only cursed animals at Hallows Fest who knew how to behave themselves, unlike the fawns and bulls and godforsaken wolves. One month to shift into humans and they all went berserk. Not the Crows, though. They carried on much in the same way they did in their bird forms, sitting in treetops, observing every tiny detail of the world below them.

"You'll keep her out of trouble and get her somewhere safe?" I pressed.

"Ghost, we don't have time—"

I shoved at Cat with my boot, and she swatted her claws at my ankle.

Raven bowed again, cocking his head to the side, the long-beaked mask and the elongated feathers he kept only making them look like a large bird-human. Ridiculous but in a harmless way. The birds had an affinity for mischief, but they were loyal and honest, and I'd always appreciated that about them, even if many other Hallows attendees viewed them as inferior.

"You have my word. I will protect with all my magic and might."

He kept his head lowered as I assessed him. Finally, I cut him a nod. "If I'm not back in time to see her home, find Dragon or Wolf. Under no circumstance does a vampire take her or follow her home, got it?"

"Yes, I will see to it."

It was sufficient but not ideal. Then again, the only threat to Blythe at this point, you know, aside from me, the most powerful demon in this part of the world, was the escaped soul roaming the forest. The ghoul was writhing under the maw of a werewolf right now, as it should be. Reluctantly, I gave up my post to the inky foul and followed Cat deeper into the forest. "How could this be?" Cat panted, jumping over a log as she scurried.

I didn't have an answer for her. There was a lot going on behind and outside of the gate that I didn't understand recently. Why was the ground groaning and lifting as if the damned were trying to shove it off their heads? What could cause them to act so bold and come so close to the surface? Was it due to my waning abilities? I had no clue, and if Judas knew, he sure as fuck wasn't telling me, nor was he around to help.

It was just my luck that every being in Ash Grove would pick the one time in almost two hundred years a woman caught my eye to act like fools: ghouls chasing her, nightmares haunting her, witches meddling, vampires lusting, my powers failing, and now the damned escaping on the same ground she walked.

What in the actual *hell* was going on?

CHAPTER 20

Blythe

LOVE BITES

Everything is ecstasy, inside... Close your eyes, let your hands and nerve-endings drop, stop breathing for 3 seconds, listen to the silence inside...and you will remember.

Jack Kerouac

Captain Vex looked around at his friends. They eyed him with reverence and loyalty, and though he looked rugged and worn, I could tell that the bearded pirate was sharp and cunning. He'd clearly earned the trust of everyone here. *It was all pretend*, I told myself, but damn if he wasn't the realest and truest pirate I'd ever seen, in both dress and actions. His masculine features shone orange in the firelight, showing his handsome, weathered, and tanned face.

He glanced at Scully and nodded, answering a question that was somehow asked without words. "If she's found us here, where the stories are held and told, she's ready to hear them."

Scully looked to me with concern on his bushy brows but jerked a nod before knocking back his drink.

The rambunctious crew settled into silence, with only the crackle and pop of the fire interrupting the quiet of night. "Stories are our treasures, girl. And we have a great many treasures between us. We seek 'em, keep 'em, and cash 'em in when we need it. I'll give you this, but you'll be answerin' my call should I need a story of my own. Understood?"

I swallowed and nodded. *Cosplay, a big game.*

Captain Vex seemed satisfied with my oath, and he began: "I haven't gotten to tell this one in a great many years." He tossed a stick into the inferno. His green and yellow parrot settled into a little ball on his shoulder, as if preparing to listen along with the rest of us.

"People think the Halloween massacre of Ash Grove happened all at once. But that's not true." Men grunted their agreements before he continued, pacing around the fire and lacing his hands behind his back. I noticed a long sword dangling at his side. It looked heavy and well used. "Folks were going missing or turning up dead for years," he continued. "Then that October, in eighteen twenty three, a dozen of Ash Grove's women would be taken, snatched into the woods never to be found. Daughters, mothers, school teachers, didn't matter, the women were pulled from their beds, from their chores, never to be seen again. Only thing found was one person a night lay dead in the town's square until . . . Until on Halloween night, they came. Revealed themselves, they did."

Silence stretched and I picked up on the sound of water lapping at the lake's shore.

"Who?" I asked, looking around attentively.

Captain Vex glanced behind me into the forest. What he was looking at, I wasn't sure. But he answered, "It was a group of wretched monsters or men at that point. It made no difference. They acted as a unit. As if one murderous bastard isn't enough, these were organized kills. They planned, plotted, and slaughtered the town in cold blood, proudly calling themselves a brotherhood."

The exposed skin on my calves pricked with goose pimples as my breath caught in my throat.

"More like a cult, if you ask me," a rough female voice remarked.

The others grunted their agreements. "Lord only knows what they did to those women they took." Chills flitted down my spine. I imagined the fear they must have felt being grabbed in their sleep . . .

The captain trailed another lap around the fire. "The afterlife was flooded with souls that night. So much so, the spirits could hardly sort through 'em all. Pissed a lot of beings off on the other side. It wasn't right, the balance of life and death being thrown off by such wretched violence. Even the killings weren't enough, and they set the town on fire after. Because of the magnitude of their actions, because death would be too small a punishment, they were cursed to spend eternity paying for their sins.

"Some say that means through their children and children's children. Some say they're still alive today and in Ash Grove." The captain leveled me a pointed look, and I felt cold anxiety prickle my skin.

He continued, "A celebration every night in October, Hallows, began as a festival to honor the dead. Some felt it was needed because of the things that started happening in the years after the massacre. As the town began to rebuild, survivors and torn-apart families moved forward but started . . . seeing things. The stories say that every night in October, a new monster comes to visit, smellin' the haunted land. It's said that on Halloween, the old townspeople, the ones they mutilated, walk the streets again. We all dress in 1800s costumes so as not to confuse them. So that they can have a normal night. But even now, hundreds of years later, the monsters are still at it. Still killing. The curse only let them extend their reign. You already know what they're called, right, Fox?"

Even the flame silenced its pop and crackle. I didn't want to know. So much of my time was spent avoiding . . . what I did. Avoiding the truth, the visions, the intrusive thoughts, the parts all pulling together like magnets. I took a deep breath as everyone turned to me, even the parrot. "The Halloween Boys."

THE PIRATE CAPTAIN'S words echoed so loudly in my mind they drowned out the medley of drums and harps a group, of what looked like people dressed as deer, played. I'd hoped to see him, the one from the stories. Ghost, they had all whispered with hushed reverence. I planned to confront him, and I'd envisioned doing it during another dance.

The music was soft and perfect for my questioning. Enough of the town's riddles and half-truths, I wanted to ask him, the skeleton man stalking me. The pirates told me enough, but I wanted to hear it from him.

Raven nudged a soft, feathery elbow at my arm. "You look tired. Shall I walk you to your car?"

I glanced around the crowd for the millionth time. With a disappointed sigh, I agreed. Tonight had been a bust, in every sense of the word. Between my blow-up fight with Ames and now feeling stood up by my dance partner, I felt like an absolute loser. Even Ezmerelda took one look at me walking back and vanished. She didn't want to be around me.

The only good to come from my disaster of an evening, aside from getting actual intel from the pirates, was my somehow scoring a new apartment and job. And Raven was easy company. "How long have you been coming to Hallows?" I asked as we weaved through horns and fur.

"A long time," he replied plainly. "But I live in Ash Grove. Most here do not."

That surprised me. "But everyone in here says they never get visitors. People in Ash Grove look at me like I have two heads. Where do all these people come from if they don't stay here?"

A month was a long time to commit to a festival, yet I was seeing the same beautiful, masked faces every evening. It didn't make sense. Travel to and from each day would be a logistical nightmare. My friend shrugged and shook their shoulders. Still in bird-mode, I guessed. "This town's history draws all sorts of special people. This festival is what Halloween is all about." His beak turned toward me, and I imagined a smile beneath it as he extended his winged arms. "Tricks, treats, a little mischief, and monsters everywhere. What's not to love?"

A grin softly touched my lips as I fell into a walk beside him. The crowd dissipated while we broke the tree line to follow the flickering jack-o'-lanterns down the way. Raven remained by my side, his feathers from his arms so long they dragged the ground alongside us. He wasn't small by any means, but he stood only an inch or so taller than me. I stole brief moments to inspect his costume, wondering who the kind soul was beneath. A dark Hyde hood covered his head, concealing any hint of hair or ears. He wore a plain buttoned vest over hundreds of feathers that wrapped around his frame. I wished I knew who he was so I could text him, so that maybe we could be friends. I broke the silence. "I think I have some leftover pizza if you want to come to my place and hang out." Part of me didn't want to be alone to think about my fight with Ames. Another part truly did want to get to know Raven better.

"I already ate, but thank you—" His long winged arm shot in front of my ribs, stopping me in my tracks. "Wait," he whispered.

My heart jumped into my chest as I stood motionless atop the faint crackles of dry leaves. A moan broke out amongst the darkness of the forest. Raven's beak turned in the direction of the sound, and he cocked his head. I peered into the darkness, straining to see the source of the sound. Suddenly a red flash and a man I recognized stumbled out from the bushes. Ezmerelda smoothed her dress and Captain Vex shoved his hat back on his head, one arm lazily wrapped around her shoulder. "Evening," he said.

Ezmerelda met my gaze and grinned, wiping red liquid from her chin. It was then I noticed the captain's neck . . . and the torn and bloody fabric on his chest.

"You're bleeding," I said in alarm, "Are you okay? I have a first aid kit in my car—"

Captain Vex burst out laughing while Ezmerelda bit back her giggle. Raven looked at me, and though I couldn't see his expression under his mask, I knew he was exasperated.

Ezmerelda licked the captain's swollen neck and he groaned. "No bandages needed. I got it. Have a nice night, Little Fox. See you tomorrow." With a playful look over her shoulder, the red-headed vampiress tugged the pirate's arm, pulling him past us toward the other side of the forest. What lay that way, I had no idea. But the sight of blood was disturbing.

"That was real blood," I whispered to Raven, in case they were still nearby. "That wasn't pretend. I saw his swollen neck. Did she really bite him?"

My friend squawked with amusement. "Looks like that's the least of what she did to him. Vex Beard has been pining for The Red Vampiress for ages. I guess he's finally making some headway. Though, you never know with the vampires. They're amorous, to say the least. Fun to spy on though. The things they talk about would astound you."

Unease tensed my muscles as we continued along the winding path. I rubbed my neck in solidarity with the pirate captain. It looked painful. "Don't you think that's taking the fantasy too far? That looked like it hurt."

Raven hummed what sounded like a tune that was vaguely familiar. "I'm deciding something about you right now," he said between hums. "I'm deciding if it's in your best interest to know more or not."

"I can handle it. I'm not a child. If they're doing drugs or if Ezmerelda and Vex have a blood kink or something, that's fine as long as it's consensual, I guess. But you can tell me. It won't scare me."

Raven hummed some more and I realized the song. "That's the least of what would scare you, Blythe. Oh, and thanks for the peanuts."

"'Gold Dust Woman' by Fleetwood Mac. I was just listening to that in my car earlier."

And then my feet hit gravel and the realization hit with the crunch. "Wait, how did you know my name and—"

But a large man standing by my car snagged my attention. He howled at the moon like an animal and leaned against my car with a big grin on his face. "Not safe to be out in these woods alone," Wolfgang said as I approached.

"I'm not alone. Raven walked me."

"Is that your imaginary friend?"

When I looked around me, my bird friend was gone. "I guess he's not one for goodbyes, but he was right here."

I swallowed. Because as much as I wanted to deny it, it was as if he'd evaporated . . . or taken flight. No, both of those were ludicrous. Ezmerelda licking crimson from the corner of her lips flashed in my mind. *Blood. "Gold Dust Woman" and peanuts . . .*

"You look like you just saw a ghost," Wolfgang crooned, angling his head. "You alright, champ?"

Swallowing my rising panic, I rubbed under my itchy mask. "It's been a long day. Why are you here again?"

"Well," he said, smiling that dazzling smile. "I was going to make something up about leaving something of mine in your car, but really . . . I was in the area and thought I'd see you home. Might as well, right? Also, I don't have a ride, so it's a win, win."

"You didn't drive here? First Ames the other night and now you?" *Suspicious.*

"Nope, I was dropped off."

I clicked my tongue. "So you do party at Hallows. Where's your costume?"

Wolfgang bopped my nose with his thumb. "Wouldn't you like to know. You're cold, let's get in. I can drive if you're tired."

The feminist in me wanted to keep control by driving my own car, but even she was over it, and Wolfgang was basically a giant teddy bear. I handed my keys over and we got in.

"Am I taking you . . . back to Ames's place?" he asked carefully, though I wasn't entirely sure why he'd assume that.

"Absolutely not," I huffed, crossing my arms against the cold car. Wolf turned up the heat and chuckled.

"I heard you two got into a tiff. Don't worry, we all get pissed at him regularly. For a therapist, he says some dumb shit sometimes. But he's an alright guy."

I rolled my eyes. "Oh, yeah? Are you a part of his villains of Hell's Gate club?"

Wolfgang's smile dropped, and he looked straight ahead. "What did he tell you?"

The seriousness in his tone took me off guard. "He said he was the villain. Is he right?" I asked pointedly.

"What do you think?"

I sighed, annoyed and wanting to get out of my pointlessly sexy outfit. "I think half the town treats him, and you and Onyx, like gods. But then there are some people who warn me that you're all bad news. I'm not sure how both of those stories can coexist."

"Maybe we're both. Gods and monsters."

I grinned, looking over at Wolf's thick frame, but he wasn't smiling. His usual lightheartedness had faded into something else, something stern and pensive. We rode in silence after I asked him to drop me at Magia Eclectics.

"Do you have a ride home?" I asked when we got out.

"I'll walk over to Ames's. Sure you don't want to join me? Kiss and make up?"

I huffed a laugh. "There won't be either of those happening, ever."

Wolfgang grumbled, looking up to my window above the dim shop. "He's not going to like you staying here, that's for sure."

"Because I'm right down the road from his place at the church?" My heart dropped. Ames would be mad I lived right down the road from him. I guessed he really was done with me after today.

Wolf didn't reply, only backed away, blowing out a puff of smoke from the cold air. "Night, Blythe. I'm around if you need me."

I gave him a weak smile of thanks before letting myself inside the shop. My room was warm and cozy. I immediately stripped out of my lacy, tight things. pulled on a loose cotton AC/DC shirt, and tied my hair into a messy bun. I'd only been at the top of Magia for a few hours, and it already felt more like home than anywhere I'd ever stayed. Thirst dried my mouth as I padded to the supply cabinet, hoping for water but super-hoping for soda. To my delight, when I opened the door, it was fully stocked with both water bottles and six packs of my favorite root beers. My eyes weighed heavy as I took a few sugary gulps. What a fucking day.

I collapsed on my new bed, utterly spent and exhausted. I was haunted by skeleton masks, dripping fangs, and crows that knew too much detail. My dreams were unsettled swirls of Ames's straining forearms above my ears, the smell of his ragged breath . . . and the fear of not seeing him again. *He won't like you staying here,* Wolf had said.

It was done. Whatever I thought we might have had was gone before it started.

Maybe it was for the best. I wouldn't be here long anyway.

CHAPTER 21

Ames

NIGHT OF THE HUNTER

Let life be beautiful like summer flowers and death like autumn leaves.
Rabindranath Tagore

The week I spent without her, I stood outside her window every night, all night, watching the street to make sure she was safe. Watching her window, hoping to catch a glimpse of a bare shoulder or her golden-brown hair. When she left and I couldn't follow her, I stayed glued to my phone, following the blue dot as she drove. When I had therapy clients, I sent Onyx or Wolf to watch her, though they were way too fucking eager to do so. When she came in for her appointment with Dr. Omar, I took my lunch break so I didn't make her uncomfortable. She wanted nothing to do with me after my failed attempt at having her, my clumsy stupidity in confessing that I wanted her. The truth was, I had never wanted a woman the way I wanted her. When I said it, I didn't only mean fucking her, though I did want to do that. I wanted her goddamn soul. And I realized what a horrific thing I was asking her: to give her soul to a demon, a devil, a monster. I didn't deserve her. So every moment she put distance between us was for the best. But I'd still follow her. I wasn't sure I could make myself stop. I had to know where she was and what she was doing at all times.

When she got her morning breakfast with Onyx, I was there in my car outside across the lot.

Blythe had left my apartment for all of an hour before the busybody-ass witches sunk their claws into her. I liked Yesenia but wasn't thrilled about her abuela, Marcelene, having access to Blythe. Access where I could not go at night. Her apartment was warded heavily, and I couldn't break through if I tried. Blythe was in a place I couldn't reach. And if it weren't for the fact I'd already caught the ghoul that was chasing her, I'd hunt Marcelene down and have a word. I didn't give a fuck if she was the coven's crone. She'd release Blythe to me; I'd make her. But she'd been fucking with me for years. This was nothing more than another power play designed by her and the other old bats. They wanted to piss me off. But it didn't hurt Blythe, not really. In fact, though it pained me to admit, she was safer staying at Magia than she'd be probably anywhere else, aside from the church with me. That goddamn shop was a fortress of energetic shields meant to keep my kind away.

And then there were the nights she threw anxious glances at me at Hallows. I dressed closer to the demon I was, and I kept the unsavories away from her and made sure someone was there to walk her to her car and take her home. But I dodged before she stared too long, and I couldn't stay and dance with her like I so desperately wanted. The damned was still missing and the graveyard was still an epic pain in my ass. The ground shook and rumbled so much now that Cat slept in a nearby tree instead of her usual spot atop the marble tomb.

I'd texted Judas. *I need your fucking help. When will you be back?*

He'd replied a day later. *When I find what I'm looking for.*

Thanks for the help, prick.

My thumbs would hover over Blythe's name, wanting to message, begging me to call. But I didn't. I would go back to being the demon that followed her, but I wouldn't bother her with more. She didn't need it. What she needed was to heal. Though Wolfgang, Onyx, and I were still working on a way to tell her that her stepdad was now dead. Or who she thought was her stepdad, who was actually a ghoul pretending, was dead. Well, worse than dead, actually, but she didn't need to know that.

It turns out Onyx was right. She didn't need to know about The Halloween Boys and what we brought on Ash Grove. Blythe didn't need to see the evil that lurked beneath our nice guy masks. My black pit of a soul fought that fact. It wanted to show her, wanted her to see us and know, but it was for her benefit I didn't. Blythe didn't deserve to live in a world of monsters like us. She needed a fresh start.

Though every evening Ezmerelda waited like a little red moth on the trail to walk her to Hallows, my blood boiled. And every night Blythe's goddamn outfits were sexier and sexier. Who was she dressing for? The Red Vampiress? I'd cornered the vampire at the start of the week. Even someone as ancient as she couldn't hide the slash of fear I tasted when I stopped her. It tasted like sour grapes, and she bared her teeth, knowing I tasted it.

"I'm her friend," she claimed, tossing her long hair over her deceptively delicate shoulder.

My gaze didn't falter. I may have been behind the paint of a skull, but Ezmerelda knew what lay beneath was far worse than any costume could portray. She'd seen my demon and the fear lingered. *Good.*

"You don't have friends," I countered. "You have fuck buddies. And Blythe won't be one of them. Don't touch her, don't give her any of your kind's fucking alcohol, and keep Vincent the fuck away from her, too."

Ezmerelda Bennet's fear twisted with indignation, the taste like overripe green apples. "Stop feeding on my emotions, demon."

"I'll do whatever the fuck I want, vampiress. And you'll obey me if you and your kind want access to my lands."

Her red gaze narrowed as she walked by me. "If you were smart, Ghost, you'd give her to us. She'd be better off under the watch of our coven than The Halloween Boys. It's only a matter of time before one of you claim her and that poor girl loses her soul."

"Try to convince me you give a shit about her soul," I said through gritted teeth.

Ezmerelda twirled on her boot as she circled me in that annoying as fuck way she did to everyone. Her time in the circus never left her. She'd always be a performer. "With us, she'd experience pleasure, not pain, and she'd only give her soul if she wanted to. There have been humans in the past who have decided not to and have aged away. With you though . . . " She jumped and grabbed a branch several feet overhead. "Her soul is gone the moment you inevitably shoot her up with your cursed cock. Sad you'd even let yourself so close, Ghost. You're truly out-eviling yourself at every turn. Haven't you put Ash Grove through enough?" She tsked sarcastically.

I was tempted to shift just to taste the fear again. To put her in her place. Though she spoke some truth and I knew it. "Your people intoxicate your victims and convince yourselves they have free will. The mental gymnastics are almost as good as your physical ones. This isn't the circus, Ezmerelda. And you will obey my commands."

A lithe giggle faded as she silently jumped between trees. "Think it over, Ghost. I could treat her better than you, and you know it."

And she was gone.

Infuriating fucking vampiress. That's what they did though. They thrived on getting in their victims' heads, convincing their prey they wanted it. Onyx thought too highly of the other half of his kind, and I kept silent too often so as not to offend him. The vampires weren't my favorite of the monsters I oversaw. But I knew they wouldn't harm her. Not after knowing I was watching her. Claimed or not, they wouldn't touch what was mine. They loved rules and order and following the letter of any law placed over them. I could at least count on that.

At the end of my nights, I'd wait in the dark of the shadows and watch one of my friends drive her home. Following behind, once she was inside, I'd assume my position under the dead tree in the square across from her window and sit in its shadows. Watching, listening, and alone.

Alone except for the crow that perched above me, seemingly doing the same thing I was. Another night I wasn't chasing the damned and sent the guys to look for it instead. I didn't care. They got to drive her, and talk to her, and eat breakfast with her, so I got to watch her through her window. It was fair.

And I thought to myself as I watched her brush her hair, I could live like this until she died peacefully of old age. I could follow her and look after her. Then when she left her physical body, I'd find her soul and follow it too. Blythe would be my new guiding light, not dissecting the limitations of my curse, not school, or careers, or even my friends. It would be this woman and this woman alone now. Perhaps stalking her was even more than I deserved. It was selfish and an obsession, but I had no urge to change it. It was what it was. I was what I was. A demon. A ghost.

And now she was cursed with me forever.

CHAPTER 22

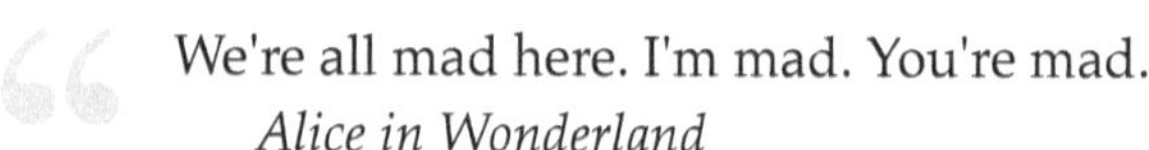

THE BRIDE OF CHARLES MOORE

The only reason I went to my therapy appointment was in hopes of seeing him. But he'd even orchestrated an eleven in the morning lunch break to avoid being near me. I guessed I was right. He wanted a quick lay, and when I proved more complicated, less thankful for his help, and interested in more than just sex, he split. Why couldn't I have just slept with him? *I want you* replayed over and over in my mind. His gruff voice, the way he moved so fast to grab my face . . . His lips were right there. I'd had eight days to think about his lips and how close they were. In my fantasies, I acted like a normal woman would and I kissed him. Pulling him close, I'd push him onto the sofa and straddle him. I'd grind on him until he begged for more, and then I'd slide between his knees and do what I should have done then. That could have been my first time having sex. But I wasn't a normal woman. I was someone who'd been chased, taunted, and toyed with her entire adult life. I'd been surrounded by death and sadness. They followed me to every town I tried to call home, along with my stepfather, who'd recently been concerningly quiet. The smallest, tiniest flicker of hope bounced in my heart that maybe, just maybe, he'd stopped his quest. That maybe something scared him off, or maybe he lost track of me somehow. I couldn't explain the blank letter and how he knew where I was . . . and maybe he truly was lurking around a corner waiting to strike . . . but for now, I'd keep doing what I was doing. I'd never stayed put after receiving a letter. I'd always ran. Maybe he didn't know what to do with that, like he never expected me to stay, and he chickened out on killing me. I could only hope.

I didn't want to die. And not just because of Ames, or Onyx and Wolf, though they had quickly taken up residence in my thoughts.

I didn't want to die anymore because I now had a crow that followed me around and laid pennies on my windowsill. And I had a creepy, cryptic friend who also happened to dress as a crow, who'd appear at Hallows each night to talk to me.

I didn't want to die anymore because the ladies at the diner pulled together a bunch of their clothes they weren't using and gave them to me at breakfast just to be nice. I actually looked forward to mornings, now. Each day after getting dressed, I'd go to the diner. I had a regular booth, and I'd sit and someone would bring coffee and waffles. Soon after, Onyx would take a seat across from me and ask me stupid questions about his crossword puzzle until I laughed. And then Wolfgang would join and gossip with us about town drama and whatever story he was writing. Wolf was the biggest gossip I'd ever met, and I loved it. They'd talk about everything except Ames and his glaring absence.

But I was thankful that at least they still seemed to care. I was thankful I hadn't lost them too.

I didn't want to die because Yesenia would stop by every morning after I opened the shop and spend hours just talking to me. She told me, not so subtly, about her family's history of being gifted in the esoteric arts. She'd learned to palm read, and see auras, and look into crystal balls from her abuela. I'd only seen Marcelene once since moving in and working at the shop, and she seemed friendlier than our first meeting, though still wary of me.

I didn't want to die because I suspected that Yesenia or Marcelene were stocking my apartment's supply closet with food and drinks.

Somehow, they knew my favorites of everything, and anything I needed was always there.

I didn't want to die and not be a part of a world where Hallows Fest didn't exist. The autumn air, the tint of orange, and smell of pumpkins and fire fed my soul. I knew the creatures now as I passed their pelts and paws. I loved it being a little fox in their midst. I didn't want it to end.

When I called the Moores to let them know I'd found another place to stay, they were kind and apologetic for the leak in the basement. I was secretly thankful it played out the way it did because this setup was infinitely better than being scared and alone in a basement. From the top of the shop, I had a full view of downtown: the flame lanterns, the nightly trick-or-treaters running past, and of course, that damned creepy church. I'd look through my window at night and find *his* stained-glass attic window and wonder what he was doing. Probably not thinking of me in the slightest. Probably getting what he needed from Cat. I thought that could be why Onyx and Wolf hadn't mentioned him. He'd already moved on.

The thought of him with someone else threatened to strangle me if I dwelled on it. Which was something else that had changed for me in that week. While the nightmares still plagued me, the daydreams were waning. The intrusion of nearly blacking out with dissociating into whatever fantasy world my brain wanted me to imagine had at least subsided momentarily. Maybe it was a step in the right direction, a sign I could grow and heal.

The Moores still insisted on having me over for dinner, which I didn't feel I could refuse. It was a Monday night and I had nothing else to do. The shop was closed on Mondays, and I'd already walked around the town, talking to all the business owners downtown whom I'd met and knew by name now. I'd walked by Lamb's Blood Church and saw Ames's motorcycle out front, and my heart clenched remembering our ride. The way I felt free for the first time in my life on the back of his bike. Why was his bike out? Probably giving *Cat* a ride.

The Moores ate early, at five in the evening. I arrived clutching a bottle of three-dollar white wine and a list of excuses for leaving early.

It's not that I didn't like them or appreciate their kindness; I did. But I hadn't been asked to dinner in my adult life, and having to make small talk with anyone felt like an enormous hurtle. It dawned on me I'd still never met Mrs. Moore. The same damn crow squawked what sounded like a laugh above me. I grinned, thinking it sounded like Raven. My mind tumbled back to his song reference and very specific mention of peanuts. He had to be messing with me, right? Raven couldn't literally be a crow . . . .I glanced up at the black bird ruffling its feathers, perched on the mossy home's gutter. Something about the way it moved . . .

Soft fur caressed my ankles. With a smile, I knelt to pet the orange cat. The door opened and Mr. Moore happily ushered me inside.

And that was where shit got really weird.

I'd never been in the upstairs of the house except for the one dark evening I scurried straight from the basement stairs to their daughter's room. From my soggy apartment, I'd assumed the rest of the old house would resemble the seventies decor. I'd expected some groovy flowers, maybe more shag carpet, some pastel tile. But what greeted me was . . . jarring.

"Welcome," Mr. Moore said. "Again, we're so sorry about the flooding. We're glad to hear you found another place to stay."

My breath caught in my chest as I took in my surroundings. Bookshelves lined the walls where hundreds, maybe thousands, of dolls sat perched, their beady little eyes seemingly staring me down. Dolls in frilly dresses covered the beige loveseat in the living room, they cascaded over the old television set, and they were piled in rusty red wagons near the walls. "Th-thank you for having me for dinner. I see you have quite the collection up here . . . ."

Mr. Moore padded into the kitchen. "Yes, don't mind the girls. They like to jump off the shelves. Sometimes they sing, too." He chuckled as I sat the wine on the round table. At the head of it sat a large doll with white hair, and next to that one, a smaller blonde doll in pigtails. I recognized it from the guest room. It was the same doll. Her glassy eyes and red-lipped smile sent unease trickling down my body.

"Um . . . Where's Mrs. Moore?" I asked, steadying myself into a seat next to the pig-tailed doll. It felt like a thousand eyes were on me. They were only toys, but they had that creepy antique look about them. These weren't the Barbies I played with as a child. These were something you passed in a thrift shop and shuddered, unsure why they unsettled you so. What would possess someone to have a home filled with the creepy little things?

My host sat a plate of steaming pork chops, mashed potatoes, and corn upon my lacy placemat and took a seat across from me. He put a hand over the larger doll's glass hand. "She's right here, dear. See, honey? I told you Miss Blythe needed a home-cooked meal."

Words stuck in my throat as my grip went clammy around my fork. Part of me wanted to laugh, but the earnest look in Mr. Moore's gaze told me he wasn't joking. I couldn't very well run out the door, though I considered it. I'd have to suck it up and get through this weird as hell meal. Despite his . . . collection . . . and belief that the doll was his wife, Mr. Moore had always been kind to me. I'd always known he was eccentric but this—

"It's nice to meet you, Mrs. Moore," I said to the . . . doll.

Taking a bite of pork, my elderly former landlord smiled. "Oh, yes, sorry, dear," he said to the large doll. "And this is our daughter, Ellie May. She's home for a week on a visit."

I nodded, taking a bite of mashed potatoes, willing my face into neutrality. "Nice to meet you, Ellie . . ."

"Ellie talks so softly she's hard to hear. She asked who you've made friends with in town. Maybe she knows them. Ellie's quite the social butterfly."

Is she?

Mr. Moore uncorked the wine and filled each of the four glasses on the table. I stared at my plate, feeling more and more unsettled. So many dolls. Mr. Moore clearly believed these toys at the table were real, and that was tragic. I guessed he didn't have guests over often, or many friends. I didn't want to make him feel judged or mocked, so I tried to pretend that this was all normal. Just a few more bites and I could pretend Yesenia called me back to the shop for emergency inventory . . . or something.

"I've met a few people . . . our age . . ." I said, looking at the smiling doll next to me. I took a gulp of cheap wine. "Of course, Yesenia at Magia, and someone you know, too. Dr. Cove."

"Who?" my host asked, cutting his meat as if this were a perfectly ordinary night.

"Dr. Ames Cove? He says he's a friend of yours. He's lived here his whole life."

"Never heard of him."

What? Either he was misremembering or Ames had lied about knowing my old landlord. Why would he do that? The night he drove me home bounced through my brain. He knew where I lived.

He knew where I lived before I told him. Mr. Moore had to be mistaken about knowing him . . . But despite his odd decorations and dinner companions . . . he'd always seemed of sound mind. Well, except for sweeping the street every morning.

"Well, honey, she left so quick I didn't have time to tell her," he said quietly to . . . Mrs. Moore.

"Excuse me?" Four more bites left.

Mr. Moore shook his head. "Dear, you ruined the surprise. You shouldn't have said anything. He said it was a secret."

I paused my fork in midair.

"W-who?" I trembled. *It couldn't be.*

My host sighed and smiled fondly at the white-haired doll. "Cat's out of the bag. My bride never could hide a thing. You're a jabber-jaw, yes you are." He chuckled.

I wiped my mouth on the cloth napkin with shaking hands. "Tell me?" I urged gently.

"Your dad wanted to surprise you. He's in town for a visit. Don't tell him we spilled the beans, alright?"

My vision went hazy, and the air went thin. "My stepfather called here? You spoke to him?"

"No, no." Mr. Moore leaned back after finishing his food. He took Mrs. Moore's tiny glass hand in his. "He came by yesterday. Seems nice enough, little . . . peculiar, though, isn't he?"

My heartbeat jumped into my throat. "My stepfather . . . was here?" There was no hiding my shaking.

"Dear, the fire's going. It's plenty warm in here. I don't know why she's shivering. Yes, Ellie, I'll ask her. Ellie wants to know if you'd like one of her petticoats to keep warm. I can throw another log on the fire—"

I stood. "Inside *this* house, you're sure he was here, Mr. Moore? It's very important that you tell me exactly what you remember."

He could have died. He could have been killed. Because of me.

"Are you okay, young lady? He was here, saw him with my own eyes. Simon's his name, right? Big ol' fella in overalls. Said he wanted to catch you when you least expected it. Says he's got you a gift you'll love."

Thousands of eyes peered into me behind black glossy glass and blue ribbons. I knocked into the chair, and it fell over. "I'm sorry," I stuttered. "I'm afraid I left the stove on at the shop. I need to—"

A shrill laugh echoed through the room and I stilled. It laughed again as both mine and Mr. Moore's gaze shot to the table. Ellie May . . . the doll . . . cackled a static automatic giggle that sounded part tiny child and part horror.

"Well, I'll be damned." Mr. Moore grinned. "This girl hasn't laughed like that in years. She likes you. Please say you'll come back for a visit?"

I tripped on a wrinkle in the carpet as I nodded. "Yes, sir. Thank you for dinner."

As my hand reached the doorknob, more laughter sounded. Only this time it wasn't just the doll at the table. Hundreds of dolls clattered with automatic and echoey laughter. Mr. Moore chuckled again in glee as I turned the knob and stumbled into the yard.

Above me, a crow squawked. I put my hands on my knees, trying to find air. Where was the air?

Something sharp pricked my scalp.

"What the hell?" I looked up in time to dodge another swoop from the bird. "Oh, you're possessed now too?" I shouted. "Great, just great," I shrieked, running to my car.

Was my stepdad still here? What if he were nearby just watching, waiting, laughing his ass off, sharpening his blade . . .

The engine cranked and I floored it out of the driveway.

I couldn't stay here any longer. This was too far. He'd stopped by. This was real. Someone else saw him. Mr. Moore, strange as he was, was lucky to be alive after that encounter. All my things were at Magia. My heart sank as hot tears fell down my cheeks. Benny the Bat was on my bed. My only constant was a stuffed animal. I choked on a sob, knowing I had to leave him behind along with Yesenia and the guys . . . Ames. I rubbed my face, trying to clear my vision enough to drive. I turned onto the highway, but instead of reaching the freeway, the road curved in a direction I didn't recall. I must have been delirious because the path led me downtown. I stopped, reversed, and went back toward the interstate. Again, the road curved, leading me past the large gray stone sign, "Welcome to Ash Grove."

"What the actual hell?" I breathed.

Reversing again, I turned toward the highway.

As I stalled, my phone buzzed. With clumsy hands, I checked my message. It was a group text between me, Onyx, Wolfgang, and Ames. Through the week we'd had the chat going, Ames had never chimed in. I didn't know why the guys added him.

Taco night at Fenrir. You guys coming? I can pick you up, B! Wolf asked.

Tears fell anew as I tossed my phone onto the dash and sped in the opposite direction of the welcome sign. I'd abandoned almost-friends before. But never one like Wolf. He was my friend. My *real* friend. This time, my sense of direction must have improved slightly because I found myself on a two-lane highway through tall trees and winding roads. I didn't recognize this route, but at least I was getting somewhere, anywhere but Ash Grove.

I felt worse than I had when I'd left home.

Alabama never had my heart. It was full of only pain and loss. My mom was buried there, and memories of my stepfather's rage tainted every corner.

But Ash Grove, with its odd residents and traditions, had felt more like home than anywhere I'd ever been. Agony slid down my cheeks as I sped down the narrow road. The sky grew dark, and a heavy fog enveloped my car. I slowed and flicked on my headlights. It looked like a freak storm was appearing.

The outline of an extremely tall man appeared several yards ahead of my car.

Panic overtook me as I slammed on the brakes, jerking forward, my seatbelt cutting into my collar. Breathing heavy, my engine sputtered. No, no, no. I cranked it again and again.

The fog was so thick now it looked blue. I flicked on my wipers, as if they could do anything against the harsh elements before me. The man. There was a man in the middle of the road. What if it was . . .

I unbuckled. Everything in me screamed at me to lock the doors and cry. But if it were my stepfather . . . I may as well face him head-on. Here and now.

This was it. I slammed my car door and walked forward, unable to see anything.

A figure appeared in front of me in a flash and grabbed my arms. I screamed.

This was the end.

CHAPTER 23

Ames

WHO DID THAT TO YOU?

Did I shift in time? Could she see me shift in the smoke? Her fear was stronger than ever. It was hard not to moan at the feel of it on my tongue. She trembled beneath my grip and her scream instantly hardened my cock.

"Where the fuck are you going?" I growled, letting the smoke dim.

She looked up at me through wet, black lashes. "Ames?"

A quick glance at my knuckles. My human knuckles. "Yes," I answered. *For now.*

A sob belted from her throat as she threw herself into my arms. It was the second time she'd done that. The second time a woman had ever done that with me. You only did that with people you felt safe with. Did she feel safe with me? Even after what happened between us?

"I'm leaving," she said through muffled cried. "I have to."

I stroked her hair and held her tight against my body. "I'm sorry I upset you, Blythe. But please stay. I'll leave you alone forever. You never have to deal with me again."

"It's not you, of course it's not you. It's him."

My fingers wove and tightened through her hair, and my demon acted of his own accord, pulling her head back. The gasp that left her lips tasted like sex as my cock strained against my jeans. "He who?" my demon voice said.

Her eyes widened like she heard the difference too. But she answered, "My stepdad, he's coming for me."

My grip on her hair loosened marginally. "No, Blythe. Onyx called today. The police caught him weeks ago. He's gone, Little Ghost," I lied.

She blinked in confusion. "They must have the wrong guy then, because he was at the Moore's looking for me."

I stilled. "When?"

"Last night," she breathed, dropping her gaze to my lips.

No. It couldn't be. "Blythe, Mr. Moore is old and not . . . all there."

She nodded. "I know . . . but he knew his name, his overalls . . . I know he's here. I feel it."

I noticed darkness swirling around my hands but averted my gaze so as not to draw attention. A month ago, I couldn't access my abilities, but now, I couldn't get them to turn off. Not when it came to her.

"You're not going anywhere."

"Ames, I can't stay. It's too dangerous for everyone involved, including you—"

"I'm going to kill him, Blythe. If that bastard is somehow alive . . . I will end him."

She froze and a chilly breeze snaked between us as I held her close. "You're just saying that," she whispered on a shaky breath.

I dropped my hand to her waist, pushing up under her T-shirt. She gasped as I touched bare skin, tugging the fabric up to her ribs. They'd faded, but the tint of yellow remained.

Anger pulled at my movements as I beheld her perfect, soft stomach. "Who did this to you?"

"What? Oh, I slipped. I'm clumsy," she lied breathlessly. It tasted like milk.

"I'm going to ask one more time. Who. Did. That. To. You?"

She swallowed, hands on my arms. "I saw his truck in New Hope. It was early, before the sun came up. I was on my way to work some shitty diner job. I stopped to shower at a truck stop. When I was done, I saw his red truck parked next to mine. I knew it was his. It had the same scratch on the side I accidentally made with the handlebar of my bike when I was sixteen. Then I heard his boots behind me and his stupid . . . whistle. Like he was calling a dog. I ran and tripped. He grabbed my ankle and dragged me backwards. I saw him then. He looked older. And meaner. So much meaner. I didn't know it was possible to look worse than he had before. The hate that filled his eyes . . . But then a Mack truck honked its horn in the parking lot. I guess I got lucky someone saw. That was about three weeks ago. I got in my car and drove and drove until I ran out of gas here."

"I need you to listen to my words, Blythe." This was it. I knew it. And if she tried to run from me now . . . I knew the demon in me wouldn't let her. She'd be afraid; perhaps she would scream again. *Ah fuck, please scream again . . . .* "I don't exaggerate. I'm going to drain his body of blood while pumping him full of poisons to keep him alive and conscious. I'm going to remove each of his appendages and he's going to feel every slice of my dull blade."

Her eyes widened and the soft nudge of fear pressed my tongue. "I'm starting with his dick. And he will bleed, and he will writhe in pain. And he won't die until I allow it. Until I show him a mercy he doesn't deserve and I decide to usher him to Hell." I laughed. "That's not even the worst part. The worst part for him comes after he dies. That's my job here. But you'll see. This is what I do, Blythe. And I know for a fact that motherfucker has never known a greater fear than meeting me."

Her big brown eyes took me in as we stood in the center of the pavement. My forest. I'd brought her here. She couldn't escape me, and she didn't even know it. But somehow, her fear morphed into something else. Something sweet like honeysuckle. "You've killed people?" What was that sweet emotion so out of place?

"Yes."

"How many?"

"Too many to count."

The honeysuckle taste flooded my mouth. Not fear . . . curiosity, admiration . . . hope. It took me off guard.

And then her next words shook me to my core. Not much surprised me after nearly two hundred years of existence, but this did. Her sweet pink lips moved as her grip firmed on my biceps. "Me too."

"What?" I took her jaw in my hands. "What did you say?"

She sniffled, so innocent. I marveled at the freckles dusting the tops of her cheeks. "I'm a killer too. A murderer."

"Who have you killed, Little Ghost?"

"You're not going to believe me. It's too . . . It doesn't make sense."

"You'd be surprised what I can believe, Blythe."

Her breath hitched as I traced circles with my thumb on the side of her neck. Surely, she was speaking in metaphors. She wasn't a killer. There was nothing dark within my Little Ghost—only light and good and everything I wasn't.

Her eyes searched mine as she held on tighter, like she thought I'd run away. *Never.*

"He charged for me with a broken bottle. We'd just buried my mom. I grabbed the butcher knife from the kitchen just in time. He ran right into me." Her voice shook, and the bitter taste of shame mixed with guilt washed over my mouth. "The blood . . . I didn't know someone could bleed so much. He went white, and the blood pooled on the kitchen tile. Ames . . ." She cried. "I didn't run away immediately. I stayed. I stayed for two days with him dead on the kitchen floor. I had to make sure . . . It doesn't make any sense, but I had to know he was dead, and it took forty-eight hours for me to be certain. The blood turned cold and dark. I forged a suicide note in his messy handwriting, left it on the table . . . and I just . . . left."

My dick swelled in pain and longing. Wanting her. She'd murdered him. I wanted to fuck her and show her how not afraid that made me. But how was he . . . No . . . *Who* was he? Who was in his body still?

"I didn't shed a tear, Ames. God, I'm so evil. But I felt better. I thought I'd leave and never look back. And I did . . . until the letters started coming. At first, I ignored them . . . but then I'd see his truck . . . and him. Him, Ames. I killed him. He was dead but he's chasing me. It doesn't make sense." She searched my stare. "You think I'm crazy and traumatized, I know—"

"I believe you, Blythe."

Fresh tears streamed down her face, and the taste of relief and sadness felt thick between us. "We'll figure this out, I swear to you."

She nodded weakly. She believed me this time, and something warmed inside me. Something warm alongside the raging inferno of hate and wrath I'd rain down on this demon who'd evaded us. This fucker who thought they could pull one over on Ghost. No, The goddamn Halloween Boys would find this thing and fucking shred it. I salivated with bloodlust as I put Blythe in the passenger seat and took over the driver's side. Reversing, I took her back home, with me.

Her home. Our home. Ash Grove.

And this time I wouldn't let either of them down.

This time I would keep them both safe.

This time, I wouldn't fail.

CHAPTER 24

Ames

FORKED TONGUES

> True love is like ghosts, which everyone talks about and few have seen.
>
> *Francois de La Rochefoucauld*

"What about your car?" was the only thing she uttered on the too-quiet drive home.

I raised an eyebrow. "You haven't figured out that we rarely drive?"

"So you and Onyx and Wolf are just . . . lurking around the woods?"

I chuckled. "Something like that, yeah."

When we arrived where the red and blue light filtered in through the stained glass, Blythe picked at her nails as she walked timidly to the window.

"You're quiet," I said, tossing her keys on the counter.

Her back was to me, but I knew she felt apprehension. She sucked in a breath, still not turning around. "You're a serial killer." A statement, not a question.

"I've murdered a lot of people, if that's what you're asking, yes." I took a step closer, catching the smallest glimpse of her fragile features in the colorful window's reflection. "But I won't hurt you."

"I know," she replied quickly. "Have you killed . . . good people?"

That was an important question. If someone could get past the murder part, if their morals were flexible enough for that, it had to be for a good reason. Unfortunately, I didn't have one. What could I tell her? I'm a cursed demon who fucked over the town a couple hundred years ago? That bloodlust and savagery runs through my veins like a living breathing entity? Should I have told her I was the bad guy in all the stories from the Bible, to ancient Greece and Rome, to occult and pagan superstition? There was no religion, no spirituality, no organized thought in this world that saw me as anything other than exactly what I was: evil. If this was happening, and it seemed it must now, she would have to know. Something was inhabiting the man she killed, she knew it, and that wasn't a natural human occurrence. Blythe was a part of my world long before I came along. But I could help her. I could save her. But I'd need to ease her in.

"I have, yes," I replied honestly. "Though not for a very long time." The confession struck in my gut, and I waited for her rejection. When it didn't come, I placed my palm in quiet test on her shoulder. She didn't flinch.

She swallowed, clutching her hands together. "I know it sounds impossible, but he was dead, Ames. And now he's following me. How do you kill a dead man?"

"There are ways," I answered smoothly. "I'll start with slicing his throat," I whispered, dropping my lips to her neck. Her breath hitched as sweet arousal hit my taste buds like honeycomb fresh from the hive. I trailed a knuckle gently down her arm as I pushed up closer to her perfect ass. "The blood gushes from the neck. It can flow down their arms, dying them red. I'll start with that." As her breathing picked up, her head fell back, resting on my chest. I wrapped my other arm around her, trailing it down her stomach, pushing her shirt aside to get another feel of her silky skin. My cock pulsated so hard it hurt, pressed flush to her, wanting to sink inside.

"Ames," she said on a breath. A plea for more, and to stop. I'd only give her one of those. And I didn't plan on stopping unless she begged. Even then . . .

I dipped my fingers beneath the waistline of her jeans, finding the thin fabric underneath. She sucked in a small moan and leaned back into me. I gave her neck another kiss as I allowed my greedy palm to cup her overtop her panties. "Then, while he's bleeding out slowly . . ." I circled her softly. "I'll saw off his dick."

Blythe let out a heavenly moan as I pushed her panties aside, slipping a finger over the wetness awaiting me. "God," she breathed.

"Furthest thing from it, darling," I whispered. "I need to taste you."

Her answering whine was enough. I swooped her into my arms and carried her to my bed. She unbuttoned her jeans, and I peeled them away from her rounded hips. "Take off your shirt," I ordered. I stepped back as she obeyed, her breasts falling like the most faultless church bells. She leaned back on her elbows, breathing ragged, biting at the corner of her lips.

"You're making me nervous just staring at me like that," she said softly. But I couldn't pull my gaze from her.

"I could stare at you for two hundred lifetimes and it wouldn't be enough to take you in." Not just a figure of speech for me. It was true.

Her lips parted beneath rosy cheeks. "We haven't even kissed yet," she answered with a smile.

I dropped to my knees before her, like a dark and desperate prayer from a monster. "We will. I'm saving it for the right moment."

I gripped her hips and pulled her closer to the edge of the bed. She gasped before leaning up on her elbows. Reaching forward, she removed my glasses, which were starting to fog. She brushed the dark curls of my hair aside as I gazed up at her overtop of her stunning pussy. "Your eyes . . . ," she trailed off. I wondered if she was piecing it together yet. I didn't give her time to work it out, to match my blue to the blue behind the paint at Hallows. My mouth found her with a hungry suck. Her moan was a hymn fit for the church I was tasting her in. Her flesh and the dripping between her thighs were an offering upon the altar for her own personal demon.

I pushed a finger inside her tight center and hissed. "Fuck, you're so tight, Little Ghost."

She hummed, writhing beneath my mouth. "I've never done this before," she panted.

I let my lips vibrate against her wetness as a grumble left my throat. "No one's tasted you before?"

"I'm . . . I'm a virgin."

I pulled back as if struck. "You've never been touched?"

"No, I have. I've been with guys, and girls, too. But just . . . messing around. Not . . . this. Or full-on sex."

My cock twitched and my demon raged like a feral animal clawing to be freed. He wanted to fuck her. I wanted to take her like that too. To paint my demon cock red with her virgin blood . . . To feel her tight walls squeeze and milk me for everything my wretched body would give. I wanted to envelope her with my seven-feet-tall form and look at her with my clear vision, my body and senses not muffled by my mortal mask. As a human, I was like a bird with weights on its wings. As a demon . . . I could ravish her the way I desired. "We don't have to do anything you don't want to," I said despite myself. Though I hated that, every urge in my body wanted to chain her down and fuck her for weeks on end. Until she was screaming and raw from pleasure. Oh, those screams . . .

"I want you," she replied, her voice so sweet, so pure. "I want you," she repeated, and I realized she was mirroring what I'd said to her. My stupid words that only half meant sex and half meant . . . more.

"Lie back, Little Ghost," I instructed. I dipped between her thighs again, and this time, there was no pulling me away. Her hips bucked at my face as I inserted a finger again. My other hand curled around her ass, pushing her into me. I lapped at her slit like the ravenous monster I was. Her physical flavor paired with the palatable honey of her arousal as it heightened. I could feel the flavor of her peak as it neared and taste the sweetness of her bliss, surprise, passion, curiosity, all emotions I never got to savor until now. I wanted to shift. My demon wanted a taste so fucking badly. Perhaps I'd indulge in one thing... she wouldn't see. Checking to make sure her eyes were closed, I let him have a bit of what he wanted. I groaned into her wet cunt, knowing what I was about to do was wrong. Since when did I give a shit?

I took her clit between my lips and sucked before nibbling with my teeth. My shifted tongue rolled out then, forked and gripping at her sweet bundle of nerves. She tightened around my finger as her grip pulled at my hair. Breathy whimpers sang along the stone walls of the church attic, an angel's little death song. The honey in my mouth intensified as I pumped in and out, hooking inside her, pressing on that delightful spot along her inner walls. Fuck, she tasted so good on my true, depraved, taste buds. "That's it, darling. Give it to me. Give me what's mine," I growled, hearing a hint of my evil. My full shift was hanging by a thread. Letting out the long, forked tongue wasn't enough. It took every ounce of power within me to keep the full change contained beneath my mortal, paper thin flesh. With sudden need, I removed my fingers and let my tongue snake inside her wanting opening. Pushing in, swirling, searching, and tasting her from within. A moan rumbled in my throat as I explored the inside of her.

She pulled my hair. "Whatever you're doing. . . it feels so good." Her head fell back onto the pillow as her back arched.

Her pleasure exploded into a cascade of sugared wine down the length of my tongue. She cried out, the most solemn and erotic declaration. One I didn't deserve, especially from her, but I'd drink every drop she offered. My mouth didn't stop its hungered swipes until she shoved at my face, breathlessly begging me to stop. I would. This time.

When she came down from her orgasm I crawled into the bed, pulling her close, my fun tongue replaced with my boring one. Her naked body felt like holding a goddess in my arms. I tangled my fingers in her hair, twirling a curl softly. "Stay with me tonight," I ordered softly. It wasn't optional, of course, but it would be easier if I could get her to think she was agreeing. I wasn't even willing to give Blythe the illusion of freedom right now. Not when something not of this world was hunting her. Not when the taste of her arousal was still slick on my lips.

"Okay," she agreed softly.

After a few moments, I got up to light the candles and fetch her water. When I returned, she'd unfortunately dressed in her shirt and panties and sat cross-legged on my bed. She pensively took sips of water as I lounged next to her, my shoulders relaxing at just having her near me. It sure beat sitting under a tree in the cold and bird shit all night. "Tell me about your childhood," she said.

I opened one eye. "Are you the therapist now?"

"Funny. But really, I don't know much about you, and it feels like you know everything about me."

Folding my palms behind my head, I closed my eyes. It wasn't something I thought of often. "I grew up on a farm not too far from here. My father was a hardworking drunk. I never could do anything right around him. My mother was a devout Catholic and dragged me to church every mass, every holiday. It was one of the only places I didn't have to plow with the horses, or reap with our godawful sickle, or feed the cattle, so as a boy up to no good, I liked it. When I got older, I liked it for other reasons. The thought of salvation and higher beings and all that."

"What do you like about that?" she asked, curiosity tanging my tongue.

I shrugged a shoulder. "I guess I always had an interest in the supernatural. I like the Bible's stories."

Even if they were about me burning in hellfire for eternity, some of them were nice.

"Any brothers or sisters?"

"Seven."

"Seven?" she asked in shock.

I smiled. "Seven of each."

"Holy shit. You're one of fifteen kids? Where are they all now?"

My ribs tightened in remembrance. "They all died a long time ago."

"I'm sorry," she whispered as she rubbed at the condensation on the outside of the glass. "I always wished I had siblings. I guess it's good I didn't because my mom could barely care for herself, much less me. But I always thought it would be fun to have someone to go through life with like that." She paused before continuing. "When did you meet Onyx and Wolfgang?"

"We all met as boys. We grew up together, climbing trees, chasing stray cats, all the mischievous things boys do, we did."

"You guys do seem like brothers."

"We are. And we added Judas in there at some point too. You'll meet him soon."

"Thanks for stopping me from leaving," she whispered. "And for accepting me for who I am . . . and what I've done."

I opened my eyes to take in her gentle gaze. "I'm the killer, Blythe, not you. You defended yourself from a monster. I am the monster."

She swallowed. "You really murder people? Like, regularly?"

"As often as I can."

"Why?"

I struggled between telling her too little and too much. "It's a . . . compulsion."

"Did you ever want to kill me?"

I raised an eyebrow, and the corner of my mouth lifted. "Only with pleasure."

She giggled and my heart warmed. "You're well on your way. That was . . . I didn't know it could feel like that."

"High praise if you've been with women. They're hard to outdo."

She shrugged. "I was just a teenager messing around. I've never had anything serious."

As she snuggled up to me in the candlelight, I pulled her to my chest. "How is it you're not more afraid of me?"

"Because I've been upstairs in Mr. Moore's house. Remind me to take you sometime so you'll have nightmares too. It's worse than any costume I've seen at Hallows, and there's some creepy characters there."

I chuckled. "Oh? Who's creepy?"

"This guy with skeleton face paint following me . . ." She sat up on her elbow and peered at me. "Would you happen to know anything about him? They call him Ghost."

I could have admitted it all right then and there, but . . . I didn't like doing anything the way I was supposed to. Where was the fun in that? "He sounds like an absolute prick, but I can take you to Hallows if you want. I don't want you to miss it if you were planning to go."

She nuzzled back into my embrace. "No, I want to just sleep tonight. Is that okay?"

"More than okay."

And she slept. Her pink lips parted slightly as I watched every breath.

All the while I locked in the rage in my chest that somewhere, right then, something hunted her. Something hunted her and it wasn't the goddamn ghoul. It lied to us, either out of its need for chaos or because it knew something. I'd find out. And I'd burn this town to the ground to find the motherfucker who was after Blythe.

I'd done it once before, and I'd do it again.

I'd burn the world for her.

CHAPTER 25

Blythe

HIDE AND SEEK

It was easier to tell a hero from villain when the stakes were only life or death. Everything in between gets harder.

Maggie Stiefvater

A bead of sweat rolled between my breasts, my chest glistening with the joy of dancing my ass off. The band tonight were pirates, and the energy they brought to the crowd was palpable. I found myself pulled into a dance with a group of people wearing deer antlers and black, furry goat masks. Anywhere else, any other time, the scene would have been absurd, but I didn't care. The deer-woman and I twirled, holding hands, until a goat-man cut in and danced with me until I was panting for breath. He didn't speak when I thanked him, but he made a flourishing bow. I vowed to find them again later. I liked them.

Needing a break, and maybe a drink, I wandered away from the concert crowd in search of the willow tree from nights prior. Maybe the witches were nearby with water bottles. I'd spent the last two nights with Ames licking and kissing between my thighs. He hadn't once asked or tried for anything more—no kisses, no removing his pants. I wasn't complaining . . . though I did want more. But I was too afraid to protest. After our last misunderstanding regarding sex, we didn't speak for a week and I almost lost him. I'd learned my lesson. If a man wanted to eat me out every night, I wasn't about to stop him.

But more than that . . . we'd stayed up late every night talking. We swapped stories about our childhoods, our old friends, and places we'd been. His chuckle was something I'd grown addicted to hearing. There was such a sadness in his soulful blue eyes that any time I could make them clear again, it sent butterflies through me.

So . . . he was a serial killer. Somehow it didn't shock me like it should have. It was even a small relief. I'd killed before, and I didn't feel an ounce of guilt over it. Not anymore. Ames had done it more than me, yes, but we were the same. And I didn't buy that he killed innocent people. That couldn't be.

I was a murderer, he was a killer, and somehow . . . it was the most peace I'd ever felt with a man in my life. Somehow, some ripple in the universe put us together.

And somehow that same universe brought my stepfather back to life . . . my stepfather who'd visited the Moores and told them he was coming for me. My dead . . . or undead stepfather.

But I had Ames, and for once, I wasn't alone in dealing with this. Ames hadn't left my side, and I doubted he would. The only time he let me go anywhere without him was to Hallows, which he said was a safe space. I begged him to come, but he'd only said, "See you later." Something pulled at my awareness . . . and maybe my hopes . . . that Ames and Ghost could be one and the same. But then, why wouldn't he have just told me? If I knew his secret, why not be honest about his Hallows identity? Was it really that huge of a deal?

The willow tree sat vacant, however. It was a lovely tree, its trunk massive and vines hanging like a leafy curtain. Maybe I'd sit for a moment and watch the folks who walked by. Parting the vines gently, I made my way to the center of the space, near the trunk. I touched the rough bark lightly. "You really are very pretty," I said with a smile. Why not talk to a tree? I'd just danced with a goat-man.

"You're pretty too," an echoey voice replied, making me jump. I looked to the tree in shock when a low laugh sounded. "It's not the tree."

Something wispy by the trunk caught my eye, and I took a step back. From around the back of the tree, something like a sheer white cloud floated over. It was long and shapeless aside from the faintest outline of a human form.

"Wow, your costume is amazing," I breathed, perplexed. How could I see through it to the vines and grass on the other side? An illusion of some sort? A mirror, maybe? People here took their costumes very seriously, I'd seen it all by now, but this had to be the best one yet. The figure tilted its head, surveying me. "Curious force, you are. How did you get here, I wonder . . . ," he or she mused. Their voice was male and female and three voices at once. A sound machine in their costume, probably. "Who called you in?"

"Oh, I don't know anyone here. I'm just passing through," I answered, grabbing a vine to fidget with while staring at the floating, translucent thing. I wasn't afraid though. Whoever this was didn't seem mean. "Ghost costumes have really come a long way from white sheets and holes cut out for eyes, huh? What's your name?" I asked, knowing they would give me their fest name and not their real one. That was what everyone here did.

The wispy costume swayed before me and hummed. "You know what? It's been so long since someone asked me that . . . I don't recall. But I do believe you should be watchful, Tree Talker. All is not what it seems here."

Something pricked in my gut, a fearful little twinge that agreed. "Do you know the ghost stories of this town?"

The spirit chuckled and brightened, like the glow of the moon. "I do."

"Will you tell me?"

"Has Ghost not shared with you who he is? Curious . . ." It pondered a moment. *What? Were they saying that what I suspected was true?*

"You look more like a ghost than he does," I remarked, eliciting another echoey laugh.

Its glow brightened. "I like you. You may hear the tale if you do something for me. Here, take this." A white arm reached out, one I hadn't seen through the reflecting illusion. It was glowing and slightly too long, the fingers not quite right . . . not quite human . . . I swallowed, reaching out to take the item. My fingers brushed against tendrils of smoke as I plucked the necklace out of the air. "Wear it and you'll always choose the right path. Though, it does put me at a disadvantage if we were to play a game . . . but I don't mind. I have a small advantage on you, being what you are, so now the game is fair."

The necklace sparkled in my palm. A deep and shimmering obsidian stone pendent lay set in golden prongs. "This is too much. I can't accept. And what game—"

The item seemingly moved of its own accord and clasped around my neck. I gasped. "Another illusion?" I asked with a shaky voice. Surely, I just didn't see them put it on me. It was dark under the tree.

The apparition rippled and spoke. "Do you want to play hide and seek?"

The question caught me off guard. I thumbed at the cool pendent on my neck. "Um, sure?"

The echoey laugh of several people, men and women, young and old, brought goosebumps to my arms. "I hear you're good at this game, Tree Talker."

Something moved and caught my attention. When I looked back, the being was gone. "Hey, you didn't say who's turn it is. Am I hiding or seeking?" My voice fell flat beneath the willow. I was alone again. My breath caught in my chest. That was one spooky and high-tech costume, that's for sure. Whoever was on the inside of it was probably laughing their ass off right now at how scared I must have looked. But the necklace . . . It felt heavy and solid. It had to have been some sort of prop or stage jewelry. I needed to get out from the heavy curtain of the tree. Taking a deep breath on the other side, I power walked toward the populated concert area. The band played a Halloween tune now, and people were laughing and clapping along. My mood lifted with every step forward. I looked down at my necklace again before stopping slowly.

The crowd around me had dissipated, and a low fog crept into the space. I took a step backwards and my shoulder blades hit something solid. Turning, I suppressed the urge to scream. The most realistic were-wolf mask I'd ever seen stared back at me from a muscular and tall form. When I looked back, another man was standing next to him. His mask was serpentine and snake-like, yet more. He was a dragon.

And the dragon spoke, addressing me. "Don't fuck with the spirits. They're . . . unpredictable."

"I'm just on my way out," I replied, trembling. Just then, the fog parted and he appeared. *Ghost* stepped up right beside me. Something in me felt fear but also hope that he would protect me from these guys who encircled me.

"Ah, the willow ghost is harmless." Ghost spoke for the first time. "Mostly. Just don't let it talk you into a game," the wolf man purred, smirking. How was a wolf mask smirking and speaking? The other wolves weren't like this one . . . yet there was something familiar about all of their voices.

Everything inside my mind screamed at me with the answer.

I shot him a quick glance. "What happens if I did agree to a game?"

Before he could reply, the dragon spoke. "It's time to do this."

"Do what?" I asked, alarmed. "Wait." I looked around at the several pairs of eyes that stared us down. "Are you The . . . Halloween Boys?"

Ghost simply stepped backwards. "Not yet."

"You're outvoted on this one," the dragon man argued. "If what she said is true, this isn't fun and games anymore."

I turned to see Ghost backing away into the woods. "No," I said, pacing after him. "You're not just going to walk away."

But he did. And by the time I made it to into the foggy, dark forest, I'd lost sight of him. I should have known better than to go chasing my masked stalker into the isolated woods. And a few weeks ago, I never would have dared. I would have run to my car in fear. On this night, I wore a tight black mini dress with fishnets and my lacy black fox mask. If I'd chosen a disguise based on how I arrived in Ash Grove, it would have been a timid rabbit, the opposite from a clever fox. I'd run my whole life. I'd watched my mother destroy herself with men and substances, and I did and said nothing. The night my mother died, I was too much of a coward to even call the police. I walked into the house and my stepfather was drinking a beer with blood on his hands. When I screamed over her lifeless body, he shrugged and lazily dialed the police. A rehearsed dance. Suicide. Like hell it was. But did I tell the cops when they interviewed me? No. I lied. I protected him because I was afraid of him. I stayed because I was afraid of him trying to find me. I thought the Devil I could see was better than the one I couldn't. I'd go to college pretending to believe his story of how my mom died and I'd never look back. I had no other family or friends to rely on. Where would I have even gone?

When he charged for me, the bravest thing I ever did was grab a knife instead of curling up into a ball as he beat and killed me, too. When he bled out on the floor, I didn't feel triumph or a surge of power and bravery. Funny how it didn't erase the fear it just . . . paralyzed it. It was why I stayed and stared at his cold, lifeless body for two days before I split. And because I was so afraid, I'd gaslit myself into questioning those two days over and over. Was he sleeping and pretending? Did I really stay two days, or two hours? I didn't want it to be true. Something so horrific couldn't possibly be real outside of horror films and scary stories.

But something happened. Something against all acts of God and laws of nature. The fucker came back to life . . . somehow. And he'd been chasing me ever since. And like the scared bunny I'd always been, I hopped away into whatever hole I could find until he came sniffing.

And then I came here, and I met Ames and his friends: Yesenia, witches, vampires, pirates and crows, the skeleton man . . . Ghost.

And I'd never felt more alive. I'd found my home amongst monsters.

I was done running. I *was* a fox now.

And now I was chasing the monster who'd been following me at Hallows. Wordlessly creeping behind me, watching, only ever offering a dance.

The stories I'd heard were infamous. They said he was the worst of the worst.

It seemed I attracted his type.

Because I was prey.

But not anymore. Now, I'd be a predator. Whether I felt like it on the inside all the time or not. I'd find my teeth and claws. And it would start with catching Ghost.

The Devil I knew.

The Ghost I knew.

I wove through the trees and fallen branches. With every step, the fog at my feet grew thicker. Anyone would have turned around. Anyone would have listened to their primal instincts pulling them away from the dark. Only the most idiotic ignored that voice. Or the ones like me with nothing more to lose.

With every crunch of dead leaves beneath my shoes, my resolve grew. I had no idea where I was going, but it didn't matter. I'd walk all night until I found him. Something inside me told me to turn right, so I did.

My therapist's, Dr. Omar's, voice played through my mind from our last meeting. She said I had extreme avoidism that roped me into dissociation: the daydreams that assaulted my waking hours and pulled me from any hope of being in the present, and the nightmares that plagued my consciousness, causing dark circles under my eyes. The things and events surrounding me were unbelievable. They defied all laws of nature. Dead men didn't chase girls to strange towns. Strange towns with residents who looked at me like they'd never seen another human before. *We don't get many visitors.*

I'd never seen Ash Grove on a map. It didn't show up on my phone's navigation, only gray roads with no bigger picture to zoom out on. I'd never heard of Hallows Fest or anything like it.

Everyone had a different ghost story. I'd been collecting each one like the pirates said they did. Maybe scattered amongst the variations, the truth would become apparent, only they all only got stranger. But they all agreed on one thing, this group called The Halloween Boys were to blame for each and every scary story here. They'd killed, and brutalized, and burnt it all down two hundred years ago.

And I was following one of them into the woods. Alone . . . somehow.

And somehow, in this place where vampires drank from pirates and crows could talk . . . here I was. I knew it even though I didn't want to. I'd deflected, ignored, and ran. Even inside my own mind, I ran and avoided. I didn't know what Ghost was . . . .

But those blue eyes. That touch . . . that smell. When I brushed his hair back last night, I saw it. I saw exactly where the paint would go. A serial killer, he'd admitted that much. I realized why Ames let me go alone to Hallows—because I wasn't alone. I probably hadn't been alone a day since coming here.

No, I didn't know what Ghost was, but I had an idea of who he was. And I was ready to face it. All of it.

And I was going to do it here and now.

I'd thought this whole time that being a clever fox was my mask. When in reality, the only mask I wore was playing dumb, hiding my smarts, my observations, not willing to act or question. I'd gone back to the library early that morning, before breakfast with the guys, before they could miss me. I told Ames I was picking up some clothes and showering at the shop. I found the newspaper the boys tried to hide from me. The Halloween Boys . . . and a faded sepia photo of Wolfgang Jack, Onyx Hart, and Ames Cove.

Looking as alive and young as they do now.

The rabbit was my mask all along. They wanted to tell me, as evidenced by the conversations I'd overheard at the church and in the car, when they thought I was sleeping. I'd pieced together that Onyx had some sort of hypnotic ability, but he overestimated how long it worked on me, and I used it to my advantage. I just hadn't been brave enough to put the puzzle together until now. I couldn't pretend any more. If my stepfather was somehow a part of the paranormal world . . . others had to be too.

My feet hit gravel and the trees cleared. The fog was blue violet and like a thick and living thing as it pulsed and swirled around me. As it waved and thinned, I made out the towered shape of a wrought iron gate. The tops were sharp spears and the energy that emanated from it was ominous. There was no lock to be seen, but when I shook the gates, they didn't budge. I couldn't exactly climb the massive two-story structure, so I stood at a standstill. I knew he was in there; I could feel it. Where else would he disappear to than a creepy cemetery in the woods?

"I know you're in here," I said just under a shout.

Just then, the gates rumbled and clanked, opening automatically.

I stepped through the threshold, and a howling wind whistled past me as the fog parted like a sea. Hundreds, maybe thousands, of decrepit gravestones jutted from the ground and rolling hills in the distance.

It was the largest and oldest cemetery I'd ever seen.

And then I saw him.

CHAPTER 26
Blythe
A SACRIFICE FIT FOR A MONSTER

He was leaning against a gravestone with his arms crossed in that alluring way of his, obsidian hair brushed back, revealing his skeleton disguise—all under a leather jacket and jeans. The only sort of modern attire I'd seen at Hallows. But I guessed a Halloween Boy could do whatever he wanted.

I'd be lying if I said a twinge of trepidation didn't shudder through me at the sight of him in such a grim setting. This place was far from the hallowed orange jack-o'-lanterns and rubber bats. There weren't wires holding balloons under sheets or bowls full of chocolates. The frigid breeze that brushed past my cheek and the blue fog were real . . . as real as the monster staring me down in a graveyard. Like a spider, confident in knowing I was stuck in his web, he didn't have to move. There was nowhere I could run, and certainly no one to hear me scream all the way out here.

Gathering my strength, I leveled my breathing and stopped several yards in front of him. "When are you going to stop following me?" The fog swirled around my ankles with disconcerting precision.

He took a step forward, face revealing nothing under the black and white paint. "When are you going to stop running?" There was the deep and graveled voice I'd expected.

I gasped as the blue mist snaked up my body, skimming my thighs and swirling around my throat. It was only air, but somehow I could feel it. The denier inside me, the avoidant, dissociative bunny, wanted to say it was all a trick . . . but I knew better. "I'm not running."

The corner of his mouth lifted as he took another step. I inched back, bumping into a mossy gravestone. My breath hitched as he reached out a painted hand. His knuckle met my cheek, softly grazing my jaw. "You will be, Little Ghost."

"You're the Ghost. The leader of The Halloween Boys."

"What else?" he asked, letting his gaze wander down my neck, to the cleavage above my dress's neckline.

I felt a rush of blood to my core as I answered, "A killer."

"More," he coaxed, stepping closer, his body only inches from mine. "You know there's more to me, don't you?"

I couldn't hide the heaving of my chest from anticipation, longing, and a bite of fear. What if this had been an elaborate game for him? What if I really was a fly lured into a trap? "You're some sort of monster. Are you a vampire?"

A dark chuckle escaped his throat as the soft graze of his hand skimmed my neck. "Unfortunately, you didn't get so lucky. I'm something much worse. But I like this game . . . ." His touch dropped to the top of my exposed breasts.

"Tell me, Ames," I breathed, feeling my knees weaken.

His mouth curved again as hunger lurked behind his blue stare. He leaned forward, breath hot on my ear, and whispered, "You're standing on me."

Confusion muddled in my mind as I looked down at the dead grass. And then I realized. Turning around, I looked closer at the dark gray and crumbling headstone. My mouth went dry as I read the inscription. "James William Cove, born November twelfth, seventeen ninety-four . . . died October thirty-first eighteen twenty-three. How?" I managed, feeling his presence against my back. I turned, searching his deep eyes.

"Who I was died with the rest of the town that day. But who I am now . . . I'm the stuff of nightmares, Blythe. The reason they say not to go into the woods alone, why people are afraid of the dark . . ." Blue fog suddenly turned black as night as it wrapped around my thighs and curved up my waist. I gasped, this time feeling the give, like an arm.

"Demon," I murmured, feeling my voice leave me.

He took another step forward, letting me feel his heat but also putting the choice in my lap of how close I wanted to get. "Even that would be better in this case. No, Blythe, I'm an Archdemon. The worst of the worst and more powerful than any god you've ever heard of in your religions."

"How? I'm standing on your grave. You had fourteen brothers and sisters on a farm, plowing with horses and sickles?" The black weaved through my hair now, as the Archdemon angled his head.

"My friends and I pissed off the Devil, and it cost us our souls. But the stories about him are true. Even his curse came with stipulations . . . appetites and oaths."

"Did you really slaughter the whole town?"

His jaw tensed as the black took hold of my wrists. I felt it then, its strength, his strength. The force could have shattered my bones in an instant. But instead, it pulled me back against his gravestone. I gasped and pulled against it, but it was useless. I wasn't getting out unless he let me. His lip twitched. "Your fear is so sweet. I can't think with you scared like this." He took another step, this time pushing himself flush to me. I could feel the bulge in his jeans press into my stomach. My core heated with wetness for him. I didn't know what it said about me that I was pinned to a dead man's grave and getting wet for a Archdemon, but I couldn't resist his pull, even without the ropes of dark. "What if I did? Would you still chase after me, Little Fox?"

"I like Little Ghost better, and yes, I would." The words tumbled out effortlessly.

His gruff chuckle trilled through my bones, and the tension on my wrists relaxed, though they remained like translucent chains. "You're more depraved than I gave you credit for." His lips hovered over mine. "I like it."

I couldn't help myself then, and I wrapped my arms around his neck as he leaned forward. I pressed my forehead to his.

"You'll never have to chase me." His deep timbre shook through me. "I will haunt you for the rest of your days and then some, Little Ghost."

"Kiss me," I answered.

His lips crashed into mine without a moment's hesitation. A small moan escaped my throat as his lips parted mine and his tongue slipped in. When it found mine, I gasped at the taste. It was like amber honeycomb. I wanted to ask if that was normal for an Archdemon, but then his hands were hitching my thighs around him. With easy effort, he picked me up and placed me on the top of his headstone. I pulled at the collar of his jacket, needing him closer, wrapping my legs around his hips. He growled in my ear before his lips found mine again, taking in my kiss hungrily.

His palms enveloped my breasts, fingers hooking into the fabric and pulling it down. The stretchy material gave, and my bare breasts poured over the edge. His mouth left mine, taking a nipple between his teeth and sucking. My head tilted back as I sighed in pleasure. After he moved to the other nipple, my hips were all but thrusting forward, begging for him. I pulled at his belt, unhooking it as his rough jaw scraped against my cleavage. My hard nipples pricked, dampened against the cold night air. He stood, tugging off his belt and surveying me. Ghost looked like evil incarnate, gazing at me behind his frightening skull paint. I removed my mask, the lace wet with perspiration against my face. "Are you sure you want your first time to be with a monster?" he asked, his belt dropping with a clatter to the ground.

"Yes," I breathed, watching as he unzipped his pants. "I want you."

He made a deep, guttural sound of appreciation as he kicked off his jeans. Pulling down the waist band of his boxers, his dick sprang free. My lips parted as I took in his considerable length. He was so well endowed, I wondered how it would fit if even his finger felt tight inside me.

"Your fear tastes like honey, Little Ghost." He cupped my jaw with both hands and planted a kiss on my lips. "You're so beautiful this entire wretched and screaming pit of a cemetery silences for you."

I slipped my hand between us to palm him. A hiss escaped his throat as I moved my cold hand slowly from base to tip. Suddenly, he pushed my dress up and over my waist. I lifted my arms and let him peel it off, leaving me sitting on a gravestone, his gravestone, in only fishnets and heels. A rough growl sounded from his throat as he pushed forward, lining my slit with his length. My breath was coming out in puffs of cold when I felt it. His arms were wrapped around me, yet something hooked into the holes of my tights, ripping them right at my core. I gasped, my voice a shrill and little thing. "The fog is you?"

"Smoke from Hell's flames," he purred. "And yes, it's me. Are you ready, Little Ghost?"

The smoke flicked lightly against my bare pussy, feeling buzzy and firm. I hissed in a small breath as I grabbed his cock and lined the tip with my opening. He sucked in a breath. "Ready for me to fuck you on my grave?"

"Yes," I whispered. "Please, Ames, *Ghost*, please."

Taking the back of my neck with one hand, his other hitched under my knee, then I felt another force catch under my other knee. *Smoke from hell*, darkness. His rounded tip eased in, stretching me into a burning circle of ecstasy. My forehead fell forward onto his chest, and I flinched as he pushed in farther. "Do you want me to stop," he hissed, his voice a shade darker than it was before.

"No, don't stop. Don't hold back," I begged. "Just like on your bike." I smiled against his shoulder, pulling back to look at his black shrouded eyes. "I can take it."

"Fuck," he groaned. With a single, massive thrust, he filled me.

And I screamed.

A woman screaming in a cemetery.

A wall of smoke pushed against my back, holding me up, as his palms dropped to the top of the grave I was seated on. I leaned back, the smoke like a taut sheet of silk. Ghost stilled, letting me adjust to his girth while his mouth found my neck. He pulled out only halfway and looked down. "Your blood looks good on my cock."

I ached at his words. He began moving in and out, filling me to the hilt and then retreating at a slow and agonizing blissful pace. I moaned as he slammed into me. Then a wisp of air found my clit, circling and pulling softly, mirroring everything his tongue was doing the night prior. The pleasure was too much to bear. My scream echoed through the graveyard as sparkles fluttered along my vision. When I came down to Earth, Ames was still inside me but frozen still. His face was down and resting on my shoulder. His breathing was rough and ragged. I nudged my hips forward and gasped as a harsh rope of smoke banded around each of my wrists, tying me back to the gravestone. "Ames?" I whispered, fighting against their hold and searching for his downcast face.

My thighs began to tremble as his breathing grew rougher. Suddenly, his shoulder blades . . . expanded. He grew wider and began to lift from the ground, lengthening. He stayed hunched over, his cock still buried in me. I began to squirm, panic pricking at my senses. I felt the grave-stone rumble beneath me, and when I looked over, massive black hands with protruding white bones were digging into the rock, causing it to crumble like dust in its grip. His clothing ripped and fell like rags, leaving stretched obsidian muscle striped with white bone. I felt his breath, long and hot at my bare chest, though I feared looking down. His hair was gone, and only the outline of the monster remained. And then he looked up. Pale-blue eyes sat on a wide face of darkness and bone, matching the rest of him. He looked like the demons from old Renaissance paintings, only stronger and fiercer. A scream pushed from my throat. His hand shot for my face, wrapping around my mouth. "Don't. Scream. I like it . . . too . . . much." He growled, wincing. Then I felt it. The stretch. My eyes grew wide, and his mouth quirked.

"Ames?" I said, muffled by his massive hand.

A dark, unholy voice responded, "There's no Ames here. This is your Archdemon, Little Ghost. And that's Hell's cock inside you." He growled, his voice different now, deeper, more sinister. The stretch continued and burned as his length expanded and filled me. Against his warning, I screamed. I couldn't help it. The terror and torment and divine feeling of it all was otherworldly. Despite the fear, and pain, my pussy tingled and pulsated. My head dipped back. Something long and wet trailed from between my breasts, up to my neck. When I looked up,

I gasped as I watched his long black forked tongue tasting my skin. It swirled over my exposed breasts, flicking and exploring. I would have been terrified if I weren't so turned on. He was staring at me with those eyes so blue they were almost white. Retreating an inch, he said, "I can't pretend that fucking a pure and gentle virgin doesn't turn me on. I'm damning you with my demon cock, Little Ghost. Keep screaming for me."

I tilted my head back in a breathy whimper, attempting to gather myself. Ames had begun having sex with me but transformed into a demon fucking me. A terrifying and huge thing, stretching me, pulling me. Wetness pooled and dripped down my ass. I cupped his face, searching those haunting eyes. He moved, then, with a thrust that sent chills through me and pushed another moan from my lips. "Oh, my god," I cried, looking down and seeing the massive appendage impaling my center. I had no idea how it was fitting, and all of it wasn't, but some was. Somehow it felt better than anything I'd ever experienced.

He growled deep with an ancient and knowing tone. "No gods, I devoured them all. Only me, fucking my virgin on my grave. Watching you take my demon fucking monster cock."

I cried out again, screaming in pleasure, pain, fear, and ecstasy as he plunged forward, the sound of my wetness proof of how turned on I was by this new form. "You're mine now, do you hear me? Fucking mine. Forever."

"Yes," I agreed, feeling another orgasm build. "Forever."

He pushed in to the hilt, or as far as he could possibly fit, and I gasped, still bound by his smoke. I wanted to reach around him, feel the bones that sat along the dark muscle. "I Claim you, Blythe Pearl." A strong wind whistled past, throwing my hair forward and then back. "I Claim you," he repeated, pushing in. Again and again, he said it, thrusting in and out. Then the tendril of smoke flicked steady at my clit again and I broke.

"What does that mean—" A shrill scream tore through me as my pleasure erupted under his massive, evil form. My Archdemon picked up the pace, thrusting harder and faster. My pussy could hardly take it.

He went so deep, stretched me so far. And then he growled, groaning like a roar through the forest. Warmth filled me as he shoved in farther, emptying himself inside me. The smoke released my wrists but caught me by my back so I didn't fall. He gently pulled out, staring down at my thighs. When he stood, he was at least seven, maybe eight, feet tall and a massive, frightening thing. "What is it?" I asked breathlessly.

When I looked down, I saw it. Black smudged all over my pussy and dripped down my thighs. Him. His wet and dark release.

Then his fists balled at his sides as I slipped off the defiled stone and stood, gaping up at him. He shut his eyes and ground his teeth. "You need to go."

"What?" Shock rippled through me. "Why—"

"Walk away calmly, Blythe. You don't know what I've done. You don't know what it means."

"I won't leave you," I breathed, panic pressing in on my chest.

A growl rumbled through his throat. "If you don't calmly walk away, I will fuck you again, harder. And I won't be able to stop. I will fuck you so hard, so many times, you'll be raw and begging me to end it. I will cover you with my demon seed until you're drenched in me, head to toe."

I swallowed, already feeling the soreness aching between my legs. "That was me being gentle," he warned. Though I still wanted more.

He tilted his head back. "That can't possibly turn you on."

"How do you know that?"

He turned his back to me, and a wave of blue smoke pressed my dress to my chest. Gently, it turned me around, pushing me toward the open gate. "I don't want to leave you, please," I begged. "Don't make me. Not now."

He made a vibrating sound in his throat as the smoke pushed me farther. "This is your last chance to get away, Blythe. To leave. I will find you, of course. I will have you again. But if you want a chance to leave, to take a break, you best take it now. Because I am a thin thread away from losing control."

"You said I wouldn't have to chase you," I breathed. "Don't leave me."

Suddenly, the smoke shoved me forward and I fell into a pile of leaves. The gates cranked and groaned as they slammed shut. I sat up in a flurry, still naked, in only ripped fishnets and heels. A growl echoed through the forest, shaking my bones. Then I saw the size of him, the full mass of how huge he was as he stalked toward the gate. Another growl rattled the wood. And now I was afraid. I grabbed my dress that was wrapped around one ankle and stood on shaking knees, fear and adrenaline propelling me forward. Without looking back, I broke into a run, grabbing onto trees and stumbling over branches and stones. Another roar shook through the woods. Darkness surrounded me, and when I looked back, a sea of blue smoke glided slowly toward me— searching. What if he told me to go because he'd hurt me now? I couldn't believe it to be true, but then again, this form, this . . . demon . . . was something I never could have imagined, not in my worst nightmares. None of the church stories or scary tales could have prepared me for the terror of what he looked like. What his terrible roar sounded like. I couldn't imagine that anything existed in this world, or others, more fearsome than him.

And he was Ames.

Somewhere in there, it was him.

And I still wanted him. And Ghost

I wanted them both.

CHAPTER 27

Ghost

RADIO SILENCE

> On the other hand, what I like my music to do to me is awaken the ghosts inside of me. Not the demons, you understand, but the ghosts.
> *David Bowie*

My bones, my blood, everything in me burned with fire for her. I needed her. Needed to seat myself deep inside her and stay. Fuck, what had I done?

Claimed.

Claimed.

Claimed.

I fucking Claimed her.

I shifted without thinking, cock inside her, without being able to stop it. I lost control and my demon took over. My true self with no restraint and only instinct enveloped every sense, and there was only her. Only Blythe taking my monster cock so good. I watched those perfect pink lips of her pussy take me as I slide in and out, sending my demon seed deep into her, spilling out of her like pure evil, and staining her milky-white skin black with me. Her red blood still coated my length. *Mine.* My Claimed.

I would have kept fucking her. I wouldn't have stopped. She was a virgin, my virgin. My fucking virgin taken atop my grave like some sort of demonic ritual. Well, if it wasn't, it should be, because goddamn . . .

Making her leave while I shifted back to mortal was for her own good. My smoke went with her, watching her, protecting her. She'd never be away from me. Ever.

But Claiming had sent electricity through my veins that I couldn't diffuse. I needed her. Needed her again. I tasted her fear from here. Her scream was what sent me . . .

I rattled against the bars of Hell's Gate. "*Open,*" I ground out with the voice of many.

You can't harm her, the gate whispered.

"Yeah, no shit, I'd never hurt her. And why do you fucking care?" I spat as the gates shook and creaked slowly open. "Fucking batshit crazy hunk of metal."

The forest stilled as I stepped out. I fucking loved being in this form. My height, my strength, my full power was finally fully restored. Though my dick was already hard and throbbing for her again. I smelled her sex. Felt her slick dew still wet against me. I growled again, low in my throat, as I drifted through the forest. My smoke had found her. Blue smoke from Hell's sacred flames floated under my Claimed, padding her step, protecting her from thorns and scrapes. I involuntarily shifted balls deep inside her. The power that thrummed through my body was stronger than ever before. Maybe Claiming had done that, or maybe Wolf was right and I just needed to get laid. Whatever the case, when I stepped outside the gate, all I wanted was her. A monster chasing its prey.

I was on the verge of tearing through the forest to find her. I'd bind her against a tree, ass up, and fuck her from behind until she'd screamed through so many orgasms the branches shook. But the stench of filth flooded my mouth . . . and I knew someone was near.

"There you are," I threatened. "Step out, coward. You know I've been looking for you."

It floated out with erratic movements, a dark, shapeless thing. Something the mortals would call an evil spirit, and they'd be wrong. There were no spirits inside the damned. The damned were once the most foul of humans. The ones who hurt women and children, who loved suffering and caused destruction to everyone in their wake. I'd put many of them in this graveyard myself. Though this particular one, I didn't remember. The damned lost their autonomy, for the most part, when I stole their disgusting souls. No name, no recognizable body, only pain, torment, and every ounce of fear and suffering they'd inflicted on others cast back to them for all eternity. They would find no rest, no peace with me. "Tell me how you got out," I demanded, feeling its fear mingled with defiance ripple from its darkness.

If it had a head, it cocked it to the side and looked up at me before a muddle of voices took over. They were radio signals. Random waves the damned could grab at like flies and string together. With no voice, it was the best they could do. A loophole in their curse. One I would have closed myself when I realized it, but I'd found that getting an answer out of them was necessary sometimes, like now, so I let the loophole remain. Static buzzed in the air as I heard a dial switch. "*We—*" a sports announcer said. "*Only want!*" A salesman. "*Her—*" A woman's sultry voice.

I snorted, crossing my arms and giving the gate a kick. *Don't kick me, asshole,* the gate rumbled as she opened.

The damned was speaking nonsense. And what would rattle an Archdemon? Next to nothing. But the words . . . *Her. Mine.*

"Yes, I noticed you all got awfully quiet when she came into the graveyard. I'll be sure to bind your every fucking sense next time so you can't even feel her presence. It's more than any of you fucking deserve."

"She is—" a woman's voice said, followed by static. "Not yours—" A child's gleeful tone. Static.

I'd had enough. My darkness shot out in a flash of night, faster, stronger than even when I'd caught the ghoul. The damned let out a screech like a train slamming on its brakes. My smoke burned and sliced and confined, wrapping around it until it was enclosed in my dark orb of energy.

Just then, a testy voice trotted forward on four paws. "I'll take it from here and let you get back to your date."

"Did you enjoying watching, Cat? I always knew you were a little freak."

She bared her teeth as she batted the large orb into the graveyard like an unholy beach ball. "I left to give you privacy. Though if you're into someone watching, I'm sure those friends of yours would be happy to. Word on the street is they like her too."

Cat was always a gossip, knowing everything, hearing everything, talking to everyone and every being. But she liked to stir trouble, too, and say things to get a rise. I ignored her, not allowing the jealousy to spike behind my ribs.

"Put this one in the deepest, farthest spot and make sure it stays there. I want an example made. This is what happens when you think you can escape my Hell."

"Yeah, yeah," she replied with a swish of her trail, prancing into the graveyard as if she were doing nothing but chasing a ball of yarn.

"No respect, I swear to the Devil," I muttered. "You know, familiars are supposed to worship their masters."

"Oh, I guess I didn't read the handbook, or I just don't give a shit," Cat replied just as the gate slammed shut.

Amusement replaced the spot where annoyance would typically be as I made my way through the woods. I could sense her, feel her with my smoke and darkness, her tender steps, the soft padding of the palm that was wrapped around my cock just moments ago. Now that was done, I could hunt down my Little Ghost and fuck her senseless on the forest floor.

Suddenly, static invaded my senses, high-pitched and drawling like a microphone off its wire. I stopped, tension crawling into my muscles as rage pressed down on my chest like a weight. This wasn't like the damned. This was worse. I sensed it then. The demon. It was knowledgeable enough to know how to fuck with my abilities as my smoke thinned under the screech of energy. For some reason, he'd chosen to wear her stepfather's skin, feasting on the fear it offered him. I felt them both: the skin, the demon.

I lost feeling and taste of her.

It was in the woods.

CHAPTER 28

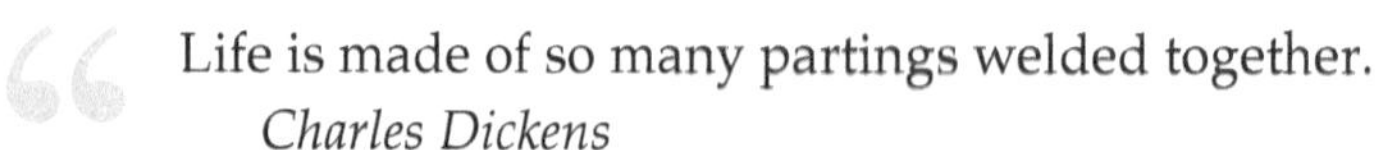

WILLOW'S GIFT

> Life is made of so many partings welded together.
> *Charles Dickens*

Every inch of my flesh shuddered in hyperawareness. Remnants of where he touched, the feel of his hands, the caress of his smoke . . . the way I stretched to take him in. Ghost was terrifying. Not the short, frail, and gangly depiction of a demon like I saw in church or in movies, he was monstrous in height and strength. Yet he was careful with me. He told me to leave to protect me from having more of him too soon . . . but he was wrong about what I could manage. Now he'd created a monster, and I felt insatiable with need. I was already aching for him to be inside me again. I wanted a better look at him, at his full form. I tugged on my dress, feeling the frigid night cling to me without his veracious warmth on top of me. I dipped a curious finger between where my thighs touched, feeling them slippery as I walked. Ebony coated my fingers. His cum was . . . unique.

I'd just lost my virginity to a demon.

My poor Catholic mother would be horrified.

And I wanted more. I wondered if his cum tasted like honey, the same as his kiss. Was he stalking me now? The thought sent a jolt of thrill through me. I wasn't sure where I was going as I wove through brush, but finally, the space cleared into an area I'd never seen before. A stone bridge arched over a wide, shallow stream. It was then I noticed the blue-violet fog that had been accompanying me had thinned to near invisible. Did that mean he was near? My pulse quickened, and I considered waiting naked on the bridge for him . . . but instead, I chose to hide. Sliding ungracefully down the muddy bank, I carefully tiptoed across wet stones covered in rushing water. The sound of breaking branches reached my ears. Leaves crunched under something heavy, stalking slowly toward me. My heart jumped in my chest. Would he take me here, under the bridge?

A *demon*. A demon who'd killed his town . . .

And if he were truly this otherworldly thing, if demons existed, then were the others at Hallows Fest . . .

A flash of white light blinded me. I fell back, bracing myself against the curved, slimy underside of the bridge. A youthful giggle of multiple voices emanated from the translucent being. "You found me," the willow spirit said. "You're good at this game. Though I did give you a necklace that guided you to the place you needed to be."

"Shh," I answered, putting a finger to my lips. "Wait," I whispered softly. "You're really a spirit, aren't you?"

The ribbon-like edges of the spirit fluttered on an invisible breeze. "I never said I wasn't. Now to figure out what you are . . ." It angled its head before straightening. "Something draws near."

I swallowed, my excitement rising. "You should go," I urged. "I'm okay."

The spirit floated backwards, it's opal sheen glistening in the bright light of the moon. The heavy footsteps hit stone now, and I held my breath. "Evil searches for you, Tree Talker. It needs you."

Ghost. "I know, but I'm safe—"

A rough voice clutched my whisper in my throat. "I can smell you, whore."

My stepfather. His voice, somehow. How did he find me all the way out here? My blood ran cold as I looked to the willow spirit in panic. Wide, deep-set eyes surveyed me curiously. A delicate finger pressed to my lips, nodding as it sought my understanding. I nodded, too shocked to move. Its tone softened, as if he decided on a different approach. "You shouldn't be hard to find . . ." The words were strained, as if speaking were a struggle. "Needed to tell you, your mother's alive. We want you to come home so we can be a family again. She says she loves you, BB."

My chest squeezed. My mother's nickname for me. How could he know that? The spirit shook its head. I knew it was a lie. Whoever, whatever, this was wanted me to come out of my foxhole. Why it didn't come down here and get me . . . I couldn't be sure.

Stomps sounded on the bridge, stopping right above me before seeming to turn and walk back the way it came. The willow spirit took my hand in its long, delicate grip, urging me out the opposite side. I followed its lead and tried to quietly climb the bank, my heels sinking into the mud. I could only hope that darkness and shadow covered me enough to escape. The fog had evaporated.

Where was Ghost?

I cast a nervous glance over my shoulder as the spirit nudged me wordlessly to the woods. I saw nothing, and a small glimmer of relief bloomed in my belly.

But then I stopped in my tracks. There he was. On wobbly knees, he swayed, one hand bracing himself on a tree. I swallowed, panic freezing me in place. "You look worse than when I last saw you on the kitchen floor," I said, shocking myself with the strength and challenge in my words. I had no fight against him, no advantage but to stall for time and hope my Archdemon chased after me.

A raspy chuckle gurgled from his throat. "You, Blythe Pearl, are indeed a ruthless little human."

He wobbled forward, and I noticed his eyes were black and unfocused, searching, like someone who'd lost their glasses. I could run.

Without a second thought, I kicked off my heel, a rock clattering beneath me. Something like an invisible grip seized me and I froze, paralyzed. "Got you. There we go. Master will be most pleased."

The force pressed in like a boa constrictor, pulling the air from my lungs. A terror-filled scream lodged in my throat, and tears pricked my eyes. I felt my bones crushing inward as breaths were harder to grab hold of. "But he won't notice if I have a little fun with you first. You smell like you've already been had by another of my kind, haven't you? You Devil-fucking slut." His tone turned deeper and magnified, something I didn't recognize and didn't belong to my dead stepfather.

This was how I'd die.

I should feel at peace with that. I'd gotten everything I'd wanted to find before death: a dance with a stranger, a festival where no one judged me, friends to joke with, and a town that took me in as its own. And a man . . . or something like a man . . . to give myself to.

It was what I had been searching for when I came here, shaking and afraid. But now . . . it wasn't enough to have and leave behind. I wanted it now. I wanted more of it, of *living*.

I couldn't go out like this. Not now. Not when life and other worlds just opened up before me. "No," I pushed out, shoving with all my feeble, human might against the indiscernible pressure caving me in. My vision started to go blurry, and I knew I was moments from a rib cracking.

A crow cawed.

And then a flash of white light rendered me sightless. I fell to the ground with a thud as white enveloped me. "Run, Tree Talker. It's your turn to hide; I'll seek."

The willow spirit had grown into a veil of vast white light as bright as sunshine. I looked to the body of my stepfather to see his face contort . . . and then drop to the ground.

And then the most terrifying sight.

One at a time, then a dozen, and then four dozen more, shoots of black screamed as they wrenched out of his lifeless body like a geyser, one after the other. A sharp and dreadful voice of a hundred screamed. Then a shoot coiled and struck like a snake. The willow spirit hissed a soft and tender sigh. "Go, little one," it urged.

Hot tears burned my eyes. "No," I pleaded, helpless to aid in what I was seeing. Another strike tore through the translucent white. And another. And then twenty more. It screamed like a clear bell being struck as I lay debilitated.

Black flashed before me as wings surrounded me. "We must go, now," the bird said.

Sniffling tears, my ears ringing with the willow spirit's agonizing cries, I pulled myself up, struggling into a run. To watch something so pure, so beautiful and innocent, be pierced and tortured . . . all because of me . . . The crow flapped its wings before me, flying at my height, leading me out of the forest. The hissing and screams faded in the background, along with the melodic rings of the spirit's last screams.

And then they stopped.

I sobbed into the night air, keeping my eyes on my bird until my feet hit familiar gravel.

Suddenly the bird jerked upwards, and I didn't see the man in front of me until it was too late. I crashed into a hard chest, trembling and soaked in mud and sweat. "Blythe, what the fuck?" Onyx's hands gripped my face frantically. A surge of clarity and calm poured over me like a waterfall and my tears stopped; my fear vanished. "Did someone hurt you—" He stopped and breathed in deeply, looking down at my black stained thighs. "He didn't. Ghost, that bastard. I'm going to kill him."

"No." I spoke up way too calmly. "My stepfather's body is filled with . . . There's so many of them. They're after me. You need to run, Onyx." What if they got here and did to him what they did to the willow spirit?

Onyx's dark brows furrowed, and his emerald-green eyes began to glow. The middle of his irises slitted like a snake. I would have screamed if it wasn't for the disconcerting calm I felt, so unmatched for my circumstance. "Get behind me," he ordered, pushing himself between me and the tree line.

"We need to run," I said softly. I may have been calm, but I sorted through the pieces in my head. Safety, we had to find shelter somewhere . . .

Onyx shot me a cocky glance over his shoulder. "I never run."

An eerie calm fell upon the lot as footsteps sounded. The figure of my stepfather limped into view. He looked so weak and decrepit, but now I knew better what lurked beneath the surface of the dead man's body.

Onyx didn't make my mistake, however, in underestimating this . . . thing. Turning his palms forward, a burst of green light lit up the lot. Green fire flicked from his hands and glowed like orbs. I felt their heat from standing behind him. The struggling voice of my stepfather gave a raspy laugh. "Half breeds always have nice tricks," it seethed.

"I always heard that lesser demons liked chasing smaller humans because they are weak. But this is ridiculous. Look at you," Onyx bit out a chuckle. "So much effort for one mortal?"

Limping forward, it snarled. "We have come to retrieve the girl. Hand her over and there will be less trouble for you."

I startled as an emerald flame encircled us. "What if I like trouble?" Onyx purred.

The face of Simon Glen looked up at an unnatural angle, as if he were being puppeteered. The sight made me shudder. His head lolled forward, eyes wide. Onyx laughed. "That's right; he's here. The Archdemon you've tried so hard to evade. And oh, smell that? He's fucking pissed."

A roar, a screech, an unholy and terrifying, blood-curdling sound shook through the lot as trees bent and broke in its wake. The rocks underfoot shook as the Archdemon, my Archdemon, stepped out from the darkness. The graying human body shook violently as Ghost walked through the flames, his stare fixed to me. He stopped and twisted a long finger through my hair, and I noticed the tight line of his sharp jaw loosen slightly. And then his smoke enveloped me, the world going silent.

"No!" I banged my fist against it. When nothing budged, I pressed my ear to the wispy wall of blue and violet, straining to hear. I could make out voices, and I could see blurry images. The dark shoots sprang from the body like before, dancing and zigzagging outside the flames. Only now there were hundreds.

"You will obey your Archdemon, legion." Ghost spoke with ferocity and rage.

They answered in unison, "We answer to one above you. You are to yield or reap the consequences."

Ghost stated with lethal calm, "I will send you back to your master with each of your heads on spears for coming near my Claimed."

A roar of hissing responded, "It is not yours to Claim."

"Like hell she isn't," Onyx replied, surprising me.

The blurry figure struck then. Onyx barely flicked his wrist, and the lesser demon went ablaze in green, writhing and falling to the ground. "Next?" he asked casually.

A dozen shot forward at Ghost then, and I screamed. Tendrils of smoke broke free in my enclosure, some caressing my cheek, one holding my hand. It was so tender, so sweet, that he was battling like a ruthless creature all while making a point to somehow hold my hand and comfort me through the barrier he'd captured me in.

But the demons fell like dead gnats as they made contact with him, like they were nothing. Forty more charged Onyx then, and I was blinded by green light. Another group surged at Ghost, whose smoke rose from the ground, enveloping and ripping heads off slender bodies. But every time one group died, three took its place. "It's a hydra-legion!" Ghost shouted to Onyx.

"Motherfucker," Onyx swore, flashes of green all I could see behind the cloud. Then suddenly, something broke through my barrier. I screamed as the enormous maw of a wolf towered over me. It was the size of a horse, at least. At the sight of my terror, its face instantly softened into that of a friendly canine, and it nudged a nose at my wrist.

Just then, a flurry of black, flapping feathers appeared. "Get on his back, now!" the bird shouted. I had no time to question why or how this bird was speaking, or the absurdity of gripping onto rough fur and climbing up a shadowy wolf-like-creature. But after fucking a demon, nothing seemed that weird anymore.

The moment I was positioned, the beast took off in a lightning flash. The screams behind me vanished. Within minutes, we were outside town, miles and miles from the grounds of Hallows. The bird reappeared, and I pieced together it was something of a translator between the beast and me. "Tell him to go back and help," I ordered the crow.

His beak shot to the dark wolf who only stared at me, as if deciding. "Go, please help them. Please," I begged.

Its snout jerked a nod before it cast a pointed glance at the crow, who squawked in answer. And then the wolf was gone, kicking up dust and disappearing.

Leaving us alone along on the outskirts of town.

CHAPTER 29

Blythe

MARK OF THE BEAST

You have witchcraft in your lips.
William Shakespeare

When I turned, I jumped in surprise. "Raven," I breathed.

"Yes," he answered, standing in human . . . well, humanish form, like I'd seen him at Hallows all those nights.

"All this time, you were my bird stalker?"

He cawed a weak laugh. "I tried to tell you, but you didn't have the ears to hear."

"Well, thanks for saving my ass." I stumbled forward, and he steadied me with his long winged arm.

His beak looked to me in concern. "I'm your familiar, Blythe. I'll always *save your ass* to the best of my ability. Now come, let's get you someplace safe."

I didn't know what that meant, my brain spinning with fear and adrenaline. "Someone should help them . . ."

"Who? The legion?"

"Not the time for jokes."

He squawked as we padded down a grassy knoll. "I'm not joking.

The Halloween Boys have faced worse. Though perhaps . . . not so many at once."

Worry constricted my heart just like the force the legion put on me earlier. And then my mind went to the willow spirit in sorrow. "The spirit of the willow. They sacrificed themself for me." My throat went raw. Raven's warm, feathered arm wrapped around my shoulder and pulled me close to his chest as we walked. "I know. It is an honor for us to . . . do that. They went happily."

The words dragged behind me like chains in the grass. How could that be true? Such a tender and light soul . . . was ripped apart by something so dark and dirty. All they wanted was a game of hide and seek. And now they were gone with a gruesome and unwarranted death. Something I brought here. It was my fault. All of this was my fault. And I'd been too blind, too afraid, too ignorant and avoidant to even want to try to help fix it until now.

"You can speak when you're in bird-form?" I asked, the words sounding odd as they fumbled out. So much had transpired so quickly.

He understood, reaching out a wing to help me down a steep step. "If needed, but I prefer not to."

We traveled in silence, finally reaching pavement and the illusion of security that civilization brought. The clock tower in the center of town displayed four-thirty in the morning. "The sun will be up soon, and they'll have to stop. Demons like the legions can't survive in light."

My heart gripped again in remembrance of the spirit's bright light. The light that saved my life.

We paused in the town square. Raven's gaze, and beak that followed, darted from left to right. "What is it?" I asked, wrapping my arms around myself against the cold.

"The Archdemon would have me take you to his church. He has the authority there and you would be safe. However—" He looked to the left. "—the crone is on equal standing as the Archdemon, and the witches are heavily warded against all manner of things."

"You mean my apartment? Magia Eclectics? There. I want to go there."

Raven looked me up and down, still pondering. "My obligation is to you and no other. Ghost will be cross, but you will be safe, if not safer there than Lamb's Blood."

"It's settled." I marched past him to Magia. As I approached the front door of the faintly purple glowing shop, Raven cawed. I startled as talons landed and gripped onto my shoulder. "Oh, so this is a thing now?" I asked rhetorically. "I just want to take a shower and go to bed. This night has been too fucking weird."

The usual *wa ha ha* greeted me as I flipped on the lights . . . and the room remained enveloped in dark. All at once, crystal balls began lighting from within. Some swirled purple, others white, or navy. A woman in a cloak walked forward, carrying a dripping candle. Three others stood behind her, also cloaked and holding candles. The old woman removed her cloak, letting her aged and feminine features dance in the flicker of candlelight and the soft glow of the orbs.

"Come with us, child," Marcelene ordered, ushering me forward.

I glanced up at Raven, who seemed nonplused, and followed. A woman lagged behind, putting a soft hand on my back. I met her gaze briefly under her flame. Yesenia. We walked upstairs to my room, and the women eyed me in the lamp light. There was Marcelene, another older woman, Yesenia, and the witch I recognized from Hallows, the one who read my aura. Or, my lack thereof.

"Did you offer yourself willingly to the Archdemon, child?" Marcelene asked abruptly.

"Abuela!" Yesenia said in shock, arm still around me.

Marcelene's mouth straightened into a straight line as she eyed my knees, up to my muddy and black-covered thighs. I felt naked and exposed under their scrutiny and suddenly wondered if I would have been better off in the foreboding attic of Lamb's Blood Church, waiting for Ames to return.

I swallowed, steadying my tired frame. I didn't contend with my stepfather's body containing a legion of demons just to be cowering under some old woman's judgmental gaze. "I did," I replied. "And I'd do it again. Yes, I know who he is and what's he's done, and no, I don't care. If that bothers you, I can go elsewhere. If not, I'd really like to shower and go to sleep."

The elder witch's mouth dropped, while the witch who read my aura lifted a hand to her mouth to conceal her grin.

Yesenia's abuela huffed, shaking her long, curly white and gray hair. "You have no idea what you've done. What you've agreed to. He will never stop now. You will never be free of him so long as your soul roams this Earth. He will always find you."

I felt Raven's talons prick at my shoulder in show of support. "I'm used to being chased by monsters. I can handle it."

Marcelene let out an exasperated sigh and puffed out her dripping taper candle. "Get some rest. We'll speak in the morning. There is much to discuss."

The women turned to leave. Yesenia pulled me in for a hug. "Blythe, I'm so glad you're okay. When we sensed the legion, it was already upon you and—"

"Yesenia," Marcelene snapped. "We have hours of spell work ahead of us. The wards need strengthening."

My friend gave a small smile and squeezed my arm. "Anything you need's in the closet. I'll see you in a few hours."

I stopped her, pulling at her long purple robe. "Will you tell him . . . that I'm safe if he comes looking?"

The beautiful witch chuckled and softly ran a finger down Raven's puffed chest. "Oh, he'll come looking, alright. But yes, we'll let him know."

It was the most I could hope for. I didn't want to go to the church alone, even with all the promises that it was a safe place. It was big and cold and creepy. I wanted to be here in the warmth and coziness, even with the older woman's disapproving tone. I wearily padded to the supply closet, fitted with bottles of water, fluffy white towels, body wash, a toothbrush and . . . Raven hopped off my shoulder onto the shelf and bent down. "A dead frog, really?" I said in disgust.

The bird cackled in the same way he did as a humanoid before scooping it into his beak. "This is a magic cabinet, isn't it? They're real witches, aren't they?"

Raven chucked back the limp amphibian and swallowed it whole. I almost gagged on the bottle of water I was downing in desperate gulps.

"My brain's had enough paranormal for the day. I'm taking a shower," I said, grabbing the shower supplies.

WHEN I EMERGED from the steam, scrubbed clean of the black between my upper thighs and the mud and blood from my knees, I pulled on a big T-shirt and walked to the window. The town was silent. Nothing to be seen but the flickering orange of jack-o'-lanterns and the rustling of the tops of decorative bundles of straw. My heart gripped, wanting to see him, wanting to know he was okay. It was insanity, what I'd been through. But it was also a strange sort of relief. I wasn't crazy. This wasn't a dissociative episode. I'd killed my stepfather and something took over his body. The same brand of something that had my core aching sore with need. Exhaustion pulled at my eyes as I fell into bed. I pulled open my eyelids long enough to see Raven perch on the windowpane. The gruesome, empty faces of the legions peppered my fading thoughts, along with the smoke my Archdemon flicked at my center . . . and then sleep pulled me under.

CHAPTER 30
Ghost

PLEASURE SUCKING

October was always the least dependable of months … full of ghosts and shadows.
Joy Fielding

The fury roiling through me was a tangible, seething darkness. Its tendrils of sacred smoke sought and slaughtered. Dragon and I had killed fifty each before realizing the legion was a hydra. The fucker was regenerating twofold for every single kill. That was a mistake on their part, because it only made my anger and blood-lust intensify.

"What the actual fuck is a hydra-fucking-legion of demons doing chasing down our girl?"

"*My* girl," I corrected, trapping a group of seventy demons squealing like pigs inside my cocoon of night. I'd made a nice entrapment for Blythe, but for these fuckers, they got the full package. The smoke would debilitate them, seeping poison into their every pore and shutting their wretched bodies down from the inside out. The hydra's cells wouldn't see it as a killing, but as a dying off, and the bastards wouldn't regenerate like the cockroaches they were.

A hundred now targeted Dragon, who stood surrounded in his green hellfire. "Need some help?" I yelled as I swatted away a dozen demons as if they were nothing but flies. They fell, sizzling and shrieking under my smoke. "I'm getting bored over here."

Dragon chuckled. "Ghost gets his balls back for a night and thinks he's better than me. Funny, dude." Hundreds fled me and flocked to him—exactly what he wanted. Taking a deep inhale, green radiated and swirled around him, blinding and hot. Then he dropped his protective ring of fire, and everything went dark. The legion cried out in victory as they struck.

A dark shadowed beast appeared next to me as I crossed my arms, watching the show. Into the air, like a firework from Hell, shot a massive, glowing, scaled outline of pure flame. Demons tried to flee but it was too late. The dragon spun and roared, its incinerating breath burning the hundreds so thoroughly that when a new hydra demon popped up to take its fallen counterpart's place, it crackled in death before its miserable life even began.

"Show off," Wolf muttered.

I snorted a laugh.

Wolf's yellow gaze shot to mine. "You're in a good mood for someone who's territory was just attacked by a fucking army."

I shrugged. "You know I needed some kills. These are basically gifts."

Wolf huffed and pawed at the ground. "You and I are going to talk. But first, I need to bite some fucking demon scum." He shot forward, circling Onyx. "You're not even going to shift? Pussy."

"You're dying to fight me in full dragon mode, aren't you, little guy?"

"Little guy?" Wolf charged, taking the neck of a screeching black shadow and pressing his venomous maw together, paralyzing it. "Shift and let's see how little I am."

Dragon seared through another wild and erratic pocket of filth. "That's your problem, Wolf. You and your kind are all brawn and teeth and no style."

"Yeah well—"

Onyx cried out in pain. A roar of fire bloomed and exploded around him, like an atomic bomb. The hydra assholes jeered as if they'd accomplished something grand. Wolf and I rushed to our friend's side as he lay on the singed gravel, clutching his arm. In a breath, my darkness located the lesser demon who'd landed the blow. I rippled pain through his insignificant form slowly, agonizingly. He screamed and writhed on the ground as I knelt by Onyx. "I got him," I said to the werewolf. He howled, long and eerie. I'd learned over the years that even the length of the werewolves' howls conveyed information to the pack, though I never knew what they were saying. Finally realizing their numbers were dissipating and dawn was approaching, demons bounced through the trees, aiming for their escape. They'd hide in trees and caves until night, when they'd grab hikers, stray pets, and burn campsites. These legion's strength was in their collective consciousness. Separated, they weren't much stronger, or smarter, than the average ghoul. For millennia, lesser demons like this were wielded by stronger forces. Archdemons, Devils, whatever other darknesses lay beyond that, too. Legions were foot soldiers of something greater. Something that didn't want to get its hands dirty. I pressed a palm over Dragon's shoulder to stop the bleeding. "I'm fine. Don't let the pack see me like this, goddamn."

"Bleeding out and still concerned with what a group of wolves thinks about you?" I asked, swirling my darkness over the jagged wound, using my poison to draw out the demon bile. Dragon hissed in pain.

"He's always been a vain motherfucker," Wolf remarked before lunging at an escapee, shaking it ferociously until it halted its futile struggle. Then everything grew silent. Wolf relaxed and trotted over, shadow trailing behind him. "They're toast now. Let's head home. We have *much* to discuss."

I rolled my eyes. "Sure, Mom."

Onyx groaned as he sat up. "That reminds me, I'm going to fucking kill you, Ghost. What happened to, *no one touch her. She deserves better. I'm not claiming her?*"

Wolfgang growled low in his massive, furry throat.

I looked to them both, incredulous, as I shifted back to human form. "Not my problem if you expected a demon to tell the truth."

Their answering snarls sent a chuckle through me as I stalked to the abandoned pickup truck beneath a nearby tree. Wolf had stashes all around town for when he'd shift and need clothing after changing back. We went through a lot of jeans. I tugged on a pair that were a little too loose and shrugged on a black hoodie. Wolf joined me and silently did the same, sans shirt.

"If you two weren't so eager to swing your shifter dicks around every time a baby demon popped up, you wouldn't be left with your bare asses out in the woods," Onyx grumbled. He looked to the sky, clutching his shoulder. I wondered if he missed his home, his parents, whoever they might be. Onyx was born an immortal and not made, like I was. His power was a deep and untapped well, along with his mind.

"That'll take a few hours to shake off," I said. "I got most the poison out, but those gashes are a bitch, even on an immortal."

"Could heal faster if you'd offer me a quick bite. What do ya say, pup?"

Wolf bared his teeth. Standing at full human height, he was still bigger than both Onyx and me. He tied his long hair back in a low ponytail. "All brawn, huh? What was that you were saying before you got your ass kicked by a baby demon?"

"Can you two cut the shit," I interrupted. "We need to debrief and figure out what in the hell is going on. Give him what he needs, Wolfgang."

With an exasperated sigh, Wolf walked over to a smug-looking Onyx, who'd paled slightly from the venom, making him look more vampiric than ever. "Neck, please, sweetie."

Wolf bent down slightly as Onyx took hold of his broad shoulders. "Make it quick, no pleasure sucking."

"But pleasure sucking's all I know," he jeered before moving at lightning-fast, predatory speed. His fangs sank into the werewolf's neck, who grunted upon impact.

Gulping down mouthful after mouthful of blood, as if chugging a beer, he detached after a minute's drink. Wiping his mouth with the back of his hand, he offered Wolf a small smirk. "Thanks, man."

Wolf ran a hand through his hair. "Fuck that horny vampire shit." His arousal was evident through his loose gray sweatpants.

"I'd take care of that," Onyx purred. "But you said no pleasure sucking."

Wolfgang adjusted his cock and huffed, stalking into the forest toward town. "Come on, assholes."

<hr>

As we hit the town square like it was our own fucking living room, which, it might as well have been after two hundred years, I paused. I couldn't sense Blythe unless my smoke was directly on her or I tasted her emotions. Which fucking annoyed the shit out of me. I could sense every being in this town, where they were, who they were with, except for her. Just another byproduct of my abilities being on the fritz. Thankfully, they were back in full, an even stronger force now. So, the fact I still couldn't sense her was irritating to say the least. But from the square, I should have been able to taste her. "Blythe isn't at Lamb's Blood. Is she at Fenrir with the wolves?" I asked.

Wolfgang and Onyx shot each other worried looks. Wolfgang rubbed his neck, massaging his two new puncture wounds. "Look, man, we were in the midst of battle. I knew she needed to get to safety, but also knew I needed to get back to help you dumbasses."

"Where is she?" I growled, near shaking. Claimed. *My* Claimed.

"I ordered her familiar to take her to safety. I assumed he'd choose Lamb's Blood, but if he didn't take her to the church, it means there was somewhere safer."

"Blythe doesn't have a familiar. She's not a goddamn witch or demon. Do you hear yourself? What if it was a morphing demon in disguise?" Panic rose in my ribs.

Wolfgang sighed, leaning his bare back against the white birch I'd slept on all week last week. "She *does* have a familiar. I didn't have time to stop and question the situation, but my werewolf instincts confirmed it. I know good animals from bad, and she's got just about the best familiar she could have. It's Raven. You know him."

"Raven? The weird-ass bird humanoid?" Onyx chuckled. "The tree-house lunatics?"

"They're good birds," Wolfgang replied lowly. "And ravens don't familiar-bond with just anyone unless they're a powerful . . ."

"She's *not* a goddamn witch. I would have sensed it. Any of us would have."

Onyx's jaw tightened and he shoved his hands in his pockets. "What *have* we sensed about her?"

Silence stretched amongst us. Nothing. We'd sensed nothing. Which wasn't normal. "It could be because she's my Claimed. That's why malevolent forces are fucking with her. It's to get to me."

"Even before she came to town?" Wolfgang asked, raising an eyebrow.

"It's possible. Now, where is she?"

"Where do you think?" His gaze flicked across the way.

My heart dropped. "You've got to be fucking kidding me."

"I know you hate the crone, but you can't deny Blythe is safe with them," Wolfgang replied softly, looking at the ground. Steam emitted from his high body temp, making it look like he was radiating smoke.

"The Raven's probably working for Marcelene, did you think of that? You put my Claimed in the hands of a fucking bird and it took her right where it wanted her. Back to them," I pointed out, frustrated, incensed.

Onyx put a hand on my shoulder. "Technically, he put her in the *wings* of a bird. Or talons?"

The look I shot him was pure warning. He stepped back. "You want to punch me? Go ahead, man. I want to rail on you, too, if I'm honest. You fucking Claimed her? You fucking piece of shit demon."

I crossed my arms. "Yeah, I'm sure I derailed both of your plans to get at her. Sorry about that. But I changed my mind. I Claimed her. So how about acting like real friends, true brothers, and being happy for me that I've Claimed someone after two hundred years, instead of acting like spoiled fucking kids."

Onyx and Wolfgang exchanged bitter glances. Wolf spoke. "She's mortal, Ames. Do you realize what you've condemned her to? This isn't just about what Onyx and I might be . . . feeling for her."

I looked to her window, only seeing the faintest outline of a raven. At least he was standing watch. Good for nothing, witches' ass-kissing fowl. When I pulled my stare away, my friends were looking toward her window too. I sighed.

We arrived in the church attic in silence and went about our tried, after-battle routines. Onyx showered first, Wolf fried up bacon and eggs, and I downed half a bottle of bourbon. As much as I wanted to slam my demon fists into the crone's wards, make them shake, make them scream . . . I knew my friend was right. She was safe. And if she did indeed have a familiar . . . If this wasn't some trick from the witches meant to fuck with me . . . I didn't know what to think of that. At the very least, she was getting rest. And she sure as fuck wouldn't be getting that if she were here. She'd be getting dicked down until she passed out from pleasure. And then I'd fuck her while she slept.

Onyx yelled from the shower, and it echoed through the stone walls. "Stop thinking with your cock, Ghost. Your drive is so high right now it's getting *me* hard."

Wolf raised an eyebrow at me, shirtless, over a frying pan of half a dozen eggs.

"We haven't done that in years, and we don't have time," I replied. Besides, my cock was stuck on Blythe at the moment. Probably forever. Though something in me stirred, pondering the thought.

After showers, *cold* showers, and several breakfasts and bottles of liquor, we huddled around the torn leather sofa and high-piled rug of my living room. We didn't have to eat, or drink, or sleep to survive, but it offered strength. What was the point of having an indestructible immortal form if our human bodies were scrawny? Wolf took a seat on the floor, while Onyx and I took to the sofa. "Obviously, a hydra legion doesn't just possess dead men and chase little girls across state lines," Wolfgang began. "Judas texted this morning. He's on his way."

Onyx snorted. "Fucking Devil, like he gives a fuck."

"We can't count on him to bail our asses out. I take it the wolves took care of the remaining legion?" I asked Wolf.

He grabbed a half-empty bottle and knocked back a swig of amber alcohol. "Yeah, they're dead. Except for the one they interrogated and got only nonsense from."

"What kind of nonsense?" I asked.

Wolf shook his head and glanced out the stained-glass window. "They're fixated on Blythe. They need her; their master needs her. They chanted it over and over."

I gripped the arm of the couch so hard it groaned beneath me.

Onyx crossed him arms. "But why? Do demons skillfully choose targets, or do they just catch a scent and get . . . fixated?"

"Could be either. Some of us are more chaotic than others." Then my exchange with the ghoul popped into my mind. "The ghoul said similar things. I ignored it at the time, thinking he was just fucking with us, but he said something about his master wanting her."

"Whoever this motherfucker is, he's putting in a lot of effort to get at a regular human girl."

"Unless she isn't a regular human girl," Onyx mused.

Irritation burned in my throat. "It doesn't matter what she is or isn't. What matters is finding out who this is because he'll send more next time, and they'll be smarter, faster. I left her in the woods on her own. I was being reckless. Anything could have happened. We keep underestimating this shit. We can stand against anything. She can't."

"So we watch her. One of us stays with her at all times," Wolf said. "I'll double my wolves' patrols. Maybe you can talk to the vampires?"

Onyx snorted. "Right, yeah, I'll just walk up the Vince and ask him to help a half breed who won't join their coven. That'll go over well. Plus, they never get involved in fights that aren't theirs. You know that. But . . . there's another coven that could help. Who's shown interest in assisting."

"No," I answered.

Wolf leveled a stare at me and turned on the game system. "Either they do their own shit and we have no clue what they're up to, or you humble yourself for once in your life and ask Marcelene for help."

A groan left my throat. "She hates me."

"Then you know she has good judgment." Onyx elbowed me in the ribs and took the controller off the coffee table.

I knew they were right as our serious talk died down into race cars and pixels on the screen.

I'd do anything for Blythe.

Even ask for help from *her*.

The crone I'd killed.

CHAPTER 31

Blythe

AREN'T HUMAN GIRLS SUPPOSED TO PICK THE VAMPIRE?

 By the pricking of my thumbs, something wicked this way comes.
William Shakespeare

My phone buzzed on the nightstand, pulling me from sleep. Sunlight filtered into the room, casting a long dark shadow of Raven, who was asleep on the windowpane. Ravens slept fully upright, huh.

I sat up, stifling my groan. My entire body ached. I grabbed my phone and my heart pulsed in my chest. *Come out, come out, Little Ghost. I miss you.*

Ames. *Ghost.*

Pulling the sheets up to my chin, I felt the ache between my thighs. I had graveyard sex with a demon last night.

And then was chased by, like, a hundred of them.

I saw a big wolf.

Onyx has . . . fire.

My bird friend is an actual bird sleeping on my window.

And I was pretty sure the shop owner was a real-life witch.

Yet the only thing I wanted to think about was how I lost my virginity. And wanted to do it again.

My thumbs tapped out a reply. *Was last night real or a dream?*

I double texted. *Are you all okay?*

The gray dots on my screen bounced as his response appeared. *It was as real as you want it to be. And we are fine. How are you?*

I answered honestly. *Sore.*

I can fix that . . . if you come here.

Blood rushed to my center, reminding me I was wet already. My demon was beckoning me. It should have terrified me. Any other girl in the horror movie would be beside herself with fear. As someone who'd lived most of her life in fear, it was shocking I wasn't more afraid. But I'd always been drawn to dark things, from my personal style to arts and interests. And I'd just learned it was all real. Not only real, but handsomely terrifying and powerful. But he was also Ames. Just James Cove somewhere deep inside him. Maybe he was a killer, and maybe the huge demon of night-twisted muscle was who he was, but he was more too. And I wanted to unravel all the pieces of him.

If whatever entity that was pursuing me let me, that is.

The witches want to talk to me, I replied.

His dots appeared and disappeared before he finally sent: *Ditch them. Crotchety old bats.*

I like bats.

I'll make you a bouquet of them.

His dark response made me smile, and I hugged my Benny Bat plush to my heart and typed: *I'll find you this afternoon . . . Ghost.*

His message was instant. *And I'll be waiting all day, Little Ghost.*

A clatter across the room made me jump. Visions jumped into my mind of the ghastly, strained faces of the demons . . . my stepfather's gray body being puppeteered by something or someone. I shivered, glancing over at a still dozing Raven. Pulling myself out of bed, I hissed at my aching legs—and other areas. I hobbled over to the source of the clatter and opened the supply closet door. A basket of blueberry muffins, a decanter of what looked like iced coffee, a plate of sausages, and a bottle of pain reliever capsules sat neatly on the shelf. I pushed on the back of the closet door and looked inside. No trap door or opening to be found . . . In fact, the closet was detached from the wall and ceiling. "Magic muffins," I said to myself, scooping the loot into my arms. It thumped onto the small breakfast table, jolting Raven awake. He stretched his wings and squawked. Grabbing dishes from the sink, I filled a bowl of water, put a muffin on a plate, and sat it on the space across from me. "Breakfast?"

Raven cocked his head and with two big flaps of feathers, he perched on the edge of the table and pecked at his food. "You know, I kind of like having you around. The dead frogs are a little weird, and you know, the fact that you can turn into a dude-like-person sometimes. But you're nice company."

The black bird looked up at me with big shimmering eyes. He dipped his beak and nudged the bottle of pills closer until they spilled over. I groaned, "Yeah, these are necessary today. Service here is pretty good, huh?" I joked.

A knock on the door sounded, and before I could slowly pull myself to a stand, Yesenia whooshed in, her long yellow skirt billowing behind her like a cloud. She sat at the breakfast table and grabbed a muffin. "*Girl*," she said, taking a bite.

I lowered myself with a hiss into the wooden chair. "Good morning," I replied.

"The crones are beside themselves," she started. "Tell me everything."

A laugh strained from my throat. "*Me* tell *you* everything? How about you tell me some stuff first."

Her eyebrows rose and she leaned back, crossing her legs. Raven still sat perched on the end of the table between us, looking at us both before pecking at his pastry. "What do you want to know?"

"You're all witches, right? Like, real witches. Not just dress up?"

She giggled. "Yes, of course we are. What gave it away, the Magia Eclectics shop, the crystal balls, or the coven in the woods?"

"Well, when you put it like that," I teased, scooping up Raven's crumbs and brushing them onto my plate. "Is everything I've been seeing at Hallows . . . real?"

"Sure is," she said simply. "Except, I think Ezmerelda uses autotune. No one's voice sounds that perfect live."

I shook my head and tossed back a pain reliever with a sip of iced coffee. "Vampires, the deer and wolves, spirits . . . pirates, all real?"

"Yes. And demons, but I think you've figured that out already. I think you've really explored that topic."

My mouth twitched in a grin. "I suspected, you know. But it's all just so unreal. This shit doesn't happen in real life, you know?"

She shrugged. "It does in Ash Grove."

"Does everyone here know about it?"

Yesenia tightened the yellow ribbon holding up half her thick, curly hair. "That's a little more complicated. Now, it's my turn to ask questions. Girl, a whole host of hot immortals at your disposal, and you go and pick the deadliest of the bunch? I mean, I like a bad boy as much as the next girl, but an Archdemon might be taking it a step too far. Aren't you girls supposed to love vampires? Isn't that a thing with normal human girls?"

"Are you not mortal?"

She sighed. "I'm not immortal, per say, but I will live a very long time. So will my husband and kids, thanks to my magic. But even when I die, I won't be gone."

I opened my mouth to ask more questions, but she shushed me. "You need to understand something before my abuela and the other crones talk to you. The older witches . . . they feel differently about things than us younger ones. They hold to a lot of old ways and traditions we've moved on from. My abuela means well, and she truly will help you, but you've just got to be patient with her . . . temperament. Her and Ghost . . . they go way back. Seriously, you couldn't have picked a worse dude."

"Thanks," I muttered. "Is he really that bad?"

Yesenia poured herself a glass of iced coffee. "Bad? Yes, he is. Will he hurt you? No, I don't think he will. The younger witches and I see The Halloween Boys differently than the crones. I think there's more to the story than the crones are willing to share. But don't tell them I told you that. I actually didn't even figure out Ghost was Ames until that talk you and I had last week. Anyway—" She took a bite of muffin and gave Raven a stroke down his chest. "Abuela and the crones are waiting for you. I'm not allowed to go. You're going to have to do all this weird shit, but trust me, just do it. You'll all get some answers, and we might find a way to keep you safer from, you know, leagues of dark forces and all that."

I held my head in my hands. "What is my life right now?"

She giggled and squeezed my arm as she stood. "Get used to it, babe. You're one of us now."

Raven cocked his head at me as I got ready, sprawling my makeup on the table. "What makeup look goes best with being interrogated by witches before a date with an Archdemon?" With a caw that was maybe a laugh, the bird hopped into its water bowl and began splashing. "A cat eye and a bold lip? That's what I was thinking too." Once my face was put together and I slipped on a green plaid skirt with a black cut-off shirt and boots, I fastened on my dark necklace from the willow spirit. I thumbed at the jewel, swallowing back guilt. Raven hopped onto my shoulder, and I grinned at us in the mirror. I may not be a witch, but I looked the part. "Stevie Nicks would be proud," I said to my feathered accessory.

When I arrived downstairs, an old woman I hadn't met before simply took me by the arm. "Your familiar must stay here." I glanced at Raven, who bristled his feathers. "He needs to stretch his wings. You may fly in and out. There are no wards against you, friend."

Raven nodded, seemingly satisfied, and hopped off my shoulder and onto the front desk of Magia. I cast him a worried look as the woman tugged my arm. I'd already grown attached to the guy.

The crone wordlessly walked me to the back of the shop and down two flights of stairs. "I had no idea this building had a basement," I remarked, only slightly unsettled by the dim candlelight and eerie quiet. The bottom of the stairs was a stone cave-like floor, glistening with ripples of turquoise. In the center was a pool of water the size of a large jacuzzi. The woman gestured toward the water and draped a towel on the railing of the stairs. "You want me to get in?" I asked.

The woman spoke then, pointing a veiny finger toward the water. "A ritual bath in moon water will cleanse you for what we need to do. Soak for thirty minutes and join us down the corridor." She gestured to a hallway on the left.

I nodded, and she walked carefully past the pool, down the way I was to go after half an hour. After tying my long hair up in a messy bun, I undressed and carefully stepped into the pool. The water was surprisingly warm, and it glowed as if lit on its own. As odd as the situation was, it wasn't unpleasant. I leaned back, letting my head rest on the rock, because hell if I was going to let magic moon water mess up my liquid liner.

With a sigh, I let my legs float and my toes poke above the surface.

Suddenly, my mind flashed crimson.

I was in a lot I recognized. It was the one I parked in for Hallows Fest. The place we'd encountered my stepfather's body and the . . . puppeteers the night before. Only now, it glowed orange, and the burnt smell of ash invaded my senses. I tried to kick in the water, thrash, wake myself up, but I couldn't escape. A bird cawed, and Raven, as a humanoid, appeared by my side. Crackles and hisses of embers flicked around us as I surveyed the forest. What was once lush and thriving, now stood decayed by char. The scene was shocking and disturbingly real. I could feel the brush of heat along my cheek. "What happened here?" I looked to my long-beaked friend, who stated simply, "You did."

But it wasn't panic that consumed me, or fear, it was something hotter. *Rage.*

With a gasp, I felt smooth water around me as I kicked and came back to myself. My hair and face were dry, so I hadn't gone under. Panting, I pulled myself out and wrapped a towel around me. Once I'd shakily pulled on my clothes, I padded toward the hallway, where a figure startled me. Another old woman stood, cloaked in purple. "It's been two hours. I came to find you."

Two hours?

"I'm sorry. I think I fell asleep." I nervously released my hair from its bun, letting it fall in soft waves.

The crone clicked her tongue, eyeing me skeptically. "Come." I followed her down a torch-lit path to a large room that was considerably more comfortable. Dried flowers and herbs swayed as they dangled from the ceiling, and hundreds of jars lined old wooden tables. "An apothecary?" I asked.

The crone dipped her head. "Sit."

I did as I was told and took a seat across from her. Between us, a rickety table moaned as she placed her boney elbows atop it. With a flick of her wrist, four items appeared before us. "Just pick the one you like the most. Don't give it too much thought."

A shallow breath landed in my chest as I looked at the objects: the head of a red rose, a purple hyacinth, white daisy, and yellow daffodil. I pointed to the mauve hyacinth. The old woman waved a hand and the objects changed, shuffling like a deck of cards before my eyes. My stomach twisted at such an obvious display of power. I pointed quicker, this time to a bat wing amongst a rabbit's foot, fish head, and pink feather. Another wave of her bony hand over the objects and they shuffled. This time my fingers grazed the item from head to tip, the dry feel of snakeskin beneath my touch. I hardly noticed the monarch butterfly model, something like a small animal pelt, and white tooth arranged next to it. At my touch, the snakeskin hummed and puckered before smoothing to its long, three-foot length. When I pulled away from my sudden fascination with the dark gray skin, I met the crone's hazel gaze. "It moved on its own?" I asked, wondering why the snakeskin animated while the others didn't.

The crone's mouth leveled into a hard line, and something like worry crinkled her forehead. "I think we'll skip stone and fire," was all she said. Her chair scraped against the stone floor as she stood. "Come."

Feeling like I failed a test, I followed. This time, we arrived in a dark room, the glow from a crystal ball in the center of a round table. Marcelene sat at the far end, next to the woman that took me to the bath. Next to Marcelene and the apothecary woman sat a third witch. "We appreciate your cooperation, Blythe. I know this must all be very sudden and strange."

I fidgeted with a beaded bracelet on my wrist. "Thank you," was all I could think to say.

"This is Victoria and Esther, and we are the elder crones of The Moon Halo Coven. And you, Blythe Pearl, are a peculiar girl." She took my hand and placed it palm up on the center of the table. Victoria, the apothecary witch, leaned in, as did Esther, the one who directed me to the bath. "Curious," Victoria murmured.

"How could this be, sister?" Esther asked, only giving my palm a quick flick of her gaze.

"This while being devoid of an aura . . . ," Victoria answered.

I looked at Marcelene, "Do you think whatever is . . . weird . . . about me is why these . . . things are following me?" I had no idea what they saw in my hand or aura, or why the bath or mystery object choosing mattered, and I didn't really care. I just wanted to know how to get rid of whatever was chasing me so I could attempt to live in some sort of peace.

"I believe so, yes," Marcelene answered carefully. She peered idly into the orb that began pulsing slowly with a faint white glow. "But . . . do you dislike the entities that are drawn to you?"

The question caught me off guard. "Do I dislike being stalked by my dead stepfather and whatever wretched things are taking over his body? Yes, I'm not enjoying the experience."

I couldn't help the edge to my tone. I'd gone through their little trails with no objections, but I wasn't up for being patronized.

"You *are* fond of a few of the dark beings that surround you, yes?" the leader of the crones asked, betraying no emotion, a simple question.

I sighed. "Yes, if you're asking about the . . . The Halloween Boys, then yes, I like them."

"And they like you profusely, fervently, even."

My irritation rose in my bones. I could see why Ghost wasn't particularly fond of them. "Your point?" I asked, crossing my arms. "I didn't come here to be shamed for my choice of friends."

"Are they only your friends?" Marcelene pulled out a small leather bag and untied the top. Turning it upside down, small bones clattered atop the purple tablecloth.

"Are you guys going to give me any answers, or just more questions and riddles?" I asked, exasperated. "Seems that's what everyone in this town prefers to do."

"No one in this place knows what to do with you, child," Marcelene replied, surveying the bones. She didn't seem put off by my surliness. "You waltz into Ash Grove, who hasn't allowed a tourist in twenty years, and you walk amongst the myths and legends. They accept you into their groups happily."

"Peculiar, indeed," Victoria whispered. "Give me your finger, please?"

"Sure," I answered, holding my hand out. The old woman took what looked like a sewing needle and pricked my thumb. I winced but didn't want to cower or show fear. The witch angled my thumb, letting a drop of blood fall atop the crystal ball.

Upon impact, the glow faded and turned . . . black. Yet somehow, it still glowed. Could black glow?

Esther gasped, putting a hand to her throat. Her stare searched me with confusion. "She's clearly alive," she breathed. "But there is nothing living about her. It's as if . . ." The apothecary witch leaned back in her chair.

"Alive? Of course I'm alive." I shook my head. "You needed to put me through all this weird stuff to figure out if I'm *alive*? Are we almost done here?"

Victoria looked to Marcelene. "But the town allowed her in. The town sees her, though we do not. What could it mean, sister?"

Esther interrupted. "She has a familiar. A raven, at that. I would have killed to have a raven familiar. Yet she is not one of us."

Marcelene tapped a slender bone, addressing me. "You are not a witch. Yet something feels so familiar about you . . ."

It wasn't that I was hoping to be, or maybe I was. Maybe any sort of explanation would have been welcomed, but my heart sank at her declaration.

"If someone isn't upfront with me soon, I'm leaving," I declared, scooting my chair back a fraction. "You may think The Halloween Boys are terrible, but they've never treated me like a science project."

"The Halloween Boys, especially that Ghost of yours, have damned you, child." She scooped up the bones and tossed them down again. With an unsatisfied huff, she pulled out a deck of cards and began shuffling with practiced speed. "The water and moon say it, the earth declares it, and your aura and palm confirm it." Her voice grew in intensity as the table began to softly vibrate. The air froze in my throat. "Your blood screams it, child." A card popped from the deck of colorful foils and landed with a flick. The two other women leaned in with wide eyes. Marcelene plucked the card and held it in front of me. The tarot card depicted a chilling outline of a skeleton holding a long, curved knife. "The card with no name. You are not of the living, Blythe. You are dead."

CHAPTER 32

Ghost

BATS, BLOWJOBS, AND BURNINGS

> You must come with me, loving me, to death; or else hate
> me, and still come with me.
> *J. Sheridan Le Fanu*, Carmilla

I leaned against my bike, peering at Magia Eclectics, deliberating on what would happen if I ordered Onyx to set it ablaze. Were they warded against dragon fire? Could they ward against an extinct species? Only one way to find out. I could walk in in my human form, but I couldn't pass any threshold past the stupid little jars of dirt and fancy rocks they sold. I wondered if that was a flaw in their wards, if me as a human passed enough of their criteria that I made it through security. I wondered where else the flaws in their shields were. Spells and curses fascinated me, only giving me a puzzle to solve, a challenge.

The door chimed, and in broad daylight, he stalked forward, long feathers swishing on the wind behind him. His plague mask looked as ridiculous as he did. I pointed as he neared. "You're on my shit list, Raven."

He stopped a healthy distance away before continuing to cross the street. "The werewolf told me to get her to safety. The witches were safer than you last night. Tonight may be different."

I straightened, the urge to shift pulsing. I never wanted to shift in daylight, but lately I couldn't turn it off. Like my demon had finally grown sick of my human skin and wanted to spend some time, years, decades, just being the monster I was. What was the point of civilized life if I'd found her? Perhaps she was all I was waiting for. "That decision isn't yours; it's mine. I decide where she goes, where she sleeps, and where is safe, got it?"

He shook his shoulders silently as I asked, "Why'd you bond to her, huh? Boredom? Tell me."

"We don't choose who we bond to. I saw her and knew and now I can do nothing but aid her and look after her. We are not enemies, Ghost. I do not mean to disrespect you."

My features softened a fraction. "I've always liked the birds."

"We know, and we do not forget." He turned to watch the shop.

"Are they giving her broom flying lessons yet?"

"She's getting her things now. Doesn't seem happy. She's well but displeased."

I huffed. "Saw that coming from a mile away. I don't know why your kind love the witches so much. They're insufferable know-it-alls."

The humanoid reached into his trench coat, pulling out a silver hand mirror. "They want to talk to you."

I glanced at the mirror. "Oh, for fuck's sake." I snatched it from his feathered grip and looked into the reflection. "Speak your nonsense, crone."

"Nice to see you too, demon."

"Archdemon," I corrected, not in the mood for Marcelene's shit.

Her face, her *young* face, stared back at me. She looked a lot like her granddaughter, Yesenia, only . . . meaner.

"You must be congratulating yourselves for corrupting this poor girl so quickly. She reeks of your foul darkness."

"Did you summon me to hear yourself talk, crone, or is there a purpose to this chat? Which, by the way, you could deign to have in person. I won't hurt you . . . again."

She cackled, covering her red lips. "Oh, I don't fear for myself. I fear what I'd do to you, Ghost. And I don't want to deal with the fallout from your overlords." She paused and clicked her tongue. "The girl is not a witch, so we don't owe her our protection."

I dropped the mirror to my side, ready to give it back to Raven, before I heard it speak again. "However . . ." I pulled it back up, meeting the witch's scowl. "We like her. There's something about her that is . . . alluring. I haven't met a being quite like her before. Her energy—"

"She's a typical, *human* girl." I interrupted. "Whatever you sense off her is from me and my brothers taking her in. I have Claimed her as mine."

"You think legions and their master followed her to Ash Grove because of your dark rituals, Archdemon? Before she met you?"

Her question was curious and not sarcastic. So, I replied, "It's possible. You know that some of us see time on a different scale than others. I don't. However, some of my kind do, as do yours."

She paused, eyeing me considerably. It'd been a hundred years or more since I'd seen her younger form—the way she looked when I killed her.

"You look the same, too," she said with a smirk. "Angrier, perhaps."

"Get out of my thoughts, witch."

With an exhale, she offered, "The coven will put protection spells around the town. Though I'm curious, Ghost. Do you or your brothers see her?"

I knew what she meant. Could any of us sense her. But the fucking absurdity of it all was that from my smoke, Dragon's touch, and Wolf's scent . . . none of us could. Thank the Devil for modern technology and the tracker I put on her car. "No."

The witch considered me a moment before adding, "Nothing not of Ash Grove will get in, but nothing will get out, either. So make use of this time and watch her closely. Our wards will fall at midnight on Halloween."

"Always a pleasure talking to the Crone of Moon Halo Coven," I edged, just to get on her nerves.

She rolled her eyes. "Burn in Hell."

"Gladly, it's my favorite thing to do. How about I take you with me next time?"

The mirror went black. I passed it to Raven, who wasn't even pretending not to listen. Familiars were always nosey as fuck.

The taste of cinnamon played on my tongue and I chuckled. Blythe stomped out of the shop, duffle bag slung over her shoulder. She stopped in front of Raven and me, dropping her bag to the ground. "They're lunatics. The young ones are nice but the old ones . . . Holy shit."

I chuckled darkly, pulling her waist flush to me. "I warned you, Little Ghost."

Her cheeks flushed, and the taste of her arousal seeped into my mouth. "You really waited outside for me all day?"

I shrugged. "Not so different from any other day since you came to town."

She shook her head. "Stalker."

"Demon," I whispered. A small breath left her lips. It turned her on —my darkness. "Raven, take her bag to Lamb's Blood. I've got her today."

His beak lowered in a bow.

"Thanks, Raven," she said softly as I held her tighter. The black bird-man shouldered her bag and left toward the church on foot. She giggled. "Won't people look at him like that?"

"I don't think he cares about anything but you." I took her hand in mine and led her to my bike. "What do you say we take a ride?"

Her eyes lit as she bit her lip in a smile. "Are we safe? Last night was scary, to say the least . . ."

I brushed a stray curl behind her ear. "You're always safe with me. They're all gone, taken care of. I'm sorry I left you alone like that. I didn't know what I'd do after we were so . . . intimate. You deserved a break, and I was right behind you—"

"It's okay. I don't blame you." She took the helmet from my handlebars. "But can I ask you something?"

"Anything." I got onto my bike and cranked the engine.

"Do spirits die?"

She straddled me, and I noticed the edges of her little plaid skirt lift, showing off those soft as fuck thighs. They needed to be stained with my seed between them again. Word had already spread through the forest about willow spirit's sacrifice. I owed the spirit a great debt for protecting my Claimed. "No, death is a misunderstood concept with your kind. It's not an end; it's merely a . . . redistribution. When you blow out a candle, is fire dead?"

Her arms tightened around my ribs. "Don't hold back."

"I never do."

***

WE DISMOUNTED next to a dark and gloomy trail, twisting down a rocky path. To my delight, Blythe wasn't afraid, only intrigued by where I might be taking her. Because her fear was basically my own personal aphrodisiac, it was for her benefit she didn't feel fear with me. Not at that moment, at least. Not in my human cloak. What looked like scattered stones soon made way into an organized rock path. "I love empty places like this," she said as I held her hand to help her down the steeper parts of the stairs.

"Like graveyards?" I asked with a sly smirk.

Her blush answered and she bit her lip. "You know I love graveyards. Especially now."

"I think you'll like what I'm about to show you. When I was a boy, I spent a lot of time in these woods. My family's old farm is a few miles west of here. I built these steps, marked this path."

"Now I'm very intrigued."

I chuckled. "Here we are." We stopped outside what looked like two narrow moss-covered boulders. "Ready to follow a monster into the dark?"

Her lip twitched in sweet smile. "You know I am."

Taking her hand, I showed her the hidden gap between the rocks. We squeezed through, and the space opened into a huge, dark cavern. I called in my smoke, and it snaked ahead of us, glowing blue. "Is it really from Hell?" she whispered. "The blue smoke?"

"Smoke from Hell's sacred fire. I have direct access to the powers of Hell."

Her curiosity danced on my tongue. How peculiar a human was so at ease with this wicked side of Heaven and Hell. The sound of rushing water preceded us as I directed our way into a larger dripping cavern. In the center, the small trickle of a waterfall cascaded into a jagged rock-filled pond. "It's beautiful," she breathed.

A smile tugged at my lips. "That's not what I wanted to show you. This is." My smoke grew brighter, the blue as bright as moonlight. "Look up."

Her gasp was audible as she held onto my bicep. A giggle floated from her throat, and I could have cried at how much I was becoming addicted to the sound of it. "Bats." She grinned, pointing to each, counting. "They're amazing," she whispered.

"I thought you'd frown upon me making them into an actual bouquet, so this is as close as I could get."

She let out a breath and leaned against the curved cave wall. "You're something else, Ames, James, Ghost . . . Which do you prefer?"

"Anything you call me is what I prefer." I took her hand and pressed it to my lips, the sweet taste of honey flicking against my tongue.

"Do you prefer being like this or like . . . last night."

I took a step closer, putting a hand on either side of the cave above her. "They both have their advantages. I feel most at home in my demon form, however."

Her breathing picked up. "Can I see you again like that?"

"You want to?"

"I'm not afraid."

A growl vibrated from low in my throat. "That's too bad," I replied darkly. He wanted out. I wanted out. "I've never turned in front of a woman before. I've never had sex with a woman like that before either." She sucked in a breath as I felt my body grow. I rose above her to staggering height. I was a foot taller than her in human form. As a demon . . . she felt even more delicate and small beneath me. My protective instincts roared within me. *Mine.*

"Can I see your hands?" she asked softly. I held them out for her inspection. Her fingers trailed the exposed bone above the ebony muscle before pressing her palm to mine, lining them together. Her hand was like a pebble in mine.

After inspecting my long fingers, she slid her palms over my forearms. Her tiny grip softly exploring where bone sat atop black ripples of thick muscle. I let her explore, not sure what she was looking for, until finally she looked up. She tilted her head to the side, looking at my face. For the first time in two hundred years, I wondered if my demon form was attractive. How could it be? Ames was an averagely handsome human man. But Ghost . . . I was built to instill terror, fear, and torment. This form wasn't created to feel the soft and tender touch of a woman. "You're big," she whispered after a moment.

I inclined my head. "I am."

"Your face looks like your mask."

"My mask looks like my face," I corrected. My blue smoke pulsed around her. She lifted a wrist, watching it swirl around her arm like a bracelet. I let out the smallest amount of warmth and pressure. She smiled. "This is you too?"

"Hell's fire is an extension of what I am, yes."

"Archdemon perks?"

A grumble of a laugh left my throat as I stared down at her in awe. "It certainly has its advantages. Like this—" The smallest command of energy and I'd bound her wrists above her head and pulled her upward. She gasped, cheeks flushing bright pink, as she dangled at my eye level. "The things I'd do to you, Blythe Pearl," I growled.

Biting her lip, I tasted her honeyed longing. "Do them, Demon Daddy."

I lifted an eyebrow. "Demon Daddy sure rolls of the tongue, doesn't it? Speaking of tongues . . ." I unfurled mine, resembling that of a snake. She shivered as I licked between her breasts and up to her chin, tasting the salt of her sweat.

"Big fan of that, but I want to taste you too," she panted. "Make me your bat."

It took me a moment to understand her. And then I remembered the thousands of bats surrounding us. My cock sprang from half to full stand. I lifted my hand and cupped her jaw, prepared to ask if she was sure, when she bit my thumb before taking it between her lush lips. A growl emanated from deep within me. In a quick movement, she yelped as the ropes of smoke shifted, hanging her upside down. I pressed a hand against the slick cave wall and let the other explore what her skirt raised to reveal. That damn little skirt.

"I wonder what my cum will look like flowing out the sides of your mouth, Little Ghost. Show me."

I heard her intake of breath before she took me with two hands, letting them roam, curving around opposite the other from tip to shaft. Then, finally, her tongue flicked forward, licking the bead on my tip that gathered in appreciation of her. "Fuck," I groaned, feeling her mouth stretch as she took me in.

Her moan vibrated against my cock. I looked down, seeing her nipples poking out from her low top, her middle and soaked panties at easy access. I let my long finger slip under the fabric and jerk, tearing them with ease. "Your cunt smells so good. Little demon fucking whore, aren't you?"

She nodded as she pursed her lips around my cock.

"Daddy Demon wants to hear you say it, Blythe," I gritted out, feeling my release build already. I pushed a finger inside her wet entrance, and she moaned. My finger alone was larger than the average human male's manhood. I watched at perfect vantage the stretch of her pink little pussy.

"Mhm . . " She pulled off, the cold air of the cave assaulting my dick. I needed her back. "I'll be your demon whore." I felt her tongue explore my shaft as she moved, her body, swaying forward and back as she hung from my ropes. Her fallen hair grazed my knees, and the sounds of her slurping made my cock pulse between her rosy cheeks.

The growl that echoed through the cave walls almost woke the bats as I thrust forward, catching her between the lips. The look of her full tits hanging upside down was delectable. My smoke twisted in her hair as I pushed another finger inside her. I pulled her hair, perhaps too hard. She screamed, and I tasted the briefest fear, but fuck if I could stop then. It only made me harder, more feral, my evil surfacing fully. The beast was out and had his cock in my sullied virgin's upside-down mouth. I thrust hard while pulling her hair, straightening her mouth with her throat. She gagged and squirmed under my grip, fresh fear tasting as good as her sweet cunt. I watched her bare ass jiggle as she writhed.

Though she was wrenching and choking as I plummeted into her throat, her hands remained firm around my shaft, moving up and down, still servicing me through her terror. If I weren't careful I'd break her jaw. *Fucking hell.* My cock grazed the walls of her airways, cutting off her breath until I pulled out, allowing her quick gasps of breath. Intensity rose within me like a volcano before erupting. I pushed as far into her throat, and my finger as far into her cunt, as I could go. She writhed, gargling a scream around my demon cock. Fear like fresh berries on my tastebuds. I growled with everything unholy in me, pouring into my Claimed little virgin turned whore. The feel of her mouth struggling to take me in, her gagging and pushing her tongue against me, all while her pussy weeped. And then her gags turned to screams. The walls containing her orgasm clamped down around my fingers. I was cutting off her air supply with my cock, hanging her upside down, threatening to break her jaw, and the bitch was cumming.

This time I did wake the bats as I roared. Their chirps and screeches enveloped us. I put an orb of blue smoke around us to protect her from being bitten, as the thousands of nocturnal creatures erratically flapped in a frenzy around us, blocking out all sight of the cave. But it didn't matter. At the graze of her teeth, my rapture tore through me like an inferno. I pulled out as I was still releasing, spilling my inky seed along her mouth and up onto her face, coating her cheeks. She licked her lips greedily, still holding herself by my cock as she hung upside down. In a swoop, I righted her, her hair a glorious tangle of my cum. My release now stained her chin and cheeks and neck. I licked my fingers of her orgasm before shoving them into her mouth for a taste, which she accepted. "Mmm...," she moaned appreciatively. "I like your taste," she said, out of breath. My smoke held her like a swing, and she wrapped her hands around the ropes of it, like an innocent little human on the Devil's playground. "You burn . . . like alcohol."

I elevated her on her swing so we were eye to eye. "Kiss me," I demanded. I wanted to feel her lips in my true form, something I'd never done, never considered before her. Without hesitation, she wrapped her arms around my neck. Her lips met mine with righteous purity.

Blythe kissed me like I was James Cove, stealing a kiss in the barn before church.

Blythe kissed me like Ames would kiss his wife before a priest on their wedding day.

Blythe kissed me like she believed she could love a fallen beast.

I kissed Blythe like the monster who stalked her in the night.

I kissed Blythe like a virtuously wicked thing I wanted to keep forever.

I kissed Blythe as if my entire woeful existence depended on it.

At this point, it did. She was everything. My only reason to roam this universe as the despicable being I was. Now I was hers.

Her slave for eternity.

Using cave water, I cleaned my perfect little Claimed girl. "Are you okay?" I asked as I gently wiped at her mouth. I'd keep the stain there forever if it were up to me, but she insisted on removing it.

"More than okay. I officially have another reason to love bats."

I chuckled, and my laughter echoed through the cave. A few of the furry, winged animals brushed by us on our hike out, delighting Blythe to no end.

"I love seeing you happy. And there are few things rarer than love for something like me."

She squeezed my hand. "I'm only human, but love is rare for me too."

My Little Ghost understood and accepted me. Somehow, an angel showed empathy toward something so fallen, so evil.

As we crested the shadows of the cave, I changed back to my human form and got dressed while Blythe tied her long, tangled, and dark-stained hair back. I still wasn't sorry she couldn't wash that out yet. I felt the full weight of my body, my shorter frame, my weaker muscles. This wasn't good enough for her. Weak ass Ames Cove wasn't what she needed. The Ghost however . . .

"Can I ask you something?" she asked as we mounted my bike.

"Of course."

"What happened to . . . my stepdad's body?"

I turned and took her hand, speaking carefully. "We thought we'd leave it up to you. The wolves have it in the meantime. If you want them to handle it, they can, but if you want to . . . for closure, that's an option too."

It was my very unprofessional opinion after decades of schooling in psychology that people should be able to do whatever the fuck they wanted to their abuser. Fuck talk-therapy. What they needed for healing was blood. To see the piece of shit that harmed them in the ground. But society hadn't caught up to that idea. Not yet, anyway.

She considered for a moment. "After I shower, can we stop by the grocery store?"

Her question caught me off guard. "Absolutely. Looking for anything in particular?"

"I want to get marshmallows. We're having a bonfire tonight."

The murderous gleam in her eye hardened my cock instantly. I growled low in my throat. "I like your style. You're a little bit wicked, aren't you, Little Ghost?"

She smiled and raised an eyebrow, repeating my words from weeks ago back to me. "Only sometimes."

THE WOLVES HAD the body waiting atop a hefty pile of wood when we arrived at Onyx's farm. He, Wolfgang, and a few of the wolves straightened when we approached. "Hey . . . ," Onyx said carefully. They were testing the waters, seeing if she was afraid or further traumatized by the events of last night. Blythe simply stomped over through the grass and tossed the marshmallows at Wolfgang's chest. "Got any sticks?"

My friends and the wolves laughed heartily as they accommodated her. Onyx passed her a lighter. "Hey," he whispered lowly. "What's your favorite color?"

Her brows rose in confusion as she accepted the green Zippo. "Black," she replied skeptically. "Why?"

Onyx shrugged. "No reason."

Blythe knelt next to the wood pile, giving the limp body of her stepfather a quick glance. "I guess I got to watch you die twice. That's nice," she remarked, flicking the lighter. A flame caught on the tinder, and faster than humanly possible, a roaring, hissing, black fire overtook the mountain of logs. Blythe gasped and took a step back as the bonfire snaked and twirled, exploding into the night sky like a fireworks show, curtesy of our very own Dragon.

I flicked Onyx a look. "Show off."

Wolfgang joked, "That vampire bravado is coming out to play."

"Yeah, yeah," our green-eyed friend replied, offering Blythe a small smile. She returned it from where she stood near the flame and mouthed, *thank you.*

The teenage wolven, Lupus and Freki, did well to lighten the mood as they tossed a frisbee back and forth. Wolfgang pleaded for Blythe to join, and when she did, the wolves howled and hollered. They were brutes, but they were lovable brutes. It was impossible to be sad with the pack. And I suspected that was why my friend had brought them along.

As much as I wanted to admonish them for being *all up in my business* with Blythe, I was thankful they were looking out for her wellbeing as fervently as I was.

Onyx gravitated toward her in the field. I unabashedly eavesdropped to make sure he stayed in line. She pulled her gaze from the wolven boys playing frisbee and addressed him, "So, you have fire powers?"

"Among other things, yes, it comes from my dragon side. I'm a hybrid, the only one of my kind, as far as I know. My mom was . . . is . . . a dragon. My father is a vampire. They abandoned me here in Ash Grove over two hundred years ago. When the curse happened on

Halloween, it removed my blinders, I guess. I thought the family I was staying with were mine, but they were just random humans. My parents left me here for some reason and erased my memory of them. But I remember. If I can ever leave Ash Grove . . ." He shrugged. My chest constricted for my friend. I had no reason to leave other than selfishness. Onyx, however, had a family, a lineage, and an entire new world to seek out. Instead of exploring, he was tethered here like an animal on a chain.

Blythe clicked her tongue in her cheek. Stray hairs from her ponytail wisped around her face in the cold autumn breeze. "Which one did the ability to drug me come from?"

He winced. "Vampire. I don't know a lot about my dragon heritage, aside from the fire."

She raised an eyebrow and tapped her foot expectantly.

"I'm sorry for making you fall asleep and giving you happy feelings? Is that what you're looking for? Because I was just keeping you safe, and I don't regret that."

Blythe blew out an exasperated breath, though she was fighting a smile. A smile that burned like a coal in my gut. She shouldn't be looking at him like that. He shouldn't have been standing so close. "If it makes you feel better, you snapped out of it way quicker than most humans," Onyx added.

Wolfgang bounded over, shirtless and dripping sweat. "What about snapping humans?"

"And *you*." She poked his bare chest. "You're a shadow monster. *Beast of the forest*?"

"More commonly known in lore as *werewolf* but I'll take it." Wolf tilted his chin and let out a forlorn howl toward the moon. The other boys stopped and followed his lead, letting out their howls. When he finished, he shot Blythe a devilish grin. She smiled, despite her crossed arms and what I assumed was a determination to act tough. My valiant Little Ghost.

"You're all hopeless," she muttered.

"That's putting it mildly," Wolf said, pulling her in for a hug. "I'm glad you're okay, pup. And hey, that bastard is dead, and we don't have to hide who we are anymore. You don't have to hide anymore either." She nodded, hugged him back before he and Onyx returned to their games.

When I noticed her break away from them and float back toward the fire, I joined her. "Want to talk?"

"Just thinking about the crones and their tests. They said that I'm not alive." She rubbed her arms. I shrugged off my leather jacket and wrapped it around her. She smiled sweetly. "Thanks."

I chuckled darkly. "What, did some cards and chicken bones tell them that?"

Her mouth quirked at the corners again. "Maybe I was hoping there was something extraordinary about me. But turns out I'm average. No, not even average, below average. Marcelene said I was verifiably dead. Maybe because I've been so depressed, so afraid for so long . . ."

"I think time has messed with her mind. And you are extraordinary, supernatural abilities or not. You're brave, and compassionate, and accepting." I tugged playfully at a lock of her long hair. "Those aren't things most humans or monsters alike possess. You definitely won't find those traits amongst many witches, that's for sure."

I picked up a stick and speared four marshmallows. "Want to do the honors, or shall I?"

She took it from my hands and poked them into the ebony blaze. After a moment of silence, she blew the flame from her treats and tugged a messy glob off, passing it to me. Then she tapped her sticky mess with mine in a salute. "Thanks for this, by the way. It's nice watching him burn." She plopped her marshmallow into her mouth.

I grinned. "I know. It becomes addictive . . . watching your enemies burn."

"You are so fucked up." She laughed.

I put my arm around her. "You're only grazing the surface of that fact, Little Ghost."

CHAPTER 33

Blythe

GHOST STORIES

> She was young and very beautiful, but pale, like the grey
> pallor of death.
> *Bram Stoker,* The Lady of the Shroud

I spent the next week back in the church attic. Raven had indeed dropped off my things . . . and organized them. I blushed at discovering he'd folded and put away my panties and bras amongst Ghost's things in his top dresser drawer. He'd also spread out my makeup on the bathroom counter and placed Benny the Bat in the center of the pillows on the bed. Bats had taken on a whole new significance for me after our sexy cave visit. Benny would be proud. And as if Raven's over-tending wasn't enough, the countertops and fridge were stocked with all my favorite foods: chips and salsa, brioche bread and crunchy peanut butter, and a five-pound bag of unsalted, shelled peanuts, which I guessed were for him. It was better than frogs, at least.

"This is ridiculous." I laughed, handing Ghost, who looked like Ames now, the jar of salsa. "It looks like I live here."

He popped open the lid for me. "No, this is perfect. The bird's scoring big points with me and he knows it. And you do live here now."

I stopped mid-crunch. "I can't just live with you. It's too soon."

He wrapped his strong arms around me from behind as I sat on his barstool. He smelled like his pine-scented body-wash, his skin still damp from his shower. "You'll find that demons grow attached quickly. Time is relative. And with a legion after you, it's either stay with me here, stay with the wolves in a shoebox they call a house, or stay with Onyx on his sprawling farm that's stuck in the eighteen hundreds. Take your pick. But whichever you choose, I'm still going with you. That's not optional."

I sighed. "I like my spot at Magia."

"When this is all over, I'll build you one just like it. Or I'll kick the witches out and take it over myself. Whatever I have to do to make you happy, I will. For now, your safety is the number one priority. We'll focus on aesthetics later." He reached over my shoulder and dipped a chip in salsa.

"So you eat?" I asked. "And sleep? Even as a demon?" I'd seen him do both all week. I'd also seen him shift into a demon. And it made some sort of sense why he liked the church. Its massive high ceilings and huge arched doorways accommodated his monstrous size.

He kissed my temple before going to the fridge and pulling out a decanter of water. He poured a glass. "Yes, if we're in mortal form, it is beneficial to care for our human body. We don't have to, we'd live without anything, but food, water, working out, it helps to strengthen our mortal forms. A lot of entities who shift to humans don't realize these bodies are like vehicles; they require maintenance. And I don't want to be weak in any form."

He placed the water glass in front of me, and I took a long sip. "Does the town know who you are?"

"So curious today, Little Ghost." He rummaged through his dresser and pulled out one of my The Doors shirts and a pair of ripped, black jeans. "Some do, some don't. Some residents were caught up in the town's curse and have been here as long as I have. Most don't realize it, though. Your Mr. Moore, Charles, is one of them. His wife died of influenza before I was born. Their daughter, Ellie May . . . We knew each other as children, before she was . . . taken. But he's forgotten over time as his body has slowly aged."

My mouth dropped. "He has a doll he calls Ellie. That's so incredibly sad, Ames. So, some of the townspeople are just . . . stuck? And they don't know what's happening? That's horrible." My heart sank. "Is there any way to help them?"

He tossed me the clothes and dropped the towel around his waist. Suddenly butterflies replaced the hole in my heart. "We've tried over the years. The witches have tried the most to free them. The curse was meant for us, not for them. What they need is death, and we can't seem to find a way to give it to them."

"How awful." I shook my head, staring down at the clothes he tossed me. "You want me to wear these, I gather?"

"I don't want you to wear anything ever. But the guys are on their way here, and I'll be damned if they see you in only a robe."

I finished my water before pulling on my jeans and shirt—no underwear. He'd probably rip them off me again soon anyway. "Can I ask you something else?" I hesitated as he stepped into jeans and a tugged on a black V-neck tee. His blue stare met mine, the only thing that looked exactly the same whether he was Ames, or the skeleton man, or Ghost. That entrancing color blue . . . The words stalled on my tongue. I had to know, though, if the answer changed anything for me. I was terrible enough to admit that it probably wouldn't, but I had to ask. "Did you guys really do it? What they say you did to the town on Halloween?"

A voice sounded behind me, and I jumped. "Sounds like it's story time in the Lord's house. Shall I preach, or would you like to?" Onyx reached over me and grabbed a handful of chips. "Hey, Blythe," he said, voice silky. His black hair glinted in the stained-glass glow. If Ames were a demon, Onyx looked like his angel counterpart. Where Ames was sharp and brooding, Onyx was chiseled and inviting. I shook off my perusal of his body, and he smirked a sideways smile, shooting me a wink. Maybe I was a nymphomaniac now. These guys were messing with me on a primal level.

Speaking of primal, Wolfgang stomped in, lacking any of the subtly or silence Onyx radiated. He tousled my hair, and I batted his thick arm away. Instead of fleeing my swats, he wrapped his big arms around me, pulling me to his barrel chest. I giggled, accepting the hug. "If you want good stories you should come listen to the elders at Fenrir. Our legends go way back. Plus the food's good."

So much had happened in such a short time: demons, demon sex, witches, shifting crows, seeing Onyx with green fire, and Wolfgang, the creature that whisked me away from danger. "I'd love to," I replied as he sat me gently back onto my feet. Ghost's eyes glowed, staring icy daggers at his friend, who only ignored him and grabbed beers from the fridge. "I was asking about how this all started for you guys. The things I've heard are infamous, to say the least."

Onyx sat on the floor, leaning against the stone wall beneath the crimson stained glass. He was idly pursuing the town's newspaper. "You missed a typo, Wolfgang."

"Like hell I did." Wolf stormed over.

"Right here, old boy. City complains about *spoty* cell coverage . . . " He pointed. "Two ts not one."

Wolf gave the paper a flick. "Want to come be my editor? It's just me and a team of old people who don't even know how to open a laptop."

"I'll stick to criminal law whenever this cursed town loosens my leash for the day, thanks."

I raised an eyebrow at Ames, who accepted a beer from Wolf. "Onyx, you're a better storyteller."

"Hey, I'm a journalist," Wolfgang complained. "My stories are pretty good."

"I'm superior, yet again," Onyx boasted. "I'll tell it. I'm good. I'm not pirate story-telling good, but I manage."

I was dying to learn more about the pirates but refrained from asking, knowing I needed to pace myself with these easily-distracted guys.

Onyx's emerald gaze reached mine as I sat cross-legged on the floor across from him. Ames took a seat behind me in the armchair, and I rested my back against his legs, feeling his fingers tangle through my hair. Onyx glanced at Ames then to me. "Are you sure you don't want to wait until Halloween? Scary stories are better on Halloween, and it's only a few nights away."

"I have a feeling there will be plenty of things for me to be scared of on Halloween in Ash Grove."

Ames's grip tugged on my hair. "Let's hope so," he murmured softly. I felt my core clench in excitement.

Onyx rolled up his newspaper and rested his forearms on his knees. "It's been a long time, and I try not to think about it, honestly." He took a deep breath, and I waited. "Ames has probably told you we all met as boys, though my story is a little different than theirs. I was already . . . what I am when I met them. I was older than what my body looked. Let's just leave it at that for now. We all had our own proclivity toward . . . dark things. Things most would shy away from, we gravitated toward. Most like the heavenly stories at church, the tales of redemption, light, and love. We leaned toward the sinful side . . . fascinated by this Satan character, the Hell mentioned, fire and brimstone, and magic. A need to kill ran through us all for our own reasons, that I'm sure we'll all share with you at some point." Ames's fingers softly petted my hair, and I wished I could turn to see his expression. Onyx continued, "We'd always been a quiet little farming town. When the boys and I were in our twenties, some new guys showed up, men no one knew. Women started disappearing without a trace, one after the other. Ames's sisters, gone. Wolfgang's mother, gone. My . . . A woman I knew, gone."

"Oh my god," I breathed, my bones chilling. Ames twirled my hair through his fingers gently, comfortingly.

"No trace, no pattern. Some were sleeping in their beds and snatched in the night, while others were out in the fields, or forest, or just hanging washings on the line when it happened. The guys and I . . . We hunted them . . . and we found them. They were these gray men, living in caves at night and walking into town like gentlemen during the day. We thought they were depraved, psychotic. We killed them, one by one, dropping their bodies in the town square each night of October —an offering to the families of the women gone missing. Looking back, we should have suspected. Should have seen the signs . . . but as you probably know, the human mind wants to convince itself of anything other than the supernatural."

I nodded, remembering my own disbelief and unwillingness to see what was right in front of me with my stepfather chasing me and Ash Grove being, well, Ash Grove.

"They were demons, and not just any. They were sent by a Devil. The women were . . . recruited. Transformed into something . . . else," Ames said, leaning forward. "Some seemed to have been granted the powers of an Archdemon, while others . . . We don't know where they went."

Onyx nodded. "The Devil didn't like us fucking with his shit, and Devils are notoriously territorial. We were taken to Hell, Wolfgang, Ames, and I, and released on Halloween as . . . what we are, though I was already a hybrid, part vampire and part dragon. We suspect Wolf may have had werewolf in his blood already. Ames was born human. The curse . . . amplified what we are. Some may think it a gift to be immortal, but after a hundred years or so, you change your mind. We cannot die; we cannot leave Ash Grove. Ash Grove has warped and taken on a life of its own. There are others like us, and humans too, who gravitated toward Ash Grove because of its magical pull. They all have the option of death, should they choose it. We do not. Though the humans cannot leave. The ones who come here will find they stay here forever. Either the dark magic reroutes them or somehow, they never feel the desire to move away."

I sorted through my thoughts a moment before asking, "They say the whole town was slaughtered by The Halloween Boys?"

"Ah yes, that." Onyx said, remembering. "It probably was. We have no memory of that night. To be honest, we still don't know all the rules of the curse, another really fun addition. We have yet to find the Devil who cursed us. He scrambled our memories of that Halloween. But yes, the entire town, or rather, everyone who was downtown that night, perished. The ones who didn't die . . . Well, they're as stuck as the ones who did. Maybe more so."

"The ones who died are stuck?"

Ames leaned forward. "There are two sections of the graveyard I took you to. One part holds the good souls who died that night. They're bound to Ash Grove, unable to move on to death and new lives. Then the other part is, well, the bad people. The ones I don't let move on."

I swallowed at the edge in his tone.

Wolfgang spoke up. "The curse may have heightened our bloodlust, or maybe it comes with what we are, but we have to kill. It's like a compulsion. Over the years, we've honed it into killing people who deserve it. When we do, Ghost takes it from there and their souls suffer forever."

"That's why you guys were interested in me. You wanted to kill my stepdad."

Wolf answered, "True, we were excited to find such a worthy kill. But it's not why we stuck around. We don't mingle with the target's victims. Well, we didn't until you."

Ames took my chin in his hand, urging me to face him. I did, looking up at him through his legs. "Remember that fight we had? You said I only wanted you because I thought you needed saving. Saving, rescuing, isn't a need I have. I don't like you because you need saving. I've killed hundreds of scumbags like your stepdad, and I never once felt like saying so much as a word to their victim. But for some reason, I can't stay away from you. I want to breathe you in and let you live in my lungs and carry you everywhere I go, Blythe."

"At the end of the night, I don't give a shit about them. It's about me, and yeah, I like it. It's about getting my death fix. Curbing my bloodlust in some tangible way. You need to understand, all I want and crave and need in this world is death. And you."

My heart fluttered and sank, and so many different feelings at once flowed through me.

"Are you all afraid? Afraid the Devil might come back and I don't know, want or take you?"

Wolfgang snorted. "Let him. Fucking coward hasn't faced us once in two hundred years. He's either forgotten us or he's waiting, keeping us in his back pocket until he wants to cash in on our abilities. But it doesn't matter. We picked up a Devil of our own: Judas. He's a part of our crew. You'll meet him soon."

"I get to meet the Devil soon? Great . . ."

Ames chuckled. "There are several Devils. They like for the world to think there's only one, though."

Onyx slapped his hands on his thighs. "Well, that was cheerful. I'm ordering a pizza. Blythe, rematch in *Super Smash Brothers*?"

I quirked a grin. "You're on." My lip burned I had to bite it so hard to keep from peppering him with questions. What's the etiquette for inquiring about someone's immortal history? A dragon and a vampire . . . How did that happen? So many questions. But I'd gotten enough answers for now.

I sat cross-legged on a worn Persian rug between a demon, a dragon vampire hybrid, and a werewolf . . . playing old video games.

It was shocking and unbelievable. I still marveled at what I'd seen each of them do. The story of how they came to be would perplex me and unravel through my mind in quiet moments. But one thing that was more surprising than anything was how they were still such guys. Like any other band of brothers, they drank beers, played video games, and made inappropriate jokes. They may have been paranormal, and they may have done terrible things, but somehow, I'd never felt more myself around any group of people. They felt familiar and safe.

The Halloween Boys were becoming more than friends.

They were becoming my home.

CHAPTER 34

Blythe

HIS TRICK, HER TREAT

> There is a child in every one of us who is still a trick-or-treater looking for a brightly-lit front porch.
> *Robert Brault*

"We have a surprise for you." Ames leaned against the railing of the church stairs. The crisp October wind ruffled the black waves of his hair. He embodied smoke and darkness even in human form. It was still hard to reconcile the two because right now, he looked like a devastatingly handsome man in a leather jacket with a hungry blue gaze. The atmosphere matched his demeanor. A cloudy, gray gloom dimmed around us, causing the pavement covered in yellow leaves to look like it was glowing—our own yellow brick road under a spooky, chilly sky.

I'd just showered and come down the winding staircase to meet the guys outside. We'd spent the week in a strangely normal routine. I'd get breakfast with everyone at the diner, laughing while Onyx and Wolfgang play-flirted with Doris. Ames would have a casual arm wrapped around me, stroking my shoulder with his thumb as I ate and watched their antics. Then we'd all go to work. Yesenia had begged me not to quit the shop and not to be scared off by the elder witches of The Moon Halo Coven. I liked my new friend a lot but wasn't eager to run into her grandmother, or the other crones, anytime soon. She promised she'd have them steer clear of the shop and give me space, while also trying to convince me to move back in. I hadn't closed the door on that possibility. I did like living above the shop better than the creaky, cold attic of Lamb's Blood Church. But the church attic had my demon . . . and my demon did that thing with his tongue.

After work we'd have dinner with Wolfgang at Fenrir, eating around the fire while kids played. I'd listen intently to any stories The Halloween Boys would share—stories about growing up together, about the many times they'd graduated high school before moving on to collecting careers and . . . targets. Apparently, Wolfgang had a collection of every article ever written about them, and the serial killer names they'd taken on over the years. I saw them more as vigilantes. Though, their definition of who should die was a bit gray at times. After dinner, Ames and I would go home and run into the difficulty of my human body needing sleep and his seemingly only needing me. It was a great problem to have. I'd never known sex could be so fun, and freeing, and intense. And on the nights I didn't go home with Ames . . . I went to Hallows with Ghost. He didn't want to be in demon form at the festival. He said the sight of him would stir up too much for too many festival-goers. So, I'd dance and visit my friends. I'd listen to Captain Vex and the pirates tell stories, or I'd visit the birds in their treehouse. Raven stuck to being a bird, perching on the tree outside Lamb's Blood and keeping watch. I opened the window in the mornings, and he'd fly in for his breakfast and bowl of water.

It was strangely comfortable and normal, though it was the craziest, most unbelievable sort of life.

"What's the surprise?" I asked, unable to hide my smile.

Wolfgang grinned, crossing his burly arms. "Onyx has it."

Onyx replied, emerald eyes giving me a quick head to toe glance that didn't escape my notice. Or Ames's. "It was my idea," he said, slyly pulling out something from behind his back.

I giggled. "Wow, my own jack-o'-lantern bucket, thanks, but there's no candy inside."

"Yeah, dummy, we've got to go get it," Wolfgang jeered, his smile bright against his copper skin.

I raised an eyebrow. They all stood a few steps beneath me in the pumpkin-cluttered courtyard of the church. "We're buying candy?"

Onyx sighed. "We're taking you trick-or-treating, B. You know how we've told you things get weird on Halloween here . . . and since there's trick-or-treating every night of October in Ash Grove . . . we're taking you tonight." He winked on the last portion of that statement, sending a flush to my face that wasn't from the crisp air.

I looked to Ames, who gave Onyx a mildly annoyed glance before relaxing at my smile. "Really? Aren't we too old for that?"

"Excuse me?" Ames put a hand to his chest. "You, kid, are a youngin'. We are old."

Wolfgang replied, "And no one's ever too old to trick-or-treat."

Onyx clapped. "That's settled, now costumes . . . Let's meet in the square in an hour?"

"Okay," I agreed, feeling a rush of excitement. "I do have lots of costumes."

While Wolf and Onyx got into Wolfgang's car, Ames snaked an arm around my waist, pulling me hard to his body. "I already know what you're going to wear. I want you to put on that lacy little top with the black skirt and trench coat. That one you wore after our fight that nearly fucking ended me."

My breath lodged in my throat as I clenched my thighs. "You noticed?"

"Of course I noticed," he growled. "And I'm fucking you in it tonight."

His lips brushed mine, sending a shiver of anticipation flowing down my skin. "I'll get my fox mask," I breathed, tugging away.

He only held tighter, not letting me move, as his kiss dipped to the crook of my neck. "I've got that taken care of too. You're not a fox tonight. You never were."

I dressed, shoving my breasts into my lacy top and shimmying on my mini skirt. I zipped up my long leather boots and let my hair hang long and straight. I was secretly excited to get to wear this getup again, this time with my stalker's undivided attention.

When I turned, he was watching me from the doorway: leather jacket, jeans, hair brushed back, hands painted—like his face. The skeleton man. My breath hitched. "We're not going to make it out of this attic if you keep looking at me like that," he drawled, holding a box and stalking forward.

I sat on the bed, pushing my knees, and breasts, together. "I don't know what you mean."

He chuckled darkly. "Like hell you don't. Here, look at me," he said, sitting beside me. He dabbed the makeup sponge in white and smeared it over my face. It was cold and wet, and from so close, I could admire his face. A face hidden behind paint, and masks, and worlds. A face from hundreds of years ago and made into something entirely new. Something darker and fearsome . . . yet tender enough to paint on my mask. After grabbing a paint brush and working in strokes of black, I giggled, with little hope I'd look anything but ridiculous. But when I walked to the mirror in the tiny bathroom, I gasped.

"It's beautiful." I sighed, lightly touching my cheeks so as to not rub it off as it dried.

"You're beautiful," he replied, coming up behind me, towering over me while he rubbed his hands down my ribs. "I've wanted to paint you like this for a while now."

I admired us both for a moment. "I look like you."

"You look like *mine*," he replied, gravel in his voice. "*My* Little Ghost. Now everyone who sees you will know it."

"Kiss me," I demanded, turning to face him. "Softly, so you don't mess up my face."

His mouth quirked a grin. The skeleton man. My skeleton man. His mouth lowered to mine, brushing at my lips tenderly. Parting them sweetly with his, he slipped in his tongue. I met it with my own and sighed at the taste of him, feeling my silk panties already dampen.

"You taste like honey," I whispered.

He pulled back, tilting his head to the side. "Do I? That's interesting because that's what you taste like to me. I can taste . . . emotions. All demons can."

Surprise flitted through me. "Really? And what emotion of mine tastes like honey?"

He leaned forward, pushing me back until my ass pressed into the cool ceramic sink. "Arousal," he purred.

My breathing picked up as I let my hands roam his hard chest. "We better go or we'll never leave," I whispered.

My skeleton man dipped, lightly sucking my earlobe. "I'll take you trick-or-treating next year."

I giggled at his persistence. "But the candy."

"I'll buy you a mountain of candy."

"It's not the same as taking it from strangers," I said, teasing but breathless. "You know, I've never fully had sex with you as Ames because you shifted inside me the first time. We've only finished together in your . . ."

"True form," he answered.

"Yes." I bit my lip. "Don't get me wrong, I love it when you go down on me every night . . . and I especially love your snake tongue. But I'm just wondering if I could have you as a human too?"

He pulled back, still holding me close, eyeing me consideringly. "I like feasting on you." He leaned in, brushing a hot whisper against my ear. "Plus, I like that you've only ever been with a demon and not a man. You're mine."

A chill shivered down my spine. "I'm still yours either way . . . and you're still a demon."

"Sounds like you want some mortal cock, is that right, Little Ghost?"

Heat pooled in my core. Ames chuckled darkly. "The honey taste in my mouth right now tells me that is a yes."

"I want all of you," I breathed, not sure how I felt about the fact he could *taste* how I felt. It was oddly intimate. "Now, please?"

"We only have a little while before the canine and the reptile start clawing at our door." With strong hands, he picked me up by the ass and sat me on the sink's edge. "But I'm sure I can make quick work of you." My skeleton man smirked.

His hands explored under my skirt until reaching my center. With a small rip, he tore a hole in my fishnets. "Second pair you've ruined," I said in his ear. I liked that he wasn't so far away as a human, especially with me sitting up higher. I could see his face, well, behind the paint. I could touch him, unlike how we were when he was shifted and I was tied by smoke.

"Get used to that," he drawled. His fingers stroked at the damp silk of my panties. "So ready for human cock, aren't you, Little Ghost? *Archdemon me* is mildly offended."

"I love your true form," I replied, my eyes drifting closed at the feel of his fingers. "But we can be closer like this. I can touch you and feel all of you."

He growled, a sound from the demon. Whether his demon self liked that reply or not, I couldn't be sure. With the clinking sound of his belt being undone, he pulled out his dick. I grabbed at it greedily, my hips straining forward in need. "Let's see how human me compares. I'll try not to shift, but no promises," he said as I palmed his length. It wasn't the ridged and enormous demon I was used to, but even for a man, Ames's girth and length were considerable. I liked how he almost fit in my hand, well, at least it took only one hand to hold him like this, not two. I refrained from saying anything, not wanting to hurt his sensitive demon feelings. I grinned to myself, thinking of his demon form being sensitive.

He nipped at my lip. "What's that smile about?"

"You."

With quick and direct force, he jerked my hips forward and plunged inside me. I moaned at the sudden invasion, holding on to him by the neck.

He moved in and out, the sounds of my honeyed arousal echoing in the small tiled bathroom. "I'm the only man or monster that gets you, understand?" he gritted out between thrusts. Leaning closer, he rested his hand on the back of the sink and thrust deeper. I screamed, and it bounced off the walls of the church attic.

"Yes, that's it, scream for your master, Little Ghost. You're mine."

"Fuck," I breathed, clutching onto his biceps and leaning back, the water faucet cutting into my spine.

"I want to hear you scream it. You're mine. God, your screams taste delectable. Almost as good as your perfect little cunt." His hand inched between us and found my sensitive spot, pressing and flicking.

Without resistance, I did as he ordered, screaming yes over and over. "I'm yours."

"That's it, Little Ghost. Now come on my mortal cock. Let me feel your little cunt squeeze it empty." His thumb and forefinger pinched at my clit. I lost control. Time and space swirled before my closed eyes, balancing on my frantic breaths as my orgasm ripped through me, tearing me apart and ruining me just like my fishnets.

He rested a palm on the mirror, and another hand gripped my hip as he picked up the pace. I loved hearing his hot breath in my ear, and seeing the face of the skeleton man, *Ames*, fucking me. "It's hard," he gritted out. "To not . . . turn into my true form . . . when I'm inside you. Especially when you scream like that."

I wrapped my legs tight around him, feeling his cock grow and expand slightly. The line of his jaw turning more jagged, the blue of his eyes became an icy, deathly shade.

I wrapped my fingers through the back of his hair. "Please try, I want to feel you like this. Please come inside me like this, Ames. You're my demon, always, and you're my man, my Ames, too."

He swore, pushing through the need to shift. After a moment, he buried himself to the hilt, shoving my hips closer into his. He cried out, holding my gaze. His fierce blues faded slightly, his jaw relaxed, and I felt his human length inside me. I held him close, both of us panting and catching our breath. "Thank you," I whispered.

He cupped my jaw in his hands, emotion dancing in his features, even behind the black and white paint. "Thank you, Blythe . . . for reminding me that I am more. That maybe there's more in here aside from . . . the dark."

I kissed him passionately, tasting honey, though that wasn't the only thing on my the tip of my tongue in that moment. I'd never felt the urge to say it, but I'd never been so close to anyone in my life. However, to tell him I loved him . . . it might have been too much for him in that moment. So, I only said, "I need tiny chocolates."

The corners of his mouth lifted. "And the tiny chocolates you shall have, Little Ghost."

We met up with the guys in the town square, thinking we'd trick-or-treat downtown around the shops and then head to a neighborhood. Fog drifted like a cloud along the cobblestone streets, and flame flickered in the old lanterns. Raven cawed and soared above me, saying hello. When I saw them walking toward us, my breath froze in my chest. Wolfgang's massive size was dressed all in black, his thick biceps straining against his black shirt. He stalked next to Onyx, who looked like a fallen angel, his inky hair brushed back, emerald eyes glowing lightly. I wondered if it was a dragon trick, and curiosity tingled in me as I wondered what he was looking for, or why they glowed this night. But it was their faces that made my heart stop: white, black accents of paint, shaded outlines of teeth and bone. Skeleton men.

Or rather, we all were painted the same.

"Looks like we added a girl to The Halloween Boys," Wolfgang said when he reached us. "You look nice." He wrapped around me in an embrace, lifting me off the ground and squeezing until I was kicking my legs and giggling.

Ames only crossed his arms and lifted a brow at his touchy-feely friend.

Onyx glanced a moment too long at my mini skirt before reaching my gaze. Something flickered there, behind the glow, but I wasn't sure what it was. His voice was coated in his usual, irreverent tone. "Or we're a Kiss cover band."

The guys chuckled as we made our way through the town streets. A black cat darted in front of us, chasing a mouse and scurrying away. Children in various costumes giggled as they visited each shop. The air had that very specific Halloween smell—like sugar, and plastic, and musty leaves, and fire. It was the best scent in the world. I felt like an idiot holding my jack-o'-lantern. The guys had pillowcases, which looked much cooler. *Trick or Treat!* they boomed, shoving at each other and chuckling. Glee flooded me at how not embarrassed they were. Shop owner after shop owner, little old ladies, and rough-looking farmer men all smiled with fondness as they filled our containers with handfuls of candy. I wondered which were truly old people and which were *stuck* people, like Mr. Moore, the ones who couldn't move forward, couldn't die. The guys knew them all by name and took the time to inquire about their lives. Wolfgang asked if Miss Edith had any lightbulbs that needed changing, to which she agreed she did, and he and Ames disappeared inside her flower shop. I stayed behind, breathing in the cool night air, and dug through my pail for the treat of my choosing. Onyx stood next to me, tall, with his typical mischievous air. "Hey, so," he started, a hint of nervousness in his tone. "I noticed you have a vintage band T-shirt collection."

I found the caramels I wanted and ripped open the package with my teeth. "Yes, I do. I try to find them in thrift shops at every place I travel through."

He scratched his stubbled chin before reaching into the back pocket of his jeans. He pulled out a rolled-up bundle of fabric. "I thought you'd like to have this one."

I tossed back a palmful of chewy caramel and shook out the shirt. "Are you kidding me? This is from nineteen sixty-five. You're a *Deadhead*?"

He rubbed the back of his neck. "It's a tour shirt from when they first got together. Not many of them out there. They played Hallows one year. I met them, nice guys."

My mouth dropped. "Wait, The Grateful Dead played Hallows Fest? Are they immortal, too?"

"They're artists, which is like being immortal, isn't it? I guess Ash Grove let them in as a treat. Sort of like it let in you."

My face flushed and something warm swirled in my middle. "You . . . Are you sure you want to give me this? It probably belongs in a rock and roll museum or something. You could sell it for a fortune."

He shrugged. "Money's boring. It's more fun to make someone smile. Do you like it?"

"Like it? I freaking love it." I dropped my bucket on the ground and launched myself into his arms for a hug. He chuckled, and I felt his fingers lightly rub my long hair. His jaw grazed the side of my head in a nuzzle.

Someone cleared their throat, and Onyx slowly loosened his grip. For some reason, a flash of shame shot through me when I met Ames's stare. Wolf looked to be holding back what he wanted to say.

"Um, look," I said, holding up the shirt. "Onyx gave me his Grateful Dead shirt to add to my collection. I was just thanking him."

"Damn, their show was fucking good, wasn't it, dude?" Wolf said, instantly lightening the mood.

While they chatted, I slipped off my trench coat and pulled the roomy shirt over my head, letting it hang to my hips. It almost covered my mini skirt and made it look like I was only wearing a shirt and fishnets, but I didn't care. It was the most thoughtful gift I'd ever received.

Out of the corner of my eye, I tried not to notice Onyx watching me, a beautiful smile pulling at the corner of his mouth as he watched me put my coat back on. Ames appeared then, blocking his friend from view and wrapping a possessive arm around my shoulder. He gave my outfit update a quick, disapproving glance.

The guys walked up ahead as we veered away from town and toward neighborhoods. We weren't too far from my old basement apartment, actually. "Are you mad at me?" I asked softly, so the guys couldn't hear. Though, I suspected with their abilities, they probably heard me anyway.

"I could never be mad at you, Little Ghost," he said, kissing my temple. "My *friends*, however, need to learn how to respect what's mine."

I glanced ahead, seeing Onyx and Wolfgang jeering and talking as usual. "They're just being nice. It's harmless."

Ames huffed an unamused sound. "A little too nice."

I rolled my eyes and shoved him playfully. "Lighten up, demon boy."

His eyebrows rose in amusement. "Demon boy, huh?"

He grabbed me around the waist, pinching at my ribs. I laughed, pushing him off. Once I wiggled out of his grip, I ran, brushing in between Onyx and Wolfgang.

"See, I told you he'd scare her off," Wolf said. "You owe me fifty bucks."

Ames caught me so quickly, I thought he must have used some of his magic. He grabbed me as I laughed and hauled me over his shoulder, casually turning to the guys. "Where to next?"

"Let me down," I demanded, though I was laughing so hard I could barely make out the words.

"We could hit a couple more houses then go sort our loot at the church?" Onyx offered.

"Sounds good to me," Wolf replied, nonchalantly ignoring my pleas and laughing.

Ames spanked my behind with a loud clap before setting me gently on the ground. I dried my eyes of the tears from laughter, when an image appeared down the street. My heart sank. As my smile faded, I walked past the guys towards the hunched figure. When I reached him, he stood, broom in hand. He smiled when he recognized me under my face paint. "Blythe, it's so good to see you again. You ran out before dessert the other week. I hope everything turned out alright."

"Oh, I'm sorry about that, Mr. Moore." The guys' words about Charles Moore being stuck here . . . for hundreds of years . . . missing his wife who passed and his daughter who was taken, snatched into the woods never to be seen again. I shuddered. "Um . . . are you okay?" I asked. There was nothing I could do, but I worried about him all the same.

"Yes, young lady, I am just fine. You and your fellas probably want some candy, don't you. I can run and grab some from the house."

Wolfgang's presence appeared next to me first. "Hey, Mr. Moore, I'm Wolfgang Jack, and this is Onyx Hart and Ames Cove."

Mr. Moore clutched his broom and nodded. "I bet you boys know my daughter Ellie. She's about your age."

I swallowed down tears.

Ames spoke, smooth and respectful, betraying a hint of his old-timey accent. "Yes, sir. Ellie May is a wonderful girl."

"She sewed a flag for our treehouse when we were younger," Onyx added, stopping next to Ames.

Mr. Moore's eyes lit up. "That sure does sound like my Ellie. Oh, Blythe, dear, did your stepfather find you?"

I felt Ames's fingers stroke comfortingly between my shoulder blades. "Yes, sir. All is well," I replied. Somehow . . . for the first time . . . no fear clawed at my senses. I was safe now. I was safe with The Halloween Boys. I looked to Ames, and he smiled like he noticed it too. Like he noticed that I didn't taste like fear at the mention of my stepfather.

"Good, good," Charles Moore said, going back to sweeping the street. I wondered how long he'd been out here in the cold, sweeping . . . sweeping . . .

Onyx offered me a tender look before walking over to the old man and placing a hand on his shoulder. "Sir, don't you think you should go inside, have some hot tea, and have a nice rest this evening? The street looks great."

Awareness and relief instantly softened Mr. Moore's wrinkled features. "You know what, young man, that sounds delightful. I think I'll do just that. You kids be safe and have a good time trick-or-treating. I'll get the big candy bars next year to make up for this one."

"Yes, sir, thank you," we all replied. I swallowed, fighting the tears at the corners of my eyes.

Onyx dared to brush a rough thumb on my chin. "Hey, he's alright. I made sure. He's going to sleep soundly with only good memories tonight." In that moment, I was very thankful for Onyx's drug-touch.

"I wish I could help him," I whispered. "I wish I could help all of them."

"Us too," Wolfgang replied. "I've looked for the lost girls for over a hundred years." He shook his head. "Ellie is among them, unfortunately."

Ames wrapped his arm around me again, and I rested my head on his shoulder. "We'll find a way to help them someday. But there's nothing you can do. You're mortal."

It was the best he could offer, though it stung. *You're mortal.* Why'd that feel so shitty?

Onyx chimed in, shoving his hands in his pockets. "Our curses are connected. If we freed ourselves from this devil's snare, we'd free them. Our Devil has been searching for the key to that for years. It's one of the reasons he's always gone, supposedly."

"Would you leave if the curse was broken?" I asked on instinct.

Onyx shot me a sideways glance. "I'd try to find my parents, my family, my people. It's been a very long time."

Behind the pumpkins and festivals and polite hellos, Ash Grove harbored pain and longing. Whatever the curse, everyone was stuck and immovable—my boys and the people here. But Ames was right. There was nothing I could do. We walked the rest of the way in silence. We stopped at a house with a yard full of crunchy dead leaves. I stood on the sidewalk, rifling through my candy. By the time I pulled out a green apple sucker, they'd raked the yard. "Miss Doris's house," Wolfgang offered to my questioning glance.

They stuffed the leaves into orange garbage bags that were on the front porch, but instead of leaving them on the side of the road, they hauled them over their shoulders, walking to a dark house across the street. They chuckled, talking softly as they walked up to the front door . . . and dumped the leaves, creating a tower blocking the front entrance. I gasped and looked around to see if anyone else noticed. "What the hell are you doing?"

Ames shrugged and wiped his hands. "Just thanking Marcelene for taking such good care of you the other day." When I turned, looking over Ames's arm that was already around my shoulder, a stream of white flowed through the air and into the tree in her yard. And then another. "You can't toilet-paper her house," I said in horror. Onyx and Wolfgang made quick work of it, pulling out toilet paper rolls from under bushes, almost liked they'd planned and executed this very thing for years. "This is so wrong."

"So you don't care that we've killed people, but you draw the line at vandalism? Interesting." Ames smirked, kissing my painted cheek.

I crossed my arms, shaking my head as the guys laughed, joining us on our walk back to the square. "You're awful."

"You're just now figuring that out, B?" Onyx's green eyes glowed again.

We weaved between the pumpkins in the yard and up the stairs of Lamb's Blood. "She's going to turn you all into toads and feed you to Raven."

Wolf chuckled. "I'd like to see her try. Her magic doesn't work on us."

"Why not?"

"There's a lot about the curse we don't know because the Devil who did it disappeared. As most Devils tend to do."

We reached the echoey stone room that led up to the attic. Wolfgang complained, "Dude, fuck all those stairs. I'm drunk as hell. Let's dump our loot and trade in the sanctuary."

"When have you been drinking?" I asked, laughing.

He gave me a wolfish smile. "We do lots of things when you aren't looking."

"Demons," I muttered and shoved open the sanctuary doors. The stained glass was floor to ceiling, and hundreds of glossy pews lined an aisle to the altar and pulpit.

"Creepy," I whispered.

Onyx shook his head and walked to the front. "You hang out with monsters, but church is creepy? I'm sorry to tell you, but I think you may be fucked in the head."

Ames shoved his friend's shoulder who chuckled and sat on the front pew. He turned his pillowcase upside down, spilling out the brightly-colored packages. I sat on the bottom step of the altar with Ames and Wolf, and we did the same. I felt like a little kid, trading candy, aiming to score everyone's caramels.

One of which fell down my shirt as I tossed back a few. "Allow me," Ames said to my surprise. He slowly pushed off my trench coat and tugged off my T-shirt, revealing my tight, lacy crop top. The candy had fallen right down the center of my cleavage. I gasped at the sudden feel of his mouth exploring the tops of my breasts, his tongue sinking down the crease. Wetness pooled in my center, and I glanced up to see Wolf and Onyx watching intently. Ames found the candy and sucked it into his mouth. "Here you go, Little Ghost," he said, grabbing the back of my neck and pulling my lips to his. He parted them roughly, pushing the orb of sugar onto my tongue.

My pulse quickened as he stood, bringing me to stand with him. "Come here," he said, leading me up the altar to what looked like a throne. "Sit."

I swallowed, looking over his shoulder, confused, as the guys looked on with hungry stares. "Are you . . . sure?"

His palm pressed against my chest, and I sat as he dropped to his knees. "This seat is called the bishop's throne, the cathedra, or the presider's chair." He spread my knees with his rough palms.

I startled at the rough rip of my new pair fishnets . . . along with my silk underwear. It was the second pair he'd torn tonight. Heat flushed my cheeks, and I bit my lip, knowing we had onlookers. "Ames," I whispered.

"The priest leads prayer and worship here, in this seat." His mouth dropped, finding my exposed folds. His back to his friends, when he lowered, I caught their greedy gazes. Onyx sat forward, elbows on his knees as he rubbed his chin, green eyes glowing. Wolfgang leaned back in the pew, arms on either side next to him, eyeing me darkly under a heavy stare. My head lolled back as his tongue swiped me, circling my wet opening, then slowly dragged up toward my bundle of nerves. "What are you doing?" I whimpered, breathless.

"Leading prayer and worship," he muttered against my wet pussy, meeting my gaze with a mouth full of me. "I told you I always wanted to be a priest."

I groaned, lolling my head back.

"Fuck," I heard Onyx whisper through the echoes of the cathedral.

Ames continued licking, plunging his long tongue inside me. I swear I felt his demon lap at my cervix. The feeling both tickling and instilling a deep buildup of pleasure.

"These sanctuaries were built to amplify sound. We can hear your every breath, even without our heightened senses."

The sound of a primal growl reached my ears. I opened my eyes to see Wolfgang palm his cock overtop his jeans. "Go ahead and sing like an angel for us," the werewolf encouraged, his voice rough and sexy.

I ran my hands through Ames's hair and pulled him up to look at me. "I can't believe you're okay with this," I panted, feeling the cold air of the church hit my wet center. He'd been so protective. Any glance, or touch his friends had offered me angered him. Confusion peppered my mind at how this was acceptable for him. Not that I minded . . . I didn't mind one bit. Their eyes on me from their pews made me feel like I was beautiful and sensual and wicked. Arousing them made me feel a sort of power I didn't know I craved.

"They can come to our church and worship you . . . from down there. Let them pray to you, baby. Watch them wish you were theirs."

My breathing accelerated, and I noticed Onyx bite his lip and bounce his heel, seemingly struggling not to charge forward and participate. He smiled when he noticed he had my attention, revealing the points of his sharp white smile. Ames went back to work, nibbling my cunt as I squirmed, feeling my juices pooling on the holy throne below me.

Onyx's fangs glinted in the moonlight, shining through the stained glass as he stood. I whimpered, watching the hybrid dragon unbutton his jeans and slowly unzip. They dropped to the ground, and he kicked them aside. He glanced over at Wolf, who stood and walked up behind him.

I gasped, watching Wolf hook his fingers into the band of Onyx's dark-green boxer briefs and shove them down. His erection sprang free. Onyx straightened, boldly allowing my eyes to assess his manhood as he tugged off his shirt. He was naked, and we were undoubtedly defiling this sacred place, but Onyx looked like he fit here—like a statue of an angel. Ames's two fingers nudged at my soaked entrance, pushing in slowly. The dry roughness of them caused me to cry out.

Wolf, standing taller and broader than Onyx, reached around, flicking Onyx's hand away and taking his cock into his large palm. I moaned as he slowly touched him, base to tip, before offering his hand to Onyx. I don't know what I expected. I'd never watched two men together, though I'd always wanted to. Onyx grinned at me before running his tongue slowly up Wolf's wrist. Suddenly, he bit down on the flesh of his palm, and I yelped in surprise. Ames chuckled against my clit as his fingers continued their agonizingly slow pace. "I smell a blood offering," he purred. My body felt as if it had been electrocuted. Every touch, the cold hard chair under me, Ames's pumping and licking, the sounds coming from the guys . . . Everything in me was hyper aware. I watched as two thick streams of crimson blood dripped down Wolf's fingertips, who then promptly lowered it from the vampire's mouth to Onyx's cock. My mouth fell open, watching his erection become coated in blood as Wolf pumped him, slowly at first, and then rougher. Onyx grunted, smiling at me with blood dripping from his pale chin. God, it was evil, and so fucking sexy. "Oh fuck," I breathed. "I'm going to come."

Ames moved then, to the side, allowing the guys full view of my pussy as he continued thrusting his fingers in and out. My demon extended his snake-like tongue, swirling my nipple. The fork shape pinched and rolled the hard buds, causing me to squirm and pant. My congregation's gazes immediately took in the sight, and they awed in appreciation. "Goddamn," Wolf said, still handling Onyx's cock.

"Let's come together, B." Onyx winked, a drop of Wolf's blood dripping from his fangs.

My resolve exploded as I screamed my bliss, echoing it through the holy halls of Lamb's Blood Church. More like *Wolf's Blood* Church now. I was the lamb amongst lions, being fucked, slaughtered, and bleeding passion before my predators.

Onyx groaned, mouth opening as he eyed my clenching cunt, still full of Ames's fingers, still riding out my orgasm. His release shot out, drenching Wolf's red knuckles in milky white. Wolfgang let go, bringing his hand to his lips and sucking his fingers, meeting my delirious gaze. "Delicious," he whispered. His eyes were wild and yellow as his long hair swayed free. *Fuck.* Each one was like my own personal sex monster.

I stood then, Ames still on his knees, looking at me with a devilish grin. "My turn," I ordered, pushing him onto his back. He undid his pants and jerked them off, then removed his shirt. He sat up on his elbows, watching me, seemingly oblivious to the guys having their own fun at the bottom of the altar. I unhooked my crop top, though my breasts were already spilling over the edges from that glorious tongue's assault. I left my torn fishnets and panties on. They were wet now, and I liked the way they accentuated my ripped silk thong still pressed between my ass cheeks. Ames palmed at his cock, "I want to turn. Let me turn, Little Ghost? Show The Halloween Boys how good you take a monster cock?"

I swallowed, hearing the ragged breathing of both men below us. When I looked over, Onyx was on his knees, taking Wolf in his mouth, both of their gazes fixed to Ames and me. When I glanced back, it wasn't Ames beneath me. All eight feet of muscled and lethal Ghost lay before me. He put his hands under his head as he watched me strain to climb on top of him and spread my legs around him. He was so wide, so big. If there had been no light filtering in, he would have been invisible. A demon concealed by darkness. When I was in position, I lined my dripping center over his throbbing, ridged cock. "That's it, Little Ghost. You're such a good girl. My little demon slut. Aren't you?"

I lowered myself slowly onto him, taking in his tip. It felt even bigger in this position. I whined, and his huge, boned hands took my hips in his grip. "Your very own corrupted and taken girl," I repeated. "Your Little Ghost."

"Mm . . . that's right. Hear that, boys? Mine. All. Fucking. Mine." He guided me gently, lowering me until I could fit no more. My thighs and pussy stretched, straining to take him in. My walls were tighter on top and his cock was enormous and throbbing. The pain felt immaculate, and I could already feel another orgasm building deep within me. The thunderous crash I'd always longed for. My demon's growl vibrated through my skin as he commanded, "Watch your parishioners worship you. How devout your subjects are." I liked the way his sharp smirk glinted in the low and colorful light of Lamb's Blood Church. He didn't have to tell me twice. The wet sounds of sucking pulled my attention, and while I adjusted to Ghost's size, I watched as Wolf braced himself on a pew, one hand on the back of Onyx's head, pushing his mouth onto him roughly. Onyx groaned, meeting my gaze with a mouth full of Wolfgang's cock. When he noticed he had my attention, he pulled off. I stared, a thrust from Ghost wincing my eyes. When I opened them, Onyx's devilish smile radiated as he gave the wolven's cock a flick of his red coated tongue. Then he moved to the side of his shaft and opened his lethal mouth before clamping down in a strong bite. Wolfgang cried out in what started in a deep moan and ended in a soulful howl that shook the candlesticks around us. Blood dripped from his girth as Onyx eyed me, still smirking, before taking his friend in between his dark crimson lips. His green eyes rolled back and he sighed, savoring the taste. I wondered what blood tasted like. Did blood from a cock taste different than from elsewhere on the body? What would it feel like if he bit me . . . down there.

It was too much, too hot to handle, and my hips began thrusting of their own accord. Erratic, and probably not sexy at all to watch, but I couldn't help it. The amplified sounds of wet bodies moving together, magnified by this place built for a much different type of song, the echoes of our collective whimpers and cries of pleasure, made my bliss peak as my hips bucked wildly. I took in every agonizing ridge of Ghost's huge demon cock. The stretch was bittersweet and wretched. I couldn't fit all of him, but I damn well tried. I locked eyes with my Archdemon as he squeezed his sharp claws into my ass, watching my stretched pussy struggle to accommodate him. I gave it my best try, pushing myself farther down than I thought possible. Ghost growled a deathly swear, and in in my periphery, both men below grunted along with him. Wolfgang finished in Onyx's mouth. The vampire drank the blood and pleasure like his own personal drug, his emerald gaze glowing. As my pleasure shredded me, I screamed, letting it bellow through the halls of the sanctuary. My demon roared alongside my song. At that same moment, I felt the warmth of Ghost's release shooting inside me, black ink slithering down my inner thighs, shading me the same colors as my ripped fishnets. He sat up, still holding me, filling me, and took my lips in his. I kissed my Archdemon, tracing the outline of his long, forked tongue with my little human mouth. Onyx stood, wiping his lips with the back of his hand, while Wolf pulled up his jeans. After minutes, or maybe an hour, of Ames and I coming down off our sex, he gently eased me off of him, and I hissed at the soreness that remained. He stood and helped me up on my wobbly knees. Grabbing my shirt, he tenderly tugged it over my head until it dropped over my bare breasts and loosely covered my hips. I glanced over at Onyx, who was still staring at me with a faraway expression. "My new favorite shirt. My *lucky* shirt." I smiled.

His answering grin warmed my heart, while Wolf walked over and put an arm around his friend. They bumped fists. "Fucking good, Dragon," Wolfgang said. "And the two of you . . . Fuck."

"You're divine," Onyx said, looking at me, green eyes glowing again. I swallowed and pulled my gaze back to Ghost, afraid of what would happen if I were sucked into that pool of emerald.

He tucked me under his arm like I was his precious, tiny thing. "You're welcome," he said lowly, though there was a lightness in his tone that pulled at the corners of my lips. He didn't regret letting them watch. Something inside me thrilled at the thought this could be the first of many similar experiences.

The Halloween Boys would surely be the death of me. Small deaths and big deaths. I wouldn't make it out of their crossfire of immortality alive. And Marcelene was right. They'd damned me to never be able to love another, to fuck another, or be with another.

My mortal soul was a small price to pay for some sort of comfort in this life. I was damned, all right.

And I was so incredibly okay with that.

CHAPTER 35

Ghost

THE THINNING OF THE VEIL

> Hope not ever to see Heaven. I have come to lead you to the other shore; into eternal darkness; into fire and into ice.
>
> *Dante Alighieri*

I was too busy admiring the rose tint of her cheeks, distracted by the tastes of her fluttering emotions and the pulse of my cock that already wanted her again. My body was still in my true form, a form I was preferring more and more often, though my experience fucking as a mortal earlier wasn't so bad, either.

I didn't sense him come inside.

The wail of the organ pierced the air and made my Little Ghost startle. I may have been vexed at my friends flirting with my Claimed, but I couldn't say I wasn't both thankful for and impressed by their instant response. It took only a singular second for each of us to position around her in earnest protection. She spun, not even knowing what happened, as she still processed the source of the music.

"Toccata and Fugue in D Minor" whined through the high ceilings of the hollow stone sanctuary. I made the slightest shift in my knee, just enough movement that Onyx knew I was about to tear the coven leader's head from his shoulders. Dragon put a hand to my chest, stilling me in place. My human form was protective, but my demon form was positively feral in its need to guard my Claimed. I'd sooner kill than ask questions, but Onyx was opposite in that regard. My way was better.

Wolfgang spoke first, feigning a casual stance, though I saw his claws emerging from his hands. I tasted his anger like char from a grill. Good, at least he'd back me up if I decided to rip this motherfucker apart. "The pipe organ has to be the ugliest instrument invented. Makes sense you'd like to play it."

There was a low chuckle over the disconcerting piece of music. The vampire spoke over his own playing. "You know, I was there when Johann wrote this. I thought it was horrid as well. But it's grown on me over time. Funny how time does that. And we, as immortals, have so much of it."

"You have about five seconds to tell me what the fuck you're doing in my house, Vincent." I growled, not in the mood for the bloodsucker's preening and arrogance—both of which he kept on full display at all times. I didn't blame Onyx for refusing to join his coven.

The music stopped, and before the last key halted its reverberation, he was in front of us, flaunting his preternatural speed. Leaning against a pew, he picked at his pointed nails. "This is the Lord's house, not yours, Ghost."

"I am the Lord," I snarled. I felt a small hand touch my palm, and I calmed slightly, feeling her behind me.

"Get on with it, Vincent." Onyx took a casual step forward, angling himself strategically between the coven leader and me.

He noticed and smirked. "I come with news. Though, I won't lie . . . I smelled a lot of tantalizing fun coming from here."

Wolfgang ignored his baiting. "What news?"

Vincent let out an exasperated sigh and straightened, his long hair glowing white in the light of the moon. "You Halloween Boys really are no fun. So serious all the time . . . and hiding your girl from me as if I haven't been looking after her since the moment she stepped her human foot into Hallows Fest." He tsked, "Not a great way to show me gratitude." I opened my mouth to respond, but he glanced up at me and lifted a pompous hand. "Nevertheless, I came to let you know that something has entered Ash Grove. Something, one of your kind, I imagine, made it past our coven on the outskirts of town."

My kind, he'd said with disgust. Vampires were self-appointed as top of the immortal food chain, though that was far from reality. Archdemons had superiority over them, and they fucking hated it. "That's impossible," I replied. "The witches have the town warded. Nothing not of Ash Grove can enter, so perhaps, once again, you and *your kind* are incorrect."

Vincent bared his teeth. "It wasn't us who brought in a goddamn legion. We've been picking off stray demon scum for weeks."

Onyx snorted. "Nice to know you saw us fighting and decided not to help until it concerned you. Typical."

The vampire leader looked at each of us with murderous rage. Good. I preferred him like this rather than the aristocrat act. "I'm warning you now, aren't I? Members of my coven have grown attached to the girl, and I have to say—" He strained a glance through our arms, finding a sliver of her gaze. "Blythe, dear, if you grow tired of the alpha-male barbarism, you're always welcome in our coven. You'll find we prefer a more . . . sophisticated standard of being."

In one swift movement, I'd shoved Onyx back and my hand wrapped swiftly around Vincent's neck. The asshole didn't flinch, I'd give him that. "You even so much as think about my Claimed, I will tear you apart, limb by limb, and scatter them across the globe. I won't burn you, bloodsucker. I'll just let your filthy pieces crawl through shit trying to put you back together. We'll see how sophisticated you are then."

The vampire tensed his jaw, a red glint sparking through his stare. He pushed off my hold and landed on his feet with a thud. "I came to warn you. Believe me or not, that's your choice." He turned to leave but stopped on his heel. "Maybe when Ghost calms down, you'll consider inviting me to your next . . . church service. I'm dying to attend."

In a flash, he was gone.

"Fucking creep," Wolfgang said. "You alright, pup?"

I turned, anger simmering, to see Blythe wrapped protectively in Wolf's hold. He loosened his grip slowly as he noticed my attention.

"I'm fine," she whispered, smoothing out her shirt. "Why do you hate him so much? It sounds like he was only warning us."

Wolf's eyebrows rose, and I tasted Onyx's amusement. They'd never dare question me in a state like this—not shifted, not angry. But she did. It was okay that she did.

"Our relationship with the vampires is strategic. Each group of immortals have their own customs, their own little fucking traps and tricks. The politics between us is complicated and spans thousands of years. You can't let anyone think you like them too much or they fall out of line. Vincent, for example, hasn't pissed me off in a decade or so, but he likes dancing close to the line just to fuck with me. I won't forget the many times he's declined to lend a hand to our efforts to break the curse . . . or to save the stolen women."

Onyx added, "Or offer me any intel on who my father is and where he may be."

She let out a sigh and rubbed her eyes. "I'm tired."

"Let's get you to bed." My strong arms scooped her up in an instant, and I carried her up to the attic. Her eyes drifted shut as she leaned into my chest, the protruding bones not bothering her. She was so accepting of me, of us, and this life. It was remarkable. Somehow, I was stronger around her, my abilities heightened, my need to be in my true form more urgent than ever. It was as if she'd given me strength. Perhaps finding your Claimed did that. I wasn't sure. All I knew was that Claiming tied our souls together for eternity. It was a bond mysterious and powerful. But my increased power was evident. Even Vincent seemed to notice. As I tucked her into bed and removed her shoes, I shifted back into a man so I could fit in the bed and lie beside her. She was so fragile, so easily frightened, and her body tired so quickly. It would be my life's work, from this point forward, to guard her against my kind. As I tugged her close, I promised, "I'll always protect you, Little Ghost, from this dark and twisted world of monsters. You're mine."

THE WOODS at Hallows were alive the night of Halloween. I loved the thinning of the veil that Halloween brought. A twisted anniversary for me and my boys. The night we'd failed, cursed, and killed. The name of the holiday that would haunt us and give us our titles.

"Vincent's high off his ass," Wolfgang spat. "The wolven have combed the forest, and there's no trace of anything, not even a damned or a stray ghoul. You may not like the witches, but they cast a damn good spell. Whatever's sending ghouls and legions after Blythe, we don't have to deal with it until after Halloween."

I kicked at a branch. "My smoke doesn't detect anything either. It's possible whatever was after her just wanted to test me, the Archdemon of Ash Grove. Once they saw they didn't stand a chance, they forfeited. Could be as simple as that."

Onyx considered while tending his campfire. The guy couldn't be in nature for any length of time without starting a fire. Dragon and pyromaniac. "Feels a little too easy, don't you think? And now that Vincent's suddenly involved . . . Vampires only care for their own."

Shrugging my shoulder, I peered into the mirror I'd propped in the crook of a maple. Skull makeup was perfect for tonight's surprise. "Not everything's a conspiracy. Blythe's a mortal under the protection of an Archdemon, a dragon-vampire hybrid, wolven, witches, and a host of other meddling immortal assholes. Who in their right mind would be stupid enough to continue pursuing her?"

The flame pulsed green. After a hundred or so years, I still didn't know what that meant, if anything. "What if whoever it is isn't in their right mind," he mused. "A being with nothing to lose."

Wolf answered as my irritation grew. "That still doesn't explain what they'd want with an average mortal. Yes, we're into her. I mean, Ghost, she's Ghost's," he recovered, not so swiftly. I rolled my eyes while slicking back my hair. My plan to give them a taste of her, to let them watch as I fucked her, backfired. They were as interested as ever. "But any creature could sooner pursue an easier human. I think we can relax," Wolfgang said as he walked over to Onyx and wrapped his arm around him in a side hug. "Don't overthink for a night, man. It's Halloween."

Onyx kept his tone casual as he asked, "So Blythe is getting the full experience downtown, huh? I noticed the cemetery emptied out quick this year."

"She's with Raven. I thought I'd let him usher her through the souls. They're meeting us at The Brew Pump." I straightened my collar. The boys and I were dressed in our eighteen hundreds finery: coats with tails, collars, the works. I hadn't seen Blythe yet, but I was certain she'd look stunning in a period-piece dress. The thought of seeing her in a dress from my time . . .

Wolfgang chuckled, pulling on his top-hat. "She has no idea what we're about to do, does she?"

My lips curved in a smile. "No clue."

***

BLYTHE

My witch friend clicked her tongue as she scanned me top to bottom. "You look like you walked straight out of a Jane Austen novel. You know, a Halloween version of Pride and Prejudice."

"I always liked Persuasion better. Only I wished she could end up with all the guys and not just one." I shrugged. "I feel so fancy." I rocked side to side, watching my large, black gown sway. It was gorgeous ebony fabric and lace, complete with long silk gloves and my lacy black mask. Yesenia had done my hair, an updo with a few face-framing curls. "It's not too poofy, is it?"

"Poofy was the style of the ladies back then. But no, not too poofy."

"Yours is less poofy than mine. And wow, purple is your color." Her gown matched mine but in a deep eggplant shade, hemmed with delicate black lace. Yesenia's dark curly hair and brown skin shimmered. She looked like a lady. I looked like a girl playing dress-up.

She passed me my red lipstick from my makeup bag. It reminded me of the color of Onyx's lips from the night before. . . blood tinted. "This shade, this is the one. And don't worry, Ames is going to lose his mind when he sees you. I'll be shocked if he doesn't declare his love and propose right then and there."

My heart catapulted into my throat. "You have to be joking. There's no way. We just met."

She giggled as I tried to steady my hand enough to apply the unforgiving hue of scarlet. "Honey, I'm surprised he hasn't already. The way he looks at you . . . It's like he wants to eat you for dessert." I blushed the same color as my lipstick. My very forward friend plucked a nice pinkish berry shade from my kit and continued, "Plus, you know who he is. What he is. That's not information we share lightly. Or at all, really. Lots of us go our entire existences never telling a soul. I imagine Ames, Ghost, has seen every person, friend, or lover he's had live and die in his time."

"Wow, that's depressing," I murmured, dabbing the corner of my lips with a tissue. "There's a liner in there named Midnight Blackberry that matches that lipstick perfectly." She thanked me and rummaged through the various tubes. Ghost couldn't be that serious about me, could he? What I felt for him was deeper than anything I'd ever experienced. I may have been sleeping with a demon, but being with him was the most heavenly experience I could have imagined. We hadn't said anything about . . . exclusivity, though the thought of him being with anyone else sent a rage of jealousy through my body. I didn't want him to be with anyone else. And he clearly didn't want his friends flirting with me. But then again, he let them watch us fuck. And I watched them. And it was the most erotic and sexiest thing that had ever happened to me. I couldn't deny that there were rosebuds of emotion burrowing into my soul toward Onyx and Wolfgang, too. And I didn't know how to feel about that.

Also on that list of things to ponder, Yesenia was right in her own morbid way. I was mortal and my time on Earth was limited. I'd grow old and die and Ghost and The Halloween Boys would live on. Suddenly, my dress matched my mood: dismal.

"Oh, they're arriving. This is so exciting. I love when the souls stop by to chat."

My breath froze. "Wait, that really happens?"

"Duh! It's why we all dress like this, so we don't confuse or upset them. They think it's Halloween in eighteen twenty-something. Just be yourself. They're all super nice. Except Patricia, steer clear of her."

My bubbly friend bounced through the shop door and opened it wide, propping it open.

"Which one is Pat—"

"Mabel! Welcome, dear. Come on in and look around. In need of some new ribbon today?"

My bones chilled as a cold rushed in that wasn't from the weather or any earthly element. It was a cold that pricked your skin, one that made you feel like someone was watching you. Two women walked in, dressed just like we were. I'd expected them to look like apparitions, like the willow spirit, or like ghosts in movies. But they looked . . . real. Normal, even. Just like anyone else. I could have passed them by on the street and had no idea they were the undead. They didn't feel like everyone else, though. A chill tightened my chest. I stood awkwardly behind the counter after gathering and hiding my makeup bag. I wasn't sure if the sight of it would confuse them.

"Marcelene, good to see you. The shop looks . . . different. You've really decorated for Samhain this year, haven't you?"

"I think we're calling it Halloween now," Mabel's friend in a light-pink dress and frilly gloves whispered. "I don't believe we've met your friend. Oh, dear, are you coming from a funeral? That black dress . . ."

"Oh," I startled. "No, it's just the nicest dress I had for tonight."

Mabel looped arms with her friend. "Alice, don't be rude." She spoke lower. "She's probably a farm girl and a funeral gown is her best. Perhaps we could go through our old dresses and see if she'd be interested . . ."

Their conversation trailed off as they pursued the store, picking up, actually picking up, items and inspecting them. Something about them surprised me and drew me in, more than any of the other creatures I'd met. These weren't demons or vampires or wolves. These were normal women just . . . shopping. And yet there was something else . . . something so familiar about them. I wanted to touch them. A little voice inside my head called out . . .

My eyes drifted closed.

I'm at Hallows Fest. Every being is dressed in their finest. The shrill hum of a mic check and a stray drum beat sound. I see Ghost leaning on the stage, talking to Onyx and Wolfgang. My heart warms at the sight of them. My guys. They were my guys now, and I felt just as protective over them as they did over me. Groups of others filtered into The Brew Pump, gazing up at the old gas station's roof. Vincent and Ezmerelda walk right in front of me but don't notice or acknowledge me. "Something isn't right," Ezmerelda says urgently, her sage-colored dress making her look even more stunning than usual. I'd never heard her voice sound serious before now. "I fucking feel it and I'm never wrong, Vince."

The coven leader's long white hair was pulled back into a braid falling down his back. He brushed a piece of lint from his blue velvet jacket. "What more can I do? I've warned them. Ghost's arrogance will be his downfall. I've said it for a century now."

"Nothing can happen to her. I won't allow it."

"Neither will I, Red Vampiress." He pulled a golden pocket watch out of his pocket and checked the time. "But don't you find it peculiar?"

"What?"

"That we are so riveted by this human. We all have our opinions when it comes to the other communities amongst us, some of us tolerating, some forming alliances. Even within those, there are exceptions. Except with this mortal . . . An Archdemon Claimed her, and a prized hybrid and alpha wolven worship her. Even the ostentatious witches have lost sleep warding the town to protect her. Day and night they chant and weave their spells. I've never seen anything like the adoration this human female brings. And yet, you and I feel it too."

Ezmerelda considered a moment.

Hooves beat against the ground. The Red Vampiress's crimson eyes shoot up in alarm. "Something's not right. I'm alerting the rest of the coven."

The small, trilling laugher of a little girl cuts through my awareness. It's eerie and echoing.

When I blinked awake, Mabel and Alice were gawking at me. *What the hell just happened?* I'd zoned out like that before but this one . . . It felt too real, like I was somehow seeing something that was actually happening right that moment. My gaze flicked to the door where Yesenia was outside speaking with a small group of ghosts. Steadying my breath, I glanced back at the women who were now directly in front of me on the other side of the checkout desk. I hadn't heard them move. But would I have? They were disembodied spirits.

"Are you well, miss . . ."

"Oh, Alice, you're right. Where are our manners? We haven't gotten your name yet."

I smiled. "Hi, I'm—"

Alice slammed her palms on the desk, making me jump. "I know your name," she said sternly, her cloudy eyes wild. My blood ran cold.

Mabel put a hand to her décolletage. "Mercy, Alice! What are you—"

"You!" Alice pointed, her delicate face contorting. "You're the one."

"I'm sorry, Alice, but you must be confused. I'm brand new to town."

"Look at her, Mabel. Please, try to remember. She's the one. It's her."

My pulse quickened while Mabel searched her friend's eyes. Then, ever so slowly, like a doll's head on a porcelain body, her head turned to me. Two pairs of eyes narrowed as gloved hands reached out slowly toward me. "Please," Mabel begged. "You're the only one who can save us."

"The one we've been waiting for." Alice began to steadily repeat. "The one we've been waiting for."

I inched out from behind the desk, my dress squishing against the wall. They turned slowly in unison and began following me, as if pulled by an invisible thread. I bolted out to find Yesenia, but she was nowhere to be seen. I flung my gaze desperately down the street, trying to find her. What was going on? Were the ghosts short-circuiting? A hand grabbed my shoulder and I jumped.

Raven as a humanoid stepped back. "Sorry, is everything alright? I was watching from the lamppost and you seemed upset in there."

"Raven, I don't know what's going on but—"

I stilled, noticing the movement around the square had halted. Not just stopped, but frozen . . . and all eyes were on me. Dozens of ghosts, looking like they stepped out of a period drama, walked toward me then. "You," one said with a strained whisper. "It's you. You've come."

Another cried in a rattling sob, "Please, help us. Please, please."

Raven wrapped his black wings around me, encompassing me in his feathered hold. I looked up to see the underside of his beak. There was no indent of a mask. He wore no mask. This was him. My body pressed into the varied intricate bones of his wings. "Hold on, Blythe," he ordered.

I gripped his leather vest.

And everything went dark.

It felt as if I were spinning upside down underwater. There was no way to decipher which way was up. No way to get air. My lungs burned. I held close to the leather vest, feathers pricking my cheeks my only hint of tangibility.

And then we landed with a thump.

"I've never tried that before." Raven stood quickly, brushing himself off and helping me to my feet.

A headache pounded between my eyebrows. "What the hell just happened?"

Raven reached into his vest pocket and pulled out a tiny multicolored bag. "Here, sugar helps. These are your favorite, right? I went through your trash." He shrugged. "It's a bird thing."

I took the orange and black wrapped caramels from his wing. "Thanks."

Raven was a compassionate and observant soul. However, he was a little bird-brained. "Do you have any idea what just happened? It's like they all turned on me. Did I do something wrong?"

"Beats me. I've seen a lot of weird things in my time. You wouldn't believe the things people do with their curtains wide open at night. Oh, and dead people are always strange. I wouldn't concern yourself. They can't hurt you."

Despite his assurances, unease prodded at my senses. "Where are we and how did we get here?" I asked, my eyes adjusting to the dark forest.

"I overshot the landing . . . and magic is how we got here. I have a little myself. It's not just all of you guys." He squawked a laugh. Taking my arm, the bird humanoid led me several yards west, where a trail of jack-o'-lanterns lit a pathway through the woods. My shoulders relaxed at the sight. I half expected Ezmerelda to drop from a branch or pop out of the woods like she had done every night I'd attended Hallows Fest, but she didn't appear. It was then it hit me that Hallows was over tomorrow. This was the last night, the crescendo. Sadness crept through me at the thought. I didn't want it to end.

"After October, does everyone leave? The festivalgoers?"

"Mostly, yes."

I made a mental note to find Ezmerelda and see if there was a way we could stay in touch. And the pirates . . . Did pirates have cell phones?

I'd spent so long running and being afraid that now I had what felt like friends, and a community, I didn't want to let them go. What would it look like when The Brew Pump sat vacant?

The shy girl, the scared girl, the one riddled with anxiety . . . had found happiness amongst the dark and strange. I adored all the monsters around me. It couldn't be over.

Speaking of The Brew Pump, that was exactly where Raven insisted we go. I wanted to look for Ghost, or the guys, but he pulled me through the festival, all the way to the concert venue. It was packed, busier than usual, and there was a buzz of excitement emanating from the crowd. "Who's playing?" I shouted over the noise.

"You'll see. The crowd is too much for me. I'm going bird mode now, alright?"

"Okay, have fun." I smiled. I loved that raven already, and I wasn't afraid to admit it.

Just then, blue smoke billowed onto the stage. The crowd went wild. A boar shifter let out a whistle, and I caught sight of the pirates and Captain Vex raising their flasks. "Happy Halloween," a deep voice rumbled over the microphone. Green flame erupted and shot into the sky at the corners of the stage.

The smoke dissolved, and my smile hurt my cheeks it was so big. I cheered along with the crowd. "This surprise performance goes out to my Little Ghost," the voice purred. I saw him then. He was stunning in his jacket, like he belonged in that clothing all along. I had no idea they were in a band. Even more so, they were *good*. Like, really freaking good. Ames played guitar and sang, along with Onyx who played bass. Wolfgang performed a drum solo that revved the crowd into a small riot. It was the most fun I'd ever had. A fitting end.

I didn't even see it coming.

GHOST

Blythe took my breath away. If I had a soul to give, I'd give it to her. But since I was damned, I'd give her my eternity. She was it. My Claimed. And tonight, I was going to tell her. Tell her that I loved her. That she was mine, forever. The look on her face when she realized we were playing would live in my dreams for the rest of my existence, along with the way her long black dress moved as she danced. She moved freely, happily, laughing, the polar opposite of the girl who came here a little over a month ago. That girl was running, lonely, sad. She'd given up hope when she stumbled into my office that day. If I were being honest, I'd given up hope too. Until her. But now we had each other, and everything would be okay. I said I'd defeat the evil chasing her and I did. It was a night to celebrate . . . though I was sorely tempted to end my set early and take her back to the graveyard to properly fuck her in that dress.

I thrummed my electric guitar, feeling the music vibrate through me, when a flash of red blocked my vision of Blythe.

I knew that hue. The color was his. It belonged to him. To his kind.

"Devil, nice to see you, but we're a little busy right now," I drawled, not caring that my mic was still on.

Onyx laughed and shouted above the noise, "Just like the Devil, always showing up when you don't need him." The crowd laughed.

Judas's black eyes searched mine for only a second before he turned, long cape fanning behind him. "They're here," he said deeply. "The one

I've been searching for. The one I've looked for for eternities. The one—"

He stopped abruptly. I shoved his big shoulder aside just in time to see it. It charged for her on all fours. Vampires were flung to the side, impaled by its horns. The ox shifter leapt, trying to protect her. Monsters and immortals flung themselves in its path to guard her. To protect my Claimed. But it was too late. The Devil disappeared, and his red mixed with my blue, setting the stage in a purple haze as I became smoke and darkness. I heard Onyx and Wolf shout behind me.

A searing pain stabbed through my back. I looked down to see a poison blade protruding from my chest.

CHAPTER 36

Blythe

ASH GROVE IS A FINE PLACE TO DIE

> Anyone could see that the wind was a special wind this night, and the darkness took on a special feel because it was All Hallows' Eve.
> *Ray Bradbury*

The last thing I remembered was its face. Its horrible, muddy red eyes with rectangle irises. Hooves reached me at the same moment a screech sounded, and talons gripped onto my shoulder. I fell, and its hooves rose above me and crashed down.

And then I was gone.

When I opened my eyes, red smoke twisted around my arms. It was just like Ghost's smoke, only this one burned and ached. It felt as if all the life force from my body were being drained. My chin was so heavy. Stray curls blocked my vision of the long, fur-covered legs. I made out horns. Blood covered horns. Friends from Hallows tried to save me. The energy to sob in terror escaped me. The tall goat-creature was mixing something at the checkout counter. We were . . . I looked around, seeing bags of chips, gums, candies, hearing the crackle of an ice box filled with sodas.

A female voice spoke. "A gasoline station. Never had these when I lived here, not invented yet. There are several haunted ones scattered around Ash Grove. They're all portals. I'm surprised no one's figured it out by now. Then again, it's always the ordinary that's overlooked, am I right?" She shrugged a furry shoulder in a way a furry shoulder shouldn't be able to move. The goat creature continued, clinking glassware. "No matter. I'm just glad I got you. I've been looking for you for years, you invisible thing you. But then some of my legions and ghouls happened upon the blood and your scent. Your sweet scent of fear was so strong so potent . . . leaving such a long trail of crumbs for us to follow. My how my master will reward me."

The creature stood on knobby two legs but had the body of a large goat, with enormous bloody horns to match. I'd seen many monsters at Hallows Fest, but nothing like this.

The giggle sounded. The giggle I'd heard in my daydream earlier . . . eerie and echoing. A little girl's laughter.

"So why not grab me? Why the letters and games?"

"Luck seems to be on your side. Somehow, every time a demon went right, you went left. And being invisible made it difficult. If you weren't actively frightened, you were damn near untraceable. Nonexistent. Sometimes we could see you through your dead father's skin. But we had to keep scaring you. What better way then with what scared you most? Your dead daddy. Wretched fellow, head full of horrible thoughts." The goat-thing continued stirring. "But then something curious happened. Your fear went away . . . and we couldn't find you again. Come to find out, you're fucking an Archdemon." Her laughter was sinister and hideous. "Wow, I sure do love a plot twist. When you're as old as I am, you always see them coming, but I didn't see this one. No, I did not."

"Who are you? Why do you want me?" My voice was strained.

It ignored me. "However, you picked the most arrogant son of a bitch Archdemon amongst us. Him and his crew are thoughtless. Wreckless. Think too highly of themselves. But hell, even the witches didn't know what you are so maybe I can't blame them for not seeing it. I mean, that's a part of your schtick right? No one can see you coming. Clever."

"What am I?"

"Hmm . . . honestly, it's easier for me if I don't tell you. Poison time!" She giggled. "You're so afraid." She laughed again. "It's delightful. Just delightful. It tastes like . . . some human thing I don't remember. You'll work just fine. I've been chasing you long enough I would hope you'd work fine, anyway."

"What—"

"Don't bother speaking. You won't be able to remember soon, anyway. Little smoke ropes, so fun. James doesn't know how to use them."

James. Who was James? My head was fuzzy, and my shoulders felt like a weight pressed upon them.

Then I remembered the talons. I searched, trying to angle my chin. "Raven," I rasped.

"Oh, your filthy crow? Over there." She gestured with a hoof.

Lying on the ground, limp, unmoving, was Raven. His perfect black wings were outstretched in the worst way. Grief stung at my ribs. "Fuck you," I ground out as hot tears flooded my eyes.

Something inside me screamed to give up. Let her have me and let it be over. And then I remembered his blue eyes, his smile. I remembered breakfasts, and crossword puzzles, and trips to Fenrir. I had to get out of here. They needed me. I needed them. My family.

"Nasty language for a lady. You don't deserve such a fine dress." She giggled again and turned to face me. "My dresses were finer. . ." Each step she made clanked against the tile floor. She was so tall and moved in an unnatural way. And aside from just the terrifying look of her and her dark fur from hoof to horn, she didn't look particularly strong. But I knew that wasn't true. The life draining quickly from my body let me know this was a powerful and malevolent force. "You're not that pretty. I was prettier than you. My hair was so blonde and fine when I tied it in blue ribbons," she said wistfully. "If you look ugly now, just wait until I'm done with you. You'll be hideous. Here, drink this." A gangly limb pushed a bubbling drink at my face. I had to be smart. I couldn't cry and panic. I needed to outsmart her. And I was running out of time.

"Liar," I choked out.

She recoiled, red eyes flashing. "Excuse me?"

"Look at you, there's no way you're more beautiful than I am. You're lying. If you're going to kill me, or do whatever it is you're going to do, you may as well be honest."

She heaved a piercing shriek so loud it shattered glass. I only hoped that somewhere, somehow, Ghost heard it. Or Onyx, or Wolf . . . the witches . . . vampires . . . somebody. *Where was everyone?*

"I was the talk of Ash Grove, to be married to the town physician. We were going to travel and have babies . . . ," she trailed off, something in her eyes shifting. But it was gone as quickly as it came. "I don't have to prove anything to you. All I have to do is bring you to my master and I'll be rewarded. Finally, I'll be freed from this wretched form for a newer, less farm animal one."

"Who's your master?" I asked as the cup touched my lips. My chin dangled now, I was almost spent. She pressed the goblet rim into me and pulled my hair, tilting me back until hot liquid dripped into my mouth and down my chin, causing me to choke as it trickled down my throat. She looked pleased. That couldn't be good.

Her goat-like head angled, and she watched me through rectangular irises. "I could play with you first though. My master would never know. It's an ugly form, to be sure, but it's better than mine. How about we trade?" She giggled. "Oh, if we trade, do I get to fuck an Archdemon too?" She laughed maniacally.

"Ames would never touch you. Pretty or not. And you won't touch him either. I won't let you," I said through gritted teeth. The ropes tightened on my wrists and a new one wrapped around my neck, squeezing like a snake. I coughed a wet choke. I didn't want to think of why my throat felt wet and sticky.

"I don't care about *James* Cove. He was so strange . . . and poor. Why would I want a farmer? He's more now than he ever was then and all thanks to my master." A sharp spear of smoke wavered in front of me. "You talk too much. Let's make it hurt more. What do you think?"

The spear shot through my shoulder. I screamed in agony as it pulsed and twisted.

It was then I realized I was going to die.

GHOST

I swore, crawling through the dirt. All I heard were the sounds of animal shifters panicking and my brothers rushing to my side. Something roared. I looked down to see the demon blade lodged in me, slowly killing me. It didn't matter. All that mattered was finding Blythe. It took her. A fucking Baphomet. Wolfgang dropped to my side, cursing.

Spitting out a wad of black blood, I said, "We have to find her. Leave me, find her."

"We're trying." He lifted me to my feet. "We have to get you to a healer immediately."

"No, just her, find Blythe."

"Judas and Onyx are on it. And the moment I drop you with a healer, I'm gone. I won't stop until she's safe, do you hear me? But you can't fucking die. Not like this. Not with a goddamn Baphomet spear."

The poison spread like a web, like it recognized its master's name. I cried out, my knees failing. I sent out a wave of blue smoke to look for her. *Find her*, I commanded it.

My vision was impeded by my speckles of nothingness. A voice rang in my ears. "I don't know if I can save him. Historically, my magic has not worked on any of the cursed of Ash Grove. But if he's her Claimed, he should be able to find her." Marcelene looked at me with a judgmental stare even now. She was dressed as a classic witch, purple pointed hat and all.

"How," I managed.

She sighed, looking to my wound and paling. Where had she come from? How was I under the willow tree. I was losing consciousness. "You don't feel her?" she asked, her wise violet eyes assessing my wound.

Onyx appeared in a blaze of green, kneeling opposite Wolf. Oh, I was lying in the grass now.

"I don't feel her," I said.

Onyx put a hand on my chest as Wolfgang cradled my head in his muscular lap. And then it flashed, like a speeding train, the imagines flooding me. Fluorescent, flickering light, packs of cigarettes . . . Blythe, hanging by blood chains. And the fucking Baphomet. I'd only been shackled by blood chains once and it was excruciating. And meeting a Baphomet . . . Fuck. Only the worst devils could create those foul beings.

Then I was back. When I opened my eyes, Judas was standing at my feet, wide-eyed. He ran a hand over his head. I'd never seen him look afraid before. *What does a Devil fear?* I wondered, feeling my sentience slip in and out. "Did you all feel and see that, too?" Onyx asked.

Wolfgang answered, "Yes. The gas station."

"What the fuck? How did you—"

"How do you think, asshole?" Marcelene said, exasperated. "Now shut up while I finish this spell." Cranky ass crone. The poison exploded in my chest like a tiny bomb. My body shook, trying to shift into demon form, but it didn't matter. I was dying. I was going to die without ever telling Blythe I loved her. My death would come with the awareness that I'd found my Claimed only to fail her. Sorrow pressed into me, and for the first time in hundreds of years, I felt the urge to cry.

Judas spoke in a rumble. "Death is here."

"What?" I asked, feeling something tingle in my blood as the witch chanted a spell. More witches gathered around us now, kneeling, waving crystals on silver strings. Even the vines of the willow trees swayed with them. "You don't mean?"

Judas replied, "A Reaper."

"Blythe's stepfather, or the one who inhabited him—"

Onyx interrupted, "We thought he was a demon. They were all demons."

Wolfgang pieced it together out loud. "We can't see him or find him. He's silent. Judas senses death. The Baphomet is a Reaper."

I argued, "Reapers don't exist anymore. They're the most powerful beings there are. Like a thousand legions of demons put together. They're death incarnate. Pure death."

"Yes. The Reaper is here. I feel it," The Devil spoke, and his word was always final. He would know.

I swore. "My Claimed is with a goddamn Reaper?"

"Our Claimed," Onyx interrupted.

"Yes," Wolfgang agreed. "Ours."

Judas only crossed his arms, still looking alarmed.

"What the fuck?" I asked, sitting up on my elbows, the pain easing a bit. A crone opened an eye long enough to roll it at me before continuing her chant. They were saving me. Reluctantly, but hell, I'd take it.

Onyx said, "We all saw her when we touched. Only Claimed matches can do that. Polyamorous groupings aren't impossible. We're her Claimed and she's ours."

"Fuck no," I spat. "No. She's mine."

Yesenia's overeager voice strained somewhere in the distance. "I turn my back for one moment and all hell breaks loose. If something happens to her, I'll never forgive myself. I'm so sorry—"

Marcelene interrupted her granddaughter, addressing me, "You're not healed, but you're good enough to get to her. Being mated is the strongest magic that exists. It's love magic, the deepest thing across all worlds. If you're each her Claimed, you need to touch and think of her and her need for you. That will get you there. I'll throw in some energy to help. Though, I'm sure with Judas back, you don't need it."

"Thank you, Marcelene," I said, meeting her gaze. "I mean it. Thanks." She could have left me for dead, killed me like I killed her. But she didn't. The crone was better than me, and I was grateful for that.

She cut a nod, her gaze softening a bit. The old bat had a soft spot for me even after all these years. "Oh, and we're sorry for vandalizing your house every year," I added.

She dropped her crystal pendulum. "I knew it was you wretched Halloween Boys—"

Onyx and Wolf touched me, and we closed our eyes. At the last moment, another hand touched my leg, and we were gone before she finished her sentence. If I was going to die fighting a goddamn Reaper, I was happy to have gotten one last dig at Marcelene in. As I tumbled through the darkness, I wondered, *How does one defeat death?*

BLYTHE

Numbness overtook me like an undertow, pulling me down into a blanket of white. This was how a daydream felt. But this wasn't a daydream, just white . . . nothingness. Funny how I assumed death would be black. Then I saw her. She sat on a throne of gray bones holding a staff. A raven perched atop it, and it eyed at me as I approached. "Can you help me?" I asked the woman.

She looked down at me, and I gasped when I realized it was my own face staring back at me. Me, but different. Twisted horns stretched above my head, and my black dress glowed in the bright white room. She thrummed her fingers on her throne, the other hand caressing her staff. No, not a staff, a scythe. Whoever this was, they weren't human, and I wasn't sure if they were good or bad yet.

"You can help you," she answered. "You've had the answers all along. If you'd only listen to yourself." The bird squawked in agreement.

"I don't understand."

"You do, though, you really do."

I looked to the bird on the scythe . . . Raven. I knew my bird. Another trick, maybe, but I didn't think she meant to harm me or she would have already. The long, arched blade and the bones reminded me of . . . some sort of Grim Reaper.

The ghost in the shop's voice rang in my ears. *It's you. You can save us. Please, please . . .*

The legion of demons . . . my stepfather . . . They couldn't see me. Ames couldn't see me.

Suddenly, we weren't alone.

Four men stood by her throne.

And four men appeared beside me. I felt his arms instantly. "Ames," I sobbed into his chest.

"I've got you," he breathed. "We're here."

"Are we dead?"

Ames glanced at a man in red I didn't recognize, and then at the woman at the throne. "I don't think so. This reminds me of Hell."

The men standing around her were fierce, and strong, with mighty wings and horns . . . and they were also nearly the mirror image of the men clutching me now. My men. The Halloween Boys.

The woman spoke in my voice. "You underestimated the girl. You thought she needed you to rescue her. You assumed this *man* chasing her must be magical to fly under the radar. You thought he wanted her only to get at you." She grinned and glanced at the demon who looked like Ames, who gave a very human-looking shrug. She continued, "Did you ever consider it was her the entire time? That perhaps she's the one with the magic, and you're all the average, ordinary monsters? She never needed your help, Ames. In fact, you're lucky she didn't kick your ass. Beware the damsel in distress. Sometimes she's death in disguise. And that's what you have here. You were too blind to see it. It's ironic that her gifts make her invisible to being seen because you saw nothing about her even with your talents. You saw what you wanted to see, and you all missed out on who she is. You thought you had a helpless lost girl to save?"

A chill ran through my spine . . . a chill and . . . darkness. It flooded into my lungs, my chest, my body, like the biggest and best breath I'd ever taken. It was me. This was me. I knew who I was. And I *could* help them all.

The woman . . . me . . . smiled at me then, and winked, before saying.

"Blythe is Death, and she needs no saving."

WE APPEARED THEN, back in the gas station. I gulped and panted, as if just emerging from the ocean. But it was real. The guys were here. Onyx stood with green flame flicking around him. Ames shifted, and Ghost stood at full, terrifying height. Wolfgang became his shadowy beast . . . and the man in red . . . he hadn't come. He was gone.

The goat demon looked between us wide-eyed. "He wants her. He won't stop until he gets her."

The chains burned at my wrist, and the spear pulsed in my shoulder. It felt so real. Then I remembered her on her throne of bones . . . Death. I was Death.

If I was truly Death . . .

I tugged, feeling that shadow seep inside me once more. It cooled my bones and steadied me as I jerked my arms forward and stood. The chains whisked away like a cloud, as did the spear, and I felt no pain.

"No," the demon screeched. "You weren't supposed to realize it. I was supposed to take you to him unaware. He wants you, and he'll have you—"

I took a step toward the creature, and she flinched. She spoke again, dropping to her furry knees. "Kill me. You're the only one who can. Death would be a freedom from what my master will do when he sees I have failed."

"Sounds good to me," Ghost growled. The boys grunted their agreements.

"Wait," I said, reaching out a hand and touching the being that bowed before me's snout. I saw it then. Who it was. Who she was. Curls and ribbons . . . Memories of the photographs in Mr. Moore's guest room flooded my awareness.

I gasped. "Ellie May?"

Something flashed across the demon's eyes. She shook her head, her ears flapping as if to shake the thought away.

"They took you, didn't they, Ellie? Your master . . . whoever he is . . . will meet me soon. You can count on that." Rage coursed through me as the realization poured in, but I softened. "Your dad misses you, Ellie. He kept your room so nice."

"No," the creature wailed. "No, I don't know that name. I answer to no name. I have no name".

"When I came here, I was a scared little girl too. And a demon found me too."

Her eyes shot up, looking faintly human in that moment. "Did he take you?" she asked, averting her red gaze.

"Yes . . . just like you were taken. Right?"

She slammed a loud hoof on the tile, shaking the building. I felt the guys flinch and move toward me, but I lifted a hand, telling them to pause. They'd kill her in a moment, rip her to shreds for taking me and trying to harm me. Her gritty voice spoke. "We're just things to be taken and *changed* and *fucked* and fucked with and used. You're no different than me. And soon you'll look like this, too, when they're finished with you."

I felt her pain, the darkness that had been planted and taken root inside her. Who could blame her? "That's not all we are," I replied softly. "We are more than what's happened to us, Ellie. Maybe they caged us because we're the scary ones. Maybe we're monsters too, all on our own. We're powerful. You don't have to stay this way. Let me help you. Let's help each other."

Her big, animalistic eyes stared into mine, flickering in pale awareness.

I didn't know why I did it, maybe instinct, and I was done ignoring that. I reached out and touched her horns. The beast fell limp at my feet. *Dead.*

Behind, she stood, glowing and gorgeous with blonde ringlet curls tied up in blue ribbons. Her long petticoat grazing the ground.

She reached out a hand. "Come with me?"

I smiled, not registering the guys' objections. Or not caring. "Of course." When I took her hand, we vanished.

We appeared on a street I recognized. Ellie looked around and smiled softly at the trick-or-treaters that whirled past her. The little kids saw her and didn't care. She was just another lost ghost. "It looks so different . . ." She put a gloved hand to her mouth in a gasp.

There he was, sweeping the street. I took her palm and held it tight. "He's been waiting for you," I said as we walked up to Mr. Moore.

"Papa?" she said, sweetly.

He stalled a moment, almost as if he were afraid to look up and not see her. I wondered how many times he'd done that for more than a century. But he did look up. And when he saw her, his lip quivered. "Ellie May . . . I've swept the road every day waiting for you. So the dirt doesn't muddy your petticoat. I know you hate that."

I swallowed back emotion and took a step back. "Papa." Her voice cracked again, tears streaming down her face. She threw herself into his arms and he caught her, their embrace saying more than lifetimes of words could.

When he pulled back, holding his daughter's petite shoulders, he said, "Let's go see your mama. Let's go home, Ellie May."

"Yes, Papa. I've missed you both so, so much."

Through cloudy eyes and hot tears streaking down my face, I walked up to them both and placed a palm on their shoulders.

Mr. Moore sighed. "Thank you. Thank you," he whispered as they both faded away.

CHAPTER 37

Blythe

LA PETITE MORT

> We stopped checking for monsters under our bed when
> we realized they were inside us.
> *Charles Darwin*

I WAS DEATH.

The street fell silent as I stood alone in their wake. My touch freed them both from their curse. It was why I was brought here. How I found Ash Grove. In running from death and demons, I found that I was Death itself. And though I may have found family in monsters and all the darkness they brought . . . the greatest monster I'd befriended was me.

And somehow my power surpassed them all.

I felt it, a chilly and exhilarating wave through my bones. I pictured the horned lady on her throne of bones, her four men at her side. She was me, somehow. She showed me the way and revealed I'd been holding all the puzzle pieces to my own mystery the entire time. I never needed to run. The chains that bound me when the Baphomet hissed were only effective because I believed they were. Because I didn't believe in myself. I watched in wonder as these magical beings were drawn to me, for some reason, and I sorted through the riddles of them and the town. But when I got close to the answer, I dodged it, not wanting to face what somewhere inside me knew was true.

I was Death.

Tingles ignited along my bare shoulders as I felt his presence. A tender, calloused touch skimmed my arms as warm breath hit my ear. "Did I tell you that you look beautiful tonight, Little Ghost?"

I spun, pulling his face to mine for a passionate kiss. He obliged without hesitation, cupping my jaw. His honeyed tongue found mine as we pressed our bodies together. Reluctantly, I pulled myself away. "You're okay," I breathed. "I'm so glad you're okay."

"I'm sorry I didn't save you," he replied solemnly, his eyes dark and jaw tight.

My fingers tugged around his jacket opening. "I never needed saving." I looked beyond him to three rogue ghosts, two women and a man, walking through the streets. "They do though. And I can help them."

His lips curved. "Yes, you can." His lips brushed my earlobe. "And that is so goddamn sexy."

My neck tingled as his tone promised to fulfill my every desire later. With another soft kiss, I made my way to the ghosts, freeing them from their purgatory.

When we stood outside of Hell's Gates, this time I didn't cower. The gate whispered, *master*, and opened with reverence. A black cat jumped from a grave and trotted over. It lowered in a bow. "Hello, I'm Cat."

I smiled. Cat. "It's nice to meet you. I'm Blythe. Are you a . . . familiar?"

Ghost snorted as the cat cleaned its whiskers. "Yes, *his.*"

A laugh left my chest. "You never told me you had a familiar?" I nudged him.

"It's not something I brag about."

The cat hissed but allowed us to pass. I giggled as we walked deeper into the cemetery. No wonder these dark and dreary places always brought me comfort. None of it made sense, but then, it all made sense, too.

Onyx and Wolfgang strode forward, like they'd been waiting, like they knew this is exactly where I'd go next. Wolfgang enveloped me in his big warm hug that felt like home. When I looked up at him, he ran a wide hand over his face, clearing away tears. "Don't scare me like that again. You can't get out of our *Mario Kart* rematch that easily."

"I wouldn't dare try." I grinned, giving him another squeeze.

Onyx stood behind me, arms crossed, eyeing me with a look I couldn't place. Emotion danced behind his glowing emerald eyes. With his black hair brushed back, and his widow's peak, along with the dark cape behind him, he looked every bit the classic vampire I knew lurked in his blood. He came closer and wordlessly put a hand on my cheek.

Suddenly, a mirage of images flooded my mind.

A woman with long, wavy blonde hair and glowing emerald eyes, *his* glowing emerald eyes, kissed Onyx's cheek. A man next to her, who was taller, broader, and the quintessential vampire, gave his shoulder a squeeze. "We love you, son. Be safe."

My vision flashed again, and I saw all three of the guys, younger, throwing rocks into a lake and laughing.

And then I saw me. I looked so sad, my skin pale and lifeless, as I rummaged through my purse at the diner.

It flashed again, and I was tugging on the T-shirt he gave me, giggling, bouncing with excitement. Then something that felt a lot like love and gratitude erupted in my chest.

When I looked at him again, the corner of his mouth quirked in a smile. Had I blacked out, or had I only just blinked? "Was that you?" I whispered.

"Was what me?" he asked, giving me a secretive wink. My heart warmed. *Onyx Hart* . . .

I shook off my overflowing emotions and dried my palms on the fluffy fabric of my dress, which was somehow still intact. "Are they all here?" I asked Ghost, who'd resumed his position in Archdemon form behind me.

"Yes, quietly waiting for you, Little Reaper."

I grinned up at him, and the pride and love beaming through his gaze took my breath away. He wasn't the least bit angered, or intimidated, by my newfound skills. We complimented each other, him and I. Death and the Archdemon. The Reaper and the Ghost.

"I don't really know what I'm doing," I admitted, padding over to two large, mossy gravestones.

Wolfgang encouraged, "Just do what feels right. Don't think too much about it. Let your instincts guide you."

I nodded, thinking that was what a wise wolf would advise. My eyes fluttered shut as I caressed the fuzzy, damp stones. With a sigh, I felt a rush of wind billow from the ground, lifting my curls and chilling my skin. When I opened my eyes, there they were, all standing and staring at me—hundreds of spirits. Men, women, children, young and old, their need and longing were palpable through the cold Halloween air. The full moon's glow shimmered across them as they stared at me expectantly. "Rest well, friends," I whispered.

Their returning smiles and soft nods evaporated as colors of pale blue, purple, and green, shot toward the sky. Maybe those were the auras the witches saw. Relief pooled through me. Peace. They finally had found peace.

Ames gently ran a hand through my hair. "For centuries, they'd paid the price for what we did, how we failed them. For centuries, we searched for a way to relieve them and we fell short." His jaw tensed with emotion. "They're finally free . . . because of you." He sucked in a breath. "Though if my head weren't so far up my own ass, I could have realized what you were . . . and they could have found death sooner. The first night I brought you here, the cemetery went quiet. Even the fucking damned tried to tell me who you were."

I placed a single, gloved finger to his lips. "You have given me more than any man, demon or otherwise, ever has, Ames. You've helped me see who I am, and not just this." I gestured around me. "But you helped me learn to chase away my loneliness, my resignation. It was always you fighting for me."

His lips dropped to mine, but before they touched, he whispered, "All because a demon fell in love."

I gasped a quick breath before his kiss found me. "I love you too," I replied, honestly, truly.

Wolfgang cleared his throat. "I hate to interrupt, but we don't have a lot of time."

When I looked, he was holding something that looked so small and floppy in his arms—a bundle of feathers. My heart clenched. "Raven," I breathed as he walked closer. "He came with me," I managed. "He came with me to face the . . ."

Wolf nodded. "He did. Raven is just about the best familiar you could hope for. Though, Blythe, he is dead."

My throat tightened as the tears I'd been holding back threatened to unleash.

"But," Wolf continued, "all animals . . . We all have our own sort of magic. It's hard to explain, but when an animal dies that was loved by someone, they don't leave. They stay, even in death, to look after their person. His soul is still close by. I think you can bring him back."

My gaze shot to his in shock. Ames rubbed my back gently, and Onyx's eyes glowed as he leaned on a nearby tombstone.

"I'll try," I said with a shaky voice. Removing my gloves, I placed my palms on his cold, silky-soft body. I didn't know what to do, or where to start, or what I was trying to accomplish exactly . . . but I thought of Raven when he found me at Hallows Fest and I needed a friend. How he made me feel at home and safe. Memories flashed through my mind of the black bird that followed me from the moment I entered Ash Grove. How he made me feel like I had a buddy. I remembered the night I actually got restful sleep for the first time in years . . . and it was as he sat perched on my windowsill, watching after me. *Thank you,* I said with my mind. *But I still need you. Please, come back?*

After several silent moments, his wing twitched. Wolfgang smiled broadly, running a hand down Raven's back. "There we go," he said proudly. "Nice work, friend."

My sobs exploded then as Raven straightened, ruffling out his feathers. He hopped onto my shoulder, and I nuzzled my head into his wing.

I had all my boys now. We were dark, and probably evil, and most certainly damned to Hell, though Ghost swore Hell wasn't so bad, but they were mine. And I was theirs.

My friends.

My family.

My home.

TWO MONTHS LATER

Snow floated out the frosty window, joining the blanket of white on the ground. The smell of evergreen and fire warmed my chest as I wrapped a blanket around my shoulders and sat on the floor in front of the stone fireplace.

A boom of laughter erupted in the kitchen, where the smell of meat, so much meat, wafted into the family room. We'd spent the last two months finding every trapped resident of Ash Grove. I'd given each of them peace, allowing them to pass on. It was funny what I'd learned about death since, well, *being* Death. It wasn't like the ominous hooded figures in movies or books, though the scythe was definitely a thing, as proven by my earlier vision, it seemed. Death was just another passage-way, and I held open the door. Raven cawed from his perch by the window. Wolfgang had built him a long, T-shaped stand. Wolf really spoiled that bird, and Raven didn't mind at all. A grin broke upon my lips.

"I love that smile." Ames lowered himself next to me. He passed me a mug swirling with steam. The smell of cinnamon and lemon tingling my nose. "Hot Toddy," he said, putting an arm around my shoulder as we leaned back on the sofa.

The Devil's words from months prior played through my mind as I sipped my spicy drink.

"She's who I've been looking for, the missing piece. A Reaper. Death itself. Blythe can break the curse. She can give the residences here peace and death, releasing you all from the hold Ash Grove has on you. You're no longer bound to the town."

He spoke with such authority, such finality. And he'd said little else. Though when I looked at him, I knew without a doubt he looked exactly like the fourth man standing around the horned lady's throne. The lady that was me.

Onyx and Wolfgang filtered in with plates piled high with food and joined us. Out of nowhere, I asked, "Do you think you were all drawn to me just because I'm Death? Like the vampires and witches were? Is that the only reason you like me?"

Wolfgang snorted. "You think we'd put up with your hair all over the shower just because you're a Reaper?"

Onyx added, "And the makeup all over the place . . . This is a historical farmhouse, not a dressing room."

"Ha, ha." I rolled my eyes. Ames grinned, tugging me to his chest. I snuggled in, inhaling his intoxicating scent. I persisted, "Your curse is broken. You can all leave Ash Grove and go as far as you want, for as long as you want. Will . . . any of you be leaving?"

The four of us had been spending time on the outskirts of Ash Grove in Onyx's farmhouse. It was quaint, and farm life was unexpectedly what I'd needed after the whole Halloween ordeal. Though I wouldn't lie, goats now freaked me the hell out. We had a chance to breathe here. And immortals, witches, and ghosts weren't knocking down my door with questions or requests.

"You're right," Wolfgang replied thoughtfully. "I can finally recruit new wolves. After so many years . . ."

I didn't know what that meant, but the awe in his voice seemed answer enough.

Onyx spoke next, his usual teasing tone somber. "I can search for my family, my mother . . . after so long."

My heart clenched. I knew his mother was the blonde woman from the vision, or memory, he'd shown me. She was beautiful, and even in that snippet, I saw and felt the love his parents had for him.

Ames let out an exasperated sigh. "I don't have to deal with that goddamn cat every day. Thank fuck."

The guys rumbled with laughter, and I couldn't help my own, too.

"We need more firewood. Be right back," Ames said, kissing my temple. He and the guys filtered into the backyard in search of logs when a new presence rippled through the living room. I'd be lying if I said I had any sort of grip on my powers. I still didn't understand the extent of what they were, or what I was, even. But I could always feel its pull. What I would have dismissed months ago, I listened to fervently now. And I knew what *he* felt like. Judas felt like the color red. And yes, I knew that didn't make sense.

He sat slumped back in the velvet armchair next to the fire, loosely clutching a glass of amber liquid. I looked over and raised an eyebrow. "Hi?"

The Devil only offered a small nod in response, his deep brown complexion dancing with gold in the firelight. He looked at home next to fire. I shuddered. I knew almost nothing about Judas. He popped in and out with no warning, no rhyme or reason. He hardly spoke to me, or anyone, really. The Devil was a mystery, and I wasn't sure if that was a good or bad thing.

I broke the silence with no preamble, something I'd learned in our few interactions that he wouldn't answer to anyway. There was no discussing the weather with the Devil. "So, you're a Devil, more powerful than anything, but you're helping them. Why?"

He shrugged a shoulder, still gazing into the fire as if he could see something in it. "You don't think me to be altruistic?" His deep timbre rattled my core. I wondered if it was because of what he was . . . or something else.

I raised an eyebrow. "They believe you're a part of their crew, their friend. And I may not know how to use my powers now, but I'll learn." I sat my mug down and faced him, rising onto my knees. "If you even think about hurting them, I am Death, and I will find a way to end you. And if there isn't a way, I'll invent one."

His eyebrows rose slightly as he finally met my gaze. With disconcerting calm he replied. "Threatening the Devil, are we?"

"You're not the only Devil," I replied, acting braver than was wise. Raven squawked in warning, bird talk for *shut the hell up, Blythe.*

To my surprise, the Devil stood and took a step toward me. When I didn't stand or back away, he let out a dark chuckle. "Look at you. So puffed up and brave now with death and your demons dancing around you. When you first came to Ash Grove, you were startled by the ring of a phone. Now look at you . . . My, how things change." My mouth dropped open. How did he . . . My thoughts were interrupted as he continued, "I'll Claim what's mine when the time comes. Be sure of that, Reaper. Notice, you're still on your knees for me." He downed his drink in one gulp, tossing his glass into the fire. He disappeared in a cloud of smoke. I coughed, waving it out of the way, just as the guys came barreling back inside.

"What'd we miss?" Wolfgang asked, falling back onto the couch.

I coughed again. "Nothing. Bourbon burns my throat, that's all." The Devil was shady as *hell*, but he needed to know I was watching him. Apparently, he'd been watching me too. I didn't know how I felt about that, but I didn't regret my warning. As the guys fell into easy conversation, several earlier talks still weighed on my mind.

"Who or what do you think made and sent the Baphomet?"

The guys went quiet, glancing at each other. They weren't telling me something. I could feel it. But ever so casually, Onyx answered. I always knew they were hiding something when they made Onyx answer. His gift of charm and way with words were distracting. But this time, I had my eyes open.

"Could be anything. It sounds like by what the Baphomet told you, that their master could be the devil who cursed us. That would explain why we couldn't sense them. I wonder if other stolen girls of Ash Grove were likewise transformed . . ." He pondered quietly for a moment. The thought of other girls being turned into those horrifying creatures . . . Onyx continued, "If anything caught on to you being a Reaper, your strength and power would be a coveted tool for any immortal to wield . . . or exploit."

My gut constricted. That last part wasn't a lie. I was still wrapping my mind around what I was, and with so little information about Reapers, it was hard to land on anything solid in my thoughts. I hadn't considered that whatever my abilities may be, they'd be sought after by others. But I was safe in Ash Grove. We all were. Which led me to my next question. "Are you all leaving Ash Grove?" I asked simply, turning my back to the fire to look at each of their faces. I wanted to cry at the thought. Ames answered first, plopping a purple grape into his mouth, "Hell no, I love Ash Grove. And you." He winked. "Curse or not. This is my home."

My heart fluttered. I liked that answer.

Onyx's jaw tensed. "This may be my last chance to find my family. Wherever they are . . . it's a long way away . . . but I have to try." His emerald gaze glowed, meeting mine, searching my eyes for something. Permission, maybe. I couldn't be sure with him. I didn't know what was fun and games and what was serious. And with Ames policing the guys' every interaction with me . . . it was difficult to sort through whatever feelings that existed between us.

Wolf hit his friend on the back. "I'm in. Let's go looking for dragons and bloodsuckers. What could go wrong?"

Onyx looked to him in surprise. "What about Fenrir?"

Wolfgang snorted. "I'm not an alpha yet. And I'm in no hurry to train a bunch of rabid pups."

"I can help," I offered. "I'll go too."

The room went silent. With hesitation looming over me, I cast a glance at Ames, who met my stare. Where I'd expected anger, only a hint of sadness danced along his features. My heart cracked a little. I didn't want to make him sad . . . but I couldn't not help Onyx when he needed me. Not when they'd all been there for me in my time of being lost, of searching. I'd been looking for a family, too, when The Halloween Boys found me. How could I not be there for Onyx?

Shadows danced around Ames when he answered, "You have my help, friend. Always."

Onyx's shoulders visibly relaxed. "You guys would really come with me?" His gaze searched his friends' before landing on mine. I swallowed, just then realizing I'd probably follow him anywhere. I'd follow any of them anywhere. If they needed me . . . that was all the reason I needed.

"We're a pack." Wolfgang shrugged.

Ames tangled his fingers through my hair. "We're family."

Onyx chuckled. "A band of assholes, more like it. Except you, Blythe. You know, except for the hair in the shower shit."

After my cheeks hurt from laughter, visions of our next adventure thrilled through me. Where would one find dragons? Were all vampires like Vincent and Ezmerelda? Where did they disappear to after Hallows? Was it possible to find someone who could tell me more about *what* exactly I was?

With love, confidence, and freedom, I said, "Wherever we go, we go together."

And though I may have been Death itself, something dark and powerful and misunderstood, as Ghost said, I was loyal to those I loved. Perhaps I'd willfully joined them on the wrong side of Heaven and old stories and legends. Despite it all, I'd found what I'd been searching for. Ash Grove had let me in for a reason . . . and I'd found my purpose here. The Halloween Boys were indeed the death of me . . . and the start of my life. Whatever spooky adventure that lay ahead of us filled me with fire and energy. Something dark and ancient lurked beneath my skin, a monster of legendary proportions, And I couldn't wait to meet her.

I'm Blythe Pearl and I am Death. A Reaper.
And I have never felt so alive.

To be continued in *The Halloween Boys Book Two: Dragon*. Flying castles, vampires, dragons, and more mysteries coming this winter.

Acknowledgments

First and foremost I want to thank my religious upbringing for failing at converting me so spectacularly that it spit me out on the other side heavenly beings and sanctuaries. Kidding, kind of.

Occult and Esoteric Masters are a thing, and I happened upon the best one for consulting for this book. Imagine sending a text message that says, "What alcoholic beverage would a murder of crows choose?" And getting a serious response back. (It's mead, by the way.) Also, envision you write a demon in the middle of the night. You text your consultant the weird thing the demon did or said. And he replies, "That's true, that's what they do, but most people don't know that." *That's not freaky at all.* Eric confirmed the underworld's enthusiastic involvement in this project, and that the demons were expressing their thanks by throwing birds at me constantly. Once it was indeed a literal raven sitting on my doormat. Anyway, having Eric Titus Albion's guidance from his decades of rubbing elbows with these creatures was invaluable. I think it added a layer to this novel like I've rarely seen before. I also wanted to be respectful of these beings and the people who follow and honor them.

And to you, dear reader... I've been an author long enough to know that some will vehemently hate this book. Some will be ambivalent. And then a special few, the ones that set my soul ablaze, will find something they needed. They'll see themselves in someone, creature, immortal, or human, and something will click. That reader will think of that scene or that moment over and over and a real sort of magic will happen through that spell. If you're like me, who has been so often put under the witchcraft of a book, it'll change something inside of you. You'll feel a little braver, a little more seen, something inside will hurt a little less, or feel a bit stronger. Those are the readers that keep me writing.

If you grew up as a little dark-heart, like I did, you always felt different. Too shy, too quiet, too nervous. You liked Halloween while everyone else liked Christmas. You loved autumn when everyone else wished for summer. It can be lonely feeling like you don't belong. Sometimes it feels easier to try to conform to what the others are doing, or just disappear entirely. But Halloween invites us to celebrate the strange. Monster romance embraces falling for the demon. Maybe you are a little different and maybe there's something dark inside you. But I'm here to tell you, in more than one hundred thousand words, that's okay. Are you a quiet little ghost? Are you death itself? You are? I think that's rad. Keep being that. You don't need anyone to save you, and you're more terrible than anything you'll find in the woods. Trust in that.

Thanks for wandering into Ash Grove. I hope you stick around for more.

Xoxo,
    Kat

Dear Reader

 Those who don't believe in magic will never find it.
   Roald Dahl

DEAR SPOOKY READER,

This book is for the curvy goth girls who never get any book rep. It's for the shy guys who no one sees the true power laying beneath their surface. For the guys or they's that also want to be witches and the girls and femmes who want to lead their own covens. For gay love, poly love, and monster fucking. I wrote GHOST: *The Halloween Boys* for all the spooky bitches. For the people who've felt different, and not special, and unseen, and unnoticed. I wrote GHOST for the monster lovers and stuffed animal huggers.

The grownups who still love trick-or-treating, who aren't afraid of the dark, and who connect to Halloween in a way some will never understand. With my deep and thorough consulting with an occult expert, personal diving in to getting to know demons, and my kid-at-halloween heart, I hope you've discovered something like you've never read before. I hope you eat it up you little dark hearts. Demons literally threw birds at me while I wrote this. I was also sent a crow friend who joined me while I sat in the silence of my car making notes.

If you enjoyed Ghost, please evangelize and a share the good word with reviews on your favorite platforms.

Thank you for reading.

Xoxo,

Graveyard Kat Blackthorne

- Sign up for my newsletter to be the first to know about new book releases
- Join my patreon for NSFW art, early chapters of Dragon, and more.
- Join me on #spicybooktok TikTok:
- See fan edits on Instagram:
- Watch me not know how to use Twitter:
- Follow me on Amazon for upcoming books:
- Join my coven on FB

Business or press inquires please email darkheartspresspub@gmail.com

Also by Kat Blackthorne

The Halloween Boys

Ghost

Dragon

Wolf

Devil

Wicked Ecstasy

The other villains of Ash Grove

Come For A Spell

Familiar Taste

Lady Venom Takes a Mistress

Gothic lesbian romance

Hot Queens

Contemporary polyamory

Hotwife

Hot Life

Let it Snow Queen

Browse by Trope for more

at katblackthorne.com